SHADOWS

OWS

THE ASHES TRILOGY

BOOK TWO

ILSA J. BICK

EGMONT
USA
NEW YORK

EGMONT

We bring stories to life

First published by Egmont USA, 2012
443 Park Avenue South, Suite 806
New York, NY 10016

Copyright © Ilsa J. Bick, 2012
All rights reserved

1 3 5 7 9 8 6 4 2

www.egmontusa.com
www.ilsajbick.com

The Library of Congress has Cataloged the hardcover edition as follows:

Bick, Ilsa J.
Shadows / Ilsa J. Bick.
p.   cm. — (The Ashes trilogy; [#2])
Summary: When Alex discovers that Rule is not a sanctuary,
she battles to survive against conniving adults, distrusting
survivors, and the Changed, who would eat her alive.
ISBN 978-1-60684-176-1 (hardcover) — ISBN 978-1-60684-378-9 (e-book)
[1. Science fiction. 2. Survival—Fiction. 3. Zombies—Fiction.] I. Title.
PZ7.B47234Sh 2012
2012007092
Trade paperback ISBN 978-1-60684-445-8

Printed in the United States of America

FOR THOSE WHO FIGHT

*People ain't the way
they used to be.*

—SHIRLEY JACKSON

FUBAR: THAT WAS JED'S NAME FOR IT. ONCE A MARINE, ALWAYS a Marine. He didn't know what to call the kids. Some said zombies, but that wasn't right. Zombies were the walking dead, and these kids were the furthest thing. *Chucky* got tossed around, probably started by a fellow vet who just couldn't keep 'Nam from rattling around his head, but the name also rang true. These kids came at you out of nowhere just like the Viet Cong.

And the Chuckies *were* nightmares, too: monsters with a daughter's face, or a son's. Just like the old movies about that twisted little doll with a maniac's soul.

That day in early October when the world went FUBAR, he was with Grace at the assisted-living facility in Michigan, outside of Watersmeet. One second, he was scraping Cream of Wheat from her lower lip. The next, he woke up God knows how much later sprawled in a puddle of soupy cereal—blood dribbling from his ears, a headache drilling his brain—and there was Grace, that muzzy look gone, and she said, "Jed, honey, I think I peed my pants."

Technically, she'd pissed her Depends, but who cared? His sweet Grace was back. It was a miracle—

And it went bust the instant they staggered into the hall and saw the bodies: nurses and aides and doctors sprawled like pick-a-sticks.

And their granddaughter, Alice, placidly eating her mother's eyes.

That was almost four months ago. Now, they were into the second week of January and in Wisconsin, not Michigan. This early in the morning, the sun's light spilled watery and weak across a powder-blue sky. The air was still and glassy with that kind of brittle, mind-numbing cold that hacked flesh and made Jed long for a strong fire as he hiked on snowshoes along the cliff trail and down into the dense thicket of evergreens edging the lake. Pausing at the sharp dogleg left that led deeper into the woods and toward shore, he did a one-eighty. Even without the telltale streamer of gray smoke, he picked out their cabin, a good quarter mile easy, perched on a forested sandstone bluff. This time of day, the cabin's large picture window was no more than an inky rectangle, and their two horses no larger than specks of buckshot.

Vietnam had left its mark inside and out, as it had with every vet Jed knew. He'd taken a bullet through the left eye, which was bad enough, but then the round's diagonal trajectory had cored down and out the back of his head. In an instant, his left eye was jelly and his right occipital lobe went from functional to oatmeal. Technically, his right eye still worked, but the brain damage meant that, after 'Nam, he couldn't read or recognize words. Color was gone, too. His waking world had existed in ashy shades of gray, although his dreams and the flashbacks were always in Technicolor. Worse, his brain had conjured eerie shimmers the Navy shrinks said were hallucinations, like visual phantom limbs.

Like Grace, though . . . these days, he was different.

Now he stood, looking up at that distant cabin. Oh, he was still blind in that left eye, the eyeball itself long gone and the socket filled with a plastic implant sheathed with flesh. He never had gotten around to getting fitted for an artificial eye, maybe because he didn't mind making other people uncomfortable. Vietnam was wedged in his brain, good and tight, like a stringy piece of meat caught between his teeth that wouldn't be dislodged for love or money. So why should everybody else forget if he couldn't?

But his good right eye still worked, nowadays better than ever, and that was what he aimed at the dark wedge of window. He waited, and in a moment, the loose folds of a gauzy drapery swam into view. His vision sharpened on the leather couch and the fitful orange pulse of the fire. Further back, deep in the house, he spied Grace, who wore . . . he concentrated, the mental crosshairs aligning. Yeah, Grace had on that fuzzy pink sweater and was spooning coffee into an old pot, probably calculating the number of grounds per tablespoon, he bet.

Damnedest thing, her and numbers, like him going all hawk-eye. Grace had been smart before, first in her nursing school class and a whiz when it came to math. He'd always thought that if she'd been born fifteen years later, she might have been a doctor or, maybe, right up there with those real-life rocket scientists. After

Michael, though, she'd never been right. So when the Alzheimer's hit . . . well, it was almost a blessing. But then the FUBAR *had* happened and unlocked some hidden vault where she'd stored every equation and calculation since the dawn of time.

She'd saved the boy. Thank forty-plus years of nursing and accumulated smarts coming back just when needed. Healing that boy mended her, at least as much as a broken heart could stitch itself together. She pretended the boy was Michael and the boy let her pretend, and Jed loved him for that with a ferocity that took his breath away.

Odd Lake lay southwest of Wisconsin's Bad River Reservation and deep in the Nicolet. His ice-fishing house—a gutted camper tacked to a flatbed trailer—squatted a good half mile from shore. Go out onto the lake a little further and hang a left around the kink, though, and there the ice turned, becoming first rotten and then disappearing completely for a good fifty, sixty feet of blue-black water before picking up again. The reason was that the lake straddled a stray spur from the Douglas Fault, a rift that unzipped the earth from Minnesota to Ashland. The water bubbling through the fissure was warmer by a few degrees, so in winter that particular stretch never completely froze. And that made Odd Lake . . . odd. Venture out far enough onto that thin ice and you might as well bend over and kiss your ass good-bye.

The boathouse was solid weathered cedar with a north door and west-facing pine slider perched on a sandspit tongue now mantled with snow. Twenty-five years ago, when Michael was sixteen and wanted his own space, they'd worked on the interior together, mounting windows and stuffing in insulation before nailing up drywall and tacking on shelves. No pipes or wiring, and nothing fancy. All his son wanted was a rack and a little quiet. Three years later, Michael joined up and still got his rack, but there was no such thing as quiet for a Marine. Seventeen years after that, three somber men in dress blues knocked at their door, and two weeks later, Michael returned from Anbar Province in a flag-draped box. Michael had plenty of quiet now.

Jed's extremely good eye caught the instant the north door opened, but my God, he bet they heard those hinges squalling all the way to the Upper Peninsula. A prancing golden retriever squirted out first. A moment later, the boy, his lanky frame a black silhouette against the white of the snow, followed. If Jed let his mind go just a little soft, he could almost make himself believe, the way that Grace did, that this *was* Michael. But then the dog spied him and barked, the boy tipped a wave, and that bittersweet moment passed.

"You're back early. How was Baxter's?" the boy asked as Jed scuffed up.

Baxter's was an old bait-and-tackle place just west of the border with the U.P.: a four-day journey round-trip and neutral territory where folks bartered and gossiped. "It was all right. Those hinges need more WD-40. I told you to keep up with that."

"I'm sorry. Got the Spitfire done, though. All I had to do was yank the ignition wires. Pull the cord now and that boat should start right up. Haven't tested it because of the noise, but you've got spark."

"Oh. Well. Good job." Jed was put off his stride. He unhooked his rifle—a Tac-Ops Bravo 51—and leaned it against the boathouse, then bent to unclip his snowshoes. The Bravo was a good enough Kate but couldn't compare to the M40 he'd used as a sniper in 'Nam. Now, *that* girl really *had* lived up to her name: Kate = Kill All The Enemy. The dog lathered his face as he messed with the snowshoes' buckles. "Down, Raleigh, you old mutt."

"Jed, what are you angry about?"

"Tell you inside." Gritting his teeth against the scream of those hinges, Jed followed the boy. The boathouse was large, big enough to accommodate his Harley, the vintage Spitfire, a couple kayaks, and his snowmobile, but still deeply cold despite the insulation. "Damn it, son, I told you not to worry about the propane. You got to stay warm. You want that leg to lock?"

"I'm fine," the boy protested, but Jed was already fussing with the heater. He was angrier than he ought to be, and knew why.

"Jed." A hand on his shoulder. "Just tell me."

So he did, talking as he worked WD-40 back and forth, first on the hinges of the north door and then on the slider's rails and rollers. When he was done, the can was half-empty and the boy was quiet. Jed said, "You're not surprised."

"No." Stirring through a toolbox, the boy selected a flex-handled socket wrench. "They say what branch?"

"No one's sure. Might be Army, might be a bunch of different branches. There haven't been any real military around here since the Navy packed their seabags and skedaddled out of that radio place down by Clam Lake. My money's on some of those private

militias. They were pretty damned organized *before* the FUBAR."
Tossing the WD-40 onto a shelf, Jed rested one cheek on the saddle
of his Road King and watched as the boy tightened the propeller
nut, testing the give and wobble. The propeller was from an abandoned twin-prop, but the airplane engine was an antique and just
powerful enough to turn his stripped-down, jury-rigged, ten-foot
Spitfire into a halfway-decent wind sled. Designed to float over ice
the way an airboat skimmed shallow water, the wind sled *should*
work, in theory anyway. Nearly four months after the world died,
Jed was still too spooked to crank up anything that loud.

"Before I left for Baxter's, Abel hinted that if I was to see any
kid *wasn't* a Chucky, I ought to bag him because he knew a couple
hunters and they'd take whoever I brought in." He paused. "He
said they'd even take a Chucky, so long as it was alive."

"For what?"

"Dunno." But he could guess. *He'd* seen enough in 'Nam, and
his father had been a guest of the Japs after his plane went down
over the Pacific. The Nazi docs weren't the only ones who liked
to experiment. Sometimes Jed wondered which Jap bug-eater on
Chichi-jima had been the first to take a good hard look at all those
tasty American airmen and think *beef on the hoof*.

"Why didn't you say anything?"

"Might just be Abel flapping his gums." This was a lie. Their only
neighbor in a seven-mile radius, Abel was on the wrong side of
eighty and never ventured far if he could help it. Still, when the
old man had shuffled to the cabin, Jed had first dismissed the visit
as nothing more than Abel's looking for another handout before

Jed took off. Jed could even sympathize. Abel was fifteen years older, alone, and forced to rely on whatever he could scrounge, snag, or snare. In a winter that was shaping up to be pretty bad, that wouldn't be much. Sparing food for his elderly neighbor was the right thing to do. But then Jed saw how those old dog's eyes darted here and there. Cataloging subtle changes? A stray piece of clothing? A door open that was ordinarily closed? Maybe. Times being the way they were, Jed and Grace had been very careful not to advertise about the boy, but Jed now thought that Abel guessed something was up. Hell, Jed wouldn't put it past that old fart to rat them out on nothing more than a hunch if it meant a good meal. Yet Jed had kept his suspicions about Abel to himself, and knew why: because the boy would leave, and he and Grace would be alone again. Simple as that.

"Whether they're military, militia, or a mix, they'll have plenty of volunteers if they're doling out food and supplies." Replacing the wrench, the boy wiped engine grease from his hands with a bandana from Jed's Rolling Thunder days. "I think we both know what this means, Jed."

The words stung. "We could hightail it to the island instead. No one'll be there. From the island, it's another thirty-five miles to the Canadian shore, and seventy before you get close to anything like a town. We'll be invisible. The only people who ever came to that island were kayakers—and not even that often because of the cliffs. Just no good place to put in and not end up with your boat splintered into toothpicks. But we could make it. Now you got that sled working, all we do is get to Superior and put in."

8

"Jed, it's the middle of winter. Even if we managed to get the snowmobile and Spitfire to Lake Superior without being caught or seen, as soon as the engine of either one kicks in, we might as well take out an ad. Plus, there's no way we can carry enough gas to refuel. If we conk out in the middle of the lake, that means we walk a very long way *and* drag along whatever supplies we can salvage, which won't be much. Once we're on the ice, we'll have no cover. If we lose the Spitfire and then hit a patch of thin ice or water, we're as good as dead."

"Then why did we build the damn wind sled in the first place?"

"You know why. You told me yourself: if we need to move out of here fast, a snowmobile can't cut across Odd Lake—not over that stretch of rotten ice. Only a wind sled would have a chance of making it. Stick to the plan, Jed. You don't even know if you have to leave here. If you do, then you and Grace kayak to that island of yours come spring. Better yet, get yourself a sailboat once you make it to Superior. There've got to be plenty lying around, and it's not like their owners are going to mind. That way, you won't have to rely on anything with a motor. A sailboat would be safer, and the weight you save *not* taking gas you can make up for with food and other supplies you're going to need."

"What about you?"

"You know what I have to do."

"Well, that's just crazy. It's suicide. You don't even know if she's still alive." He saw the change in the boy's face: a streak of pain, there and gone as swiftly as a comet. "What?"

"You know that tight feeling you get waiting for a firefight? Well, that's how I feel now, and it's only getting stronger. She's alive and in trouble, Jed. I've got to leave, soon, or I'm going to explode."

He *did* know the feeling. Waiting around for an attack you knew was coming was an exercise in slowly losing your mind. Some of the worst knock-down, drag-out brawls he'd gotten into had been in that lull. Jed let go of a long sigh because there was no use arguing, and he understood how the boy felt about the girl. Hell, Jed would've done the same for Grace.

"Can you wait?" When the boy hesitated, he added, "A week, ten days at the most; that's all I'm asking."

"Can I ask why?"

All of a sudden, it was very hard to swallow. "Michael's birthday. I know Grace has held back enough flour and sugar to bake a cake. It would mean a lot to her." He paused, then added, roughly, "Me, too."

"Then, of course, I'll stay," Tom Eden said. "No problem."

He'd lied.

Tom watched as Jed trudged back up the trail and disappeared into a thick screen of tamarack and hemlock. Now that he was better, Tom came up to the cabin only for meals, which was safer all the way around. Just no telling who might show up, and Jed and Grace were already in danger for sheltering him. He owed them his life. If they'd chosen another route west or hadn't gotten curious about those three dead kids sprawled in that convenience store lot, he would have died. As it was, by the time the fever broke and his delirium passed, four days were gone, and he was in Wisconsin.

God, poor Alex. Despite the deep cold, a hot-white burn flared in his chest, and he had to clamp back on a moan. She must've been frantic when she returned and found him gone. That's how he would've felt. And she *had* come back; he knew it. She was stubborn, a fighter. He would never have given up on her—

All of a sudden and out of thin air, there came a tiny, frightened whimper.

No. His breath thinned and died. Tom went absolutely still. Had he been a different person in any other place and time, he might have glanced at the dog or thought there must be a small animal, like a chipmunk or maybe even a squirrel, scuttling by. But Tom was not someone else. After Afghanistan, he could never be anyone else—and, maybe, not even himself.

The whimper—really, a choked sob—came again.

Ignore it, just like the doctors said. Come on, breathe. He dug the heels of his hands into his temples as he pulled in a long, cold draw, let it out, sucked in again. *Just breathe, this isn't real, this isn't—*

"Puh-puh-plee." Other than *candee* and *meester*, this probably had been the only English the little girl knew, and oh Jesus, he would know that voice anywhere. She rattled off something in rapid-fire Pashto he didn't understand and then said again, "Plee, plee . . ."

"No," he whispered. "You're not there. Go away, go—" He squeezed his eyes tight, as if doing that would block out the rest, but it was already much too late. He could feel the flashback biting into his brain, digging in with its claws. His head swam, and a thick layer of dust suddenly clogged his throat. *That's not real. There's no dust. I'm in Wisconsin; it's winter. I am not hearing this.* He tried clamping down on his thoughts and muscling himself back under control, but now the Afghan sun was baking him alive; he was hot, so hot, and there was grit between his teeth and on his tongue, and he could hear the hollow *boom-boom-boom* of distant weapons fire. The blast suit was suddenly there, too: a seventy-pound cocoon of hard armor and polyurethane padding that weighed him down just as heavily as these chains of memory.

A crackle of static. "For God's sake, Tom!" A sputter and then Jim—his best friend, a person he trusted with his life—said through the headphone over Tom's right ear, "Jesus, Tom, come on, man, get out, just cut—"

No, Jim, you're dead. Tom was panting now. He couldn't help it. *You're dead, Jim, I shot you—*

"Amereekan." Not a girl now, but a boy: no less frightened and just as young, his trembling voice dribbling in through the ambient mike by Tom's left ear: "Amereekan, please, Amereekan, please, please . . ."

"Leave me *alone*," Tom ground out. He'd once told a shrink that being caught in a flashback was like having your mind sucked down the throat of an inky whirlpool. You were just *there*, in a nightmare swirl of images that became more and more like real things and not only shadows of memory. "Get out of my head. I can't save you. I can't save anybody, I can't—"

"Tom." Another girl, but a much older voice—and someone he also knew, oh, so well. "Tom, help me, please."

Alex. Everything, all of him, went dead inside. He couldn't feel his heart at all. She wasn't there; he knew that. But he would give his life to see her again, and if he turned around—if he opened his eyes and peered into that awful past—she would be there, on her knees, in the rubble, beneath a merciless sun. That, he thought, he couldn't bear. *No, God, don't do this, please, don't—*

"Tom," Alex said again, and her voice was shaking; she was pleading and she sounded so much like that little girl! "Tom, don't do this. Don't leave me here to—"

"Alex, I can't. Oh, God, *please*," Tom rasped. He was not going to look. This was not real and Alex was not there; she was *never* part of that horror. "God, please stop this, pl—"

"Tom, come *on*." Jim was back. His friend's voice crackled with urgency. "Forget it, man, you got to get out. Cut the wire, come on, grab the kid and get out! Leave her, Tom, leave the girl, you've got to get—"

"*STOP!*" he roared. The shrinks always said he ought to calmly talk himself down, but then again, they weren't trapped in this endless loop. "Stop, *please*, just *stop!*"

That worked. In the next instant, Tom felt his brain abruptly disengage as the flashback finally let go. That was always the same, too, and if he had to put words to it, the sensation was like bulleting through a brittle pane of window glass, his body shattering from one world to the next.

At his side, the dog, Raleigh, nudged Tom's good thigh and let out a short, sharp yip.

"He-hey, b-boy," Tom said. He was shuddering, and he felt his knees beginning to hinge. Gripping the doorjamb with his right hand, Tom held on tight until the wood bit his flesh. The pain wasn't bad, but it was enough. It was, in fact, perfect. The dog let out another rough *wuff*, and then leaned in as if trying to prop Tom up the way a bookend kept a stack of flimsy paperbacks from tumbling to the floor.

"Thanks, boy. I kn-know." He let out a long, trembling breath. "Sit down before I fa-fall down."

Groaning, Tom stretched out on an old army cot. The springs complained, and he winced as his mangled muscles caught and then grudgingly relaxed. Beneath his parka, he could feel his shirt sticking to the skin between his shoulder blades. Gradually, he got his breathing under control, and that sick, woozy, light-headed feeling passed. Satisfied now, the dog did three turns and settled with a sigh onto an olive-drab blanket.

Jesus. Tom armed sweat from his forehead. That had been bad, but he thought he knew why. The ache in his heart—the absence that was Alex—was a scream that only got louder and stronger with each day that passed.

I've got to leave, get back to Michigan, before I lose my mind.

And he *could* manage it now. Tom ran a hand over his right thigh where Harlan had shot him the day they'd lost Ellie. He had another new scar on his neck: a souvenir from that fight in the convenience store parking lot when that kid had tried to tear out his throat. But it was the leg that had been the worst, that had nearly finished him. The wound had healed to a fist-sized crater tented with thick, shiny, taut scar tissue. He'd lost some strength, although his limp was improving and he could muster a fast jog now. Still, the leg might be a problem, especially in the backcountry. Jed would want him to take one of their two horses, but of course, he'd refuse. If Jed and Grace had to leave this place for any reason, they'd need their animals. So maybe steal a horse somewhere else? He'd cover the eighty-plus miles to the Michigan border a lot faster if he did. But any animal—or person, for that matter—was also an added responsibility, something he'd told Ellie himself right before they left the Waucamaw. They couldn't rescue everyone.

For all the good I did Ellie. The thought forced a lump to his throat. In his mind, he'd always known that their survival came down to a very simple equation: either he had the strength and the will to do whatever it took to keep Alex and Ellie alive, or the people he had come to care for would die. And so he had failed. Again. When it counted, he hadn't been able to save Ellie. Thinking of the little girl still hurt, although the nightmares had finally faded. The chances Ellie was still alive were between slim and none. Ellie was dead, and that was on him. He didn't like it, but he *could* let go.

Alex was . . . different. God, he wished he'd found the courage to tell her everything, the whole terrible mess, what he'd done and at what price. Of all people, *she* would have understood, and that would have saved him. He pressed a palm to his chest and felt the hard thump of his heart. The pain whenever he thought about her was something raw, an ache that was more than grief and sharper than sorrow. It was longing. It was need. It was the sense of something that wasn't over and he hoped never would be. He simply refused to believe that she was lost to him.

And she was in danger. He just *knew*. That had to be why his mind put her in Afghanistan, too, where death might be under a rock or in a bag of trash or strapped to—

Don't go there; don't think it. A groan tried pushing its way past his teeth. He thought he still had time to save Alex but not much. He might already be too late.

Please, God. He flung an arm over his eyes. *Please, help me. I'm not asking for a miracle. Just keep her safe a little while longer until I can get to her, that's all. Please.*

Of course, nothing happened. No lightning bolts, no heavenly choirs, no angels. The dog only groaned, and the heater hummed. A sudden fist of wind shook the boathouse and rattled the boards, but that was just a lot of air.

That was all right. What mattered was how he felt and what he knew. Alex was alive and he was going back. He would find her, or die trying.

"Hang on, Alex," he whispered. "Hang on."

PART ONE: SACRIFICE

1

Oh God, help me, please, help me. Alex felt her mind begin to slip, as if the world was ice and begun to tilt and she was going to slide right off and fall away into forever if she didn't hang on tight. Her heart was trying to blast right out of her chest. She was shaking, all over, the hay hook in its belt loop bouncing against her right thigh. The pyramid, row after row of skulls, loomed at her back: all that remained of those who'd stumbled into this killing field before her. And of course, there was the smell—that familiar reek of roadkill and boiled sewage.

This can't be happening; it's not happening.

But it was. They were right there, no more than a hundred feet from where she groveled in the snow. Five Changed. Two girls. Three boys.

She watched, not daring to move, as they fanned out in a rough semicircle. Three wore camo gear: a punky middle schooler, a sullen girl with the livid slash of a scar on one cheek, and a greasy-haired kid with terminal acne. Stirring the snow into arabesque whirls, a stray breath of wind tugged at the fraying ends of some bizarre, stenciled kerchiefs knotted around the kids' throats and biceps. Many more rags fluttered from buttonholes like colorful fringes on buckskin.

The remaining two kids, a boy and a girl with wolf skins draped over their heads and shoulders, were about her age. Their faces were hidden, but what pulled her mind out of the well of her terror was how *familiar* the boy seemed. Why? Her eyes ticked over bits and pieces: the jut of his chin, the firm line of his jaw, and his eyes—hard, glittery as a crow's. She couldn't tell their color; those eyes might be brown or mossy green—

Or a deep, smoky blue, as dark and strange as ancient ice.

Oh no. It couldn't be. It had been months. Tom was dead. This couldn't be Tom, could it? Frantic now not just with fear but dread, she pulled in a huge breath, trying to tease out Wolf Boy's scent. Tom's was musky and complex, a heady aroma that never failed to find its way deep into her chest. She would know him by scent alone, anywhere, but all she got now was that overpowering stench and the reek of her fear.

But I feel like I should know him. He looks so famil—

Her stomach bottomed out as the wolf-girl stepped past the others to halt less than twenty feet away. Aside from the whole wolf thing, she looked like the kind of privileged, moneyed kid Alex had always hated. No mistaking that black widow logo over the left breast; that was some serious designer skiwear. Her outfit made those rags or bandanas or whatever she'd tied around her wrists seem almost classy. And because the girl was so close, Alex also got a very good look at that corn knife, a wicked thing that was crusted with gore and as long as the kid's forearm.

Alex's eyes flicked to Nathan's rifle, the one Jess had forced him to give her. She'd dropped it when she'd come upon the skulls and vomited her guts out, and now the weapon was on the snow ten feet to her right. She could go for it, but even if her aim was true and she managed to squeeze off a shot, she'd be dead a second later.

Because four of these Changed were packing. A small Beretta for the runty middle schooler; a scoped big-bore lever-action for the wolf-boy, who was so maddeningly familiar. Slash, the girl with the scar, held a bolt-action, but it was Acne's rifle that really snagged her interest, because it was outfitted with a gas piston to prevent jams. That made complete sense when you were someplace where a weapon might get fouled pretty easily: say, Iraq, Afghanistan—or the deep woods in winter. So, chance? Had Acne simply lucked out? Grabbed the first rifle he saw? She didn't think so, not from the way he held that weapon. Hang around enough people who know their guns and you learn to spot someone who is really comfortable versus a person who'd be happier with a live cobra. Besides, this was the U.P., and she'd once lived in Wisconsin, where everyone hunted. So she bet this kid knew guns. They all must.

She got where this was going, too. Her end was inked in blood and a motley scrawl of shredded clothes and hacked bones.

Well, no use being coy. She tugged off her gloves with her teeth, keeping one eye on Spider as her shaking fingers fumbled with the bindings of her snowshoes. When she stepped out of them, the snow squealed beneath her weight, but she only sank an inch. Good. Still moving with care, she thumbed off her backpack. There was a jackknife with the rest of the gear Jess had stowed, but the blade was a toothpick against that corn knife. Still, the pack had some heft. Maybe ten, fifteen pounds. She choked up on the straps with her left hand. Might be useful if she got close enough to—

Her thoughts derailed as the air suddenly thickened, and another odor, a complex pop of fresh sap cooked with green pine, wormed into that roadkill reek. What *was* that? She saw Spider shoot a glance at Wolf, and then, a second later, that stinging charry smell got stronger. All the Changed were tossing looks back and forth now, and they were *grinning,* like they shared some private joke.

Her mind flashed to that long, awful road into Rule—and the instant she'd realized the wolves were there because of how *heavy* the air grew as the alpha's scent bloomed: still *wolf* but also *no threat.*

So was this communication? Complex thoughts couldn't be conveyed just through smell, could they? She didn't know. Bees danced. Birds sang, but entire flocks moved as one and with virtually no sound at all. Those wolves hadn't so much as growled, and now these kids were looking at one another as the air boiled.

Like there's something suddenly here that wasn't just a few seconds ago. The air's crowded. Alex's head went a little hollow. *But that can't be. They can't read minds.*

Could they? No, that was crazy. Still, was it less crazy than her funky super-sense of smell? *She'd* changed, just not the same way.

Well, she knew a way to find out—about the telepathy, anyway. Because she had two choices: let Spider kill her, or—

Her questing fingers closed over that hay hook and twisted it free: eighteen inches of cold-rolled steel as thick as her thumb, as sharp as an ice pick.

Or—

2

She exploded, catapulting across the snow, unfurling, leading with the hay hook and aiming right for Spider's face because that wicked curve of steel was what she wanted the girl to see. Deadly enough, but only if she got a good, hard slash that snagged something: an arm, a leg. Not going to happen. Spider's corn knife was a longer, bladed weapon with a lot of cutting area. One good chop and the fight would be over.

She drove for Spider, saw the other girl's flinch and look of utter shock—and that answered an important question. The Changed might read each other, but they could not read her.

Breaking from her paralysis, Spider brought the corn knife up and around in a wide, curving arc. At the very last second, Alex flicked her wrist and changed her line of attack, driving for Spider's chest now instead of her face. Spider tried to adjust, but momentum was her enemy now. The corn knife whizzed past and sliced only air.

Alex bulleted into her. The blunt curve of the hook speared Spider's chest, dead-center and hard enough that Alex felt the impact shiver up her arm and ball in her shoulder. Spider let out a loud *ungh*, and then she was backpedaling, trying to bring the knife down again. Alex saw the blade coming, and she uncoiled, swinging the pack in a deadly roundhouse, the weight of it like a heavy stone. Her eyes never left the corn knife, and she had just enough time to think how lucky she was that the blade wasn't double-edged.

There was a hollow *thud* as the pack hammered the girl's chin. Spider's head snapped back, and then the girl was spinning away in a swirl of blonde hair and wolf skin. Off-balance, Alex tried to pivot, but the tamped snow was slick. She felt the slide start; fought to regain her balance but couldn't find it. The snow blurred, rushed for her face as she fell, the hook driving into hard pack. The snow had some give but not a lot, and she screamed as the impact shuddered through bone and wrenched her right shoulder. She lost her grip on the hook, and then she was gasping, on her side: left hand still knotted in her pack; her right hand on fire, the wrist singing with pain, the fingers already numb. *Oh God, oh God, is it broken, did I break it . . . where's Spider, where . . . ?* She pulled in a frantic, sobbing breath. Her right elbow bawled; she couldn't move her fingers. *Broken or cracked or maybe the nerves, and oh God, where is Spider, where is she?*

Her head swirled with panic and pain. Both nearly killed her. As it was, she only just felt the attack coming, sensed it before she knew what was happening: a shuffle, the scuff of a boot in snow, a sudden rush of air. She snatched her head back just in time to catch a blur of white and black.

Spider: on her feet, rearing up, looming. Her lips curled, baring teeth that seemed very white and impossibly sharp. That girl could tear a person's throat out with those teeth.

Where's the knife, where's the knife, where is it? Her eyes jerked to Spider's right hand. Empty. *Nothing there, no knife, no knife, where is it?* Had she dropped it? But Spider's stance was all wrong; she was leading with her right shoulder, shuffling forward, her silver eyes flitting to a spot behind and to Alex's right. What? The knife was *behind* her? Alex started to crane around for a peek. *If I can get to it first—*

Then she thought, *Wait, leading with her right.* She gasped. *Left hand . . . she switched hands!*

Screeching, Spider brought the corn knife down in a vicious, left-handed chop. For a split second, all Alex could do was watch that blade come—and then, at the very last second, shock let her go. Releasing her pack, Alex snatched her left arm out of the blade's line and tried to roll. The blade cleaved air with a whistle, swishing past her ear to cut snow, the steel so close that Alex smelled the lingering copper of old blood and even the ghost of sweat from the farmer who'd once hacked at thick, stubborn stalks in September when the harvest was done.

Alex had the luxury of a half-second to think: *Close.*

And then there was pain, a lot of it, ice and fire roaring up her throat to crash out in a shriek. Twisting, she saw the corn knife buried up to the handle—and blood spraying a crimson starburst. Spider's knife had sliced a long strip of skin and meaty muscle that now dangled in a grotesque flap from Alex's left shoulder. Spider's face, dripply with blood, swam into view, and then Alex saw the knife coming up again—

"No!" Still turtled on her back, Alex tucked and kicked and jack-hammered her right boot into Spider's face. There was a splintery, crackly sound. The girl's head whipped back with a brisk snap, like a crash dummy's, and her jaws clamped with a dull *thock*. Spider let out a gargling, bubbling screech.

Most important of all, Spider lost her grip on the knife.

Knife, knife, the knife, her brain yammered, *go for the knife!* Alex moved. Rolling, she planted her boots, clawed to her feet. *Where's the knife, where is it?* She threw a fast glance left, and there it was, smeary with blood, just a few feet from the skulls.

Really, it came down to who was faster.

Alex plunged across the snow, her left shoulder still singing, blood slicking her wrist, her heart banging a wild, frenzied beat. Reaching down, she made a grab, felt her fingers curl around the wooden handle, and then she was jamming her right boot into the snow, pivoting, the grinning skulls blurring as she swung around, started to sweep up, elbow cocked, knife in hand—

What she saw next stopped her dead.

Something round and black and empty as a socket in a sightless skull hung less than six inches from her face.

A red fan of horror unfurled in her chest.

Nathan's rifle.

And then Spider squeezed the trigger.

3

Snick.

No boom.

A half-second later, she realized she was still alive.

A jam? A misfire? There was a round in the breech; Nathan had said so. Whatever. Didn't matter. She heard Spider suck in a surprised gasp, caught a glimpse of Spider's eyes going round—

Alex's right hand flashed. The thick blade clanged against the Browning's barrel, knocking the bore aside. The impact tumbled the knife from her fingers to the snow. No time to sweep it up again; she had to keep the business end of that rifle out of her face. Instead, she sprang for the barrel, got her hands around it, and yanked.

Recovering from her surprise, Spider did the smart thing. She didn't try wrestling the rifle away but drove forward. Scuttling back on her heels, Alex tried keeping her balance, but Spider was strong, with two good arms, and Alex knew this was one battle with gravity she would lose.

She teetered, the trees swirling as the world canted and slewed.

Spider swept forward with one leg, hooking Alex's ankles, sending Alex crashing against the pyramid. Pain rocketed up Alex's spine. She felt the skulls shift as the upper tiers toppled with dull clunks like marbles rattling onto wood. The lower levels, cemented with iced blood and frozen gristle, made for a sturdy, very convenient platform, and Spider knew it. Stiff-arming the rifle, the girl bore down, trying to grind the barrel against Alex's throat. Spider wasn't as tall as Alex, but she also wasn't hurt as badly, and gravity was on her side. Alex's arms began to shudder as her overstrained muscles weakened. Blood pattered onto her lips and into her eyes from Spider's ruined nose.

All at once, Alex's elbows gave. She had nothing left. The rifle came down as savagely as a guillotine. She felt a sudden grab of panic as her air cut out and her vision purpled. It was the parking lot all over again, only this time she had no knife and Tom would not come to her rescue. She bucked, but her feet dangled and she had no leverage.

So she did the only thing left. She went limp, half by instinct, half by design. Stopped pushing, stopped flailing. Just . . . let go.

She heard Spider gasp as the girl fell into her. Quick as a snake, Alex craned, lashed out, and sank her teeth into Spider's left cheek. Spider jerked, and then she was wailing. The pressure on Alex's throat was suddenly gone as Spider reared back so far that Alex's head lifted from the ruined pyramid. But Alex didn't let go. Sucking air through her teeth, she sawed her jaws from side to side. Alex felt the sudden give as Spider's skin tore, and then she was into muscle. Spider's blood, warm and brackish, bubbled into her mouth. Something ripped with a sound like wet cloth tearing in two. Bellowing, Spider stumbled back, one hand with its bracelet of colored rag clapped to her spurting cheek.

And Alex had the rifle now.

She surged to her feet. Her mouth was filled with Spider's blood and a meaty chunk of the girl's cheek. Alex spat, never taking her eyes from the girl, and then she was winding up like a batter and swinging, hard and fast The butt whirred, cleaving air. At the very last second, Spider sensed it coming; flinching, she ducked and made an abortive move to the right, which probably saved her life. The stock smashed into Spider's left temple with a loud, hollow sound like a heavy butcher's knife against a cutting board. Spider's head whipped right as jets of blood flew in long tongues. Spider's silver eyes rolled up to whites as her knees unhinged, and then the girl collapsed to the snow like a sack of soiled laundry.

Dizzy with pain, Alex swayed over the girl. Spider's face was a mess. Blood painted her jaw, and more streamed from the girl's nose, fiddleheads of steam curling into the still air where hot blood melted into snow. Spider's breath came in long, bubbling snores.

End it. Alex's stomach curdled at the taste in her mouth, sour and puckery with dying blood, the raw meat of Spider's flesh, and the lingering, metallic tang of spent adrenaline. Her throat felt like the neck of a brittle vase, every swallow bright and glassy. A high, whining buzz competed with the boom of her heart, but not so much that she didn't hear the crunch and squeal of snow and knew: the others were coming for her.

Kill Spider at least. Put a bullet in her head and then take one of them in the bargain. Tom wouldn't go down without a fight, and neither would Chris. Fight, damn you. Don't make it easy.

Her grip tightened on the rifle, but then she remembered something: the look on Spider's face at the moment the Browning *hadn't* fired. The rifle was loaded with .270-caliber Magnum shorts and one already in the breech. She'd seen it herself. If she tried again, the weapon might very well explode in her hands. People died like that, too. She could use the rifle as a club, keep them at bay, but all they had to do was wait for her to tire herself out.

Has to be another way. The useless rifle slipped from her fingers. *There has to be something I can do.* But what? They had superior numbers. From the looks of this place, hers was a scenario they'd watched unfold a hundred times before. Well—she flicked a quick glance at the gurgling Spider—maybe not. Beating Spider hadn't bought her anything except a little more time.

But every second I'm alive is one more moment I still have a chance to do something. She watched as they sidestepped the unconscious girl—and never wavered but just kept coming, silent and implacable, that weird choke of hot turpentine and resin mixed with roadkill so strong it was as if that scent somehow yoked them together the way beads ranged on a strong cord.

All right, she accepted that there was nowhere to go. Even if she bolted, beyond the circle the snow would be too deep. Could she surprise them again, the way she had Spider? Do something they wouldn't expect? Yes, that might work, especially if she could get hold of a weapon . . . but what could she use? *Come on, come on, think!* She took another quick step back, pressing up against what remained of the pyramid as the Changed drew so close that Wolf could've reached out and taken her hand.

But only if he put down Spider's corn knife first.

4

Her blood iced. Hips braced against the ruined tumble of frozen flesh and bone, she tried not to flinch as Wolf's gaze dragged over her body. His nostrils suddenly flared as he inhaled, long and deep, pulling in her scent. A moment later the too-pink tip of his tongue eeled from his mouth to skim his lips in a slow, sensual glide.

Oh God. Wolf was *tasting* her, *savoring* her scent the way a snake sampled the air. Her eyes flicked to the others. They were all standing there, mouths open, tongues writhing, drinking her in. A scream bubbled in her throat, and she felt her breath coming faster and faster. *No, don't.* She muscled herself under control. *This is what they want; they want you to panic; come on, don't lose it, don't lose it!*

Wolf edged closer. She could feel the hum of his anticipation; saw it in the set of his body, smelled his need on the air, read it in the way his gaze roved as if undressing her with his eyes. His was hunger and more: it was possession, deep and primal and sensual and awful in its power. *He* wants *me, and he'll have me, he'll—*

And that was when something very, very strange happened.

For just the briefest of moments, something so fleeting it was more an impression than an actual thought, an image swam into her brain—of her, stretched on the snow, clothes gone, and Wolf, crouching over her body, his tongue dragging over every inch of her skin—and she *felt* when his hands feathered down and between her—

No! Gasping, she cringed away, both from the scene playing itself out in her mind and this boy. *Get out of my head, get out of my head!* In the next instant, her mind seemed to snap back with a shock as physical as a slap. Her awareness sharpened to a laser-bright focus, and as she came back to herself, she felt her fingers clamped on icy bone.

And then the skull cupped in her right palm *moved.*

"Aahhhh!" Her shriek was wild, inarticulate, enraged. Wolf's arm was already coming up, steel flashing in the early light, but she had the skull now, was swinging with all she had left, thinking, *Hit him, and when he drops the kni—*

Something slammed against her right temple. The blow was so vicious, so stunning, Alex's mind blanked and stuttered the way a bad CD skips a track. She went down like a stone, the skull tumbling from her nerveless fingers. Through a swirl of pain, she saw Slash, the girl with the scar, standing over her, a cocked fist ready to strike again.

Even if Alex could have fought back, Acne never gave her the chance. He dropped onto her legs. A moment later, Slash straddled her chest and ground her knees into Alex's shoulders. A surge of white-hot pain flooded her chest, and Alex let out an agonized shout as Slash forced Alex's wounded left arm to straighten, tacking Alex's wrist to the snow with both hands.

Wolf loomed. He made sure she saw the knife, too. But it was when he drew back and she saw where he stood and read the tilt and angle of his body that Alex finally understood what would happen next.

He wasn't going to kill her, not yet. Oh no. Too easy. Too quick.

First, he would chop off her arm.

God, no, no! Her heart boomed. Frantic, she heaved and surged, but it was a waste of energy. The others were too heavy. She was pinned, and this was how it was going to end: in the snow, arms and limbs hacked away, her body emptying her life in a hot red river that would melt through the snow until there was nothing more for her heart to pump. She'd done enough amputations with Kincaid to know that you had to clamp off those arteries fast before they could spring back into muscle, or else you might as well just cut the poor guy's throat. But what if the Changed were so good at this that they knew which arteries to pinch? What if they kept her from dying fast and made her linger, carving her up, eating her alive, one juicy, quivering mouthful at a time? She might last a long, long time, because she didn't think anyone could die from pain. Maybe, for them, watching her suffer was part of the fun.

The corn knife flashed before her eyes. In her terror, the blade seemed a foot long and then ten feet and then a mile. Her vision was so keen that she picked out every nick, every scar where that razor-sharp edge had bitten into bone. The sewage stink of the Changed mushroomed and swelled—

And then she smelled something else, just behind that roadkill reek: not turpentine or resin, but a misty swarm of shadows from the deepest woods on the coldest, darkest night.

It was a scent she also knew, very well.

No, it can't be. This close, she could make out the boy's eyes, dark and deep as pits behind that wolf-skin mask. *He's got the same eyes, the same scent. But that's crazy, that's—*

The knife hacked down with a whir.

5

The heavy steel blade buried itself in snow with a meaty, muffled *boomph*. A quick lightning jag of heat and fresh pain streaked across her chest and blazed into her jaw. Her vision flashed dead-white, then fractured, turning jagged as a single great talon of pain dug into her. Yet there was a clarity in her mind, like a brilliant pane of clear glass, and she realized that while the pain was very bad, it was not the bright agony she expected if Wolf had just hacked off her arm.

Her eyes inched left.

Her arm was still there. So was her hand. But Wolf held a scrap of something drippy and wet and very red and—

Oh my God. Her breath, bottled in her chest, came in a sobbing rush. What Spider had begun, Wolf had finished. Horrified, she could only watch as Wolf inspected a flap of parka and skin and dying muscle.

Her muscle. Her heart was banging in her ears. *Her* flesh.

With a delicate, almost comical daintiness, Wolf tweezed the shredded, bloody parka as if removing a scrap of butcher paper from a freshly carved steak. Then, palming snow, he swiped the meat clean of gore and held it high, studying that slab of her flesh with a curious, strained intensity, smoothing the skin with his thumb. Looking for . . . what? She couldn't begin to imagine.

Satisfied, although with what she couldn't guess, Wolf threw her a quick, speculative look, and she had the insane thought that in another time and place, he might even have winked as if to say, *Watch this.*

And then he offered her flesh to Beretta.

Her gorge bolted up her throat. She gagged as Beretta teased the meat with his tongue, lapping her blood the way a kid licks the melt of an ice-cream cone. There was that queer, ripping sound of wet cloth again, and Beretta's jaws worked and he began to chew.

This isn't happening; this can't be happening. Numb, she watched as they ate, sampling her and licking their lips like those guys on *Top Chef* trying to decide if maybe the sauce needed a tad more salt. She felt her center skidding again. Soon she'd tumble off the thinning ice of her sanity altogether. Or maybe she'd just snap, her mind breaking like a dry twig, and start screaming. They'd have to cut her throat just to shut her up.

Now that they were so close, she also made out those weird, colored rags. They weren't single pieces but a patchwork sewn together with crude, irregular stitches that reminded her of Frankenstein's monster.

And the rags were not cloth.

They were leather.

They were skin.

Those colors weren't *just* colors either, but designs. A withered butterfly. A wrinkled coil of barbed wire. A tattered American flag. In the leather knotted around Wolf's throat, she made out a faded red heart and FRANK done in a fancy, black cursive swoop.

Now she knew why Wolf had used snow to scrub blood from that flap of her skin. He was looking for a good tattoo. The Changed were wearing . . . people.

Oh no no no no no oh God oh God oh God! A scream balled in her throat as Wolf took the last bit of her flesh and flipped back his cowl. So she saw his face. She got a very, very good look.

No. Something shifted in a deep crevice of her brain. *No. That's not right. I'm wrong. I have to be.*

But she wasn't. God help her, she wasn't.

6

The eyes were identical.

So were the nose and the high plains of his cheeks.

The face was a carbon copy. So was his mouth. Those lips were the twins of those that had pressed hers, and with a heat that fired a liquid ache in her thighs. The hair was longer but just as black. Even that shadowy scent was the same.

The only difference—and it was huge, because it was the margin between life and death—was a pale pink worm of a scar. The scar meandered from the angle of his left jaw, right below the ear, and then tracked across the hump of his Adam's apple before its tail disappeared beneath the collar of his parka.

Her parents had enjoyed talking shop at the dinner table. Having listened to her mother, who'd been an emergency room doctor, talk about cases and her cop father chime in with his own, first-responder stories, Alex knew how some people went about suicide and, especially, where to cut and how. Of course, a freak accident—say, a car crash—or a fight or even an operation might have produced the same scar, but she didn't think so. His skin was otherwise unmarred, too, though she would later wonder about his wrists and arms. Some people also scarred very badly. Thickness didn't necessarily translate to depth. But working by Kincaid's side as she had these last few months meant she now knew her fair share of anatomy.

To her eye, this cut had been wicked, a vicious slice long and deep enough to have slashed open the boy's jugular and, maybe, his carotid. Maybe—probably—both. Cut the carotid and a strong, young heart can empty the body in a crimson jet in a matter of about sixty to ninety seconds. That he hadn't bled out and had survived . . . well, his parents had probably seen that as a miracle and, maybe, some kind of sign.

By all rights, this boy should be dead. Once upon a time, he'd sure wanted to be. Call it an educated hunch. Later she would wonder what or who had saved him. Later still, she would find her answer, for all the good that would do, lucky her.

Other than the scar, there was no difference. Each could have inhabited either side of a mirror, albeit one with a crack. Each was a carbon copy of the other, perfect and identical in every detail, save that one flaw.

No wonder these Changed circled past Rule. No wonder.

Wolf was Chris.

And now, finally, she began to scream.

PART TWO:
THE ENEMY OF YOUR ENEMY

7

She'd vomited before bed and then once, quietly, during the night, spitting and retching into a chamber pot until there was nothing left but watery phlegm that burned her nose. Sleep finally spidered over her brain, laying a gray, dreamless web so thick that when the door slammed and the dog started barking, Lena jolted awake in a confused tangle, only half-convinced she'd heard anything at all. What? Her mind was gluey, but the barking didn't let up. Still druggy with sleep, she winced against the sound. Had to be Ghost. Why was Alex's dog barking?

"Shut *up*." Groaning, she rolled, mashing her pillow against her ears. "Lemme sleep, pl—"

"Sarah?" Someone was pounding up the stairs. "Lena? Wake up, wake up!"

"Tori?" Lena struggled to a woozy sit as her door flew open. Tori's hair was frizzed as a used Brillo pad, and the girl's eyes were wild. "What—"

"*Girl?*" A man's voice, roaring somewhere downstairs as Ghost kept up his yapping. "Girl, get down here! We need help!"

"What the hell?" Lena's mouth was sour with vomit. The stink of it hung in a fog over her bed. "Tori, who is that? What's going on?"

"*Chris!*" Tori blurted. Her knuckles jammed against her teeth. "Chris's *hurt*. They said he's hurt real *bad*."

"What?" Now fully alert, Lena swung her legs over the edge of her bed, grimacing as her feet hit hardwood. Even through socks, the floor was icy, colder than it should be. She stood up too quickly, and a sweep of nausea left her dizzy. *Oh God, not now.* Gulping back a surge of rancid bile, she gripped the mattress, steadied herself, and then grabbed her jeans from a bedpost. "How did he get hurt? Where's Jess?"

"She's *gone!*" Tori wailed, as Sarah, their third housemate, crowded into the room. "So is Alex!"

"Relax. Alex probably didn't come back from the hospice, that's all," Lena said, shucking her nightgown. Her skin pebbled with gooseflesh and she shivered. Why was it so cold?

"No, no," Tori shook her head in a vigorous negative. "Her door's open, but her bed's still made and—"

"Come on," Sarah said, as Lena shrugged into a sweatshirt. "Let's find out what's going on."

In the kitchen, there were two guards, one bearded and one not, in winter whites. Through the window, Lena spied a third—she thought his name was John—staggering up the side steps.

With a body.

"Oh my God." Lena's heart catapulted into her mouth as John ducked inside on a pillow of bitter air. Chris was draped over the guard's shoulders, and as John staggered across the kitchen, blood drizzled from the boy's hair to ink the floor in thick, scarlet coins.

"Where can I put him?" John was sweating so much, steam curled from his head.

"This way." Sarah threw open the wide double doors between the kitchen and Jess's sitting room. Lurching after, John stooped to ease Chris off his shoulders and onto a couch. "Watch it, watch it," John chanted as Chris's weight shifted and his body slid to one side. "Don't let him—"

"I've got him," Lena said, cradling Chris's head. His hair was tacky, and she felt the blood squelch between her fingers as she applied pressure. The smudged hollows of his eyes were brown as coffee. His lips were glassy, nearly transparent. A red tongue of blood slicked the right side of his face and dribbled down his neck, and at the sight, she felt her unruly stomach do another slow roll. "What happened?"

"Got kicked in the head." John was puffing. A large splash of Chris's blood stained the guard's shoulders crimson. "Night shied and threw him, and then she let fly. Jess's hurt, too."

"What?" Sarah and Lena said at the same time. "How?" Lena asked.

"John, we got to go," the bearded guard cut in. "We got to get Doc and we got to do it fast before—"

"Just call him on your radio," Lena said. The battery-powered radios were pre-sixties relics, used sparingly and only in true emergencies, but this surely qualified. She nodded toward the bulky, olive-green handset clipped to John's belt. "Kincaid could be here in—"

"Can't do that," the other guard warned. "Everyone'll—"

"You think I don't know that?" John snapped.

"What are you talking about?" Lena asked at the same time that Tori said, "I don't understand. Why not use your radio?"

John ignored them both. "Nathan's coming," he said to the guards. "Someone's also got to get Jess's horse."

"I'm on it," the bearded guard said.

"Jess was out riding?" Lena said. "*Now?* It's *freezing*."

"All right, come on," John said. He hurried from the room, the guards a step behind.

"Hey, wait a minute." All Lena knew about head injuries was that they were bad, and Chris was still bleeding. "Chris needs a doctor!"

"And we'll get him. Just hold tight. We'll be ba—" But whatever else John said was hacked off by the slam of the kitchen door.

"Hold *tight*?" Tori echoed.

"It's all we can do," Sarah tossed over her shoulder as she ducked back into the kitchen. "Lena, don't let up that pressure. I'll be right back. Tori, get a fire started in here."

"This is just wrong," Lena said. Through the front window, she watched the men boost onto their horses. John's rifle hung in a bright red scabbard secured to the off-side of a dapple gray, while each guard's crossbow was fitted to a scabbard off-side and just behind the cantle. The men thundered off toward the woods, leaving Night, Chris's blood bay, prancing on his tether.

"Wait," Tori said. She hadn't made a move toward the hearth. "Aren't those archers?"

"Yeah," Lena said—and that was very weird. The archers monitored the woods edging the Zone, which lay southwest of the village. So if the archers were *here*, did that mean Chris had been out *there*?

"Why would Chris be in the Zone? No one's allowed out there," Tori wondered aloud, echoing Lena's thoughts. "The supply party was headed for Wisconsin, and that's a straight shot *west*. Last I heard, they're not due back for a couple days."

"I don't know." Lena felt the slow, insistent leak of Chris's warm blood through her fingers. Where was Sarah with those towels? "I guess Chris got back early."

"But why would he go through the Zone?" Tori persisted. "He's got to know that the guards would never allow him back into the village if he came that way."

"Maybe he didn't come that way," Lena said.

"But then what?" Tori pressed.

"I don't know," Lena said again, and then looked over as Sarah bustled up with dish towels. "Do you understand any of this?"

"No. Here, let up a second," Sarah said, slipping a balled towel against Chris's head and then nodding at Lena. "Okay, hold that while I tie it down."

"One of us has to go for Kincaid," Lena said as Sarah twisted a second towel and then looped it around Chris's head in a make-shift bandage.

"No, what we've got to do now is tend to Chris," said Sarah.

"But you don't need two of us." Shuddering, Lena smeared her sticky palm on her thigh, painting her jeans with a purple exclamation mark. "I'll get Kincaid. On Night, I could be there in fifteen, twenty minutes max."

"I need you here."

"More than we need a doctor?"

"Yes." Sarah pushed up from the couch. "We've got to strip him down, see if he's hurt anywhere else. I'll get some hot water. I filled the reservoir last night, so we—"

"You can't," Tori broke in. "There's no hot water. The stove's out. That's why it's so cold in the house."

"What?" Sarah stared. "Jess never lets the stove go."

"Well, she did last night, which is strange, because I know she was up late. I came down for some tea a little after midnight, and Nathan was inside, with Jess. They were in the kitchen, and I kind of overheard them . . ." Tori fumbled. "You know, on the stairs."

"You mean, you were eavesdropping," Sarah said.

Tori flushed to the roots of her hair. "Well, I—"

"Oh, shut up, Sarah," Lena said. "What did they say, Tori?"

"Nathan said that Greg brought in a boy, a Spared, and he was hurt pretty bad."

"A boy?" That grabbed Lena's attention. "When? From where? Last night?"

"No. Afternoon. And I think he came from around Oren, but I-I'm not sure. I didn't get the rest because Jess must've heard me and she told Nathan to hush and then I . . ." Tori's throat moved in a nervous swallow. "You know, I went back to my room."

"So you wouldn't be caught spying," Sarah said.

"God, would you give it a *rest*?" Lena snapped. To Tori: "Did you hear anything else?"

"No, but there was something else kind of weird." Tori's forehead crinkled in a sudden frown. "I could've sworn that Alex's door was shut last night. So why is it open now?"

"Because Alex probably stayed to help Kincaid, and Jess got some clothes together for her, that's why," Sarah said, briskly. "There's no mystery here, and we have things to do now. You get the fire going, Tori. I'll see to the woodstove." Sarah looked at Lena. "We'll need clean cloths. Bandages, too, and whatever else you can find. The first-aid kit's in Jess's bathroom linen closet, second shelf."

Now Lena didn't want to leave. If Chris regained consciousness and if they *had* found a Spared . . .

Slow down. You don't know what this means. But Chris kept his word. He's back early. He went to Oren, and maybe the boy he found—

"Lena." She looked up to see Sarah studying her with narrowed eyes. "What?" Sarah demanded.

"Nothing." She turned away before Sarah could ask anything more and pushed into the kitchen. Prancing up, tail wagging furiously, Ghost suddenly skidded to a halt five feet away.

"What is it, boy?" The Weimaraner's body was rigid, and as Lena reached to give the pup a reassuring pat, the dog ducked away. She halted, confused. "Ghost? What—"

"Lena!" It was Sarah. "I need that kit!"

"Coming!" Brushing past the dog, Lena hurried to the connecting door, which led to a short hall and Jess's room. The bedroom had a funky, frigid, old-lady odor of too-sweet talcum powder and musty farts. Lena's eyes slid from bed to night table to an old-fashioned vanity. A long wool skirt and sweater were draped over a walnut rocker. Her gaze lingered on the neatly made bed.

Jess never went to sleep, but she changed, because those are the clothes she wore yesterday. Which meant Jess went riding in her nightgown? Okay, just more weirdness on top of an already bizarre morning. Turning, she headed for the bathroom, but as she passed Jess's open closet, her gaze dropped and snagged on a wink of brass. Her first thought was that Jess had dropped an earring. But then her brain caught up with what she was seeing.

And she thought: *What?*

8

In the life she'd had before Rule, Lena often thought of blowing Crusher Karl's head off. Her stepfather had been an avid hunter; most Amish were. The problem was that Crusher Karl hadn't owned a handgun, and his shotgun and rifles were just too big. Worse, her stepfather kept them all in a padlocked cupboard to which he had the only key. (So when she saw her chance a year ago, she'd used the knife. Whatever worked.)

Now, in Jess's bedroom, she stared as her mind tried to make sense of what she saw, because what lay on that floor didn't belong and yet there it was, as round and fat and real as a dog turd.

A shotgun shell.

The shell was capped with shiny brass, and words and numbers were stenciled on the sides of the black cartridge: HD ULTIMATE HOME DEFENSE 1250 – 1¼ 2×4. And in fancier letters, REMINGTON.

Jess had a *shotgun*? News to her. She threw a glance over the closet floor. Shoes—and a step stool.

Something on the closet shelf, she bet. She looked up, her gaze ticking over two neat stacks of boxes before snagging on a black tongue of quilted fabric that dangled just over the lip of the shelf.

The step stool made it easy, and she saw at once that the shotgun case was empty. An open cardboard box of cartridges squatted nearby. There were slots for the shells, and she counted ten slots in all. Only three shells remained. Add in the one on the floor, and that meant the shotgun held six rounds. That tallied. Crusher Karl always made a big show of loading: five in the magazine and one in the breech. Jess must've been in a hurry, too, because she'd fumbled then dropped the shell and never bothered to pick it up.

There was something else on the shelf, too, at the very back: a square, black, soft-sided case.

Lena stared at that for a long moment. She knew, instantly, what it was, and where it belonged. The pack was Alex's and *belonged* in Alex's room, on her desk where she always kept it. Lena had no idea what was inside, but she did know that the pack had no business being in Jess's room. Like, none.

So. What. The. He—

A loud, high scream ripped the air. Gasping, Lena nearly slipped off the step stool as Tori—and yes, it was Tori—screamed again, and then Lena was scrambling down, stuffing the shotgun shell into a sweatshirt pocket, and dashing into Jess's bathroom.

This is crazy. She snatched up an armful of towels and the bright-orange first-aid kit and pounded out of Jess's room. *First Chris and now Jess—and where's Alex? Why is her case in Jess's room? Why would Jess need a shotgun?* Heart thumping, she burst into the kitchen, then pulled up fast, her jaw dropping as she got a really good look.

Jess lolled in Nathan's arms, her hair flowing in a gray river that brushed the floor. Blood streamed over the old woman's face and splashed her chest in a broad red bib. She looked terrible. Hell, she looked dead.

"Oh my God, what *happened*?" Lena asked, aghast. "Who *did* this?"

Nathan's face was granite. "Alex."

9

"*Alex?*" Lena said. "Why?"

"I don't have time for this," Nathan said, and then jerked his head at John. "Give me a hand here. You, Sarah, bring me a propane heater, and let's get this front room warmed up, fast."

"What about *Kincaid*?" Lena shouted, but Nathan didn't slow. As Sarah darted past, Lena snagged her arm. "This is nuts. I'm going for the doctor."

"No." Sarah shook free. "You're not going anywhere."

"Why not?" She pushed her way past Ghost and Nathan's dog. Growling, lips curling to reveal teeth, both animals lowered their heads, then danced aside as she flung her armful of supplies onto the kitchen table. "Does this make sense? Do you think Alex would do something like *that* to an old lady?"

"Maybe," Sarah huffed, backing out of a kitchen closet with a propane heater. "Jess is tough, and you did plenty when you ran."

Lena's face flamed. "That was different. It was a guard, an old *guy*."

"I can see it, though. I think Alex has the guts to do whatever it takes. Remember, she's killed Changed."

"Those are just stories."

Sarah gave Lena a smug little grin. "Not according to Peter."

Oh, Sarah *would* bring up Peter just to rub it in. She wasn't at all surprised that the idea of Peter with Sarah hurt just as much now as before. She had used Peter, yes. But not everything with him had been a lie, then—or since.

"Tori, give me a hand here." Sarah jerked her head at Lena. "You, finish the woodstove. I'll do Jess's after we set up the heater."

Lena opened her mouth to argue, then said, instead, "We'll need more wood." Without waiting for a reply, she shrugged into her coat, grabbed up the now-filled ash pail, and hurried out of the house. But instead of heading around back, she set the pail down, ducked her head, and motored over the icy walk for the street. To hell with this. She was going for Kin—

"Hey!"

Gasping, Lena tore her gaze from her feet too late and smacked face-first into the boy's chest so hard that she thumped back onto her tailbone.

"Whoa! Hey, Lena, you okay?" Greg dropped to one knee as his golden retriever bristled and tried muscling past. "Daisy, back up, *sit*!"

"Ow." Her butt killed. Still, if she could get Greg into the house, she might have a chance. Grabbing his hand, she let him haul her up. "Yeah, I'm okay. Sorry. What are you doing here?"

"I brought the flatbed . . . Daisy, *stop*!" Turning, the boy grabbed his dog's collar and wrestled the growling animal to a sit. "What's the matter with you? Sheesh." To Lena: "I had to hitch up down a ways, what with all the horses out front. Ah . . . is Chris inside? I saw Night."

"Yeah, he's—"

"Oh crap." Greg looked unhappy. "He's going to be pissed I left Alex at the hospice."

"Wait, what? When?"

"Last night. I was supposed to stay until she was done and then take her home, only I was just so beat and she told me to go on. Wouldn't you know it that the one time I go is when Chris comes back early."

"Greg, Alex is gone."

"What?" His eyebrows drew together beneath a froth of muddy-brown curls. "She can't be. She's with Doc."

"Not anymore." Then something else registered. "Greg, how long have you been back? Why were you at the hospice?"

"Chris and us guys, we split off from Peter at the Wisconsin border a couple days ago and went north. Brought back this kid."

So they *had* found a Spared. It was all Lena could do not to grab Greg by the lapels. "Where?"

"Some old barn northwest of Oren. He was pretty bad off. His heart stopped while we were still a couple miles outside Rule."

She hoped the despair didn't show on her face. "Is he . . . ?"

"Dunno. But he's real sick. Doc and Alex worked, like, six, seven hours and then Doc was so wiped, she stayed. You're sure she's not here?"

"Positive. They're saying she ran. Nathan said she beat up Jess, too."

"What? *Alex?* No way. She'd never do something like that."

Privately, Lena thought there was just no telling. Ask her a couple years before her stepfather entered the picture if *she'd* have the courage to slip a butcher knife up her sleeve, and she'd have wondered what you'd been drinking. "Greg, how can you not know any of this? Don't they radio or send a runner when something like this happens?"

She watched Greg think about that. "Yeah." His frown deepened. "Weird that I haven't heard anything. I don't think anyone else has either. How'd Chris get hurt?"

"Nathan said Night shied and kicked him."

"Night?" Greg was incredulous. "You're kidding. I've seen Chris shot at. Even then, he never loses his saddle. Night's real steady."

"Well, there's a first time for everything. Look, we need Kincaid. Do you have a radio?"

"No, but . . ." Waving for her to follow, Greg jogged to the horses. "Chris does. Ho there, Night." The horse was shivering and snorting, and a fine frill of ice had formed on the animal's mane. At Greg's touch, the horse's muscles quivered, and then Night was stamping hard enough that Lena danced out of the way before one of those hooves could come down and break a foot. The other three horses began to toss their heads in sympathy.

"Whoa, what's got into you?" Greg put a calming hand on Night's neck. "You're all lathered up, boy. Ease down. Lena, grab his bridle while I check out the saddlebags."

"Sure." She didn't love animals, but there'd been plenty on Crusher Karl's farm and she knew what she was doing. Lena hooked a hand over the horse's bridle and murmured nonsense: "Good boy, there's a boy, good boy." But she was thinking: *Tori was right. They found a Spared by Oren. They brought back a* boy.

There was a squawk, followed by a fizz and then a series of mechanical clicks. At the sudden noise, Night suddenly swung his rump and Daisy, already jumpy, started barking again.

"Daisy, shut *up!*" She wrestled with the big blood bay as the golden pranced around her legs, still yapping. "What's that sound?"

"Message on the handset," Greg said, unbuckling a saddlebag.

"You guys don't talk?" She swatted at the growling dog. *"Quit* it."

"No, we use Morse. Saves the batteries and we still got a good eighty-, ninety-mile range. A hundred at night." Greg staggered as Night and a small sorrel gelding backed into one another. "Grab that sorrel, would you? I'm gonna get kicked."

"Easy, boy," she said, hooking the sorrel's halter. Bobbing, the gelding snorted and stamped. "Guys, just take it—" The words died on her tongue.

"Lena?" Greg looked at her over Night's saddle. "You okay?"

"Fine," she said. The word came out a bit flat, almost unreal, which was how she felt, too, because what she now spied on Nathan's saddle didn't quite compute.

She knew John rode the dapple gray, and the chestnut was Jess's. John's rifle was still in its red saddle scabbard. Chris's gun was seated in a scabbard on Night's off-side, barrel down and butt at horn height. Jess's chestnut mare had no scabbard.

The sorrel gelding, Nathan's horse, did: a short leather tube with big brass buckles. The scabbard held a pump shotgun—and there was blood, a fair amount, smeared on the stock. Hair, too. Some was long and gray, which would tally if Alex had smashed Jess hard enough to break her face. But there was also a gluey clump of shorter, very dark hair.

Chris's hair was black. Chris had a head wound.

But John said Night kicked him. Her eyes dropped to Night's hooves. Clean as a whistle. Of course, the snow might've scrubbed away blood and hair. But nothing explained the shotgun, and she'd found that shell. So was this gun Jess's? It might be, and that meant Nathan and the guards were lying about Chris. But why?

"Got it," Greg said. The olive-green walkie-talkie was rectangular and bulky, with a whippy antenna. Head cocked, Greg listened to the clicks a moment, and then his mouth sagged in shock. "Oh *shit*."

"What?" A door slammed and she saw Nathan and John spill down the stairs, coming for their horses at a dead run. John had his handset out, too. Dread knotted her stomach. "Greg, *what?*"

"Peter." Greg's face was white as chalk. "It's *Peter.*"

10

"So now what? We, like, totally *bombed*," Tyler said as his horse minced over rutted ice. The kid said he was fourteen, but Peter thought Tyler was lying. Still, the boy had stamina, and that was lucky. The majority of Peter's men were wheezy geezers who hunted and knew their guns, but that was it. Only two, Lang and Weller, who'd found their way to Rule a week after the world died, had combat experience. A lucky break, too. Both were grizzled Vietnam vets who'd served in the same unit. After hearing *that*, Peter had given them sanctuary on the spot. Although Lang was from Wisconsin, Weller was from Michigan and had worked the old iron mine south of Rule once upon a time. Of course, the mine was way before Peter's time, and Weller was his grandfather's age, which translated to older than dirt. But Lang and Weller were good men who not only knew weapons but understood battle tactics. These days, men like that were gold.

The old Yeager mine was ancient history, too: closed for decades, blockaded to keep out the curious. So, of course, the place was a complete kid magnet. It was only after he was a deputy that Peter recognized the mine for the freaking death trap that it was. But when *he* was a kid, the mine possessed an irresistible draw: a fabulous and forbidden warren of decaying, labyrinthine tunnels that were as dark and mysterious as a Roman catacomb. That he might actually *die* in a tunnel collapse; that one misstep might send him hurtling down a hidden escape shaft or forgotten blasthole to bust on the rocks like a blood balloon or, even worse, only break his legs so that he died from thirst slowly and in great pain; that given the right conditions, a tunnel could flood in a few minutes and much faster than any kid could run; that a person could keel over from swamp gas and suffocate before he knew what hit him—all that danger added to the thrill. Peter and his friends—and later, their girlfriends—had spent a lot of time there, exploring, partying, smoking, drinking. Making out. There were all sorts of interesting things you could do in the dark. Every kid in the area knew the mine, which, he now thought, explained an awful lot.

"We did okay," Peter said to Tyler now, but he was worried. *Okay* translated to *not enough to keep people in line*. Out of four wagons, only two were loaded. One swayed under several hundred pounds of gasoline-splashed hay—probably a loss, but Peter hoped to salvage feed from deeper in each bale—and four baaing sheep. The other wagon was chockablock with a motley assortment of propane tanks, a couple roadside flares, canned vegetables, sacks of flour and dried beans, bottles of cooking oil. They'd salvaged some puke-awful crap from a dinky Hmong place outside Clam Lake in Wisconsin: cans and jars with labels of nasty things he didn't even know *were* food.

The problem was he needed the other settlements' coopera-tion. Never mind Rule. If he couldn't dole out supplies to those outliers, groups that were too small to be true villages but still large enough to be useful, they wouldn't keep up their end of the bargain. If that happened? Bad news for everybody.

"I guess." Tyler hesitated, then said, "I keep seeing that old lady, you know? Like, I dream about the fire and the animals, how they screamed and then she . . . when she took her gun and—"

"No one told her to eat that bullet."

"But we killed her husband."

"Hey." Indignant, Peter took up his reins a little too fast. Surprised, Fable snorted then slithered, her hooves clattering on ice. Dead Man's Alley was steep as a ski jump but a straight, fast, twenty-mile shot all the way back to Rule. Given his druthers, he wouldn't be here, for all kinds of reasons. Still, he was reasonably sure the Changed were bedded down for the day by now, and he just didn't like the looks of that pewter sky, or the smell of blued steel. The storm that had been brewing and dogging them ever since Wisconsin was coming for sure. "That old guy shot first, and then we had no choice. It's not rocket science."

"But we were taking just about everything they had," Tyler said.

"Who said life is fair?" Peter said. The butt of a Desert Eagle fisted into the small of his back. He'd pried the weapon from some guy they'd found slumped on the steps of a Winnebago. At least, Peter thought the body was a he. No head, minus a foot and the left hand, just some leathery tendons and skin hanging off long bones like bark curls from birch. But the weapon was sweet, a real bone-breaker, judging from the exit craters blown out of two kids sprawled nearby. The kids were popsicles; scavengers didn't touch the Changed. Anyway, he took the Eagle and a couple bricks of ammo he found stashed in the trailer. "It's us or them, me or you. Now, I'm sorry about that old lady and everyone else I've had to shoot, but I got a responsibility. What I take from others, I put into your mouth."

Which wasn't strictly true. Not everything they salvaged ended up in Rule, but only Peter knew the reasons why. The equation was deceptively simple: supplies equaled cooperation. Yet it was a complex and delicate calculus that governed their survival. He didn't care how the outlying groups north and west of Rule decided whose time was up; that was their business. Hold a lottery, do eeny-meeny-miny-mo, whatever. Just so long as *someone* drew that short straw and got booted out to face . . . well, the same thing that preyed on anyone Rule Banned and sent into the Zone. Everyone knew the Changed were out there, of course. Most just didn't understand why they stayed.

To his mind, what he'd negotiated with the outliers was a one-hand-washes-the-other kind of thing. Peter wasn't a bad guy, but a bargain was a bargain and you couldn't make exceptions. Open the door just a little bit, let someone bend the rules, and the other groups got wind? Bring down the whole system, and then Rule was dead.

"I know it's harsh," he said to Tyler. "But no one said the end of the world would be easy. There's nobody going to save us but us."

"I guess." Tyler was quiet a moment, then changed the subject. "Do you believe the stories? About the military getting bounty hunters to round up Spared?"

"I don't know what to believe," he said, but that was a lie, too. Crack a rumor and often as not there was a pearl of truth. That the military had a starring role wasn't much of a surprise either. If only a third of the rumors were true, Rule was especially vulnerable. With sixty some odd kids, there just were too many Spared concentrated in too small an area. They had the Zone, but if the military really *was* involved, they had firepower that could reduce Rule to rubble. Might be time to break up the settlement, figure out safe havens where they could hide the younger kids if—

Beneath him, he felt Fable lurch in a quick, clattering stutter step. At the same moment, Tyler yelped and pitched forward, one foot still hooked in a stirrup, as his horse crashed to the ice. Lunging, Peter tried a grab, but then Fable's legs gave, cut out from under. The mare came down very hard and with so much force that Peter heard the *crack*, a sound like a tree limb snapped over one knee.

Fable let go of a high, bawling scream.

A split second later, Peter was airborne.

11

Peter had no time to think, much less react. White rushed for his face, and then he smacked hard against the ice, his vision cutting out for a split second like a dropped call from a cell. There was a gap, like a sudden gasp in time, before he faded back, the feeling in his arms and legs coming in shocks and jabs, as if something with spikes and claws was scrambling over his skin. Someone was screaming his name, but he couldn't answer. Every breath was a struggle. His own horse was still shrieking, and oh God, the *noise* coming out of Fable's mouth hurt like nails hammered into his skull.

"Fable," he croaked, the mare's name riding on nothing more than a wheeze. Where was she? Rolling onto his left arm, he craned to look back up the hill, and that was when his heart turned over in his chest.

Bleating with terror and pain, Fable sprawled, thrashing, three good hooves pedaling air. But her right foreleg . . . *Oh girl.* A surge of pity and grief flooded into Peter's chest. What he saw was a ruin: just a shattered stalk of bloody bone. Blood jetted from the severed artery to the ice, where it seeped in thick rivulets, flowing into ruts and dyeing the road a bright ruby-red. Fable was already dead. The poor thing just didn't know it ye—

To his left, a tiny white geyser spurted from the snow at the very periphery of his vision. Confused, he had just enough time to think: *Animal?* A split second later, he caught a singular, distinctive *snap* followed by a whooshing *HAAAAHHH*.

And then Peter knew exactly what was going on, because sound is slow compared to a high-velocity bullet.

"Peter!" It was Weller, somewhere behind and up the hill. "Shooters! Move, *move!*"

Rolling, his body still screaming, Peter planted his hands and feet. *Tyler—Tyler was thrown; so where is the kid, where is he?* Peter threw a wild look over his left shoulder and spotted the boy's horse perhaps twenty yards further on. A single glance was enough. The animal was still and very dead, its neck twisted so far around that the horse's bulging eyes stared up the hill and right into his. Tyler was nowhere in sight.

Snow exploded to his right. Ice spray, sharp as broken glass, nipped his cheeks. More *kerrr-SNAP*s now and then yawning sighs as bullets streaked past. Another jump of snow and then a *snap* followed by a *HAAAAHHH*. He eyed the angle where bullet met snow and then knew where the shooters were.

On my left, up high, shooting down. But why am I not dead? I should be.

"Peter!" Weller, again, alongside the third wagon and still, somehow, astride his dancing roan. Men spilled from their horses amidst a confused gabble of barking dogs and the staccato stamp of horse hooves. "Peter, I'm coming for—"

"No, stay where you are!" Peter gestured in a frantic semaphore. "They're on the left, up the hill! Get everyone behind the wagons!"

Snap—and then a nearly instantaneous, almost womanly shriek from a horse pulling the first, and closest, wagon. A fraction of a second later, the animal dropped, dead in its traces before it hit the ice. The animal's weight dragged on the far horse, which stumbled as the driver tried, frantically, to adjust.

That was when Peter saw the barbed wire, stretched across the road at precisely the right height.

Ambush. But how did they know? I didn't decide to come this way until five hours ago, when I sent the runner, Lang, ahead.

Braying, the horse tried backing away even as the wire tore its flesh. Another *snap*. The driver flung out his arms in a cartoonish gesture of surprise and crumpled as the horse finally panicked and reared, coming down with a clash of hooves that burst the driver's skull like a cantaloupe. There was a series of loud cracks, like brittle bones, as the horse shafts disintegrated. And then the wagon was thundering over the ice in a shower of sparks: a thousand pounds of squalling metal and rumbling wood coming right at him.

Peter sprang left. He felt the tug and suck of air at his neck as the wagon screamed by. Thudding to the road, he swarmed over the rutted ice. *Have to move, have to move, have to move, move, move!* He scuttled up Dead Man's Alley on hands and knees, his boots slip-sliding on ice and horse blood.

Fable was still alive, but her legs had ceased their frantic run on air. Her one visible eye rolled, trying to keep him in sight. This close, he smelled her rank sweat and the aluminum tang of her blood. Her leg was shredded, the skin hanging in bloody ribbons where the bone had ripped through. As he dropped into the sheltering hollow along her belly, his horse moaned and tried to roll to her feet.

"Easy." Pulling the Eagle free, he put the muzzle to the horse's ear. "I'm sorry, girl," he said, and took up the slack on the trigger.

"Peter?"

"I'm all right!" Blinking against tears and the fine misty blowback of Fable's blood, Peter looked back toward his men. The remaining wagons were gathered in a rough stagger, and his people were shielded for the moment. Peter counted five more horses down and at least as many men. There was a throaty growl of weapons fire as his men fought back, but Peter knew they were outmatched and outgunned. As if to underscore the point, he saw the head of a faun-colored mutt, which had been cowering beneath a wagon, suddenly explode. What was left keeled over, legs jittering, blood spurting in thick ropes from the raw stump of its neck.

Rage grabbed Peter's gut. Targeting men, even horses, was one thing, but killing that poor dog was a taunt. Like flipping the bird. Same as that crazy lady torching her barn and—

Wait a minute. His thoughts coalesced to an icy clarity. *She soaked the hay with—*

"M-Mom?" A voice, frightened and too young: *"Daaad?"*

Oh shit. "Tyler?" He didn't dare raise his head. "Tyler, stay there! Stay—"

"Mom." Tyler's voice was watery and weak. "Mom."

Peter shut his eyes, just for a second, and thought about it. The smart play was to leave the boy. From the sound of his voice, Tyler was hurt pretty bad and probably beyond any real help. So, go to Tyler and he'd accomplish nothing. Get himself pinned down and maybe even killed. Besides, captains lost men all the time. Shit happened.

The thing was—no one had ever accused him of being too smart.

Peter took off from a low crouch, darting down the hill as fast as he could. Didn't bother weaving. The road was too rotten and treacherous with Fable's blood. He was just as likely to break his neck as take a bullet. Over the thunder of his heart, he heard his men screaming as bullets buzzed around like angry hornets. Something plucked at his back, but then he was coming up on Tyler's horse—fifteen yards, ten, five . . .

The horse's hindquarters gave a sudden, spastic jolt. For a split second, he thought the horse was still alive, then realized the shooters were leading, anticipating his next move. *Have to jump for it.* Ten feet away, he dug in with his left boot, pivoted, swerved right—and then felt something smack into his left side, really hard, like this one cow, a nasty milker he'd never learned to avoid as a kid. Stumbling, he launched himself in a flat, ungainly dive. His head and chest cleared the horse, but then he ran out of air and came down half in and half out of a hollow formed by the horse's belly.

And found Tyler.

Or, rather, what was left.

12

Tyler's horse had fallen at an awkward angle. Judging from the blood splashed over the animal's poll, it had driven into the ice headfirst and broken its neck. Unfortunately, Tyler's foot never had come free of that stirrup. So when the horse collapsed, the boy's body had gotten pinned from the waist down beneath a thousand pounds of dead meat.

Oh my . . . Peter's stunned gaze tracked from the shelf of the boy's ribs to the sharp drop-off where Tyler's pelvis thinned to the thickness of a piece of construction paper before disappearing in a very wide, very red pool. A gory, steaming spool of intestines and blood-smeared fat spilled through a rip in the boy's belly. The horse's weight had been so great and the bag of the boy's body so fragile that whatever hadn't flattened had simply burst.

Peter's blood turned to slush. Tyler's steaming guts slowly undulated and bunched like thick, moist worms because the connections weren't quite severed, the body not yet ready to give up. Like the jittering legs of the headless dog. Like Fable's doomed run. Tyler's insides smelled, too, rank and feral as a gutted deer.

"D-Daaaad?" Fresh blood, red as lava, bubbled over Tyler's lips. There was something wrong with his eyes, too. The left fixed on Peter, but the right roved off-center, searching for a target it would never find.

"I'm h-here," Peter said, and then realized that his teeth were chattering. He was, suddenly, very cold. His right leg moved, but there was something wrong with his left. It wouldn't budge, like it no longer belonged, and he was still draped over the horse's body, not completely under cover. Latching onto the withers, he pulled. Pain clutched his left side. When he moved, something squelched. His parka was soaked. He put a numb hand to his side. Liquid nudged his palm in a rhythmic surge like water from a bubbler, and his hand came back glistening.

I'm shot. Another twist of pain now, worse than before. *Artery . . . bleeding out—*

The air came alive with those hornets again and then someone tumbled over Tyler's horse, dropping in a heap alongside. "Peter?" someone said, and then Peter felt hands grab his shoulders and pull. The pain was unbearable, and Peter screamed.

"Aw, *Jesus.*" Then Weller must've gotten a good look at Tyler, because his voice trailed to a hoarse groan. *"Shit."*

"W-Weller." Peter was trembling so badly he bit his tongue. How much time did he have? Two minutes? Three? "L-listen . . ."

"No." Shoving the sodden parka to one side, Weller jammed his knee into Peter's back, ignoring Peter's agonized shout. There came a long, meaty rip, and then Weller was fisting a wad of cloth into Peter's side. A bomb of agony exploded in his gut, jerking loose another breathless scream, but Weller only rolled Peter onto his back, then cinched something down tight around Peter's belly as bullets zipped and whirred. "Using my belt," Weller grunted. "God *damn* you, don't you die, Peter, not now, not when we've come this—"

"*No. L-listen.*" Peter's tongue was thick, the words mired deep, as difficult to extract as molten chewing gum from the deep treads of a boot. But he had to say something important; Weller had to *know*. "H-haay—"

"Hey yourself. Now shut up and let me—"

"No." Peter's head moved in a feeble roll. Weller would take time tending to him that his men didn't have. "H-h-hay . . . *fi-fire*—"

"Fire. Jesus, you mean the *hay*?" Weller said, and Peter heard the moment the idea clicked. "Yeah. All that gasoline, there'll be smoke, and the wind's behind us. If we can duck behind a wagon . . ."

Yes, yes! Peter nodded as hard as he could, which probably didn't amount to more than a jiggle. "G-go. H-hurry. Radio R-Rule for h-help."

"You're telling me to leave? Peter, even if we make it through, it might be hours before we could mount any kind of rescue."

"You *have* to. G-get the guys out." For a long moment, Weller's seamed face was so blank, Peter wasn't sure the older man understood. "L-leave m-me. Get th-them *out*."

"That an order?" Weller said, roughly. "You understand, you're telling me to leave you behind."

"Y-y-yesss." Peter chattered. "*G-g-go.*"

"All right." And then Weller did a curious thing. He took Peter's head between his hands, leaned down, and kissed Peter on the forehead.

"When the time comes," Weller murmured, "you remember my Mandy. You remember it was me did this." And then he was gone.

What? Peter tried focusing on the words, but it was like trying to tear through cobwebs with one hand. *Mandy? Or . . . Manny? Who? What did Weller . . .* But then his thoughts disintegrated completely as a blossom of fresh pain unfurled in a deep blood rose in the center of his chest. There was more gunfire, but Peter heard that only faintly and as nothing more substantial than distant pops, like the bang snaps he and his friends used to throw at one another on a dare. All that mattered was Weller had left, and that was good because there was no time to waste. It was getting harder to breathe past the deadening fist closing around his lungs. Almost not worth the effort.

"Daaad." An airy moan. "Daaad . . ."

"S'okay, T-Ty." Peter tried reaching for the boy's hand. He wasn't sure his fingers worked. He was shuddering uncontrollably now, and yet his arms no longer felt as if they were even there at all. He thought his hand closed around something, but it had all the life and warmth of a stone. "I'm h-here."

Tyler said nothing. But was there a slight pressure? He wasn't sure. And then—*when?*—Peter heard a *whump* and a louder boom. Explosion? Maybe. Too tired to lift his head. Just get it shot off anyway.

Things were going soft. The light was fading, drawing out of the morning like the blood in his veins. *My fault.* A thick, churning fog drifted across his vision. Or maybe thunderclouds, the storm finally catching up. *Tyler's just a kid. Not right . . . not . . . Chris . . . have to get word to him . . . explain . . . tell him about . . . about . . .*

The thought fizzled. Tell Chris . . . what? He didn't know. His ragged thoughts were fraying, his mind unraveling, and then something dark blossomed before his eyes, blotting out the light. The sky had torn. Space bled through, but it was full dark, without stars, and Peter was sinking, falling fast in a final swoon, falling and falling and falling into a black and silent forever.

Sometime after.

Later.

How long? No idea. Time didn't really matter anymore.

He was floating, not falling now. His body was as shimmery as a soap bubble, his thoughts no more substantial than mist.

Dying . . . lifted . . . angels . . . but where . . .

A sudden, hard jolt of white pain ruptured the darkness, and he moaned.

"Hey," someone said. "Got us a live one."

13

When they hauled her to her feet, she couldn't believe she was still alive. A thick fog of unreality settled over Alex's mind, muffling even the insistent mutter of pain from her hacked shoulder.

A brother. Chris had a brother. He'd never mentioned one, much less a twin, but there was no doubt. Same face, and floating above that roadkill reek, that shadowy scent was a dead ringer, too. The only difference was that healed slash drawn across Wolf's neck. He might have other scars. Perhaps he'd been in a really bad accident. She could be wrong about the suicide thing, but her gut said not. Regardless, the fact remained that these boys, Chris and Wolf, were brothers. No, more than that: they were identical *twins*.

Which meant that if she'd guessed right and Chris *was* Jess's grandson—and Yeager's—so was Wolf. Had Jess and Yeager been *married*? It occurred to her that she hadn't a clue about Jess's history, or even her last name. All Alex knew was that Jess said she'd seen her daughters die. *Chris* had said that his mom left when he was just a baby. He'd never known her.

So what if Chris's mother—one of Jess's daughters—had run

back to Rule but with only Wolf? Of course, the boy wouldn't have been Wolf then; he'd have had a name and friends, a *life*.

But why? She stared, stupid with shock and bewilderment, as Wolf approached with her snowshoes in one hand and the backpack Jess had supplied in the other. He'd shucked the wolf skin, pushing the lupine mask back like a hood. *Why only you, and not Chris?* There was nothing she could glean from his scent either, which remained as inscrutable as his expression. In this, Chris was the same as well: guarded and secretive, good at erecting barriers, putting up walls. When he let her in and opened himself, however, there was a sweetness there. Chris's only desire had been to care for and protect her—and look where that had gotten them both.

Numb, she could only watch as Wolf bent to a knee, took hold of her left boot, and guided her foot into a snowshoe, gently clipping her in the way he might a child and with something almost like tenderness. He followed suit with the right. When he was finished, he pushed to his feet and slid a hand around her uninjured arm. Wolf tugged—and she followed, heart hammering, on legs as stiff as wooden pegs. What choice did she have anyway? Whatever Wolf and the others had in mind would not happen here. If they'd wanted to place her head on that pyramid, Wolf would've cut her throat, not skinned a slice of Alex bologna.

So she went: out of the circle, past the flayed wolves—the empty sockets of all those skulls staring after and into forever—and away from Rule. Away from Jess and Nathan, the other girls, Kincaid. Away from Chris and into whatever future awaited.

Which, she thought, might be very short.

* * *

After a half hour or so, her brain kicked in again as the shock drained away. Her head ached, a steady pounding like the beat of a bass drum. Her shoulder throbbed in harmony with her pulse and hurt like hell. With the wound open to the wind and cold, now that Wolf had so nicely sliced away that portion of her parka and shirt, the pain was like nails being hammered into the exposed meat. Her nose was full with the tang of wet rust from congealing blood, though some still oozed in a warm, wet trickle down her forearm to seep into the ruined sleeve of her parka. Her wrist was damp, too, the glove a little squelchy. No pumpers, as Kincaid would say, and no glimmer of bone, which she supposed was all good, but the knowledge that she wouldn't bleed to death gave only slim comfort.

Still, if she made it through the next few hours, she'd have to figure a way to take care of her arm. She flicked a quick, sideways glance at her backpack hooked over Wolf's right shoulder. Had Jess included a first-aid kit? She couldn't remember. But wasn't it a good sign that Wolf had bothered to bring the pack in the first place? She worried the thought, turning it over, considering. It *might* be, if the Changed planned on keeping her alive for a little while. She didn't think they were into energy bars and trail mix, but a captive would need food.

Job one was to keep track of where she was and where she might be headed, maybe devise a plan to get away. Yes, but to go where? Not back to Rule. She thought of the whistle her father had given her, which she'd found in the lining of that boy's jacket.

Chris discovered the boy up north, near Oren. So that's where she should head. For all she knew, Chris might even go *back*.

But do I want that? The memory of Chris, unconscious and face-down in the snow, sent an arrow through her chest. That was her fault. Chris had tried to save her. All Chris had ever wanted was for her to be safe. She wished she could warn him now about Jess and Nathan and their crazy scheming. And this boy, his brother—what the hell was *that* about?

Oh, Chris, be careful. There are more shadows and secrets in Rule than you kn—

Her left snowshoe skittered on an icy patch. Suddenly off-balance, she let out a little grunt of surprise. Her left foot skipped into thin air, but then Wolf's hold on her arm tightened to steady her.

"Tha—" The word was automatic, a reflex. She let the breeze claim it. *This is not your friend.* Looking at Wolf was too discon-certing.

Then, she thought about the fact that she had *slipped*—and frowned down at the path. The way was very well-traveled, the snowpack compressed and slick. That made sense, she guessed; the Changed had to have come from somewhere else. The killing grounds were all about ritual. But when had the last good storm been? Yes, there'd been snow a little more than a week ago, she remembered. And yet *this* path was worn down enough that she could feel her snowshoes slew and skid.

Just like a game trail. Which means that either they or other Changed come through pretty often.

Ahead, she could see Acne laboring under the weight of the still-gurgling Spider draped over his shoulders. Blood from the girl's ruined nose left a vermillion ribbon in the snow.

And that made her wonder: were the Changed following a circuit? Made sense, all things considered, but there was still the problem of supply and demand, wasn't there? As the winter deepened, the flow of refugees had dwindled, a blessing in some ways because Rule had food and supply issues of its own. Of the few refugees who straggled in, only a handful were allowed to remain. Most were turned away.

Her nose suddenly filled with a steaming welter of odors. Dead ahead, she thought. A furtive, sidelong glance at Wolf revealed that the boy was unconcerned. Something cold and charry, like old wood smoke, and—she inhaled again—a fizz, slightly sweet . . . spoiled fruit? For reasons she couldn't fathom, her mind jumped to the hospice back at Rule and the thick miasma that filled the halls where the very few terminal patients waited to die. This scent was similar. But that would mean . . .

Oh boy. Her heart thudded to her toes. She was getting a very bad feeling about this. *Yeah, but you might be wrong. This could be old.*

Another hundred yards and they stepped into a shallow clearing. A tumble of gray stone, common to rudimentary campsites, stood to her left. Okay, given the charry scent, that added up, but judging from the snow cover, no fire had burned in that hearth for some time. Further on and to her right, close to the tree line, a series of irregular drifts abutted a three-sided wooden structure. No one there. All right, not bad but not necessary good either, because that fruity fizz was much stronger, the air more turgid and somehow rancid, like meat starting to go bad. Her eyes sharpened on the camp shelter, but aside from a stack of empty, olive-green nylon duffels on a solitary bench, the shelter was empty. Too small to comfortably house the Changed, too, come to think of it.

Which begged an interesting question. Where did Wolf and the others live? Other than *her* backpack dangling from Wolf's right shoulder, these Changed carried nothing but weapons and, probably, some extra ammo stashed in their parkas. There was no gear piled alongside the shelter. That fire pit hadn't seen action for months. Wolf's clothes and those of the other Changed were well-worn but not filthy. So either they shucked dirty clothes as they went along, or cleaned up. One thing was clear, however: these Changed hadn't been out here, in the snow, roughing it, since the Zap.

So this isn't the last stop. Rule must be on the way between point A and point B. Her eyes strayed over the shelter again, then clicked to the woods beyond. A slight trough, judging from the slouch and dip, meandered between trees, heading vaguely northwest. Perhaps twenty yards further, her gaze snagged on a smudgy slate-blue hash mark halfway up the trunk of a sturdy oak. A blaze. So this *was* or had been a trail at one point. Given the shelter and hearth, this made sense, too.

Using established trails to get around, maybe even to follow a kind of circuit. They have to be putting inside somewhere. If I planned to hang around, that's what I would do. Use a couple abandoned houses as base camps. Her eyes strayed to that shelter again. *Lay in a store of ammo and supplies and then move from one to the next, give game a chance to come back before I—*

By the shelter, one of the drifts stirred. She blinked. For a crazy second, she flashed to a Jack London novel she'd read in seventh-grade English and thought, *sled dogs.* Burrowing into snow was how Buck and the other dogs got through the night. Yet the mélange of warmed odors which pillowed out was full and round—and all wrong. Besides, dogs hated the Changed.

She watched as the lumps of snow broke apart. Two clenched fists punched through and then more fists and arms and now legs and heads—

People.

14

Three women and two men, all well along in years, struggled up from the snow. With no fire, rudimentary snow caves would be their best option. She'd have done the same thing.

Ten eyes set in five slack faces watched her watching them. They said nothing. Neither did she. They were—she sniffed—what? Not frightened. No one could stay scared to death all the time. Aside from their rancid flesh and that fruity fizz, these old people smelled like cold oatmeal, an odor that was almost no odor at all. *Apathetic:* that's what their scent said. She even understood. Endure a couple rounds of chemo that didn't kill the monster and only made you puke your guts out, and see just how interested in living *you* were. You really, truly didn't give a shit.

She also thought, though, that pasty guy in the middle was legitimately sick. His illness hung like the fetor of a stagnant, scum-choked swamp. A diabetic? Or starvation? Maybe both, judging from the loose flesh and hard planes and edges of bone tenting skin on the faces of the others. And now her association to the hospice wing where the terminal waited to die made sense. A body smelled like that when it was eating itself to stay alive.

They've been here at least an hour and probably longer. So why didn't they run? Wolf tugged, and she staggered forward as Beretta waded into the knot of bodies and began fishing for something in the snow. The oldsters shrank back, jostling and bunching the way skittish zebras clustered as the lions gathered. *There's no guard. It can't be just that they're scared . . .*

Her thoughts stumbled as something icy brushed her left wrist. She looked down and saw that Beretta held a rope, hard and stiff with cold and as thick around as her thumb. She sucked in a startled gasp. *What the hell?* She followed its length and saw how it looped from one oldster to the next. Now that she was closer, she realized their wrists were bound. So were their ankles. More rope snaked from their legs and was tied off to the support beams of the old camp shelter.

Hobbled. That's why these old people hadn't run. They couldn't. The Changed were gathering them up like cattle to be kept until it was time to slaughter—

"No!" Horror blasted through her body on a harsh wind. If she let them tie her up, she wouldn't be able to fight; it would be the end, like giving in to the monster. Gasping, she bucked and wrenched away, shaking free of Wolf's grip, and then she was swinging with her good right arm, whipping around, screaming, screaming, *screaming,* "No, no, *no,* I won't *let* you!"

Startled, the scent of his surprise spiking her nose, Beretta jerked up just as her fist jackhammered his jaw. With the tidal wave

of adrenaline-fueled fear surging through her veins, she felt nothing and heard the impact only as a distant, airy *crack,* like a punch
landed in a television show: a sound effect with no substance. Later,
when she studied her bruised knuckles, she would think it was a
miracle she hadn't broken her hand. The blow dumped Beretta
on his ass, and then she was staggering, off-balance both from
her own momentum and the snowshoes still strapped to her feet.
Out of the corner of her eye, she saw Slash making a grab, and
she shrieked again, tried ducking out from under, but the rigid toe
of her left snowshoe jammed into deep snow. Her knee twisted,
and she cried out again, this time with pain. She would've gone
down, maybe even broken her leg, but she felt a hand—Slash's, she
thought—clutch the nape of her neck and squeeze.

Oh no you don't, bitch. Another starburst of pain as the jammed
shoe came loose, and then she'd planted her feet and was uncoiling, surging up, her fist driving—

At the last second, she realized that it wasn't Slash who had her.

Quick as a snake, Wolf lashed out, his hand closing around her
wrist, stopping her fist in midair.

Please, God. Panting, she strained to complete the swing, but his
grip was iron. Her body quivered, a coiled spring under too much
pressure. *Let me finish this. Help me just one more time.*

"You shouldn't fight." An old lady's quaver. Alex had no idea
which of the three women had spoken and wasn't about to take her
eyes off Wolf to check. "It'll only make them mad," the old lady said.

"Quiet, Ruby." A man's rumble. "She wants it to end sooner
than later, that's her business."

Yes, but at least she'd go down fighting, not *cowed* and broken like these old people. If Wolf let up, just for a second, she would finish what she started. He probably knew that, too, although his dark eyes were as fathomless as deep wells and unreadable. His breath, scented with a coppery tang of half-digested meat, slanted over her cheeks. That was her blood in his mouth, on his tongue—

His body shifted then. The change was subtle: the set of his feet, the way he held his shoulders. The hand at the back of her neck tightened, and then she realized: he was pulling her closer.

The better to bite out your throat. She saw his lips peel back and the slow slink of his tongue. The Changed's thick funk of dead animal and stewed guts flooded her nose and mouth. *The better to drink nice, warm—*

Her thoughts stuttered as another, more familiar scent of cool shadows intensified, wreathing her like smoke . . . and now, there came the faint but unmistakable effervescence of crisp, sweet apples.

Chris. It was Chris's smell but much more pointed, insistent, and it touched her, found its way into her chest as it—and Chris—had before. In a different time and place, this would be that dizzying moment of anticipation right before he crushed her mouth to his and then—

Something deep in her mind turned over . . . and . . . flexed.

No. My God, what is *that?* The sensation was nearly indescribable, a kind of deep mental shift, as if some part of her brain had suddenly decided to stretch and twist around to search for a better view. Her head was simultaneously both muzzy—and *crowded.*

She remembered the instant Wolf's consciousness had slithered into hers and settled there; how she'd felt her body under his hands and his mouth dragging over—

No, don't. What was happening to her? She was losing her mind. That had to be it. She was finally cracking up, going insane—and who wouldn't? *Help me, please, somebody help me.* But there would be no rescue. She was on her own. Whatever happened next was up to her.

Do something. The choke of Wolf's excitement was gagging. Her mind was clouding. She was going to lose it; God, she was losing it . . . *Break it, do something, do anything, but do it now.*

She spat into his face.

Gasping, Wolf started back. A fleeting expression of shock sparrowed through his eyes. Later, she would remember and wonder about that.

But inside her skull, deep in her brain, something let go. There was a sudden hitch, like the clunk of a lock, and then the release of a catch as whatever gripped her consciousness relaxed. She expelled a long, shaky breath of relief. She might die in the next second, but at least she wasn't drowning in whatever passed for Wolf's mind.

For one long moment, the wolf-boy only stared. She willed herself not to look away. Her eyes fixed on the foamy slick of her saliva slithering down his upper lip like thick snot.

Then the air suddenly snapped with that sharp, expectant tang. A second later, she felt Beretta and Slash moving in to flank her and hook an arm.

She'd been right. Wolf had just given a command, and that

was interesting. However the Changed *spoke*, that particular tangy scent was a signal. Were there more odors, gradations of some kind that added up to meaning but that, for the moment, her nose just couldn't detect? Maybe. If she lived long enough, she might even figure out their vocabulary, but that still might not do her much good. She wasn't even sure she wanted to understand them.

She watched Wolf raise a hand and smear away her spit. His eyes never left hers. They were inches apart, so close she saw his scar eel and squirm over his Adam's apple when he swallowed. So close that all Wolf had to do was lean in a little and use his teeth.

But he did not.

Instead, the monster with Chris's face smiled.

15

Chris knew something was up when the entire Council trooped in, trailed by guards. Nathan slouched as if held up by a string. Weller was haunted and hollow-eyed. The others were only grim. When his grandfather, Yeager, ordered Jet, Chris's black shepherd, into the kitchen with the other animals, Chris knew this something was likely to be very bad. His grandfather also wanted Kincaid to wait with the girls and their new housemother, a grisly woman named Hammerbach, who would be there for the foreseeable future until—unless—Jess came out of her coma. But Chris nixed that. The more witnesses, the better protected he felt, and this wasn't a trial. Not yet, anyway. Besides, he wanted to make sure Lena heard what he said in case they questioned her. No use both of them going down.

He was in deep, deep trouble. But why, exactly? He had no idea. Alex had been gone for eight days. Those same days of *his* life had vanished with her, *poof.* He'd been at Jess's for more than a week, and barely remembered any of it. What also nagged him was that his memories of the couple days *before*—when he'd still been on the road, away from Rule—were a jumble. The only thing he recalled with any clarity was that one last, precious moment when Alex's horse had reared and she'd looked back, and their eyes locked. But that was it. The rest was only a big, white blank.

"I don't understand why you broke off the search. You don't know that Peter's dead," Chris said. He'd elected to stand. Sitting was too pathetic. But his head was swirling, and he felt gutted as a shriveled pumpkin with nothing left but the shell. "There's no body. He's still out there somewhere."

"Chris, it's Saturday, for God's sake." Weller's voice was a weary croak. "Eight days since the ambush, and there's nothing, no trace, not a sign of either Peter or Tyler, and no trail either. I couldn't tell you if those bastards went east or west, north or south, but I do know this: that boy, Tyler—there was no way he was gonna live another five minutes. As for Peter . . . I did the best I could. He's young, strong. He might have made it, but it's more than likely that he didn't. I don't like it, but I accept that he's gone."

"Well, I don't," Chris said. "It makes no sense. If I were a raider, I would just strip the bodies. I wouldn't *take* them."

"Maybe they weren't raiders," Weller said, simply.

"How do you mean?" Then Chris gasped. "The Changed? No, that's impossible. They're not that organized."

"As far as we know," Weller said.

That had never occurred to Chris, and the idea shook him.

But there were a lot of bodies. The rescue party didn't make it out there until noon. Plenty of time for the Changed to grab as much fresh meat as they wanted. But why take only Peter and—

"Wait a minute." He looked back at Weller. "Peter and Tyler were the only Spared."

"Yes, we noticed that." Blind in one eye, Stiemke rarely spoke, only listened like a drowsing lizard. Now Stiemke tilted his head to one side, his left eyelid twitching to reveal a thumbnail of milky iris. "What do *you* think that means?"

"Me?" Chris frowned. "I don't know."

"Weller said there were rumors," his grandfather, Yeager, prompted. His eyes, black as freshly mined coal, narrowed. "Something about bounty hunters?"

"That's right. We heard the military was recruiting locals to hand over Spared and round up Changed. You think bounty hunters set up an ambush just to capture Peter and Tyler?"

"And *you*, if you'd been there." An imposing man in his black robes, Ernst always looked and sounded a little like Darth Vader, minus the heavy breathing. "The question is, how did the shooters know where to stage the ambush? How did they know where to intercept the runner, Lang?" Lang's horse was found ten miles from Rule, a frozen worm of blood in its left ear and a big piece missing from the right side of its face where the bullet had blasted through. Lang, though, was simply gone.

"I don't know. We don't follow the same roads all the time for this very reason." Chris looked at Weller. "Tell them."

"I already did." Weller's eyes slipped to the floor. "Peter said you guys talked about taking Dead Man four, maybe five days back, right before you split off to go north."

Had they? "I honestly don't remember."

Behind him, he heard Kincaid speak up for the first time. "That's normal with a concussion, Rev. Boy's going to be spotty."

"The point is Chris knew ahead of time," Yeager said.

"I guess I knew it was a possibility," Chris said. Then it finally clicked. "Wait, you think *I* had something to do with this? That's crazy. I would never—"

"Then why leave your men?"

"I didn't *leave* anybody. I already *told* you. We caught a rumor of Spared near Oren."

"Ah yes." From his seat on the far right, Born let out a raspy cackle. "You and your famous rumors. Why is it that Weller has no recollection of such a story?"

Shuffling uneasily, Weller threw Chris a pained, apologetic look. "Chris, I—"

"Don't worry about it." The fire was high and the room stuffy and overheated, but he didn't think that had much to do with the sudden sweat starting on his upper lip. Peter had asked no questions, so Chris had fed him no lies. But now these old men wanted answers he could not risk giving.

"Weller didn't know because he wasn't there," he said to Born. "Peter and I scouted a farmstead just east of the border, and this old guy told us." They *had* visited a farmstead, too, although it was long deserted.

"And you always follow up a rumor."

"Of course. What else do you think we have to go on? Listen, we're stealing and *killing* so you can sit there and say you can't trust me?"

Kincaid's voice floated up in a warning. "Easy, Chris."

"I'm fine." He kept his eyes trained on the Council, his gaze flicking from one judge to the next. "Look, you guys aren't out there, but *I* am—me and Peter and some kids like Tyler and anyone else who isn't so ancient he needs diapers so he doesn't piss the bed."

"Chris," Kincaid said. "Don't—"

"I'll handle this, Doctor, thank you." Yeager's bird-bright eyes never wavered from Chris's face. "Watch your language, young man. Don't presume to challenge us."

"I'm *not*," Chris said. Oh, he wanted to, though. Blame the concussion or losing Alex and now Peter, but he was suddenly sick to death of these old men. "I just don't get what you're driving at. I would never hurt Peter, ever."

"Fine." His grandfather glided from his chair on a whisper of black robes. He extended his hands, palms up. "Then all you have to do is answer our questions."

Chris hesitated for the briefest of moments, then told his first lie. "Sure, I have nothing to hide," he said, and then slid his hands onto his grandfather's palms. The old man's flesh felt artificial, like slick plastic, and the hairs on Chris's neck prickled. "What do you want?"

"First, I want you to sit down," Yeager said.

"No." He saw the old man's face crease with surprise. Good. If he could keep his grandfather off-balance, do the unexpected, maybe he had a chance. *Whatever I say next* has *to be the truth.* "I'd rather stand."

"I see." As if to reassert his authority, Yeager looked at the guard hovering by Kincaid's shoulder. "I think it's time the doctor and the others waited in the kitchen."

"No," Chris said again. He aimed a quick glance over his shoulder. His eyes brushed over Lena's pale face, but she was still as a sphinx. He turned back to the Council. "I've got nothing to be ashamed of. Do you?"

"That's not how things are done, young man." Prigge's lips puckered like a prissy schoolteacher's. "*We* decide, not you."

"This isn't a trial. What are you going to do? Shoot them or me? Are you that afraid of what I'm going to say?" When Prigge didn't reply, Chris's eyes shifted back to Yeager. "Go on, what do you want to know?"

His grandfather's expression hadn't changed, and his face, almost waxy, was blank as a mannequin's. Only his eyes showed any sign of life, and they were glittery now, like those of a vulture eyeing roadkill. "Did you have anything to do with the ambush?"

"No."

"But you *did* advise Peter to take Dead Man's Alley," Ernst said.

"I already said I don't remember."

"Even if Chris did, that's not a crime," Kincaid put in.

"We're aware of that," said Prigge.

"Then stop accusing him." Chris recognized Lena's voice. "You have no *right*."

"Be quiet, girl." Yeager waited a beat, then asked Chris, "Why did you bypass Oren and head for the Amish settlement?"

His heart sank. The only way his grandfather could know that was if he'd talked to Greg or one of the others. They would've told, too, because *they* had no reason to lie. If he could just keep his answers brief. . . . "We heard there might be Spared."

"But how did you know *where* to look?" Ernst said. "The others said you went from farm to farm but never into any of the out-buildings—until you came to a *specific* barn."

The air squeezed from his lungs. The adrenaline burst was tailing off, and Chris's mouth tasted of crushed metal and fear. "I can't tell you that."

Someone gasped. He felt Kincaid tense, and he saw the other guards toss looks he couldn't read. Nathan's eyes were slits.

Yeager's grip shifted as if checking Chris's pulse. "Why not?"

Keep it short, keep it sweet, but make it the truth. "Because I promised."

"Your promise is to *me*," Yeager suddenly spat. "I took you in, and I can just as easily put you out. You *will* answer."

Chris said nothing.

"Better say, boy," Born warned. "Truth will out."

"Stop." It was Lena again. "Leave him alone. This isn't his fault!"

"Be quiet, girl." His grandfather's fingers tightened to wires. "Answer me."

Chris throttled back the impulse to wrench his hands free. If he did, he'd start whaling on the old man, and might not stop—and that was the truth, too. He said nothing.

Yeager said, "*Why* did you stay a full day after Greg and the others left? Was it to see if there were others? Did you find them? *Who* told you where to look?"

Can't say. Yes. No. Hey, you tell me; then we'll both know. The silence thickened. His pulse banged so loudly he thought everyone in the room had to hear it, but he still said nothing.

"All right." Yeager peered up at Chris. "Do you care for Alex?"

The abrupt turn threw him. He felt the heat rush all the way to his scalp, and the answer—the truth—came out before he could call it back. "You know I do," he said, hoarsely.

"But she lied, boy." Born gave his dog's laugh. "She *used* you."

"No." *Not true, not true. We kissed, and I felt what she felt. That was no lie.* "It wasn't like that."

"Of course it was. She wouldn't be the first girl here to manipulate a boy to get her way."

"That's not fair," Lena said. She suddenly started forward, ducking to avoid the guard. "It's not the same at all. Don't poison this for him."

"You, girl." Hammerbach lumbered after her, but she was an old woman who had once been very large and was now much too slow. "Come back. This is not your place."

"Screw you," Lena said, and then she was standing on Chris's right, the guard a step behind. "You have no idea what happened. Maybe Alex thought she didn't have a choice."

"Of course she did," Yeager snapped. "You, Lena, of all people, ought to understand *that*. You're an expert where betrayal's concerned."

"Leave her out of this," Chris said. "We're talking about Alex and me."

"So we are," Yeager said. "Alex is just a girl, and yet the guards said she had a shotgun and supplies. So who gave those to her? Who helped her?"

That was a very good question. "I don't know," Chris said. "Ask the guards."

"Don't think we haven't," Ernst rumbled.

"Right. Of course, you take their word for it. It's just me you doubt."

"In light of the ambush and your convenient absence? The fact that the girl needed help to get out and then succeeded?" Born said. "What would you do in our place? Wouldn't you wonder?"

"I tried to *stop* her," Chris said. "Did the guards tell you that?"

"It doesn't matter, Chris. Can't you see it? They've already made up their minds," Lena said. Her eyes were bright with unshed tears as she rounded on Yeager. "You think he's guilty, and even if Alex did come back, you'd make sure she never set foot in Rule or saw Chris again."

"Because she broke the *rules!*" Yeager's face was the color of a plum. "She *defied* us, and she had help, and I will know *who!*"

"And I said I don't know!" Chris jerked free. His wrists burned as if scorched. "You *need* us *and* you get to be the boss of how we feel, who we decide to care about? We go out, we take all the risks! We *die* out there while you sit here in your robes and judge us, and it's still not enough. You want everything. You want what I think and what I fee—"

"*Quiet!*" His grandfather's hand blurred. The slap was so hard and so fast the sound was like brittle ice cracking in two. Chris's head snapped to one side, his breath snatched from his lungs in a surprised, pained hiss. *"Don't* presume to lecture me! Your allegiance is to me and to Rule, and we will have no Judases in our midst!" His grandfather slapped him again, much harder. "I will break you, boy, I will *break* you!"

"Yeager," Kincaid said, appalled. He made a move, but a guard grabbed his arms. "Rev, please, listen to what you're *saying!"*

"You need me," Chris croaked. His ears rang. The coppery taste of his blood made him want to vomit. "You need my voice, but only to prove you're still in charge. You already know enough, or else you wouldn't have brought all these guards. I can't win this, and you know it. If I tell you, you lock me up. If I don't say anything, you lock me up." He surprised himself with a bloody, bubbly little laugh. "You want me to choose, but there's only one right answer for you."

"I want to hear it." His grandfather's lips were so thin they were no more than a fissure in stone. "From your mouth."

"To God's ear?" Chris laughed again. He dragged his hand across his lips, inking his skin red. His grandfather was Rule, and Chris would bend, or the old man would keep at him until he did. *Not going to happen.* "You're not God. There *is* no god, and if there is, he's one sick bastard to put you old farts in charge."

I've gone nuts, he marveled. He saw his grandfather's hand draw back again. *I could deck this old guy, but then I'd be just like him, and like Dad. I know how I feel about Alex. No one can take that away.*

Lena slid between them. *"Stop!* You don't need his voice. You can have mine."

"I don't *want* yours, girl," Yeager said.

"Too bad," Lena said.

"Lena, it's okay." Chris put his hands on her shoulders. "I've had a lot of experience with bullies."

"Me, too," she said. To Yeager: "You want to know who helped Alex, I'll tell you."

She leveled a finger at Nathan. "Him."

16

Nathan actually flinched. "What? That's nuts."

"No, it's *not*." Lena stared down at Yeager. Oh, it was all she could do to keep from scratching the old creep's eyes out. If she had a knife, she'd do him the way she'd done Crusher Karl a year before this nightmare began and not be sorry, not one bit. The world had come crashing down, and still all she'd managed was to swap one abusive asshole for another. "It was Nathan, and probably Jess, too. They were always hanging around together. The night before Alex left, Tori said Nathan and Jess were talking, and then it was Nathan who brought Jess back, but oh, look, now she's in a coma. You *don't* think that's just a little too convenient?"

"Convenient?" Kincaid echoed. She heard the surprise in the doctor's voice. "Wait just a minute. What the hell are you implying?"

"And I'll bet Kincaid's in on it." Lena didn't look around. "He and Jess are really tight, too."

"Whoa, whoa," Kincaid said.

"Lena, be quiet." Chris's hands tightened on her shoulders. "This isn't helping."

Yeah, but it can't hurt. I don't think things can get much worse. "Chris had nothing to do with it." She kept her eyes on Yeager, who stared as if she'd suddenly sprouted a second head. "I'm telling you it was Nathan, and I can prove it."

"She's just—" Nathan began, but the old reverend lifted a hand, and the guard fell silent.

"What are you saying, girl?" Yeager asked.

It's Lena, *asshole.* "The shotgun, the one they said Alex took? I saw it. It was hooked onto Nathan's saddle with one of those leather tube things . . . a scabbard. It's not back in Jess's room, so—"

"What?" It was Hammerbach. "You, girl, you've been in Jess's room, among her things?"

"I don't give two shits about her stuff. But I'm telling you, Jess has a shotgun. The case is in her closet." Dipping a hand into her pocket, she tweezed out the shotgun shell and handed it to Yeager. "There's a box of these on the same shelf. This shell was on the floor. She probably dropped it when she was loading the shotgun, because there are three shells left in a box of ten."

"*I* didn't know Jess had a gun," Tori said wonderingly. Sarah only shook her head.

"Me neither," said Lena. "Only Nathan says Alex got hold of it. But how? Either she knew about it and forced Jess to give it to her, or Jess handed it over herself. Whatever. It's not back in the closet, which means that Nathan still has it, and I'll bet it's got the same shells."

Yeager stared at the black Remington cartridge and then craned up to look at Nathan. "Is this true? Do you have the shotgun?"

"Yes, I retrieved it after Alex tossed it. That's my job."

"Yeah, but did you clean it, asshole?" Lena shot back.

There was a short silence, which Yeager broke. "Why is that important?"

"Because," Lena said, "there was blood on the stock and hair and—"

"Alex *hit* Jess," Nathan said, contempt dripping from every word. "What do you expect?"

Yeah, yeah, bite me. "But not all the hair was Jess's. Some was, but there was other hair, darker and shorter, that didn't match. The only person with hair like that who got bashed in the head the same day was Chris." She looked at Yeager. "Nathan made up a story about Night to cover himself, and maybe Jess . . . I don't know. But I looked at Night's hooves right after they brought him back, and they were clean."

"Snow probably did that," Nathan said.

"Maybe. But then there's the thing about Alex pitching the shotgun. Why would she do that? Does that make sense? She goes to all this trouble to get *two* guns; she's got a good rifle *and* the shotgun, and then she throws one *away*?" She saw the sudden narrowing of Yeager's eyes as he digested this.

"She panicked," Nathan offered, but even to Lena it sounded feeble.

"So you say." Yeager evidently heard the same thing, because he jerked his head at one of the other guards, who nodded and slid out of the front room, heading for the door. "I presume you won't mind if we have a look at this shotgun."

"No," Nathan said, but Lena thought there was nothing else he could say.

"I don't understand this." Chris looked dazed. The imprint of his grandfather's hand was a purple stencil on his cheek. "Why would Nathan . . ."

"It couldn't just be Nathan. It had to be both of them, together, Jess *and* Nathan," Lena said. "Because that case—the black one that was so important to Alex? It's in Jess's room, on the same shelf."

Chris's mouth unhinged. "Alex left it behind? She'd never do that."

"But it's there. I can show you."

"I think," Yeager said, "that this is something we'd all like to see."

17

The shotgun's stock told its story well enough. Chris's eyes panned from the weapon the guard had retrieved from Nathan's quarters to that black padded case and back again. The Remington's stock was crusted with dried blood in which hair, gray and black, was easily visible, preserved like insects in amber.

Unzipping the case, Chris folded back the top, but he already knew from the weight that the two sturdy bags, filled with gray ash, were still there. *Alex would never leave them behind*. He feathered the air over the case's contents, unwilling to touch them. These belonged to Alex, and her parents deserved respect. Handling them more than necessary was like walking over their graves.

"I don't believe it." Weller, who'd retrieved the case from Jess's room, stared down, wide-eyed. "It was *them*? Jess and Nathan?"

"So it appears. Please," Yeager said to Nathan, "tell us you have an explanation."

"*I'll* explain it," Weller broke in, and rounded on the other guard. "You son of a bitch, you were in on it. Either you hit Chris and Jess both, or she did Chris and then you did *her* to make your story stick."

"But why?" Tori asked. She and Sarah stood with their arms around one another, as if holding each other up.

"I know why," Chris said, grimly. "I came back too early. I was supposed to meet up with Peter, but I decided to ride straight through. At the checkpoint, one of the guards mentioned he'd seen Alex on Kincaid's horse, and so I knew something was wrong, and then . . ." His fists bunched in frustration. "I just don't *remember*. I can see Alex on the horse, and then it's this blank stretch until I woke up here."

"You don't need to remember. I'll tell you how it went down. You ruined their plans, and then they had to improvise." Weller threw Nathan a murderous look. "Nice touch, doing Jess. I'll just bet you guys were sweating bullets, worrying Chris would remember what happened. What I want to know is what else you've done. You had to intercept the runner, Lang. He was the only one who knew where we were and what route we were going to take to get back to Rule. You must have had guys waiting and then tipped off those bounty hunters. You son of a—"

Uncoiling, Weller slammed his fist in a solid uppercut. Nathan's head snapped back on the stalk of his neck, blood fanned in a fine mist, and then Weller drove the bony ridge of his forehead into Nathan's face.

"Weller!" Kincaid shouted. "Weller, stop!"

No, don't stop. Chris was gritting his teeth so hard the muscles corded in his neck. *Alex is gone, and so is Peter, and this asshole deserves everything he gets.*

Nathan's knees buckled, but Weller was still on him, drunk-walking him back, muscling the other man across the room. The old men of the Council scattered in a startled flutter and swirl of black robes, like a murder of crows. Nathan had his hands up now, and he was tucking, protecting his face, not even trying to fight back. Cursing, Weller aimed a vicious kick at Nathan's groin. Nathan gargled a breathless screech, and then he was folding in two, retching, still trying to dance away, butting against a small display table, going down in a crash of wood and porcelain figurines. The dogs, still sequestered in the kitchen, began to bark.

"Enough, *enough!*" Yeager shouted. Plum-colored splotches splashed the old man's withered cheeks. "Weller, stop! We need answers first, and then you can do what you like, but stop *now.*"

"Rev, you . . . you don't understand." Huffing, Weller staggered to his feet. On the floor, Nathan was curled into a tight, unmoving ball. "The guys guarding the Zone, John and Randy and Dale—they got to be in on it, too. Ain't that right, Nathan? Huh?" Weller let fly another kick to Nathan's middle, and the other man grunted out a gurgled moan. "*Ain't* it?"

"Kill him now, and he's of no use to us," Yeager said. "You'll get your chance, I promise you."

"Wouldn't miss it." Weller spat, then armed blood from his face. "Rev, we got to get those other men before they run, too. And I'd post a couple guys on Jess, if I was you."

"She's no threat," Kincaid said. "The woman's in a coma. Without equipment or power, it's hard enough to keep her stable as it is. I barely have enough of the right medicine."

"Yeah, like the little girl said, that's real convenient," Weller said. "How do we know you aren't *keeping* her in a coma with all these drugs of yours?"

Kincaid's face flooded with genuine shock. "What are you saying? I took an *oath*."

"Yeah, only maybe not to Rule," Weller said. To Yeager: "That girl's right about another thing, too. Kincaid and Jess, they're real tight. I think we got to keep an eye on her. Maybe if Kincaid's not allowed near her, she'll wake up."

"Or she might not," Kincaid said. "Rev, you keep me from doing my job, you might kill her."

"Perhaps she deserves nothing less. Go, Weller. Do whatever you think is best," Yeager said, and then turned to Chris as Weller ducked out. "You will also reap what you sow. You *do* understand that?"

"Yes," Chris said. He thought his voice was steady, but he felt the sweat pearls on his upper lip. The world as he knew it was again coming to an end. He'd seen it happen, with his own eyes, right in this room. Nathan and Jess and . . . and *Kincaid*?

They killed Alex. They sent her out of Rule and into the Zone. They murdered her just as surely as if they'd put a gun to her head and pulled the trigger.

"Good," Yeager said. "I would hate to think that any blood kin of mine, however tainted, is a fool. You have defied me; you have sided with those who would ruin me, the Council, *Rule*. You have chosen a *girl* over me, and that will not stand. Alex is done, too. If she returns, I will not give her sanctuary."

"She wouldn't crawl back to you. She's survived before,

without our help, and she'll do it again." God, he wished he believed that.

"You know her that well?"

"I know how I feel about her." He willed his gaze not to waver. *She* would fight this old man. She would never back down, and neither would he. As soon as he saw his opportunity, he *would* go after her, because, maybe, there was still a chance. "You can't take that away."

"True. But I *will* take you." Yeager's eyes drifted to Kincaid and Lena, and then locked, once more, on him. "I will take you all."

18

It was what Crusher Karl would've called a filthy night. When the large drays pitched a fit—dancing and kicking when the guards boosted them onto the running boards—they almost went nowhere, which would've suited Lena just fine. The wagon was open, and a single lantern bounced and swayed as the thickening snow drew down in a dense, billowing curtain that swirled and eddied and muffled all sound. They might as well have been in a tornado in a bell jar or snow globe. The wind snatched and plucked at her hair because they hadn't let her get a hat, and her ears were so icy they burned. The lantern was a swinging fuzzy blur, and their guard, a mountain of a man, had been reduced to a white hump.

A sudden gust scoured her face. Lena winced, blinking as tears pooled. She wanted to wipe them away, but her fingers were numb even in gloves because of the plasticuffs. When the guard zipped them on, she tried tensing her muscles, but then he'd slapped her hard enough to sting.

"None of that funny business, girl," the guard said, wrapping a chain around her waist that he locked to a thick metal O-ring. "Seth might be old, but Seth ain't stupid."

"No, Seth's just an asshole who can't speak in the first person," she said, but there was no fight in it and she'd only groaned when Seth yanked the plasticuffs so tight the zip sounded like a wood saw.

Now, she straightened, gritting her teeth against the bite of plastic in skin. Her wrists were wet. *Blood.* Just one more thing. She ducked her head, smearing her burning eyes on her shoulder.

"You okay?" Chris asked. He was on her right, his head and chest and shoulders frothy with snow.

"No. I can't feel my hands. These cuffs are too tight."

"Yeah, me neither. Shouldn't be much longer."

"Do you know where he's taking us?" She'd realized as soon as they turned out of Jess's street that they weren't headed into town but east.

"Torture house," Kincaid said. When he looked down at her, a mound of snow slid from the brim of his Stetson and plopped into his lap.

"What?"

"Well, they call it the interrogation center, but . . . oh yeah." Kincaid swayed as the wagon dipped in and out of ruts. "Sometimes the boys get overly *enthusiastic*. Afterward, they call me and I get to patch up whoever they're working over so they can start in again."

"Torture?" Her voice thinned to a squeak. "You mean, they're going to—" She whipped her head around to Chris. "You *know* about this?"

The light was bad, but she saw him hesitate. "Well, I—"

"Oh my God, you do." Her bravado had evaporated, and she wondered again what the hell she'd been thinking. She didn't even *like* Alex. And if Chris *knew* they were torturing people, why didn't he do something to stop it?

"They'll just try to scare you," Chris was saying. "You'll be fine, I promise."

"That's not a promise you can make, Chris. 'Sides, my guess is she *does* have information." Kincaid eyed Lena. "Do you?"

"I don't have anything to say to you," she said. "You're one of *them*."

"Oh, right. I'm so glad you reminded me I'm one of the bad guys, in case these cuffs weren't enough."

"How can you joke around?" She was feeling sick again and badly needed to pee.

"I wasn't aware I was." Kincaid paused and then his tone changed. "You're from up around Oren."

"So what? It's not a crime," she said, and then thought, *Shit, I make it* sound *like it is.*

"You don't owe him any explanations, Lena," Chris put in.

"I can talk for myself."

"I'm just saying—"

"Whoa, whoa," Kincaid said. "If you two can't do better than that, you'll be sunk in ten seconds, maybe less. Chris, you of all people ought to know that."

"Is there a question in there?" Chris asked.

"Should there be?" When Chris said nothing, Kincaid went on:

"Chris, it's what your grandfather asked. How do you know where to look for these kids you keep finding?"

More silence. Lena could feel Chris shutting down, throwing up barriers. A torture house, and Chris *knew* about it . . .

"You got some kind of system," Kincaid said. "Has to be it. You got this clockwork-like thing going, if I'm remembering it right. Of course, if you had a little *help*." Kincaid's Stetson moved fractionally, and Lena felt the burn of the old man's eyes on her face. "Someone kind of local, maybe? Clue you in where to look, or how?"

Chris jumped in before she could reply. "Like you said, you're here, too, Doc. You want to tell me what happened with Alex?"

"I honestly don't know, Chris," Kincaid said. "The last time I saw Alex, she was fine. If it was anything, I think it had something to do with that boy—"

There was a sudden bright flash. On the driver's box, Seth jerked at the same moment that Chris threw himself against Lena in a chatter of metal chain. She thudded to the wooden bed in a tangled heap, crying out as the chain around her waist bound and dug.

"Chris?" she managed. "What—"

"Someone's shooting." His head craned a cautious few inches. The wagon had lurched to a halt. "Seth's down. Thank God the horses didn't spook. Kincaid, you all right?"

"Yeah." Lena heard the drag of metal against wood as the old man shifted. "We're still in Rule," Kincaid said. "Who the hell—"

Lena's ears pricked at the muffled clop of hooves. "Stay down,"

Chris murmured. She felt him squirming onto his back. "You, too, Doc."

There was movement by the driver's box as a shape—man-sized, snow-shrouded—slid into the ball of lantern light. When the man turned to peer in their direction, Lena almost let out a yelp. The man had no face.

Idiot. Her pulse raced. *He's got on a ski mask, that's all.*

The form slipped away. She sensed him creeping alongside the wagon. There was a dip, and then the wagon jostled as the man hoisted himself up—

Chris lashed out with both feet. There was a grunt as Chris's boot thudded against the man's chest, and then the faceless man was swaying, one hand hooked over the lip. Chris's boot thrashed again, the sole smashing the man's fingers. The man howled as Chris swarmed up. His bound hands were in front now, and Chris let loose with a double-fisted, backhanded swing—

"*No*, Chris!" Someone launched himself from Kincaid's side of the wagon. Surprised, Chris let out a yell as the man wrapped him up. They thudded in a thrashing tangle on top of Lena and Kincaid. Lena's head banged against the wood; Kincaid was shouting, "*Hold on, hold on, hold on!*" But Chris was still fighting, and then this second man was screaming, "Stop, Chris, it's Weller, it's *Weller!*"

"Weller?" She heard the surprise in Chris's voice. "What are you—"

"We got to be fast," Weller said. A click, and then a spear of yellow light. "Let me get your hands, Chris. Nathan, you okay?"

"Yeah." The man Chris had kicked peeled off a black balaclava. "But I'm kinda tired of getting beat up," Nathan said.

"What," Chris asked, "are you guys doing?"

"What's it look like?" Weller tossed Chris's cuffs aside. "Saving your butts."

19

"Oren?" Chris said. The storm was settling in for a nice hard blow. Snowmelt trickled down Chris's neck, and he was starting to feel the cold, the sudden gusts driving icy flakes that needled his cheeks. They were still crouched in the wagon, although Weller now occupied the driver's box. He'd tumbled Seth's body in an unceremonious tangle to the ground. The body was already mantled with new snow. Besides his own roan and Nathan's sorrel, both laden with bulging saddlebags, Weller had also brought a lean gray. The horses stomped and blew, intermittently shaking snow from their bodies with a jangle of hardware. "Let me see if I got this straight. You *want* us to run, now, in *this.*"

"Yeah," Weller drawled. Nathan's lower lip was swollen to the size of a fat bratwurst, so Weller was doing most of the talking. For a guy who'd grown up in Michigan, he seemed to enjoy channeling cowboy-lite. "That's why I brought the gear. 'Course, I wasn't expecting you'd have to light out with the girl, but seeing as how she's lived with them . . ."

"But I wasn't born Amish," Lena put in. She huddled to Chris's left and hugged herself against the cold. Weller had shucked his own woolen watch cap, several sizes too large, which she'd jammed down around her ears. The crumpled peak sagged. She looked like a dispirited elf. "My mom married into it, and she was a complete flake. And it's not like my stepfather was *beloved* or anything. I know the settlement but not that well, and I sure never heard of any old guy named Isaac Hunter."

"Even if he's a real person, you've never met him," Chris said to Weller.

"Jess says he's still alive."

"And how does she know? And who's Hunter? And let's say I do find him. How do you or Jess know that these kids hiding out around Oren are with him?"

"He's right," Lena said. "The group I was with had ten kids. One of them, Jayden, said there were a lot of groups, but they're scattered, so people can't find them. They don't even know where the others are half the time. Jayden said it was safer that way, but he never mentioned any adult being in charge. We were on our own."

"Trust me, wherever these kids are, they don't want to be found. I know. I've been looking for months," Chris said. "And this idea you've got that I should convince them to come back to Rule, like some half-assed army, because you think no one here's going to open fire on Spared, all so I can take over? It's completely nuts. Even if I agreed—and I'm not—why wouldn't I go north? It's a hell of a lot faster than detouring east."

"Because if you lay me enough of a trail east, everyone'll look *that* way and not at Oren," Weller said. "This blow's a good thing. The Council might be hot to go after you, but I could make a good case that we shouldn't budge until the worst of this is over. So you'll have a decent head start. Say, tack east fifty, sixty miles—"

"*Fifty* mi—" Chris goggled. "Even with no storm and on horses, the snow's deep. Do you know how long that's going to take?"

"Sure. But then you loop back and head northwest."

"But it takes three or four days to get to Oren in *good* weather," Lena protested.

"With the extra mileage, we won't make it to Oren for ten, twelve days. Maybe two *weeks*. That's a long time to be out in the *snow*," Chris said.

"So you're roughing it." Weller shrugged like this was no big deal. "Won't be pleasant, and you'll get cold—"

"And probably hungry."

"So you hunt, same as if you were going on a supply run. You know how to do that. It's not like you don't have some good gear here. Of course, I wasn't expecting to hustle three of you out of the village, so you only got two sleeping bags. That should make things a little"—he cocked his head toward Lena—"interesting."

"God, you're disgusting," Lena said.

Weller brushed past her comment. "But by the time we follow, the trail'll be cold."

"Oh, ha-ha. Cold. I get it." Lena's voice dripped derision. "*Irony.*"

"Lena." She was giving Chris a headache. He turned his attention back to Weller. "You think you have this all figured out? You guys are *crazy*."

"Okay, we're crazy." Weller was matter-of-fact. "Guess you won't mind us dropping you off at the torture house then."

"Don't be stupid." Peter hadn't allowed him into the torture house, an order Chris never questioned. But he wasn't brain-dead. He'd marched his share of prisoners there. Most were men, but there were more than a few women, too. Not that you could tell the difference, necessarily, because once things got to a certain point behind those walls . . . well, all the screams sounded alike. Once, he'd caught a glimpse of a wagon rolling away, and from the lumps and hummocks beneath a swath of blood-soaked canvas heaped on the wagon's backboard, he knew, exactly, how most prisoners left. "What kind of choice is *no* choice?"

"One you just don't happen to like," Weller said.

"You got a *point*?" The doctor had stayed silent, but now Kincaid's voice shook with rage. "Do you and Nathan and the others even understand what you've done here, what you're asking of this boy? What the hell kind of game are you men playing?"

"No game." Weller's expression was obscured by snow and shadow, but his tone took on an angry edge. "I'm sorry we didn't keep you in the loop, Doc—"

"In the loop? In the goddamned *loop*?" Kincaid shouted. "We're talking a girl's *life*!"

"Wait a minute, what do you mean, *in* the loop?" Chris was incredulous. "Doc, you were part of this?"

"Told you," Lena muttered. She backhanded snow from her face. "They're all in it together."

"No, not all of it and not all the way," Kincaid said darkly. "If I'd have known what they were planning for Alex, I would've stopped them."

Yeah, Chris thought, *but* only *what they had planned for Alex?* It wasn't a comforting thought, because that meant Kincaid agreed with this crazy scheme, at least in part. Worse, the old doctor had actually *known* that, eventually, these men would ask *him* to . . . what? Save them? Save Rule?

"Alex might still be okay," Nathan said, only the words came out wet and mushy because of the lip: *Alesh* and *shill.* "She's a smart kid." *Sheeshashmarkid.*

"Oh, you think her chances are pretty good, do you?" Kincaid said.

"Doc," Nathan said doggedly, "you got to believe me. I'm sick about what happened with Alex. That was not the way it was supposed to go down."

"Well, how the hell *else* could it have—"

"Doc." Putting a restraining hand on the doctor's arm, Chris debated for a split second. Easy enough to let these men fight amongst themselves, but like it or not, they were his ticket out of Rule, and he knew it. "Tell me what was supposed to go down, Nathan. I'm not promising anything—"

Weller cut in. "You're not exactly in what you'd call a strong position to—"

"Yeah, but as I get it, you need me. So shut up, Weller." Ignoring Weller's spluttering, Chris drilled Nathan with a hard stare. "Tell me what happened, *exactly.*"

"Well . . ." Nathan cut his eyes away. "What Lena said . . . about your horse . . . she was right." *Horsh.*

"Yeah." Lena snorted. "No shit, Sherlock."

"It wasn't Night?" Chris's hand crept to the wound on his scalp, and the bristle of stitches there. "*You* hit me?"

"No." Nathan shook his head and kept talking to his hands. "That was Jess."

"*Je—*"

"She had to, Chris."

"She *had* to? That's no reason!"

"Well, me and some of the men, we hauled you off, but you just wouldn't quit."

"Because Alex was out there!" Chris shouted. "What the hell did you expect me to do? Let her go?"

"Chris, you got to understand that what Jess did was the only way to stop you going after Alex," Nathan slurred. "You got back early. There was nothing else we could do."

"Don't tell me that," Chris seethed. "Of course there was. You could let me *get* her. You could let me *save* her! Even if she'd crossed out of the Zone, you could have just *shut up* about it and let me bring her back!"

"That's not what Jess wanted," Nathan said, wetly. Like that was some sort of explanation. "She said you had to know what you were walking into. You're the only one left who can make things right, Chris. You were always the only one. If you just took off, without thinking of all the consequences, sorting the whole thing through, that would be your heart talking."

"How else *should* I feel?" Chris managed. Rage balled in his throat. "All I ever wanted was to keep Alex safe."

"Jess said you needed to want more. She was willing to die to make that happen, too. You know Jess wanted me to kill her?"

God, I wish you had. Better her than Alex. "I'll bet she did. Just something else to put on Alex." When Nathan hesitated, Chris knew he'd guessed right. "So why didn't you?"

"I . . . I couldn't do it."

"But Alex, you let go. Alex, you can let *walk* into—"

"I'm not proud of what happened. I just need you to under-stand why I did what I did, that's all." Nathan finally raised his eyes to find Kincaid. "I'm sorry we cut you out of it, Doc. Trust me, though: the less you knew, the better."

"Well, I don't trust you and you can never make this right, Nathan," Kincaid said. His voice was low and hollow, his fury an echo of Chris's own. "That girl is gone. You shut Jess up all right, and now she might die, too. Tell yourself anything you want, but you'll never be clean again."

"And you're not just as bad?" Lena demanded. "You knew they were planning something, but you never warned Chris or Alex or—"

"Let it go, Lena," Chris interrupted. "It's done and let's just deal, okay?" He turned to Nathan again. "This Hunter guy, why is he important?"

"Jess said he's got history," Nathan said. "Isaac will carry weight with the Council."

"Yeah, but how?" When Nathan didn't reply, Chris threw a look at Weller. "My God, you don't *know*. Neither of you do."

Weller's face was a stolid mask. "We took Jess at her word.

She's been in Rule longer than any of us, from a time long before Yeager took over. She knows how the Council works and where the secrets are buried, which closets got skeletons."

"But you don't know which ones," Lena said.

"Even if you did . . . that was *enough* for you?" Chris cried. "Don't you see how crazy that is?"

"She has history," Nathan persisted.

Chris opened his mouth to protest again but decided it wasn't worth the breath. They were all insane. Jess had come up with some crazy-ass plan that was *no* plan and these old men had gone along.

"Bet you still think we're nuts," Weller said.

"That makes two of us," Lena chimed.

Weller paid her no mind. "But let me ask you something, Chris. You ever have trouble with any order Peter gave?"

A tiny warning *ping* went off in his brain. "How do you mean?" Chris asked.

"I thought it was pretty clear. You ever disagree with Peter?"

"Sometimes."

"You ever go around him?"

"Weller," Kincaid warned. "This is not his fault."

"It's okay, Doc." Chris studied Weller for a long moment. "I tried never to question Peter in front of the other men, if that's what you're asking."

"Why not?"

Because I trusted him. Peter was the older brother I never had. "I didn't always agree," Chris said. "Sometimes we could talk about it. Other times he wouldn't budge."

"And then you followed orders." Weller mouthed the words as though they had a very bad taste.

"I had to. The Council decided, and Peter gave the orders. I was just doing what I was supposed to, that's all." He knew that sounded weak and pushed on. "I don't see you guys doing anything different."

"No?" Weller spread his arms. "Then what the hell do you call this?"

"Crazy," Lena said, flatly. "If you guys don't like what the Council's doing, *you* fix it."

"We can't," Nathan said. "That's not how Rule works. We'd never convince enough people. It's 'go along to get along.' Anyway, a challenge to the Council—"

"Can only come from within the Council," Chris finished, impatiently. "Or from a blood relation of someone already in the Council. Yeah, yeah, I know; I got that. But what makes you think that anyone will listen to me?"

"You expose what's going on," Nathan said. "You show people the reasons for it, and then they got to face up to the fact that they and the Council—and *Peter*—have made a deal with the Devil."

"Peter?" A cold leaked into his bones that had nothing to do with the storm. "What kind of deal? What are you saying?"

"What's beyond the Zone, Chris?"

"I don't know."

"Why not?"

"Because. I've never gone. It . . . it's not allowed. Whenever we've left for supplies, Peter . . ."

"Peter chose the routes," Weller put in. "*Peter* always decided. Peter had the Council's ear. And what about the Banned? Haven't you wondered about that particular punishment? When you're forced out of the village, it's forever. But why? This is a good Christian community, right? So why no second chance? Where's all that good Christian forgiveness? And that's set in stone, too. Go beyond a certain point, cross a foot out of the Zone, and you can never return. So could it be that the Banned might bring back stories the Council would be just as happy we didn't hear?"

Stop talking. When Chris swallowed, it sounded like thunder. *I don't want to hear this; I don't want to know.*

"Chris," Nathan said, "haven't you wondered why the Changed don't attack Rule anymore?"

Somehow, he managed to drag his voice from his chest. "No."

"And why not?"

"I don't know, I just haven't," Chris said. "Why should I care, so long as I don't have to fight them?"

"But does that make sense? You fight them on the road. You know they're not dead. They're getting along and they're not going away, isn't that true?"

"So?"

"Think, Chris. Even this far into winter, we've still had raiders. Refugees still trickle in. And yet we haven't faced the Changed, in Rule's territory, for over two months. Why?"

"There are too many of us. They know we'll kill them."

"But we shelter them," Weller interrupted. "Isn't that so?"

"What? *No.* If we find them, we kill them."

"Really?" Weller asked. "We bring back little kids. Isn't it just as likely they might eventually Change once they're old enough?"

"If age is the only factor," Kincaid put in. "We don't even know that much."

"What?" Chris was dumbfounded. "We . . . That's not how the Change works."

"Well, now, we don't know how it works, or that it's over," Kincaid said. "For that matter, we can't be certain the Spared are really safe in the long run."

"What do you mean you're not certain?" Lena suddenly shrilled. "How can it not be *over*?"

"Because it might not be."

"But we're *Spared*." Lena's voice rang with a new note of desperation. "It's been *months*. How can we not be *safe*?"

"Because we don't know why you were Spared in the first place, or why there are so few of you. What do you, Lena, have in common with Alex or Sarah or Chris? Or Peter?"

This was too much to absorb. Chris could feel his thoughts storming around and around the limits of his skull. "What does any of this have to do with the Banned? Or the Zone?"

"It's pretty simple, Chris," Weller said. "Why is the southwest corner, where we send the Banned, the least guarded?"

"I don't *know*," Chris said. "What are you saying? What are you talking about?"

"We're talking about what's beyond the Zone. We're talking about why Peter sends the Banned *there*, and nowhere else. Why *Peter* decides that certain routes should be traveled only at certain times." Weller leaned forward. "We're *talking* about why Peter has us stealing children. Why are we taking kids, by force, from their families?"

"Oh shit, oh *shit*," Lena said before Chris could answer. "*You* did it. You staged the ambush to get Peter out of the way!"

"Don't be stupid, girl," Weller said. "Peter had things to answer for, I'll give you that. But I tried to save that boy."

"Things to answer for?" Chris echoed. "What things?"

"Answer me this, Chris," Weller said. "Where are the children of Rule? Where are the grandkids?"

"They . . . well, they Changed, right? Didn't you . . . you must've killed them."

"But where are the graves? We buried everyone native to Rule, even the Changed we had to shoot. But how many kids do you think there were in a village of two thousand? I can tell you, for a fact, that there aren't near enough graves out there. So what I'm asking is . . . where are the rest of them?"

"I—" Chris's voice came in a harsh croak. "I don't know. They left. They ran away. They're . . . they're *gone*."

"Really?" Weller leaned forward. "And what makes you so sure?"

20

Nothing. No dreams, no sound. No thought. Just . . . nothing.

Then, pain: a red shriek that went on and on and on. Voices, too, but they bled into one another: *hold him watch out he's tanking working as fast as I* . . . Screams and other sounds, but they were garbled and elusive as thin mist. Only at the end—right before his fade to black—did his mind grab at a single, clear thought: those awful, bloody screams were his.

More blank. More dark. Every once in a while, his mind sputtered to life like an ancient engine that refused to turn over, no matter how gently that pedal was goosed. Sometimes, he heard himself moan and there were other shrieks, but those felt detached and . . . elsewhere, like voices trapped in those floaty cartoon bubbles.

A longer blank.

Then, all at once, he jammed to consciousness in a great searing, molten shriek of pain. The transition was shattering. His body was a white blaze of agony, but he was in the dark. His eyes wouldn't open. Or they might be wide open and he just didn't know it.

Oh God, I'm blind, I'm blind, I'm . . . A scream boiled from his throat, and then he was straining, trying to move—and couldn't.

"Easy," someone said. "Take it easy, I'm right here."

He couldn't tell if the voice belonged to a man or woman. "I . . . I . . . ," he wheezed. He tried turning his head, but another red arrow of pain pierced him to the core, and he let go of another scream.

"Stop." This time, a hand touched his shoulder. "Try not to panic."

If he wasn't hurting so much, he might've laughed. *My God, what is wrong with me?* He could smell himself: sour flesh, old blood, and fear. "Can't . . . *s-see* . . . can't *m-move.*"

"That's because of the restraints, boy-o." This voice definitely belonged to a man. Peter heard the hard boom of command but also a rough weariness he associated with the old. "You're a fighter, I'll give you that."

Restraints? His heart crowded into his mouth. "K-Kincaid . . . wh-where . . ."

"Easy." The first voice again: a soothing contralto. A woman. "You've been out so long that we put bandages over your eyes to keep the corneas from ulcerating. Take it easy." Her fingers spidered over his cheeks and then she tugged. His skin bunched as the gluey adhesive let go. Air sighed over his closed lids. "Try now."

The simple act of opening his eyes took tremendous concentration. His muscles were creaky, like long-unused gears mucky with coagulated oil and grime. A sliver of light appeared and then his lids were rolling back. Another lurch of panic clawed his chest.

"Bloo." He wanted to cry. His tongue was thick, a flap of muscle that refused to cooperate. *"Blooor."*

"Blurry?" Beads of water dripped onto his forehead. "Close your eyes again . . . that's good. Just give it a couple minutes, okay? I had to use animal tranks. I'm sorry about that, but it's the best we have. Good thing you're strong as a horse and your heart's young. Otherwise, we wouldn't be having this conversation."

The cloth felt so good and cool and wet. He stopped fighting and let her work. There was a gurgle and splash, and then she was swabbing his forehead, his face, the underside of his neck. Her fingers worked at buttons, and then she was sponging his chest. He moaned, this time with relief.

"Yeah, I'll bet that feels good." The cloth went away again, and then she was tugging a shirt over his chest and drawing up a rough blanket that smelled of old wool and death. "Try opening your eyes now."

He did. His vision was still foggy, but he could make out green canvas above his head. A tent. His gaze roved over a metal pole at his left shoulder, and a bottle of clear liquid that dripped fluid into the big vein at the crook of his elbow through a plastic tube. Leather restraints with big metal buckles were clamped around his wrists. From the pressure around his ankles, he knew his feet were tied down, too.

Some kind of infirmary. The air smelled chilly and damp. He lay beneath several blankets on a metal stretcher that felt flimsy and too light, like one of those pop-up gurneys EMTs used. *Military?*

"Better?" Above and to the left, the woman's face took on angles and substance. She wasn't heavy but solid and blunt. Her hair was scraped back into a knot at the nape of her neck. Her murky eyes were set in weathered skin. She was much older than he expected: maybe mid-seventies or early eighties. Her fatigues were dated, like they were from a surplus store. But the flash on her left shoulder looked new: a Colonial flag with a Roman numeral III dead-center in that circlet of thirteen stars.

Oh shit. Before the world went bust, he'd been a sheriff's deputy. So he knew exactly what that flash meant.

"Who are you people?" he whispered.

The booming voice came again from his right. "Relax, boy-o, you're among friends. Have to admit, though, you gave us quite a scare." The man was blocky and solid, and his head was huge, like a chunk of granite furred with a thick shock of white hair cropped flat and square as a broom. His chest was so barrel-shaped and big around that his arms seemed an afterthought: stubby and thick and tacked on. He wasn't tall but massive and compact, tough as an ox. His uniform was different, too: jet-black from head to toe, but with that same shoulder flash and a single yellow star pinned to either lapel of the old man's fleece-lined, black-leather bomber jacket. A bulky walkie-talkie—of the same vintage as the military surplus units Rule used—was clipped to his left hip. A holster rode on his right, a faint glimmer of pearl shining from the revolver's grip.

"You were gone eight days, boy-o. Glad you saw fit to rejoin us." The blocky man's lips pulled into a grin. "We had a bet going about whether you'd make it. Happy to say that I was on the winning side. Name's Finn. This fine woman is Dr. Mather. And you are . . . ?"

Eight days. He'd been here more than a *week*? If Rule was looking for him, they'd have given up by now. Chris wouldn't want to; he knew that. But even Chris wouldn't be able to justify a search forever. "Where am I?" he asked.

"You're safe and you're alive."

"But wh-where . . . what about my m-men?" His voice was rusty as an old hinge. "There was a boy."

"Hold on," Finn said. Turning aside, he poured water from a plastic jug, then slid in a straw. "You're probably dry as a desert."

The straw was tantalizingly close. The water's scent made him dizzy. Still, he hesitated. He sensed he would be crossing some line if he took water from this man.

"Go on, take it, boy-o. I don't bite—not like those Chuckies." Finn tilted his head at the far side of the tent. Peter's eyes swept right and he saw what he hadn't spotted before. More gurneys, with bodies: two boys, one girl. All were restrained and completely out, probably drugged from fluid dripped into their veins through plastic tubes.

Finn said, "Soon as we decide to let those little darlings wake up, we'll put them in our holding area with the other six. Ten's all we can safely handle and feed. Nasty little buggers. You're the first normal your age the hunters have brought in. Be interesting to see what happens over time."

What did *that* mean? And hunters. *Bounty* hunters? *Oh God.* Capturing him and Tyler had been the objective all along. He remembered the snow coming alive with icy geysers. They could have killed him but hadn't.

They tried pinning me down, but then I ran to Tyler and that's when I got hit. They shot me as a last resort because they didn't want me getting away.

He stared up at Finn. "Where's the boy?"

"I'm afraid he's gone. But rest assured we put Tyler to very good use."

What? "I . . . I don't . . ."

"Come on, no more questions. Drink up, boy-o. You've lost a lot of blood. You're O-negative, did you know that? Pretty rare, and while that's good if *I* need blood, Mather could only transfuse *you* with the same blood type. Lucky for you, Peter, we're not talking something contagious."

What did *that* mean? And Finn already knew his name—and Tyler's. Of course, he must. The bounty hunters knew who they were and where they'd been heading.

They were tipped off, but how? I didn't decide on Dead Man until that morning. That was when he'd sent Lang ahead. Had Finn's bounty hunters ambushed his runner? That had to be it.

"Where am I?" he rasped.

"Why, you're in my territory, Peter, and I've got the water you want and *need*. Come on now." Finn proffered the cup again. "No more questions."

Despite his fear, he desperately wanted a drink. He let Finn slide the straw between his lips. The water—cold and blessedly wet—flooded over his tongue. He thought he was going to faint. He sucked the cup dry in three gasping gulps.

"Excellent. Keep that down and you can have more in a little while." Finn looked over at Mather. "Bring in Davey, will you? He and Peter should get acquainted."

"Yes, sir." Mather fired off a salute, then brushed past the Changed on their gurneys. Watching her go, Peter realized something else.

"You . . ." His gaze snagged on an old caged shop light. The light wasn't soft or pleasant but very hard, a spray of bright yellow that hurt and burned shadowy afterimages on Peter's retinas. But he couldn't make himself look away. "You've got *light*."

"Some," Finn said. "We have enough juice to warm a few tents: the infirmary here and where Mather does her surgery and . . . other work. Our depot is fairly well-stocked—vehicles are virtually useless, though we have a few older trucks—but we use what we have very sparingly."

Generators. And a depot. He was sure now. It all tallied, right down to that shoulder flash. The Roman numeral III stood for the Three Percent. That was the statistic private militias liked to throw around because only that small percentage of the American colonists actually fought the British in the Revolutionary War. So this wasn't just a camp of survivors. This was a private militia compound that probably existed well before the world died.

"You know, as unfortunate as it was that you got shot, that did give us a chance to disprove another theory," Finn said.

Despite the water, his mouth was puckery and parched again. "Wh-what do you m-mean?"

"Well, you lost all that blood. Strong or not, *young* or not, you'd have died if Mather hadn't found a donor."

What had the old man said? *Lucky for you, it's not contagious.*

Oh God. "You . . ." The words wanted to wedge in his throat and stay there. "You gave me *blood* f-from . . ."

"Yes, I did, and here you woke up still you." Finn drew his hand over his brow. "Whew. Talk about a nail-biter."

The words tripped over his teeth. "How m-much?"

"Every last drop. Bled that little Chucky dry. Even that animal knew he was going. You could see it in his eyes. I got right up in his face. Little prick tried taking off my nose, but old habits die hard. I cut off his eyelids so I could watch the whole thing. It was very *gratifying.*"

He was as close to screaming as he'd ever been in his life. "You're militia, right? But who are you people? What the hell do you *want*?"

Finn's expression darkened. "We're what's left, and you will show the proper respect, or so help me God, I will carve you into kibbles and feed you to the Chuckies a piece at a time. I'll save the eyes for last. Eyes, they really like. Something about that little *pop.*"

The tent's flaps parted. Through the gap, Peter saw the slant of snow. Mather ducked in, followed a moment later by a man.

Oh my God.

"Where would you like it, sir?" Lang—*his* man, *his* runner— snapped a crisp salute. Lang's snow-salted uniform was identical to Mather's, and he carried an automatic rifle. He spared Peter not a single glance.

"Right here." Finn patted an empty gurney, then slipped Peter a wink. "Don't take it too hard now, boy-o. Lang served under my command in 'Nam." Finn said it as if the country were a sweet potato. "Imagine how pleased I was when he reported how much you respected his combat skills."

Lang was Finn's man. A sweep of dread blackened his brain as he remembered something else. Lang and Weller had served in Vietnam *together*.

But that doesn't prove anything. Weller tried to save my life. But wait. Something Weller had said suddenly marched before his inner eye like that electronic ticker tape at Times Square: *You remember when your time comes, it was* me *did this.*

Oh Jesus. A deep and darkling sickness crept through his veins like a contagion born on a plague wind. Weller hadn't saved his life. Weller was under *orders* to keep him alive. But why?

"Busy putting two and two together?" Finn lifted an eyebrow. "They said you were a smart boy."

They. So, only Lang and Weller? Or were there more? How many men had Peter thought loyal but who were really working against Rule? *And it's personal for Weller. This is a grudge, something to do with me, but what?* "What do you want?" he rasped.

"God moves in a mysterious way, Peter, His wonders to perform. He rides upon the storm and deep in unfathomable mines." Finn's eyes sparkled. "Why, I believe you *know* all about mines, don't you?"

Mines. All the breath left his lungs, and the words struck him dumb. How did Finn know that? No one outside the Council did, not even Chris. *Especially* not Chris.

Finn turned as Lang held back the flap and two more people

bullied in on a frigid cloud of fresh snow. Finn's man, bald and bucktoothed, had his hands firmly clamped around a long metal rod Peter recognized at once as an animal control pole, the type with a swivel head. That was important, because no matter how much a wild dog might fight, it could not strangle itself on that nylon noose. A good thing, too, because this animal was putting up quite a fight.

Only . . . it wasn't a dog.

21

The boy was no older than Tyler, completely naked and so scrawny the birdcage of his ribs showed. His skin was scored with healing cuts and scrapes, angry sores, and frozen mud, and from the smell, shit caked his feet. He made no sound at all, but then again the noose was tight, the fat worms of his veins bulging as he thrashed.

"Come on, ya little bastard." Bucktooth's lips peeled back as he gave the cable a vicious tug. Gagging, the boy's knees hinged.

"Barnes!" Finn snapped. There was a stinging *crack* as Finn's open palms connected with Barnes's ears. Barnes didn't even manage a scream, and went down in a heap. Finn grabbed up the pole, then loosened the noose until the boy sucked in a long, thin, shrieking breath. Cursing, Finn aimed a kick at the felled Barnes, but the old guy was already unconscious.

"Sir," Mather said to Finn. "I think this might not be the best—"

"Shut up." In a flash, Finn had his revolver out. The silvered muzzle hung an inch from Mather's nose. "Not another word, Doctor."

"Yes, sir," Mather said.

"That's two," Finn said.

The sound of the shot was enormous. Mather's skull blew out the back in a red mist. She dropped like a tree.

Finn turned to Lang, who was white-faced and absolutely still. "Get someone in here to clean up the mess. And tell Doctor Grier he's just been promoted."

Lang ducked his head once, then scuttled out. Peter lay still as death. He watched Finn turn back to the boy, who was on his knees now. The boy's filthy hands were still clamped down around the noose, but he was breathing normally. A froth of red spit foamed his lips.

"There now, Davey," Finn crooned as gently as one might try to calm a feral dog. "That's better, isn't it? Are you hungry, boy? Want something to eat?" He looked up as Lang returned with two other men. "Lang, grab hold of Davey here," he said, handing over the control pole. "You two, hold up with Barnes and Mather a minute. They're not going anywhere. Help Lang put Davey in restraints." He patted the empty gurney beside Peter's. "Right here, next to his new roomie."

As the guards hurried to comply, Finn turned his attention to the late Mather's instrument tray. Humming, he finger-walked the instruments, then selected a hefty, thick scalpel. The metal winked a hard, bright yellow as Finn stooped over Mather's body. The old woman's eyes were still jammed open. Her mouth gawped in a slack, surprised O. Finn reached in, reeled out Mather's tongue, and began to saw.

He's crazy. Peter's throat convulsed, and then he was rolling his head to one side and vomiting the water he'd just drunk along with a thick gob of sour phlegm and mucus. He gulped air as the room spun. *He's nuts, he's insane.*

"There we go," Finn said. Peter opened his eyes to find Finn standing over the gurney to his right. The boy was firmly tethered in leather restraints. The boy's chest heaved. His glittery crow's eyes were fixed on Finn's glistening, gore-soaked hands. "Care for a bite, Davey?"

The boy gasped as the first thick, ruby teardrop splashed to his lips. A mad hunger chased over the boy's face as he tongued the blood then opened wider, craning his neck so the blood could drip directly into his mouth. To Peter, he looked like a baby bird waiting for its mother to cram a worm down its throat. Peter thought of how *he* must have looked to Finn as the old man offered him water. There was, in fact, no difference.

Then, viper-quick, the boy's head darted. Finn jerked back just as Davey's teeth clashed and bit air where Finn's pinky had been.

"Bad boy." Finn gave the boy's cheek a quick, hard flick. "No, Davey, no biting."

Snarling, the Changed boy surged again. Finn backhanded him with a punch this time, right below the boy's eye, and then waited as the guards strapped a wide band of leather across the boy's forehead.

"All right, let's try again." Finn sliced off another chunk of Mather's tongue with the scalpel. It took three more tries and as many punches before Davey let Finn drop the drippy meat into his mouth without snapping at the old man's fingers. Peter watched as the boy held the morsel in his mouth then worked the meat from cheek to cheek.

"Go on." Finn sounded just like a kindly old grandpa slipping his favorite grandson a Hershey's Kiss, sure to spoil his appetite, on the sly. Without looking around, he added, "It's quite interesting, actually. I've studied a number of them now. You *do* realize that the . . . what do you call it? The Change? From my observations, it's not over yet, boy-o, not by a long shot."

Something turned over in his chest. The Change wasn't *over*? The thinking part of his brain had known this was a possibility, but no one in Rule had seen that happen to a Spared.

No one's safe? Peter felt his mind cringing away. *No, he's wrong. I'm Spared. It's not going to happen to me, or Chris, or any of the other Spared. It's been too long; it's been* months. *That can't be right.*

"Do you know what I wonder?" Finn's face turned a little dreamy. "I *wonder* what it would be like."

"What?" Peter managed. He slicked his lips. "You mean . . . to Change?"

"Yes. Self-awareness is a blessing and a curse, Peter. You know when you're coming down with a cold. There are signs and symptoms. So what is the Change like? Do you sense it? Would you even know? You must. The dying have this sixth sense when the end is near. Even the insane know when their hold on reality slips. They may lie to themselves, of course, but . . . they know."

"I . . . I d-don't . . ." He was shaking. His teeth wouldn't stop chattering. "I don't c-care. I don't w-want t-to know. It d-doesn't matter."

"Oh, but it does, and you *should* care. To understand your enemy—beat him at his own game—you must allow yourself to inhabit his brain, see with his eyes. Now, this is not to say 'seen one Chucky, seen them all.' Oh no. For example, take what happens to a Chucky once he's completely turned, like our Davey here," Finn waved a hand at the boy. "A fresh Chucky is an animal. Some stay wild. Others evolve, and some appear to be smarter than others. It's the bell curve in action, boy-o. Why, I bet there's a Chucky rocket scientist in the mix, somewhere. Oh, I'd so love to catch a normal kid a good *long* time before he goes native so I can measure the rate at which he reacquires function. I'm *especially* interested in the ones turning now. Their course must be so different from the first wave, don't you agree? And how do they communicate? We know some work together, travel in bands and packs and gangs and tribes and so forth, while others are loners. So are we talking telepathy? Subaudible vocalizations? Scent? Body language? Alone? In combination?"

"What are you talking about?" Peter whispered. He was now thoroughly and deeply afraid for the first time since the world went dark. "You want to see if I'm going to Change? I'm not. It's been too long. You want to know about Rule? You can torture me, but I won't tell you." When Finn didn't reply, Peter said, "For God's sake, what do you *want*?"

"You mean a smart boy like you can't figure it out?" Dropping to one knee, Finn used a thumb to pull down Mather's lower eyelid, then slid the scalpel into the pink tissue tethering Mather's right eyeball to its socket. He worked the blade, scraping bone.

"You disappoint me, Peter. Despite what the movies say, not all Vietnam vets are crazy. Some of us even get to be senators. Me, I'm a student of the natural world. Like Darwin, come to think of it. Evolution, natural selection, survival of the fittest—all unfolding before our eyes. We are the authors of the new origin of species, boy-o."

"What—" Peter was sick with horror. "What are you going to do with me?"

"Isn't it obvious?" Finn said. Mather's eye dangled from his fingers by a bloody stalk of nerve. "Experiment."

PART THREE:
THE SHORT STRAW

22

Eight days gone.

Alex had kept track, scratching a hash mark into the toe of her right boot with the metal prong of her watchband. Over the past eight days, she figured they'd covered anywhere from fifty to sixty miles. Getting her bearings was a challenge. The days were overcast, the nights starless, and their group kept to the deep woods. But she thought they were moving on a kind of circuit, going first west but looping north. They stopped at regular intervals, too, during which time the Changed hunted, chowed down, caught a little shut-eye.

The good news, all things considered, was that she wasn't dead yet.

The bad news: she might draw that short straw, and soon.

It all came down to the math.

Eight days ago, on that first Saturday morning, the Changed had six Happy Meals to choose from, counting Alex. After all the ruckus, she'd assumed she was next on the menu. Yet it seemed that the

Changed—well, Wolf anyway—had different ideas. Although conscious, Spider was still groggy, so Wolf had wandered up and down, eyeing the herd, that gory corn knife in hand. Twice, he lingered over Alex, now trussed between the old lady, Ruby, and the sickly guy whose name, she would discover, was Brian. Wolf's eyes touched on her, then flitted away before jumping back. Playing with her? She wasn't sure. Maybe he was as puzzled as she. Were their experiences similar? Did he feel what she had, that odd sidestep into *her* consciousness? Could he *read* her? No, she didn't think so. During the fight on the snow, she'd surprised Spider— and then she remembered how Wolf had been *startled* when she let that gob of spit fly.

So maybe it doesn't go both ways. She'd given Wolf a narrow look as he moved down the line, studying each captive. *Maybe I can use that somehow.*

In the end, Wolf had chosen a small woman, tiny and brown as a wren, for that Saturday's main course. What puzzled and then appalled her was how the woman didn't struggle or protest. None of the others did either. Instead, they watched, impassively, as Acne and Beretta took the woman out of the line and led her, stumbling, across the snow a short ten yards to where Wolf waited. When they released her, the woman tottered but didn't fall. She stood, swaying, head down, shoulders slumped. Having replaced his cowl so his face was visible only from the nose down, Wolf waited a long beat, then knotted his fist in the woman's hair. The little woman let out a small cry as Wolf gave her head a vicious wrench that exposed her throat and made her back arch like a bow.

That's when it hit Alex. Wolf was going to kill her right there, in front of them. Her stomach tried to crawl into her chest. *I can't watch this.* Repulsed, still furious, she looked away. *I won't give them the satisfac—*

The blow was stunning, a ferocious, open-palmed *smack* that sent Alex's head whipping to the right. There was a sharp stab of pain as her teeth clamped her tongue. Her mind hitched, and she tottered, her balance already precarious because her ankles were still hobbled together, and she nearly went down. She was saved only because the sickly guy, Brian, had enough bulk to steady her.

"Please." Brian actually tried pulling away, as if worried that he might give the appearance of being helpful. "Just do what they want."

"Like hell." Her face felt like a bomb had gone off in her cheek. It was a wonder her jaw wasn't broken. Panting, she pushed away and looked to see which of the Changed had blindsided her. To her complete lack of surprise, Slash was there and, judging from the loose set of her shoulders, more than happy to let go with another sucker punch.

"Listen to Brian, *please.*" It was the old lady, Ruby, at her other elbow. "Don't fight them. Just do what they want."

"No." Head ringing, a warm brackish taste filling her mouth, Alex spat blood. "How can you just *stand* there?"

"Because it's better than getting beat up." To her left, a surly-looking woman with the hard edge of an ex-biker queen snorted. "If you're smart, you'll just be thankful they gave you a pass and shut the hell up."

"Sharon's right." Ruby's eyes were wild. "Just go along. You—" Whatever else Ruby had been about to say ended in an *ulp* as Slash slid her hand around the old woman's twig of a neck and squeezed.

"What are you *doing*?" Alex cried. Ruby's eyes bugged; her scrawny limbs thrashed in a spastic herky-jerky dance as her mouth flew open, but there was no sound, not even a squawk. "Stop!"

"Sweet Jesus." It was a barrel-chested man, near the end of the line, whom she would later learn was Ruby's husband, Ray. His face was ashen with horror. "For God's sake, just cooperate and she'll let her go!"

"All right." When Slash only bared her teeth in a ferocious grin, Alex screamed, "All right, all right, you bitch, you *win*! I'll look, okay? Just let her go!"

Still grinning, Slash held onto Ruby's neck for another fraction of a second, then spread her fingers.

"*Gunh!*" Gagging, her face the color of a fresh bruise, Ruby tumbled to the snow, nearly pulling Alex down as well. Alex half-turned, moving on instinct to help the retching old woman to her feet, before she caught movement and looked up to see Slash closing in again.

"I'm not." Straightening, Alex raised her bound wrists in a hasty surrender. "I'm not helping. Okay? See? I'm watching."

"Atta girl," the ex-biker queen muttered. Her name was Sharon, but Alex wouldn't know that until an hour after Wolf gouged the little woman's eyes from their sockets, sucking each from a finger like the soft chewy center of a naked Tootsie Pop.

"You're learning," Sharon said as Wolf closed in. "Go along to get along."

Another thing Alex learned that very first day? Spider might like the corn knife.

But Wolf liked his teeth.

And then they were five.

After breakfast, the Changed crammed the little woman's drippy remains into those nylon duffels. Then they all moved out. Another few hours on the trail put them in at a rustic, though roomy, hunting cabin. Judging from the condition of the snow, Wolf's gang had been back and forth a few times. A quartet of car batteries, connected in a series by wires, nestled on the snowy porch and probably once provided enough juice to run lights. Either the batteries were drained, however, or the Changed didn't care for or need light. Instead, Acne and Beretta carried in armloads of splits from a tarpaulin-covered woodpile wedged against a dilapidated shed. Soon two columns of gray wood smoke chugged from both a chimney and stove flue. The Changed bunked in the cabin while Alex and the others roomed in the old shed, a drafty place that reeked of ancient engine oil and dead mice. For warmth, they had a squat propane camp heater, and one another, although their ropes were removed, leaving them free to roam around the shed under Acne's watchful eye.

They'd returned the backpack Jess had given her. Ruby said this was standard: "We always come with something, and whatever we have, we share." There was something odd about the way Ruby said that, as if it was just assumed that anyone captured would have supplies. That actually didn't make sense. People could be snatched at random, but Ruth had said *always*. But Alex's arm was screaming by then, and she didn't have the energy to ask any more questions.

She caught some luck. Inside the pack, Jess had squirreled a battered first-aid kit that looked as if it hadn't seen daylight since the early Mesozoic era. The alcohol swabs were long dry. The gauze packs were still intact, however, and several foils of antiseptic goo were squishy enough that she thought they'd do the trick. No antibiotics to swallow, but maybe she wouldn't need them. While the others squabbled over energy bars and MREs, she melted snow in an empty can and let the water boil then cool to where she wouldn't scald herself.

The pain was ferocious, like something with talons and teeth gnawing her flesh to the bone. It was so bad her stomach somersaulted and then rolled on a tidal heave of nausea. She stopped what she was doing to hang her head between her knees. *God.* Her face and neck were filmed in a fine, greasy sweat. She gulped air, working not to pant. How had Tom *not* passed out? She was having a hard time with only hot water and gauze. Tom had withstood a superheated *knife.*

Oh, Tom. Her throat knotted. A wave of shame and grief swept through her. She managed to stopper the moan, but she felt the tears leaking down her cheeks. She thought of how hard she'd struggled to hang onto him: his face, his scent, the way he looked at her. How he made her feel. *But I gave up. I should have fought harder, found a way out, but it was easier just to go along.*

She wasn't an idiot. She knew she was being illogical. Someone—something—had gotten to him. Tom was dead, and that was not her fault. She'd done the best she could. So why did she feel this crush of guilt, like she was the one to blame? Tom wouldn't want that. The one sensible thing Jess had ever said was that Tom's sacrifice—all he'd done and suffered through to keep her and Ellie alive—shouldn't be for nothing. Tom would want her to go on with her life, not beat up on herself.

Tom, I'm trying, but what am I fighting for? *Staying alive just to stay alive isn't enough.*

She felt a sudden, irrational urge to laugh. God, she was worrying about the meaning of life when she was probably going to wind up minced into sushi.

"Hey." She looked up to find Sharon, the ex-biker queen, eyeing her. The woman clutched an MRE meal pack in one hand and was busy forking in cheesy noodles. "You all right?" Sharon asked, through a gluey mouthful of half-chewed pasta.

Sharon didn't sound all that concerned, really. *Probably hoping I keel over and then it's just that much more food for her.* That snot-yellow goo on Sharon's chin wasn't doing wonders for Alex's stomach either. The others were similarly stuffing their faces, and the listless, vacant looks they turned on her were incurious at best.

"Yeah." Smearing away the wet with the backs of her hands, she pulled in a tremulous breath. She'd be damned if she cried in front of these people. Not one had offered to help her. No, all they were interested in was filling their bellies. "The shoulder just hurts, that's all."

"Hunh. Well, you know the old saying." Sharon chewed, swallowed, used the heel of one hand to swab her chin.

"Which one?" Sharon seemed to be a font of meaningless homilies, and Alex really wasn't interested. *God, how can they eat after what they've seen? Maybe I'll end up the same way—if I live long enough, that is. It's like being afraid. How long can horror really last before you just numb out?* "No pain, no gain? It's always darkest before the dawn?"

"Naw." Sharon sucked her hand clean. "No matter how bad you think things are now?" She forked up another mouthful of wormy noodles. "They can always get worse."

They stayed put overnight that first Saturday, a delay she later learned was unusual. By twilight, the Changed normally moved on. Privately, Alex suspected that beating the crap out of Spider had something to do with the layover.

On Sunday, at dusk, they all set out again. The dense cloud cover choking the sky that afternoon hadn't broken, and the night was black as pitch. With no stars, she could only guess at a bearing but thought they were still heading north or northwest.

Another thing: the Changed often used flashlights and lanterns, but only intermittently. While Alex and the others struggled and stumbled, the Changed were shadows, moving with relative ease through the forest. Like panthers, she thought, or wolves. She knew from high school bio that the eyes of nocturnal animals were different, though she couldn't recall exactly how. This ability begged another question, too: were the Changed done Changing?

All told—going by Ellie's Mickey Mouse watch—they walked until three Monday morning and managed maybe six miles before putting in at another campsite. No shelter this time around. Acne and Slash lashed them to each other and then a trio of stout oaks before heading out to hunt. Again clad in his wolf skin, Wolf led the pack. Only Spider stayed behind, huddled over a fire, while they burrowed into the snow and waited.

When the Changed returned at first light, they brought fresh faces: a doughy woman and a bluff man shaped like a fireplug who said, later, that his name was Otis. The woman was Claire, but it was Otis who told them her name. Not five minutes after the Changed returned, Wolf went to work with his teeth and then Claire was way past caring about little niceties like an introduction.

On Wednesday, Day 5, she thought she was done.

By then, Spider had recovered enough to do the honors. Prowling through their number, she favored Alex with a good long stare. Spider's hatred was so palpable you didn't need spidey-sense to see it. Where the others withered at the slightest eye contact, however, Alex wouldn't let herself waver. In fact, she rather enjoyed the view. Spider's face was a mess. No perky little nose now, and all that good orthodontia gone to hell. Spider's bruises were turning a sickly greenish-black. Her left cheek was so badly swollen that her eye was only a silver slit.

When they cut me loose, go for it. Alex tensed, rehearsing the moves in her mind. *Run at her, get in under the knife, and . . .*

In the next instant, that nip of resin stung her nose, and she thought, *Uh oh.* Her eyes inched left, and then her pulse skipped.

Wolf's face was a studied blank, though she saw the small muscles of his jaw twitch and that scar dance. The space around and above her head seemed to fizzle and spark. The air took on a scorched stink, like the lingering of ozone after an electrical storm. Spider's back stiffened as the other Changed's heads swiveled from her to Wolf and then back again.

Fighting about which one was going to have her, she thought. *One way or the other, I'm done.* The tang of desperation left her mouth puckery and parched. Having seen what Wolf could do— what he enjoyed—she didn't see how she could get out of this. It was one thing to head-butt Spider and grab a knife. But those clashing jaws . . .

He's heavier and I can't outrun them. They'll pin me down and then Wolf will . . .

All of a sudden, Spider faltered. A deep tremor rippled through the girl's body, and her ruined lips twisted as that chemical nip— fear and rage combined—filled the air. Recoiling, the girl back-pedaled several quick steps, then spun in a snap of wolf fur, marching down the line to stop in front of poor Otis.

My God. If she hadn't just seen this, she wouldn't have believed it. *Wolf let me live. Wolf* fought *Spider, got her to back off.* This, she figured, might not work out so well in the end, and for all sorts of reasons. Spider already hated her guts. *And right backatcha, girlfriend*. But Alex didn't understand. Why was Wolf keeping her alive? Just so *he* could be the one to end her? Terrific. This might not be any more complicated than what you did with an ice-cream sundae. She didn't know a single kid who didn't save that cherry for last.

So how much longer did she really have?

Day 6: Thursday.

A little before four that morning, Brian—the one Alex had pegged as the diabetic—collapsed. After all those miles struggling through deep snow, his feet were black with a creeping gangrene that macerated his flesh up to his knees and poisoned his blood. He was so out of it Alex thought he didn't really catch on until, maybe, the third or fourth cut.

Then Brian began to scream. Ten seconds. Maybe twenty. Clearly tired of the fuss, Spider drew a vicious, backhanded slice. All of a sudden, Brian's shrieks cut out as a drippy red smile stretched across his neck.

And then Brian's head unhinged. Just opened up and flopped so far back that his startled eyes locked on Alex *upside down*. Chin on top, eyes on bottom, the back of his head resting between his shoulders as his blood spurted in twin red ropes. At the sight, her mind slewed and she thought, crazily, *Just like that android in* Alien.

Now, they were four.

Saturday, early morning: Day 8.

Otis was a scatter of bones. Alex couldn't even remember what the man had looked like. The Changed had reduced poor, sick Brian to a quivering mound of hacked mush yet hadn't so much as tasted a mouthful, probably for the same reason that no one in his right mind ate rotted green bologna. So, with only four of them left, if the Changed didn't add to the herd, she had a week and a half to live, tops.

She also knew that Wolf was getting . . . hungrier. A good burger wasn't going to do the trick either. Call it intuition or her spidey-sense, but she just *knew*. Wolf's hunger radiated like heat shimmers from baked asphalt. Sometimes he touched her. Nothing flat-out *obscene*, but his hand might brush and then linger on her arm, his shadowy scent strengthening, growing headier by the second. Once, he'd reached past her shoulder—for what, she didn't remember—and then their faces were only inches apart. Again. Close enough that she saw his scar throb like something living as his heart quickened. His nostrils flared as his lips parted and he drew her in, like a snake, and the pulse of his hunger intensified and changed into something very nearly physical, as palpable and real as an embrace.

And, God help her, the longer she remained with these Changed—and especially around Wolf—the more this very strange, shimmery, swimmy feeling veiled her mind. Despite all the horrors, when Wolf touched her or came near, her heart skipped with equal parts attraction and deepening dread. She was . . . *doubling* somehow, her boundaries dissolving as a shadowy second self slipped from her body to straddle a divide: not quite empathy but very close.

The idea sent a shudder of revulsion through her skin and raised gooseflesh. In sophomore sociology, she'd read about prisoners and kidnap victims and what happened when a hostage began to sympathize with and see the world through a kidnapper's eyes. There were famous examples, too: Patty Hearst; the victims from the Swedish bank robbery where the Stockholm Syndrome got its name.

But I'm not like them. That is so not happening, not ever.

Yet she felt the tug. She let herself reach past that reek of decay to a familiar aroma of cool mist and swarming shadows that she savored and rolled through her mouth and allowed to linger on her tongue. So close. She shut her eyes. Her pulse throbbed. So *close*. If she truly let herself go, she could almost believe that this boy was Chris, because they were two sides of the same coin, one light and the other a dark doppelgänger. Neither was evil. Both were true to who they were.

But Wolf is the enemy. He will always be the enemy. Remember that. He'll kill you, eventually. He'll have no choice. It's what he is.

23

Saturday had come so quickly, and now this very last day with him was nearly done.

Grace aimed a glance out the picture window. The sun was a suggestion more than a fact, a dimming smudge hidden behind a thick drapery of pewter clouds that rapidly shaded to gunmetal gray as her eye moved north. The tamaracks lining Odd's west bank were a thicket of dark bristles and vertical slashes, like a stockade, against the fresh-fallen snow. The storm had swept through this region of Wisconsin a day ago and was now well on its way east to Michigan, but there was no telling if the storm might reverse course. Storms stalled around Lake Superior all the time. She'd hoped *that* might delay him, but he was bound and determined to leave.

So. This is it. A sort of last meal, she thought, and then got a little impatient with herself. *Don't mope. Don't make this harder for him than it has to be.*

Well, he would leave with a full belly if she had anything to say about it. Nearly everything was ready: potatoes, a venison stew, a trio of baked apples, and a nice pan of cornbread. All that needed doing was the cake, and *that* was the real challenge. Grace eyed the heavy cast-iron Dutch oven nestled in glowing coals. Burn rates varied; the shapes of the coals were important. Heat was mechanical energy converted into thermal energy, but *temperature* was determined by kinetic energy. So complicated.

So much preparation, but the simple pleasure of imagining the look on his face made it worthwhile. The table was strewn with tinsel from some long-ago Christmas. She'd unearthed ancient wrapping paper for the scarf and four pairs of wool socks knitted on the sly. Out of what remained, she fashioned a twinkly silver banner with his name—his real name—in big cutout letters.

Of course, she had always known. Her head might be stuffed with numbers, but she wasn't in orbit. She only pretended sometimes. Grace had never been a stupid woman.

Take the afternoon, five years ago, when the Marines knocked at her door. The odds they'd dropped by for coffee and crumb cake weren't high. A very nice corporal caught her on the way down. She apologized, but the corporal said that when the heart sinks, everybody falls.

Flipping the timer, she drew another hash mark on a scrap of old envelope. She stared at the tiny grains slithering in an avalanche down that miniature mountain. A single grain was a millimeter; factor in volume and there were three thousand grains per three-minute timer, a thousand grains a minute, sixteen-point-six-six-six-six-six-into-infinity grains per second . . .

God, I'm not asking for much. Just let the cake come out all right, okay? Just this one last thing.

Another flip. Another hash mark. Six down, seven to go. Jed had strict instructions not to come back up from the boathouse for another forty-five minutes. So, plenty of time. The cake needed another nineteen, Grace figured. Twenty-one minutes, tops.

Too bad she had only ten.

24

"I wish you'd take the horse," Jed said.

"And I'm going to say the same thing I said the other eighty times
you asked." Tom rolled a flannel shirt into a tight tube and slid it into
his backpack, then hefted the pack in both hands. All told, he'd be
carrying about thirty pounds on his back, which he could handle just
fine. He'd taken long treks on snowshoes, sprinting up hills, timing
his pace with Jed's old Timex. The leg still grabbed and locked, but he
could go a good half day without much of a break. "You need both
horses, and you know it. Besides, you're giving me plenty as it is."

Jed's face puckered like he was sucking a lemon drop. "Even if I
were to tell you it was a birthday present?"

"My birthday was in December."

"Late birthday present then."

"No."

Pause. "Grace would like it."

"*Jed.*"

"All right, all right." Sighing, Jed hooked his thumbs in his parka's
pockets. "You are a very stubborn boy, Tom Eden."

"So I've been told." After a moment's silence, he said, "How surprised should I act? I mean, considering you've told me about the cake."

"Oh, that cake!" Jed slapped his thigh. "My God, I must've aged ten years listening to her go on about chemistry and all these equations and molecular coefficients. The only physics I ever needed was bullet trajectories and wind speed."

"I think you had fun."

"Oh yeah. Grace always was smart as a whip. Michael took after her more than me. He was gonna . . ." The old man took a hard swallow. "He was fixed on engineering school, but the money was a problem, so he joined up. Then he figured out how much he liked the Marines and that was that. I thought maybe when Alice came along, he might stop to think about what would happen to her and Deb if he was to get himself killed, but he was stubborn just like you. Once his heart was set on a path, there was no talking to him."

Jed looked so miserable that Tom had to fight the impulse to blurt out that, fine, he would stay. There was no way around this; his leaving would hurt, and there was nothing he could do about that.

The Coleman hissed. He let Jed break the silence. "I got something else for you."

"You shouldn't," Tom said, quietly. "You've given me so much already."

"And not nearly half what you're worth," Jed said, fiercely. The deep crevices along the sides of his nose were wet.

Tom said nothing. Jed unzipped the Road King's right saddle-bag, reached in, and fished out a bulging, plastic accordion document pouch, tied with string. "You got maps, and I put down how to get where me and Grace are going come spring. There's a list, too," he added as Tom unwound the string. "Folks who might come in handy. I know I told you not to trust anyone, but if they're still around, these are good people."

Tom fingered the envelope, then drew out a brittle piece of paper so old that the edges were frayed, though the ink was new. "Who are they?"

"Vets, most of them. We rode Rolling Thunder together. And here." Jed dug inside his shirt and slipped something from around his neck. "You take these. Show them to anyone on that list, and they'll know you're okay."

The tags, warm from Jed's body heat, were not a matched set. The edge of the older tag was crimped, and there was no social; just Jed's name, service number, blood type, and religion. The design of the other he was very familiar with, because his meat tag tattoo had the same information. His own tags, with their rubber silencers, were tucked in an old sock drawer back in a house that, more than likely, was now nothing but ashes.

"I shouldn't take these."

"Tom, you're young. You think you can go it alone, but you ought to know by now that you can't. You're going to need help. Now, you take those." Jed paused. "Humor an old fool. Do it for me, if nothing else."

Jed had a point. If Vietnam veterans were anything like vets nowadays, the network was tight, and the bonds were for life. Draping the tags around his neck, he tucked them inside his shirt. "Where's your other tag?"

"With Michael. That tag of his there is the one they brought to the house. Night before the funeral, though, I slipped one of mine in there with him, so he wouldn't be alone." Jed put his hand on Tom's shoulder. "Now you won't be either."

There was a knock at the front door. Three, actually: sharp and evenly spaced.

Darn it. Grace's brows pulled down in a frown. Jed was early, but . . . he always used the south door. Anyway, he wouldn't knock.

More raps: "Grace, it's me."

Her shoulders relaxed, but only a little. She knew the voice, but it was the wrong place at the wrong time. She would have to figure out a way to get rid of him. He couldn't see the table, the gifts.

"Grace?"

Well, shoot. She threw a quick glance at the timer, now halfway through this ninth cycle. It shouldn't take more than twenty seconds to answer the door. Plenty of time.

One-one-thousand, two-one-thousand . . . I'll just say he can't stay. She headed out of the west room and took the short hall to the front door. *Three-one-thousand, four . . . I'll be firm, and then I'll shut the door and I won't answer again, no matter what . . . Six-one-thousand.* She dragged open the front door, wincing against a wintry blast. *Seven—*

Everything she needed to say piled up like those grains of sand on that miniature mountain. Her mouth opened, but not a word tumbled out. She recognized the old man in his black parka and too-large bombardier hat, pulled so far down he had to tip his head back to see where he was going.

The other two—hard and grim-faced and also old, because just about everyone was these days—she didn't recognize at all.

Three men. For one brief moment, she felt a weird sense of déjà vu. She wasn't at the cabin, and the world hadn't gone to hell, and the Marines had only just arrived as she wandered out of the kitchen with measuring spoons—because, for the life of her, she couldn't remember what those spoons were for.

Then her eyes shifted to the horses.

Three men, two rifles.

But *six* horses.

These men, that's three. She felt the air drying her tongue, her voice evaporating the way the fizz in pop died. *A horse for him, too, but not me or Jed—because they're not here for us, and that makes four.*

So where are the other two men?

She looked at the old man in that ridiculously outsized hat. "Abel?"

25

Saturday night.

"I don't like it. They've been gone way too long, practically since dawn, and they don't hunt during the day. Plus, they got a bonfire going in the *snow*. What sense does that make?" Sharon dug a grimy fingernail into a huge, weeping sore pocking her right cheek. The ulceration, mushy and liverish, occupied the bull's-eye of a faded green-gray tattoo of a web like a squashed spider. Sharon tossed a glare at Acne, perched on a low coffee table to the left of a crackling fire Alex had gotten started, and then turned an equally suspicious eye on Alex. "How come they ain't come back to camp?"

"How should I know?" Alex asked, although this place could hardly be called a camp. From the metallic scent of hard ice and what she'd been able to make out in the failing light, the Changed had claimed someone's old lake place: a swank and very large Victorian with gingerbread, a porch swing, and even a flagpole. Acne and Slash, the pack's muscle, had herded them into a small guesthouse that held the long-stale whiff of sulfur and rancid fat from an ancient breakfast of fried eggs. Compared to the run-down sheds and frigid lean-tos of the past week, this place was a mansion. "I don't know any more than you do."

Sharon coughed a laugh. Alex had known used gym socks with better breath. "That's horseshit," Sharon said. "I got eyes. So does that boyfriend of yours."

"Christ," Ray said. Once a fleshy man, his gut now sagged like an empty paper bag. Putting an arm around his wife's shoulders, he hugged Ruby closer. "Aren't things bad enough?"

"I'm just saying what we're all thinking," Sharon snapped. From his perch, Acne turned to look at them, and Sharon brayed, "Hey, you son of a bitch, when you gonna feed us?"

"Sharon." Ruby's voice quivered like the string of a bow drawn to the breaking point. "Don't provoke them."

Sharon glowered. "Well, I wouldn't, except we're *hungry*. We need *food*, unless you want us all skin and bones, ya assholes!"

Given that Sharon had more ink per square inch than anyone Alex had ever known and that the Changed had a distinctive taste for, ah, unusual *accessories* like tattooed skin-kerchiefs and bandanas, Alex had a sneaking suspicion the Changed would be just as happy if Sharon was nothing *but* skin. Easier to peel. A mean thought, but then again, Sharon wasn't her favorite person.

"You know why they haven't fed us, Sharon," Ruby said. "Because they haven't found anyone else. It's just . . . bad luck."

"Luck? Got nothing to do with it. We're all going to end up stew meat, except maybe little Miss Alex here." Sharon squinted. "Don't think I don't see the way you and that wolf-boy keep making googly eyes at each other. That's one itch he's got that I'm thinking only you can scratch."

"Sharon," Ray said, without much heat. "Put a cork in it."

"It's all right, Ray," Alex said.

"Yeah, *Ray*," Sharon said. "Me and Alex are just talking while we all sit on our butts, waiting to die."

"But must you be so hateful?" Ruby forked hair from her face with a hand that was all brittle bone tented with frail skin. "We're all in the same boat."

"Wanna bet? I think *one* of us has got herself a pretty nice little life raft. So where you think your boyfriend's got himself to, Alex?" Sharon grinned, not a pleasant sight. Her mouth was a gap-toothed tangle of discolored, off-kilter pegs. "Think maybe he ran out, got hisself a new girlfriend? Or maybe him and that blonde are—"

Alex zoned out. This was a tune she knew by heart. Turning aside, she carefully teased flannel and gauze from her shoulder. Her left arm throbbed and she could almost see the heat shimmers. Although she kept the wound as clean as possible, the shakes had started up a little after noon, if Mickey could be trusted.

God, not an infection. If that happened, she might as well lie down in the snow right now. As she unwound the last strip, she had to bite down on her lower lip to corral a whimper. That whiff of spoilage was unmistakable. Patches of her muscle were a soupy snot-green. *Okay, try not to panic. Clean it, maybe scrounge up some alcohol and antibiotics if they let you. That's a nice house. There's got to be a medicine cabinet somewhere.*

"Oooohhh." Sharon's tongue wormed over the ruins that passed for her teeth. "That looks pretty bad. You know, you could leave it rot. Get like Brian there and they'll only kill you."

Oh, well, that made her feel so much better. She wished she could think of something pithy, but her hunger clawed her stomach and her mind was dried up as a prune. So all she said was, "Just go to hell, okay?"

"Too late." But the wind seemed to have gone out of Sharon's proverbial sails because she turned away from Alex to Ruby. "Here's what I'm thinking," she said, confidentially. "I'm thinking the reason those little monsters ain't come back with anyone in the last couple days? It's because there was nobody waiting, which *means* the others aren't honoring the agreement anymore."

"Either that, or there's no one left *to* send out," Ray said.

"What are you talking about?" *Nobody waiting?* She'd never heard them talk this way, and Alex was curious, almost despite herself. They all might share food, but she really didn't know much about the others. Understandable: no one wanted to get too chummy with someone they'd then have to watch get turned into hamburger. "What agreement? What do you mean, no one left to send out?"

"Well, *you* know." Ray lobbed a puzzled look at Ruby and then back to Alex. "Sent out the way you were. The same way we've all been sent."

"I ran away. I escaped. I wasn't sent," Alex said, but then she recalled that, given the circumstances, she *had* been told exactly where to go—and Jess's shotgun had been nothing if not persuasive.

Then she felt her brain catch up to the words Ray and the others had actually used. "Sent . . . you mean, turned out? On purpose? Why? Did you do something wrong?" That would be the most likely explanation, she imagined. Rule probably wasn't the only village that meted out expulsions for bad behavior.

"Course not," Sharon put in. She sounded genuinely insulted. "Just drew the short straw is all."

"The short . . ." Alex gaped. "You had a *lottery*?"

"That's how we did it," Ray said, with a shrug. "It's up to each village or group to decide how they go about it, of course."

"But you could've stayed," Ruby said, quietly. "You shouldn't have come, Ray."

Ray's jaws worked. "You're my wife. You go, I go."

"Neither of you had to do anything!" Out of the corner of her eye, she saw Acne's head turn for a look, but she was too appalled by what Ray was saying—what they were all *suggesting*—to care.

"Of course we did. It's for the greater good," Ruby said.

"You've been around Sharon too long," Alex said.

"Watch it," Sharon said.

Alex ignored her. "What good does it serve for you to die? To voluntarily walk out of town to get eaten? Why would you even cooperate with something like that? Why would you ever agree?"

"You're from Rule," Sharon said. Her voice was suddenly low and shaky with anger. "You're from that goddamned village, and you're lecturing us? You're the ones came up with the idea in the first—" She broke off when she saw the look on Alex's face. "What?"

"I . . ." In her confusion—distracted by the sudden, heavy welter of odors—Alex almost blurted something stupid that would've given her away. But then Acne stiffened from his slouch so abruptly that the others also realized something was very wrong.

"What?" Sharon demanded again as Acne stood and aimed the business end of his rifle at them. She looked at Ray and Ruby. "Jesus, maybe they got someone."

"I hope so," Ray said. "I got to have something to eat."

That must be how it works. Mind still reeling, Alex followed the others as Acne herded them toward the door at gunpoint. *That's what Ruby meant that very first day about* sharing. *Whoever gets sent out also brings a little food. Not much, but enough so the Changed can build up a herd and move on.*

She watched as Acne made Ray open the door. The fire cringed as a gale of frigid air and thick snow swept in. Thirty yards away, Slash had turned from the sputtering bonfire to the woods.

She smells them, too, just like Acne. Just like me, *and I did it from behind a closed door.* Okay, this wasn't good. Her spidey-sense was definitely getting stronger, and because of that, she knew what Acne and Slash did.

And for her money? If what she smelled was true?

They'd all just drawn that short straw.

26

If not for the flashlight, Jed might have spotted what was wrong before he and Tom were well up the hill and only fifty yards from running out of woods. But he was focused on the shine of snow at his feet and only just happened to glance up at the cabin—and that's when he noticed, immediately, what wasn't right.

With the day gone, the west window was a pulsing orange sliver with light thrown by Grace's cook fire. On any other night, Grace might have lit a candle or the Coleman, but she'd wanted the cabin as dark as possible for the surprise. Still, he saw Grace's silhouette quite clearly, as well as the letters taped to an exposed beam above the table: WE LOVE YOU, TOM. So all that was fine.

But then he spotted how those shimmering words danced and fluttered and the tinsel winked—and *that*, he reasoned, was because there must be a draft, which would only happen if someone were shutting the front door.

So Jed knew, instantly: something was very, very wrong. If he'd had any doubts, that stupid bombardier hat was a dead giveaway.

Fine-tuning his hawk-eye until its owner's face jumped into stark relief was only a formality.

Abel. Jed watched his neighbor move deeper into the room. *What the hell . . .*

Then he saw that Abel wasn't alone. His companion, also male, was blunt and jowly. A hair past seventy, Jed thought, but that rifle looked pretty perky.

"Well, shoot," Jed said, and pulled up so suddenly that Tom nearly piled into him. "I forgot that darned Phillips. Grace was complaining about one of the chair legs wobbling."

"I'll get it." Tom shrugged the pack a bit higher on his shoulders. "I can always use the exercise."

"Mind if I keep the flashlight?"

"No problem. I've been up and down in these woods so much I could find my way blindfolded. Come on, Raleigh, let's go for a jog."

"I'll wait right here," Jed lied. He stayed put until the boy's footfalls faded back into the woods before flicking off the flashlight. It might already be too late. That light was as good as a flare, but the woods might have shielded him.

Unhooking the carry strap of his rifle from his shoulder, Jed moved up the trail in a low crouch, his good eye angled to keep the cabin in view. Abel would not have come with just one bounty hunter. Jed was unlikely to cooperate. If Tom ran, they'd have to chase him. Abel was a worthless piece of trash, so that meant one old man guarding Jed and Grace while another old man went after Tom. That would be risky. Tom was young and strong and, even with a gimp leg, plenty fast now. So there had to be at least two other men, maybe even three.

He winced as a whippy tangle of brush grabbed at his parka. The sound was thunderous in the dead cold, and he held his breath, every nerve quivering as he listened. Nothing. No shush of snow or crackle of a branch. He was alone.

He saw that Grace had moved farther back into the room now and closer to the window. Abel and the hunter followed, drawn along on an invisible tether. His heart fired with pride. Yes, that was his girl. She'd figured how to play them—get the fools into position—because, of all the people in the universe, she would understand how gravity tugged at even the fastest bullet. But if she gave him a clear shot—

His Bravo 51 was chambered, ready to go, the detents already adjusted for his height. Working fast, he clicked out the legs, seated the bipod into the snow, and then stretched out full length. Snugging the butt to his right shoulder, he put his very good eye to the scope—and almost laughed. He didn't need a scope now, did he? But habits died hard. The hunter's head bloomed in the sight, the magnification so great that Jed saw that the man's eyes were brown.

One shot. That'll do the trick. Abel'll freeze and then I'll pop him, too.

He only hoped Grace had the sense to stay put until both men were down. Then, do it the way they'd already planned in case of emergency: lock herself first in the bedroom and then the bathroom. There would surely be other hunters, but the shots would draw them into the house. While they were busy breaking down doors, she would have time to get out through the bathroom window. By then, *he* would be close enough to grab her. If he wasn't, she knew to go around to the root cellar and padlock the doors after her. Those doors were solid, with good iron hinges. Take too many bullets to punch through that, and the hunters wouldn't want to waste them on her anyway.

Tom was the only wild card, a way this all might go south in a hurry. The boy would hear that first shot. Lord, Jed hoped the boy realized that blundering *toward* gunfire would be a mistake.

Use your noodle, son. Circle around and—

A hard knob of metal pressed against the crown of his head. "I wouldn't," the hunter said.

Jed froze but thought: *Be fast, be quick.* There was simply no time to figure another way, and surrender was not an option. Grace would understand. Even better, she would know exactly what to do next. God, he hoped Tom would, too.

Be smart, son. Think about what you hear, and get clear.

"Then I guess it's good," he said to this man whose face he did not and would never know, "that you're not me."

27

Beretta crashed out of the woods first. He was breathing hard, panting like a dog. His jacket was ripped, and a patchwork of cuts and deep scratches crisscrossed his face. He'd lost a glove along the way, too. Acne got to him just as Beretta's knees wobbled, and then Acne was half carrying, half dragging the other boy toward the fire as more Changed shot out of the woods—on skis.

"Oh God," Ruby quailed. *"More?"*

Probably another squad, Alex guessed. The newcomers were evenly divided between girls and boys, in more or less the same outfit: white on white, with matching balaclavas, so that only the dark holes of their eyes showed, like sockets in skulls. Each wore a wildly colored bandana made of tattooed skin tied around his or her forehead, like a kamikaze pilot. Gliding to a stop, they began shucking camouflage assault packs.

"Jesus, they got some serious gear," Ray said.

He was right, but Alex knew the packs didn't belong to these new Changed. The scents of the original owners were very fresh. She inhaled again, more deeply. *Oh my God, there's food.* Cinnamon and raisins, peanuts and chocolate, and crackers, there were crackers and . . . saliva poured into her mouth, and she could feel her knees start to shiver. She thought there might even be a wedge of *cheese*. Her hunger was so great that even the knowledge that the packs' owners had been alive only a short time ago didn't make much of a dent. She just wanted the food.

Spider's scent suddenly cut at her nose, and then she spied the girl, on skis, floating out of the woods like a bad dream. Blood freckled Spider's wolf skin and parka. Along the way, her hair had come undone to tumble around her face. Her wound oozed pus, but the silver shine in her eyes was bright and excited, the blood fever giving her skin a glow.

But instead of Wolf, a lanky boy she'd never seen before pulled at the snow by her side. The boy's snow-white outfit was misted with blood and reeked of iron, scorched metal, burnt powder.

Blowback, she thought. The shot had been up close, too. The kid was pretty buff, like a sleek, red-spotted snow leopard. Kicking off his skis, the boy came up behind Spider and pressed against the girl, reaching up to cup her breasts. Eyes closed, neck arched, Spider leaned back into the boy, grinding her hips, her arms snaking up to pull his head down to the angle of her neck. Their mingled scent—roadkill and iron and Spider's rot—thickened, their excitement steaming up to turn the air turgid and so heavy Alex thought she might choke. She could feel the other newcomers coming alive, and then they were all knotting together in a frenzy of feverish mouths and groping hands.

"Hey, get a room, you little bastards!" Sharon shouted.

"Holy God," Ray said. "They're going to have an orgy out here, on the snow?"

She doubted it. This was bloodlust and, she thought, the release that came from surviving some kind of battle. That would explain the many packs that did not belong to them, the scent of spent powder, Beretta's injury, and the blood.

But Wolf . . . She concentrated, trying to reach past the general stink—so many new scents and, over it all, the arching fever of sex—but she couldn't smell him. *Oh my God, he's not—*

"Where's the other boy?" Ruby asked. "The wolf one?"

"Dead, if we're lucky." Sharon jabbed Alex with a knobby elbow. "Cheer up. That pimply one seems awful sweet. If you don't like him, those other boys look ready for a little horizontal mambo."

Alex said nothing, but she was surprised that the idea that Wolf might be dead actually *hurt*. As if she'd lost something, too.

No, don't you dare. He was a monster and never your friend.

She forced her attention back to the newcomers. Spider and Leopard were still sucking face, but their smell was less intense now. Even a sex-crazed Changed wasn't about to get down and dirty in the snow when there was that nice house and, probably, plenty of bedrooms. Maybe even a wet bar and Jacuzzi, which wouldn't work, but it was the principle of the thing. The others had calmed, too, and were clustering around Beretta the way football players huddled over a downed teammate. Now that they were closer to the fire, she caught the quicksilver shine of long knives strapped to the newcomers' backs. They were packing, too, lots and lots of firepower: rifles and matte-black handguns in cross-carry holsters and gleaming bullets on bandoliers. And was that one kid wearing a *grenade* belt?

"Shit," Ray said in a hushed undertone. "They're like some kind of crazy-ass ninja kill squad."

That was, she thought, exactly right. So, friends? Allies? Or just a different tribe who happened to link up for a little neighborly potlatch? Her eyes brushed over Spider and Leopard, noted the way their hands ran over one another. That any Changed actually *had* sex made her flesh crawl.

But there had been Wolf, and that hunger, she thought. Maybe sex and hunger are all part of the same stew.

"Lot of guns," Sharon murmured.

"Yeah," Alex breathed, glad to focus on *anything* other than Spider and Leopard exploring each other's tonsils. She eyed one kid brandishing an Uzi. Where the hell had they gotten assault weapons? "But there are too *many* guns. These can't all be theirs. I think the weapons are like their booty or something, just like the packs. The question is, who did they fight?"

"Who's *crazy* enough to fight them, you mean," Sharon said.

"Who cares? About time someone had some balls." Ray paused then leaned in closer. "Listen, they're all over there, and we're *here*. Know what I'm saying?"

"Bad idea," Sharon muttered.

For once, Alex agreed. "They've still got guns. They'll hunt us down easy, if the storm doesn't kill us first."

"But maybe not," Ray hissed. "You saw them. They're *wired*, distracted. Come on, Alex, you're the one always going on about getting off our butts."

"Yeah," Sharon said, "but getting shot in the back isn't what she had—"

An angry shout erupted from the woods. Even Acne jumped, and then all the Changed were squinting past snow and into the dark.

"Jesus," Ray breathed. "Who—"

Oh no. Even if she hadn't seen the look Acne and Slash tossed one another, or read it in the body language of the others, or remembered that, with rare exceptions, the Changed did not speak or make many sounds—she would know. Still, she sampled the air, let it drift over her tongue, hoping that maybe she was wrong.

She wasn't.

28

First, there was a *crack* and then a glassy splash as the picture window exploded. Jagged shards rained onto hardwood. Something whirred, cleaving air as it spun past her right ear, and then there was a softer *puh* as the bullet smacked into bone and flesh. The man's head snapped back at nearly the same moment his skull blew out with a sound that was dull and wet, like a pumpkin squashed by a truck. The man toppled.

Grace had never been athletic. Her body was frail and she wasn't very strong, but hate and grief gave her courage and speed. Swooping past an uncomprehending Abel, who still stood with the hunter's brains slopping from his absurd hat, she snatched up a frying pan with her right hand, pivoted, and swung. The pan swished, and even as it bore down on its target, she was thinking, *Too bad it's not a golf club; a club would be so much faster, with more angular momentum, less mass to overcome . . .*

Abel was just turning. There was a hollow thud, like a head of lettuce smashed onto a cutting board to dislodge the stem, followed almost instantly by a tremendous, wet, mucky *crunch*.

Abel's face caved in an explosion of blood. There was a pattering sound, like rice on wood, as Abel's teeth ticked to the floor. Abel didn't cry out. His body jerked back a few steps and his arms shot up and out, like he was a geeky kid trying to master the jitterbug. Then he was falling, straight back. His head bounced against the rough planked floor. His eyes were open, and so was his mouth, and she could see the bloody, broken stumps where his teeth had lived only seconds before. The rest of his face was a crater. His chest wasn't moving, but his feet and fingers were still jittering as the last of his brain died.

Total time, from the moment the bullet rocketed through the window to now: seven seconds. Maybe a hair more.

Get to the bedroom. The pan clanged to the wood. *The speed of sound depends on the square root of the absolute temperature divided by molar mass.* The second hunter had left her alone with Abel and his now-dead partner. Which meant that he and the men she hadn't seen yet would hear the sound of the shot in the woods and then the rain of glass just a tad slower than if it had been summer, because sound was a bit sluggish in cold air. She had, she thought, anywhere from nine to fifteen seconds, but there were too many variables and she couldn't account for all of them.

If whoever's out there goes around the house to listen, I've got more time. If they don't . . . I'm coming, Jed, I'm coming. She started across the room, but she was wearing fuzzy slippers, and she felt the skid begin, her balance go. Her feet flew out from under as if she'd tried running over ice, and then she was falling. The impact was solid and very hard, and she took the brunt of it on first her right leg and then the hip. She heard two sharp, brittle snaps, and then pain exploded in her pelvis and zoomed up her spine. Grace screamed, sucked in a breath for another one, and then there was blood and gore in her mouth, clogging her nose, because she'd landed facedown in the widening pool of the men's blood. She hacked out a weak, retching cough. Her right leg was twisted, splayed at a bizarre angle, and the pain was so ferocious she was afraid to move. A second later, she realized she couldn't.

Got to. The coppery smell of all this blood was making her sick. A surge of vomit lurched up her chest and into her mouth. Her hip was screaming, and the pain was making hash of her thoughts. *The amount of blood in the body is dependent on mass, and I'm so tiny . . . Got to move, got to get to the bedroom . . . Jed, Jed . . .* Over the bang of her heart, she heard the click and then the creak of the door.

Someone coming. Have to get up, get up, get up! But she couldn't move. She was gasping like a dying trout; she couldn't raise her head. Even the calculator in her brain had seized. How much blood hummed through her veins? Her mind had stalled; the numbers wouldn't come.

She watched the blood pool vibrate and ripple as someone in heavy winter boots walked toward her. Then the boots hove into view, and they were different, not what she'd expected: a stained desert-style tan instead of black or dark brown. The rusty stink of blood was so heavy, she only belatedly noticed their smell: thick and somehow a little sweet.

Gasoline.

There was a burst of static and then a series of clicks, very distinct and crisp. They reminded Grace of cicadas on a hot summer's day. A cicada's click rate was related to temperature, but these weren't rhythmic. A code. It might even be Morse code coming from a radio. There was a pause, and then the owner of the boots clicked a reply.

The pattern meant nothing to Grace. Her brother had been an Eagle Scout. He might've been able to tell her what the clicks meant, but he was dead. So, she knew, was she.

High above the boots, a new voice, one Grace knew could not have come from the men she'd seen, said, "So, it's a boy. *Tom.*" Lingering over the word, savoring the name. "Where is he?"

Run, Tom. Her tongue was coated with an old man's blood and her curdled vomit. The pain in her hip and leg kept time with her heart.

"Let me tell you something. Normally, I'd turn someone like you into hamburger, maybe even a couple of rump roasts for the Chuckies. But this cabin is hell and gone, and you're such a skinny old bird, you're not worth the effort. So I'll make an exception in your case."

Run, Tom. With the window gone, the room was growing very cold. *Run, run . . .*

"So here's what I'll do," the voice said. "Tell me where he is and I'll kill you now. A bullet to the brain, and nighty-night. Don't tell me and . . ."

The air is freezing; it's all about timing. Muzzle velocity is dependent on—

"I'll let the fire do that instead. You'll probably die of smoke inhalation before the fire does its work, or maybe your lungs will boil and you'll suffocate. Or maybe not. Maybe you'll be awake the whole time the fire eats you alive."

The speed of sound is—

"So I'll count to three."

No, it won't be three, not precisely. The speed of a thought is three hundred milliseconds, and then the time to perform the action is dependent on—

"One."

Not precisely three. She pulled in a breath and held it. *Three seconds and just enough left over, so if he's close—*

"Two."

Run, Tom, run, run—

"Thr—"

"*Ruuuuuun, Tom, Ruuuuunnnnn!*" Grace screamed, the words bursting from her mouth because the thought was there, at the front of her brain, and there was just enough time, there was just enough—

29

Six more ninja-kids trudged from the woods. They were working hard, their breaths coming in white chuffs. Each pulled a long, scalloped, fire-engine-colored plastic sled.

"Oh Lord." Ruby's hand fluttered to her mouth. "They've got *children*."

Twelve in all. Very dead. Girls and boys. Two to a sled, and carelessly sprawled across one another in a tangle of limp arms and legs and dragging hair like corpses from a concentration camp. She picked out a few head shots. No mistaking that drippy third eye or the misshapen skulls. But most had their throats cut and wore wide bibs of iced blood. Some—most—had died with their eyes wide open, and their mouths, too, frozen in a final, silent scream.

The lingering odor of the dead children's fear and terror lodged in her throat, but she also smelled a whisper of gun oil, powder. Solvent—and a drift of ashes scraped from a blackened hearth. Then, she knew: these weren't *only* children.

They had been soldiers.

Two more ninja-kids huffed into view. They, too, were dragging something along, working up a real sweat like cattlemen wrestling a bucking bull that just wouldn't quit.

Which wasn't far from the truth.

He was tall like Chris and Wolf but had Tom's muscle. His hair, very blond, was tied back with a twist of leather in a short ponytail. She pegged him as pretty close to Chris's age, give or take a year. His parka was torn wide open, and a huge blood-spider was splayed over his shirt, low and on the left. More blood smeared his face and the hollow of his throat. His hands, naked to the cold, were crimson.

"B-bastards." The boy was fighting, gasping, his breath coming in hitching, pained sobs. "Should've killed you when I had the chan—" He let out a high shriek as Acne slammed a fist into the kid's gut. The boy's knees jackknifed as the two ninjas let go. Retching, the kid dropped to the snow, trying to brace his injured side with one bloody hand.

"P-please, let him go." The boy's face was etched deep with despair and pain. "*Please*. You can *have* me, but let—"

"*Daniel?*" The word was shrill, a spear of sound hurtling from the dark woods. "*Dannnnielllll?*"

"Oh shit," Sharon said.

No. A sudden film of tears burned her eyes and splintered the firelight and all those bodies into a smeary rainbow. *Please, not another one; not this, too.*

The cry came again but was inarticulate this time and not a

word but a line of pure sound as thin and bright as a laser. A moment later, one last ninja pushed into the light. He was hauling something, staggering a little with the effort but grinning fiercely the way a fisherman did when he'd just landed the catch of a lifetime.

"Oh, sweet Jesus," Ray said.

30

When the shot came, Tom was pawing through the tool chest, a small penlight clamped between his teeth to free his hands. At the sound, Tom jumped, his teeth clicking metal. The dog yipped then growled.

What the hell? What is Jed shooting at? Then he caught the slight separation, the overlapping echoes, and his brain, so conditioned to gunfire, instantly understood: *two* shots, with only a half-second's separation, if that. And close.

Jed! The Phillips clattered to the concrete. He killed the penlight, slung off his pack, and unhooked his rifle. Shucking a round into the chamber on the run, he was nearly out the door when he caught himself. *Easy. Whatever's happened has already gone down. Run into an ambush and you won't be able to help anyone.*

Two shots, three possibilities: two shooters, both firing at Jed at virtually the same moment. Or Jed got a shot off first and the other guy spotted him at the last second. Or Jed squeezed off a round as a warning and then the other guy—

No. Can't think that, not yet.

"Raleigh, *down*," he hissed. The dog obeyed, instantly. Dropping to a crouch, he listened. Nothing. No shots. No shouting. No Jed. A hard knuckle of dread dug at his chest. He had to get out of the boathouse. The big slider opened west and onto the lake; the one door was hinged on the right, but that was only good if there was no one already on the trail. The slider, then. Take the ice all the way back to—

Another sound: high, thin. The dog let go of a whimper. Tom's ears tingled. What was that? A shout? No, a scream and—

A distant *crack*.

A third shot. Further away, to the north. The cabin.

Grace? What air he'd held in his lungs came in a sudden, hard exhalation close to a sob. He rested his forehead on his rifle. The metal was cold enough to burn. *My fault, I shouldn't have waited.*

"Kid!" The shout was so close, Tom nearly vaulted out of his skin. By his side, the dog sprang to its feet and let out a low, menacing *ruff*. "Kid, we don't want to hurt you! Just come on out!"

We. So, two men? Three? Or the guy could be bluffing. But he knew now, beyond a shadow of a doubt: Jed was dead, too.

You bastards, I'll kill you. His lungs were lead. *I'll kill you, I'll—*

"Kid, we can do this hard, or we can do this easy. We don't want to hurt you, but if you take a shot, we *will* shoot back. So open the door, then come out slow, hands up."

Maybe fifty yards away, Tom thought, and from his perspective, a little to the right, which made sense because the woods were there. That decided it.

"What do you want?" He didn't really care, but he needed to buy just a little more time.

"Just need you to come with us." In the next instant, the darkness erupted in yellow light that fired the sliding window above Tom's head. The light played over the boathouse right and then left and then right again. They did him a favor because now he saw the machines very well: the wind sled on the right and a little ahead of the snowmobile. Jed's Road King was tucked further back, across from the cot and propane heater.

The dog whimpered again. An instant later, he caught the smell, too: a faint char of wood smoke. He knew a fair amount about smoke and fire, and his nose had no trouble teasing apart the odors. Saturate wood with gas or another accelerant and the smell was very different. Burning cloth and synthetics had a chemical reek. The cabin was going up.

The bastards were smart, trying to get on top of him. They knew he'd have nowhere to go. The boathouse would be next, too. Burn him out.

"Smell that, kid?" The voice was much closer now. "Come on, you're just making this harder on yourself."

Scooping up his pack, he moved fast, dumping his gear in the wind sled's rear seat, sliding the rifle into the footwell, thinking through what he had to do—the exact sequence.

It really came down to how fast they figured it out. And if they could find a way to follow him. He glanced at the snow-mobile. In the grainy light, the hole left when he'd pulled the ignition assembly was an eyeless socket. But the loop of cord still dangled. So they just might.

The snowmobile's faster. It's got a light. One can shoot while the other drives.

No choice.

"Come on, kid!" The lights bobbed as the hunters closed in. The interior of the boathouse was graying now.

"Raleigh, come," he hissed, patting the rear seat. As the dog scampered into the wind sled, Tom darted to the slider. "Good boy. Stay." He hooked his right hand through the cast-iron latch, set his feet, braced himself on his stronger left leg. Pulled in a deep breath. Once done, he was committed.

Do it.

He yanked, almost too hard. The slider rolled easily, thanks to all Jed's WD-40, the metal wheels whispering over the rails like a bowling ball over polished wood. A gust of very cold air ballooned into the boathouse, pulling with it the stink of burning wood and melting plastics. Then he was pivoting, leaping back toward the sled. Outside, the light suddenly shifted as the hunters caught on. Five seconds, maybe ten. Vaulting into the Spitfire's front seat, he jabbed at the ignition, pumping the accelerator to drive fuel into the engine. There was a millisecond's delay, and then the engine ground, coughed, spluttered—

And did not catch.

Come on, come on, come on! From outside, there came a shout. The lights bobbed; he heard the thrash of brambles and icy wood. They were coming, fast. Gritting his teeth, he forced himself to give the engine two precious seconds he did not have and then tried again.

If it floods, I'm dead. Sweat trickled down his neck. *They'll be around the corner, and if I'm still sitting here—*

The engine came to life in a spluttering crescendo roar.

And he began to move.

31

The little boy was dark-haired and bright-eyed with terror, but Alex saw the resemblance immediately. There was a splash of crimson on the boy's face and more blood on his hands, too, but nowhere else that she could see. So maybe the blood was his brother's.

"Daniel!" the little boy cried. "Daniel, are you okay?"

"It's all right, Jack." Daniel struggled to his knees. "Stay calm, okay?"

"But what are they going to do to us?" Jack's voice was tight, and his lips were drawn back in a bright, hard rictus. He was very young, no older than Ellie. Huge tears were rolling down his cheeks, where they mixed with gore, so that it seemed like he was weeping blood. "Are they going to eat us?"

"No." Daniel heaved to his feet, pushing up on his thighs. It was costing him, too; his arms trembled and Alex saw how his breath grabbed and hitched. "You're going to be fine. It's all right."

It was not all right. Acne was helping Beretta to his feet. Spider and Leopard and the others were gathering around Daniel and Jack the same way Wolf and his crew had watched as she and Spider fought. Of course, Spider had that corn knife, too. Already thick and feverish and frenzied, the air suddenly bunched and roiled.

"Oh God," she said.

To her left, Sharon darted a look. "What?"

Alex didn't reply. She couldn't. But she had enough experience with the Changed and knew when she smelled it.

Daniel and Jack didn't have much time.

And neither did they.

32

A wind sled is not like a snowmobile. The principle's closer to that of an airboat: a strong engine producing enough air to propel a boat over shallow water or ice. There are two controls: a throttle for power and a wheel or a stick that controls the rudder and directs the air.

The problem with a wind sled? No brake. The only ways to stop are to dump air or power down. And a wind sled is clumsy. This thing doesn't turn on a dime. Jerk the rudder too quickly, spill enough air, and you guarantee a stall.

As soon as he felt the Spitfire move, Tom jammed the throttle, slotting it all the way forward. The sled responded with a thumping lurch and then shot from the boathouse so quickly he was thrown back against the dog. His foot slid on the accelerator, and he heard the engine instantly dip and grumble as the Spitfire slowed to nothing more than a slow walk. Gasping, he righted, then mashed the accelerator hard.

Bulleting away from the boathouse in a cloud of diesel, the sled sped over the spit and onto snow-mantled ice with a solid thump.

The ride was rough; every imperfection and dip in the snow and ice came through as a hard bounce and jitter, but he was moving. Odd's layout spread before his mind's eye. Jed's ice-fishing house was off to his right at about one o'clock. Best to give it a wide berth, bank left, head for the jink.

Something flickered, liquid and orange, and his eyes flicked right. The cabin was a torch. Huge flames boiled from the shattered picture window and splashed over the eaves. Inside that front room, the fire, bright as lava, streamed up the walls and over the ceiling. Even at this distance, he saw the moment a propane tank went, because the fire hitched, pulled back in an ice-blue gasp. The fireball exploded into the night with so much force he heard the boom over the sled's roar.

He was so stunned that he didn't realize he was slowing until the engine guttered. Too late, he dropped his boot again, but the Spitfire was already sliding to a halt. In the sudden silence, he caught a shrill sputter, like the scream of a buzz saw.

Jed's snowmobile.

Come on! He jabbed the ignition, but the engine had flooded and all he got was a click and a whir and a whole lot of nothing. Heart pounding, he forced himself to wait for it . . . wait for it . . . then cranked the engine again. This time, he was rewarded with a bellow. The wind sled lurched and began to pick up speed.

He shot a look over his shoulder. The single eye of the snowmobile's headlight was steady. They weren't moving. Why not? Then he saw the lake spread beneath him in a shimmery silver carpet. *Reflection.* They were lighting him up so they could—

He felt something—big, huge—rush for him. Startled, he faced front just in time to see Jed's icehouse and his own shadow suddenly leap out of the gloom. Gasping, he wrenched the wheel, banked left. The camper swept by in a dizzying swirl as the sled fishtailed, dumped air, slowed down. There was a hard *bang* as the Spitfire's fiberglass hull slapped and bounced off the camper's wood runners. Then, a bright spark danced at the corner of his right eye. A split second later, there was a sharp *ting* as the bullet smashed sheet metal.

Now he knew why they'd stayed on shore. The icehouse's metal shell reflected light just like the snow. Four hundred yards and change, with a scoped rifle, was nothing.

Go, go! Hammering the accelerator, he spun the wind sled into a wide, drunken port turn. The Spitfire yawed. Behind, he felt the dog scrambling to keep its balance, but they were moving now, gaining speed, heading for the jink, fine rooster tails of ice and snow dusting to a billowing cloud.

He knew what they would do now. The snowmobile was old but much more powerful and faster. All he had was a head start. He could hear nothing above the engine roar now. Speed turned the cold air into a scythe that sliced at his exposed flesh. He was blasting across the lake, flying blind, going on memory, relying on luck. As the Spitfire took the jink, he threw a glance over his shoulder and saw the night turn blue and then brighten as the snowmobile's light lanced through the dark in a tight, neat arc.

Running out of time. Where *was* it? How long had he been on the ice? Two minutes? Four? He should *be* there soo—

He felt the moment the ice and snowpack changed. There was a lurch and then a dip as the ice roughened, and then he was bouncing as the hull smacked rutted and refrozen ripples. Another bounce and the ride got rougher, his teeth chattering as the wind sled hit thinner ice over the rift.

If anything, he should go faster. Pound the accelerator and get the hell out of there. Those hunters were close, gaining by the second, and they would be on him, so he needed to go, to go, to *gogogo*!

Instead, he eased his foot from the accelerator. His speed dropped, the engine grumbled; ice and snow grabbed the hull. He felt the wind sled slow and stumble. There was a hard *thunk* as the bow skipped over a knee of ice, and then the Spitfire bounced and smacked over a welter of ice floes, their seams stitched with ice that was whisper-thin, no more than two inches thick. Good enough for him. Perfect. He slowed and slowed and watched the darkness gray, then blue, then silver as the churn of the snow-mobile grew louder and louder . . .

Now! He stamped down hard. The engine swelled as the Spitfire screamed to full throttle and plowed over the ice, its hull slapping up and then down like a flat stone skipping across a pond. There was a tremendous *bang* and then—all of a sudden—he was over open water. Cold spray sheeted up all around, but he kept on, straight and true, bracing himself for the sudden lurch he knew would come as soon as the sled regained the ice and snow. He prayed his speed was enough to plane the boat, compensate for the weight of him and his gear and the dog. God, the *dog*. He hoped Raleigh was smart enough to hunker down, or else the impact might throw—

The Spitfire's bow barreled onto the ice with a jolt and a hop, and then he was past the rift, screaming over the surface. He felt the lake hardening again, the jolts dying. A hard cut to the right, and then he was spilling air, curling around so the bow faced back the way he'd just come.

"Raleigh, *down!*" Cutting the engine, he swept up his rifle, slotting it as he pivoted from the waist, ready to fire—

Just as the snowmobile broke through.

33

"What the hell do they want?" Ray twisted right and left. "What's going on?"

No one answered. The Changed had closed round in a circle. Alex and the others were lined up directly across from Daniel, who was still flanked by two ninja-kids. Another held Jack by the scruff of his neck. Spider was beside the boy, loose and limber, corn knife in hand. Jack's fear-smell—curdled milk and hot urine—was so strong Alex tasted it.

Acne elbowed his way through, followed by Beretta and Leopard. Pain bit into Beretta's face, but he was steadier on his feet now. His *danger* smell made her pulse skip. Acne clutched two rifles, his own with that gas piston, and another she recognized at once: the Browning X-Bolt that Nathan had given her before that mad dash from Rule.

This close, she also got a good look at the handgun tucked in Leopard's waistband. She would know a Glock anywhere.

"What do you want from me?" Daniel said. It was costing him to stand. He was hunched into a comma, an arm clamped to his side. "I told you. You can have me. I won't fight you anymore. Just let Jack go."

Beretta stared at Daniel for a long second. Acne strode forward, the Browning outstretched.

"What?" Daniel stared at the rifle as if Acne was trying to hand him a python. "I'm not taking that. Give you a chance to shoot me? Fine. You want to kill me, just do it, but—"

"Don't you get it, kid?" Sharon's tone was flat. "You get to choose: shoot one of us or little Jackie-boy there gets his throat cut."

Alex's mouth dried up. She smelled how on the mark Sharon was. This was tit for tat: give me this, I give you that, and we'll call it even.

"What?" Ray said. He pushed Ruby behind him. "What the hell?"

"Daniel." Jack's eyes were buggy with terror. "Daniel, Daniel, Daniel . . ."

"I won't do it," Daniel gasped. A hard shudder rippled through his body, and one of the ninjas grabbed him before he could fall. Daniel shook him off with a strangled curse. "You can't make me like you. I'm not a *murderer*."

"Well, I guess they think you *are* like them," Sharon ground out. If doom could speak, Alex thought it would have this old woman's voice. "Whatever you and your friends did, you pissed them off, and now they're gonna make you pay."

No, not just pay. The air was so clogged with the stink of the Changed and the dead and her fellow prisoners—and now with

Daniel's horror and Jack's terror—that it was as if she was breathing them all in: their histories, their fates. She was certain this was a test. A trial.

A rite.

"Please. You said you'd let Jack go." Daniel turned to Beretta and Acne. "I'm responsible. *I* organized the attack. Kill me, but leave Jack and these other people out of it, *please*."

"What happens if he doesn't choose?" Ray threw a wild look at Sharon as if she might know the answer. "He doesn't *have* to."

"I think they got other ideas," Sharon said.

"I can't do this." Daniel's gaze skipped from one to the other. When his eyes landed on Alex, they grabbed and held. "They can't ask me to *do* this."

They could. And they were. She wanted to say something, *anything*. In a movie or a book, this was where the heroine volunteered. Stepped up, did the right thing. It should be her. She did not want to die, but the monster lived inside her head. It had yellow eyes and needle-teeth. It was growing a face. It was a cancer, and she was going to die anyway. Tom would've done it. Chris, too. That little kid deserved a chance.

None of the others will. She could smell it. A bone-cold finger dragged down her spine a knob at a time. *Just do it, do it now before you chicken—*

At the corner of her left eye, something blurred, moving fast—

"Ray!" she shouted. *"No!"*

34

The change was sudden and immediate. One moment, the snow-mobile was growling over the ice; the next, the light swept heavenward as the heavier treads at the rear plunged into open water. The engine's hornet-scream cut out. Beyond the headlight, he made out the men, dark as seals. One was already in the water. The guy in front was scrambling over the windscreen onto the fairing. The snowmobile slewed left, and then he heard a ferocious splashing sound and screams: "I'M CAUGHT I'M CAUGHT IT'S PULLING ME UNDER IT'S PUL—"

The sled listed again and the voice cut out. A second later, the light slid from view.

Tom lowered the rifle. His breath came hard and fast. His pulse thundered. Behind, he felt the sled shift as the dog pushed to its feet.

The other man was still railing, his voice reedy with shock: "*Please!*" The guy sounded old, too. "*Please,* I know you're out there! Help me, please, help me, please! Please, you can't just let me *die!*"

Oh, but I can. These men had killed Jed and Grace. The cabin was gone. This was the enemy.

"Please." More splashing. "I can't . . . I can't feel my legs and—"

Tom clambered out of the sled. "Stay," he said to the dog, and then he was loping across the ice. The break was a good fifty yards away, so he didn't go far—maybe fifty, sixty feet. Shucking his parka, he dropped and spread himself over the snow and ice, taking the rest in a low crawl. It occurred to him, only belatedly, that the hunter might have a pistol, but he figured the old guy probably wasn't suicidal. Pop Tom and he would still drown.

"I'm coming. Keep talking." He felt the ice change under his body, listened for telltale pops and cracks. He squirmed forward as fast as he could. "Talk to me."

"Oh, th-thank Ch-Chr-Christ. H-h-here." The old guy was winded, out of breath; his voice stuttered with cold and fright. "C-ca-can't g-get ou-out of m-my c-coat . . . duh-duh-dragging m-me . . ."

"I'm almost there." Tom heard the slop of water over ice, and then his right hand was suddenly wet. Close enough. Four inches would hold a person's weight. Three might. Two would not. With no light from that sickly green moon and not even the glow from the blazing cabin to light his way, the night was pitch-black. He had no idea if the guy was even on his side of the break. "Move toward my voice. Can you move?"

Splashes, and then the old guy said, "Y-yuh."

Coming from his left, and very close. "Hold on," Tom said—

And then he made his first mistake.

Digging in with the toes of his boots, he twisted, using his belly as a pivot point, but he wasn't paying attention, hadn't thought through how his body was now parallel to the rift—on a thin lip of rotten ice.

"I'm going to toss you my coat," he said. "As soon as you feel it, grab on and—"

Two things happened at the same time.

Tom let out a surprised grunt as the old guy's hand swam out of the dark and clamped down on his right wrist. Before he could pull away, he felt the drag on his arm as the old hunter tried scrambling out of the water, using Tom the way someone might climb a rope ladder.

"Hey, no, *stop!*" Tom shouted. He tried yanking back, but the guy's fingers dug into him like talons, and Tom had no leverage. He felt himself slipping sideways, and then there was water around his legs, and he was still sliding—

That was when he made his second mistake—the precisely wrong move at precisely the wrong moment—because he was scared.

As soon as the icy water swirled around his legs, Tom let out a yell and tried rearing up onto his knees. His center of gravity shifted.

The ice let out a high, animal-like squeal. There was a *pop* as crisp as a gunshot, followed by a groan and—

CRACK!

And then Tom was in the water, too.

35

"*No*, Ray!" Ruby shrilled. "*Stop!*"

But Ray was past the point of no return. He bulled in with so much speed and force that none of the Changed had time to react. Wrapping one hand around the Browning, Ray planted the other on Acne's chest and shoved. Acne's arms windmilled as his boots tangled, dumping him on his ass with a heavy thump.

There was a sound of shotguns being racked and bolts being thrown and handguns being drawn, and then Ray was standing there, dead center in a bristle of weapons, as perfect a bull's-eye as ever existed. Except he'd jammed the Browning against Beretta's forehead, and he was screaming, spit flying: "I'll shoot him, I'll shoot him, *I'll fucking shoot him!*"

"*Ray!*" Ruby keened, and she started forward, her hand outstretched. "R—"

There was an orange flicker, like a bright coal. Ruby stopped dead in her tracks, her eyes growing so huge they were nothing but white with dark motes at their centers. The air ballooned with the stink of wet metal. Something thick and liquid splashed snow.

And then Ruby was screeching, wailing, *screaming*: *"Aaaaahhhhh, aaahhhhhh, aaaahhhhhh!"*

36

Tom yelped in surprise, then choked as cold water gushed down his throat. His airway closed and knotted. A wild, animal panic flooded his veins. He began to thrash, not thinking now at all, terror sheeting a red blaze over his mind. He needed air—where was it? His mouth worked, opening and closing in convulsive, silent gasps as the muscles of his throat fought him, trying to keep his windpipe safe because the lizard part of his brain thought he was drowning. Then, grudgingly, his throat relaxed and he inhaled in a great shriek. He pulled in another breath and then another— and that was all he had time for.

The old hunter leapt onto his back, trying to clamber out of the water. "S-stop!" Tom spluttered, but the old guy was freaked. A split second later, Tom went completely under. The water burned. It was inky; no light at all. Above, on his shoulders, he could feel the old guy's boots churning, struggling to gain a foothold. He kicked Tom in the forehead. Maybe, in air, Tom would've blacked out completely, but the water slowed the boot down. Still, the blow landed, solid enough to hurt. He clawed at the water, grabbing for the old guy's legs, enough so he realized where the surface was.

His head shattered into thin air. The old guy was at him again, monkeying onto his back, his fingers spidering over Tom's shoulders, knotting in his hair. His stringy arms latched around Tom's neck in a stranglehold, and then he was dragging Tom down again. Tom couldn't reach him, couldn't break his hold, didn't have the leverage. It was all Tom could do just to catch a breath as the weight of the old man crushed his throat. Not much time left. The more he fought, the less energy he had to keep afloat. His pulse pounded. Only one thing left to do, but he could feel his mind jabbering: *Are you nuts, are you crazy, are you insane?*

Against all reason and instinct, he let himself drop, straight down, slipping beneath the ice.

And pulled them both under.

37

"*Aaaaahhhhhh!*" Ruby screeched. "*Aaahhhhhhh, aaaahhhh, aaahhhh!*"

On the snow, Ruby's left hand lay with the fingers curled like a dead tarantula. Still shrieking, her right hand starred in a bony claw, Ruby stared down at the empty space where her left hand had been only seconds before as her blood jetted from severed arteries.

"Jesus!" Sharon leapt onto Ruby, wrapping her up, bringing the still-screaming woman down to the snow. Clamping both huge hands around Ruby's wrist, Sharon squeezed. "You sons of bitches, you sons of *bitches!*"

"*Ruuubeeeeee!*" Ray bawled. He made one abortive step toward his wife, and then checked himself, swinging the Browning back to Beretta. "Get up, you son of a bitch, *get up*! We're walking out of here, and if one of you twitches, if one of you *moves*—"

No one twitched or moved, but Beretta did not get up either. The air was electric, fizzy with scents and meanings. There were so many that Alex only had time to think how strange it was that with all these weapons, no one had fired. The only one who'd acted at all was the ninja-kid from Leopard's crew who'd hacked Ruby's hand. Another ninja could've taken off Ray's head with the same speed. With all these weapons, all they had to do was take Ray down. Although the Browning's pull was medium—only five pounds of pressure—the chances that Ray's finger would exert that much as the bullets chewed through his clothes and into his body were small. Not zero, but so infinitesimal as to make no difference. For that matter, Acne was right there and could take Ray's feet out from under him with a single powerful kick. Any of them could do *anything*. Ruby was an afterthought, a display and show of power—and Ray should already be dead.

Oh my God. She gasped as the lightbulb flashed in her brain. *He already* is. *This was never about* choice *because it's the Browning. It's Nathan's rifle, and that very first day, when Spider pulled the trigger, it wouldn't—*

"Ray!" she screamed. "Ray, *no*, the rifle doesn't—"

Ray squeezed the trigger.

38

As soon as they slipped beneath the ice, Tom felt the old man begin to fight, but the stranglehold around Tom's throat didn't let up. Even with the added weight, his lungs held air and air gave him buoyancy. He would bob like a cork until he drowned.

So Tom tucked and dove, straight down, pulling hard with his arms. It went against all logic. His mind screamed at him to stop, stop! Air was above. Below was death. That was precisely why he did it.

The old man let go.

In an instant, Tom was twisting back, coming around, trying to remember which way was up—because, in all that terrible blackness, he had no idea. He could feel the old man thrashing not far away. Hands grabbed for him out of the dark; fingers bunched in his shirt. Cocking his elbow, Tom pistoned his right fist. He felt the impact, then heard the man's scream, muted by water. Something shuddered past his face: bubbles, boiling for the surface. Kicking away, he followed them and left the old man behind in the dark.

Almost almost almost almost . . . The word had weight and

substance; it was in the pounding of his heart and the bright burn in his chest. He had to be almost there; he had to be *almost almost almost* . . .

Then he heard something new, frantic and rhythmic. Raleigh. Raleigh, on the surface, *barking*. He followed the sound. With the last of his strength, he surged up, fingers splayed—

And hit a sheet of solid ice.

39

Nonononono! The burn in Tom's lungs was so bad and his need for air so huge, a great ball of panic tried blasting past his lips in a scream. He pounded a fist into the ice. Pressing right up to the shelf, he kicked and strained, tried to bully his way through to air. *Air air air come on comeoncomeoncomeon*—

The dog barked again. Where? From his right? He didn't know. The water was cold enough to burn and black as oil; he was blind and more terrified than ever before—and that brought an awful clarity as well. Think, or he was dead.

Follow the sound, follow the dog; Raleigh, bark again, come on, boy, come on, please... Another bark, and this time, he grabbed onto the sound of the dog like a lifeline. With the very last of his strength, he kicked away from the suck and grab of the darkness and walked his hands along the underside of the ice, his gloved fingers futilely scratching, biting, searching for any chink, the tiniest break.

And then, he *was* done: breakpoint. It was over, and he knew it. He couldn't hold his breath another second. He just couldn't. He was finished, and before he could think about it, his throat convulsed and then he was flailing as the spent air rushed from his lungs in a *scream*—

His right hand shot out of the water and into nothing. Into *air*. He surged up, his head shattering into empty space and blessed air, and then he was coughing and spluttering, drawing in one shrieking breath after another. Chunks of ice bobbed and smacked against his chest and arms as he thrashed. His lungs wouldn't work well. He couldn't get enough air; he didn't even have the breath to scream.

Got to get out, get out get out get out! Terror bolted into his throat and stayed there. Drowning was his nightmare. More than being shot or bleeding out or getting himself blown to teeny tiny bits— drowning was right up there with burning to death, and he was going to drown; he was going to die. The cold was a giant palm that cupped his body and drew away heat. He was getting weak and so tired. Let up on kicking for even a few seconds and he started to sink again. He heard his arms slap water, but the sound was receding, thinning as panic swamped his brain.

Slow down, slow down, slow down. He was gasping. His head began to whirl. He would pass out if he couldn't stop hyperventilating, but he just couldn't get a handle on the rat-panic scrambling around in his head. *You've still got time, come on, come on, slow down, slow*—

Raleigh whimpered.

"R-R-Raleigh." His lips were numb and he was shivering hard enough to bite his tongue. To his horror, the pain was only a distant pinprick. If there was blood, he couldn't taste it. "Come h-here, b-b-boy." The dog whined, and he thought it must be dead ahead. *Not too far away.* "R-Raleigh, come on."

The dog responded with a small *huff.* Was the dog closer? He couldn't tell. He put out a gloved hand, slapped more water, and then headed for the place in the dark where he thought the dog must be. He breasted the surface, half-swimming but mostly treading water and slapping until his fingers brushed something hard that did not bob away. The edge of the break. He thrust a hand out even further, patting the darkness and then, layered over the ice, a denser mélange of compacted snow. No dog. So it was still far away and he was running out of time.

Reaching out with both hands, he pushed aside snow until he got to the ice, then flattened his palms and dug in. The gloves curled only grudgingly, and he realized the fabric had frozen to the ice. Could he use that? Maybe keep himself from drowning by letting his arms freeze to the ice?

No good. I'll still die of hypothermia. Have to get out of the water. He scissored his legs as hard as he could. His body popped up, lurched forward like an ungainly seal. Not far. Even without his parka, he was sodden, his clothes waterlogged and very heavy. He didn't have the strength. But his chest was on the surface now, beginning to freeze to the ice, and that was a start.

He sensed movement. The dog. Moving away? He was so weak he could only whisper the dog's name. Nothing. Then, the black closed down, and Raleigh snuffled at his ear.

"Oh God." Tom sobbed out a breath. Slipping one cautious hand from a glove, he reached up until he felt the dog's ruff. The dog responded by licking his fingers. The urge to grab onto the animal was so great he had to force himself to go slowly. No fast moves, nothing sudden . . . easy, easy . . . and then Tom's fingers slid up and under the dog's collar.

The dog didn't shy away. Tom pulled a little harder and then tensed his right arm. At the sudden tug, the dog began to back away, which was fine, exactly what he needed as he kicked and swam his way through snow.

And then he was out, completely, flopping like a hooked trout onto the ice. Water streamed from his body. He lay on his back, spread-eagled, sucking air as the dog licked water from his face.

Get up, he thought. *Get up or you'll freeze to the ice. Come on, get up, get off the ice, get warm.*

Oh, but the dog's tongue *was* warm, and so was its breath, and he was so tired. Numb, actually. No feeling in his feet or hands, and so cold he wasn't even shivering. He just had to rest a few seconds was all.

Don't pass out. He thought his eyes were open, but it was so dark. The dog nosed his neck and then he felt its paw on his chest. *Come on, get up, don't pass out, you can't pass out—*

He was still thinking that when he did.

40

Ray pulled the trigger. The Browning's action clicked and snapped—

And that was all.

Clearly waiting for the boom, Ray held his stance for a fraction of a second, then blinked and stared, stupidly, at the useless weapon.

"No." He tossed away the Browning with a fast, quick flick as if the metal had suddenly flared red-hot. Gulping, he stumbled back a step, hands up, palms out. "N-no, no!"

Leopard moved. His right hand flashed, and then the Glock's muzzle, wicked and black, dug into the nude space just above Ray's nose.

"*Don't!*" Alex and Daniel cried at the same moment.

"Stop!" Daniel shouted. "Don't do this!"

"Rubeee?" Ray's eyes, wild with terror, rolled in their sockets, trying to find his wife, but she had fainted in a bright, blood-red lake. "*Ru—*"

There was a sudden tongue of muzzle flash, and the Glock bucked.

41

The shot echoed and dissolved, shredded by snow and wind. The air became leaden with the reek of burned hair and cooked brain and fresh death—and the Changed, always the fume and choke of the Changed. Sharon still had Ruby's wrist in a death grip. Blood splashed the big woman from the neck down. Ruby was limp and still.

Stepping away from Ray's body, Leopard slid his Glock into his waistband as Acne helped Beretta to his feet. Spider still hovered over Jack, whose face was white as milky glass. Only the boy's eyes showed any sign of life, and they ticked from the ruin of Ray's head to his brother. Daniel was the color of ash and still as a statue in a swirl of snow, like the dead air at a hurricane's heart.

Of all people, Sharon broke the silence. "There, you got what you wanted. The choice was made. Doesn't matter if the boy did it or not."

Oh, yes, it did. Alex understood why the Changed had offered only that particular weapon. She also realized something else.

Nathan's rifle had not misfired or jammed after all. If that were true, the barrel would've blown apart.

She thought back to Nathan's reluctance and Jess's insistence. Piece of cake, really. Remove the bolt action, slip out the firing pin or fatigue the spring, replace the bolt—and no one would be the wiser. She could see Nathan playacting, because she was certain Jess would've anticipated that, all things being equal, Alex would try to fight back when the Changed attacked and might even get off a shot.

So the Browning was never meant to fire. The old woman wouldn't want to risk Alex turning the tables and killing her grandson.

Which means that she knew. Wolf was out there, waiting. Jess knew.

Alex had been right about something else, too. This was a test. The Changed must've inspected the rifle and known it was useless. They'd only wanted to see what Daniel would do. Why, she didn't know, but the final outcome—what would happen next—was never in doubt.

"Don't do this," she said. Heads swiveled; the eyes of all the Changed locked. "You have the other kids. You have *us*. How much more do you need? You have enough to last you a good long time. You don't *need* to do this."

"What?" She saw the slow dawn of horror on Daniel's face as he finally understood. "No." He looked around, wildly. "Please, let him go, *please*."

"Daniel?" Jack's voice rose, and then the little boy's head craned around to Spider, who was planting her feet: all the better to keep

her balance. Her wound dripped crocodile tears of bloody pus.
"Daniel?" Jack said. *"Daniel?"*

"No!" Alex screamed it, and so did Daniel. She sprang for Spider,
but then Leopard's crew converged. They slammed her, bucking
and kicking, to the snow. "He's just a boy!" she cried. "He's just a
little *boy!*"

Across the circle, she saw Daniel suddenly churning through
the snow, his face contorted in a spasm of love and fury and despair.

"No, please, God, no!" he shrieked. *"Nonononononono!"*

It took five of them to hold Daniel down.

It took Spider only a minute.

PART FOUR:
IN THE VALLEY OF THE SHADOW, IN THE HOUR OF THE MONSTER

42

"Come on!" Sharon bawled. She hunched over an unconscious Ruby, now sprawled on a braided rug before the guesthouse fireplace. A strong woman and big, not even Sharon could stop the thin, fitful blood-geysers pumping from Ruby's severed wrist. The rug was slowly turning a deep rust color as Ruby's arteries emptied. "Come on, come on, come on!"

"Just a sec, just a sec!" Fumbling, Alex stripped the lace from her boot and then crowded in beside Sharon. She lashed the lace around Ruby's forearm a few inches down from the old woman's bloodstained elbow—once, twice. For a moment, she worried the polypropylene would saw right through Ruby's skin, which was frail and paper-thin. *Well, screw that.* She put some muscle into it, cinched down hard. "Okay, ease up."

The big woman's fingers cautiously relaxed. The steady crimson pump dribbled to an ooze.

"Christ." Sharon was panting. Her sweat-drenched face was matted with hanks of her bullet-gray hair. Drying blood fanned her chest and neck. "What the hell are we going to do?"

"I don't know. Hang on." When they'd staggered back to the guesthouse with Ruby, Acne and Slash had followed, dumping six of the camo packs in after them. Now, Alex snatched up one and pawed through the contents: food, clothes. She tried not to pay attention to the smells of trail mix and MREs, the spike of a packet of peppermint gum. Or the clothes either: floral soap, talcum warmed by a child's skin. She found no ammunition in the pack, and the Changed's muscle had pulled anything remotely resembling a weapon. So, no knives or scissors either.

Come on, come on, these kids were prepared; there's got to be something. She tumbled out another pack, gave the contents a quick going-over, her eyes brushing over a pair of boy's pajamas: Spider-Man. She grabbed up a third pack.

"What are you looking for?" Sharon asked. Her voice was limp as a spent balloon. Ruby's blood shellacked both arms to her elbows.

"Medical supplies." Alex upended the pack in a shower of pink and purple that smelled of vanilla and little girl. "These kids were ready to be on the road for a while."

Fourth try: pay dirt. She sifted through tubes of antibiotic ointment, bandages, antiseptic wipes, alcohol, gauze, tape, Kerlix. And pills, lots of pills: over-the-counter packets of cold tablets, Tylenol, ibuprofen, cough drops. But there was a clutch of more potent stuff: prescription painkillers like Percocet and Vicodin, a handful of tiny green Valiums, and—the mother lode—antibiotics: big pink horse-pills of long-acting erythromycin and chalky-white amoxicillin.

Okay, almost in business, but there was still one hell of a problem. The second she took off that tourniquet, the bleeding would start right up. During the few amputations she'd done with Kincaid, he'd talked about isolating nerve from muscle to minimize phantom limb pain and how to clamp off blood vessels; what suture to use now that were was no power for electrocautery . . .

Cautery. She gasped. *That's it.*

"What?" Sharon asked as Alex pushed to her feet.

Tom. She raced to the kitchen, started yanking open cupboards and pulling drawers. Tom had told her what to do; he'd talked her through it. She'd *done* this once before. *Come on, come on, I smelled it before, I know I did, I know it's here.*

"What are you doing?" Sharon asked.

"Metal holds heat." She ripped open another cupboard. Dust mice and crumbs. The Changed had been smart enough to remove the obvious: knives, forks, anything that jumped out as a potential weapon. But not everything. There *was* something. All she had to do was follow her nose . . .

"So?"

"*So,* if I can find something metal and get it hot enough, I can use that to stop the bleeding." As soon as she levered open the oven door, she smelled cooked sulfur, ancient grease. *Gotcha.* The skillet was upside down on the rack: cast-iron, very small, speckled with rust, a little sticky from stale Crisco. Good enough. Grabbing a cooking mitt and the pan, she scuttled back. When they'd first arrived, she'd built up the fire to burn hot and fast through that first load of wood, mainly to warm the chimney and create the airflow to keep the fire going. The fire now had dwindled to red-hot embers. Slipping on the mitt, she reached in with a long split of oak.

"Get me more logs," she said. She used the split to shove aside spent wood. "There, in the firebox."

Laying the wood in a grid, she knelt, blew on the embers, and was rewarded with a flower of flame. She jockeyed the skillet into a nest of red-orange coals.

"You sure this will work?" Sharon said.

"No, but it's better than nothing." She waited until the smell of scorched iron filled the guesthouse and then levered the skillet from the fire. The heat rolled off the iron, leaked through the mitt where the gray, fire-resistant covering had flaked away.

"Hold her down," she said to Sharon. Ruby was still out, but Alex didn't think that would last more than a nanosecond. "No matter what, don't let up until I tell you to."

"I'm on it." Sharon straddled Ruby, pushing her knees into the little woman's shoulders. She grabbed Ruby's left arm in both hands. "Go."

Has to work. Gritting her teeth, she jammed the hot skillet onto Ruby's raw stump.

There was a pop and then a sizzle. Ruby flopped. Her legs pistoned straight out. Her head jerked and then her eyes were wide and so was her mouth and she was bucking and thrashing and screaming, screaming, *screaming* . . .

"Hold her, hold her!" Alex shouted. The smell was coming

on, thick and heavy: the unmistakable aroma of fried meat and molten fat. Alex heard the fizz of boiling blood. Saliva suddenly flooded her mouth, spilled over her tongue, as her brain registered that this was meat, it was *meat*, this was the aroma of *food*. Hamburgers on the grill. Juicy steaks.

Come on, don't lose it; it doesn't mean anything.

Her body didn't care. A huge hunger-rat clawed at her belly. To her horror, her stomach let out a long, very loud growl.

But then, for once, it happened the way things are supposed to in make-believe: Ruby passed out.

"Thank Christ," Sharon breathed.

Alex had one precious second when she really thought everything would be all right; that she could chalk up her hunger for Ruby's meat to some ghost of an ancient past when cavemen hunkered over roast saber-toothed tiger.

But then her mind shifted. Again. The sensation was almost like a sound: a dry rustle as the monster flexed its muscles. Out of nowhere, that swimmy feeling washed over and through her mind, spiking the hairs on her neck. A whir bloomed in her brain—black sound—and then her mouth filled with the wet, mushy funk of warm iron and something so slick it tasted like boiled snot.

"No!" she gasped. Her gorge, sour and hot, pushed up through her chest, and then she was spinning up and away. The skillet thudded to the hardwood with a dull clang, and Sharon was shouting: *What, what, what?* She didn't care. Alex bolted for the door at a dead run, and then she was out in the storm, the snow swirling in a white rush, the wind clawing her hair. No guard at the door. None was needed because of the storm.

Through the snow, across the clearing, the Changed were feasting. The party was just getting started. She had no idea where they'd taken Daniel, but she saw what they'd done to Jack.

Against the jump of orange flames, the spit turned like something out of a grade-B movie: the carcass threaded onto forked wood lashed together with, of all things, extension cords. The stench of scorched rubber competed with the aroma of broiled meat and crisped fat.

Spider was right there, in the thick of it, cheeks bulging, her skin ruddy with firelight and excitement. She was pressing a fistful of something to Leopard's mouth—

And Alex felt the edge of his teeth ghosting over her own fingers.

God. An icy knife of horror cut her chest. *No.* She watched as Leopard pulled Spider closer—

And it was *her* skin that crawled as Leopard's tongue dragged over Spider's neck.

Oh my God. It was happening again, her mind slewing sideways, stepping away—and into *Spider.*

No! A surge of bile roared from her mouth to splatter to the snow. *She isn't me; I'm not her. I'm not one of them, I'm not!*

"Hey!" Sharon called. "Get your ass back here!"

God, what's happening to me? Alex's muscles were shuddery and weak. Sagging against the door, she pressed her sweaty face to icy wood. *I'm not Spider. I'm Alex and I'm here, I'm here, I'm right here.*

But then she thought she heard just the faintest whisper sighing up from a deep, dark crevice of her mind. Or maybe she didn't really hear anything, and it was a hallucination conjured from her addled, sick brain. Whatever. It was there, sardonic and small.

Maybe, it—the monster—said. *But so am I. So am I.*

43

"You did good." Sharon vacuumed in a mouthful of trail mix and chomped. With the other hand, she plucked at a red and black flannel shirt they'd draped over Ruby. The little woman had swum to a kind of twilight awareness long enough for Alex to feed her an erythromycin and Percocet before sinking back. Alex had worried about the dose because Ruby was so small, but knocking her out seemed both prudent and humane. Time enough to deal with the night's horrors tomorrow.

"I would never have thought to use the frying pan." Sharon smoothed the shirt under Ruby's chin. "That was real smart, Alex."

"Yeah. Well." Alex palmed a pink tablet of erythromycin. After bandaging Ruby up and then taking care of her shoulder, she'd sifted through the pill bottles, debating which was best, and decided upon erythromycin, a drug she was familiar with from her work with Kincaid. The pills had belonged to a Bev Ulrich, who had been a very bad patient, only taking four tablets when her doctor specifically prescribed two a day for fourteen days, or *else.* Or maybe Bev had been a very good patient, only the Zap happened and then bronchitis was the least of her problems.

The label said to drink plenty of water and take the medicine on a full stomach. Yeah, right. She could hear Aunt Hannah: *Not bloody likely.*

What am I going to do? The thought of her aunt made the tiny black letters on the prescription label squiggle and shimmer. Erythromycin sure wouldn't cure what ailed her, but she dry-swallowed the antibiotic, which caught and hung in her throat. *It's winning, Aunt Hannah. After all this, the monster's finally going to win.*

"Hey." Sharon fished out a bottled water and twisted off the cap. "Better chase that if you want it to go down."

"Thanks." She tipped the bottle to her mouth, wincing a little at the taste. The water smelled of blood and iron and dead Jack—

"You okay?" Sharon asked around peanuts.

"Sure." The smell of soggy nuts and sickly sweet raisins was turning her stomach. "It's just . . ." She gave a hard swallow and felt the antibiotic knuckle its way down her chest. "How can you eat after what happened?"

She expected an explosion, but Sharon only swallowed, shrugged, said, "Me starving isn't going to help that little boy. He's dead, and I'm sorry about that, but I'm not dead and neither are you. Now get some food in your stomach. You look like shit."

"What do you care if I eat?" Alex gave her a sidelong glance. "If I don't, it's just that much more for you, right?"

"That's true, but you're smarter. If I get hurt, you know what to do. I'm hedging my bets. So here." Sharon tossed her an MRE.

"Eat that before I force it down your gullet like my grandpa did his geese."

"Geese?"

"Yeah." Sharon snorted. "He thought he was going to get rich making that Frenchie food, outta liver?"

"Foie gras."

"That's it. He had this big metal tube." Sharon's hands bracketed a good foot of air. "About yay long. I had to hold the goose's head while he shoveled in the grain. Maybe two pounds of feed, four times a day? Poor things, they would struggle and choke . . . used to make me cry. That old man never did get rich neither. He was so impatient he ended up with more geese with busted guts than ones he could carve the livers out of. Near about went broke on that scheme, and good riddance to bad rubbish. But I got in plenty of practice with force-feeding. I don't think you want to find out just how much."

That, Alex thought, was about as close to an apology as she would ever get from Sharon. Alex's eyes skimmed the label of the MRE: spaghetti with meat sauce. Just the thought of wormy noodles swimming in red sauce made her stomach lurch. But she forced her trembling fingers to work open the box and pouches. The MRE came with a heater pack, but when she tried adding water, she slopped it onto her jeans.

"Whoa, whoa, hang on. Let me do it." Deftly plucking the MRE and heater pack from Alex, Sharon added water, then slid the MRE into its heater pouch. "You worried about that boy, Daniel? Think they're carving him up, too?"

A bald way to put it, but this was Sharon. "I doubt it. They always make us watch, like they did with . . ." She paused. "I just don't understand why they haven't put him here with us. What could they want with him?"

"How about information? You heard the boy: ambushing those bastards was his idea. So maybe they think they'll get more out of him. If I was them, that's what I'd do. Except"—Sharon's face puckered in a frown—"I don't know *how*. They aren't exactly the talkative types, you know what I'm saying?"

This was true, but Daniel had said something important to the Changed: *You said you'd let him go*. What had he meant? The Changed made occasional sounds, but they didn't speak. She didn't know if they could. Maybe the speech centers in their brains had shorted out. So how could—how *did*—the Changed *say* anything to someone who hadn't become one of them? *She* understood them, but only sort of and occasionally, and even that was mediated only by smell and those weird slip-slides. What she got was more inference than anything else, which wasn't the same as an actual exchange of information, and Wolf had never given any indication that he understood *her*. What she had with the Changed was like a bizarre kind of empathy, like a sixth sense that was growing stronger.

Because *she* was Changing?

No. Even as she thought that, she felt her mind working to shove the idea away. *No, it's been too long, and Tom said that when his friend, Jim, began to Change, he got confused; he forgot things.*

But she already knew that the Change didn't happen to little kids or older people, and kids hadn't Changed at the same rate. Some Changed right away, within minutes, on that first day, while others went for days. Which might mean that *how* you Changed depended on *who* you were. A boy's hormones weren't the same as a girl's; the brain of a little kid wasn't the same as that of a fourteen-year-old. Her scrambled mind had about as much in common with a normal person's as a cat did with an orangutan.

Or maybe the Zap had triggered something *in* the monster. Kincaid said there was no telling if the monster was dead or dormant—or still alive but morphing, maybe even evolving. *Organizing itself* was how Kincaid put it.

But *God*. The idea of *it* actually becoming its own *thing* brought the gooseflesh to her arms, and she felt a shiver work its way up her spine. That was just a little creepy. But it could happen. When she'd been diagnosed, she'd read a ton. Anything by Oliver Sacks she embraced like a bible. So she knew that, for reasons doctors didn't understand, certain tumors became *things*: grew their own teeth and skin, sprouted hair and cartilage and eyeballs, like little mini-me's. Completely freaked her out.

Tumors caused seizures, too, especially as more and more of the brain was either taken over by tumor or squished and shoved and elbowed out of the way. Seizures might trigger out-of-body experiences, which were, exactly, what she'd experienced.

So, in the end, the only thing her switcheroos might prove was that the monster was sending up a little red flare to signal the end of this particular game: *two-minute warning, sweetheart*. Which meant her choices about what to do weren't that different from before this nightmare began back in October, when she'd run off to the Waucamaw: she could stay on the train—go to the very end of the line where those tracks would give out—or jump off.

"But I heard of this going on," Sharon continued.

"What?" She was so deep in her own thoughts that she had to work to tease out the thread of their conversation, and then realized she really had no idea what the older woman was talking about. "What going on?"

"Bands of kids fighting those monsters. Makes sense when you think about it. The kids who haven't turned—they're the only ones fit enough to track the Chuckies. Don't get me wrong; I can point and shoot, but heading out through the snow, skiing and camping out . . ." Her lips twisted in a wry, self-deprecating grimace as she tugged at a flaccid wattle beneath her jaw, deforming the tired strands of that spiderweb tattoo. "A little too much meat, and a few too many years."

"What about in your group, the people you lived with before?" Alex asked. "Did some of you fight? Were there kids?"

Sharon busied herself readying another MRE. "Not really. All our kids—well, grandkids, mostly—they turned. The three who didn't were practically babies. The rest of us were too busy scrounging around for food and staying warm to worry much about fighting."

All our kids turned. She bit back the urge to grill the old woman on just how that happened and what the signs were. *What would it be like to watch your grandchildren Change? What would you do? Kill them?* There had to be some adults who just couldn't pull the trigger, or who wouldn't give up hope. But then it would be as Larry had said a thousand years ago in the Waucamaw: how do you live with yourself afterward, either way?

She chose to leave it alone. "Do you know anything else about kids like Daniel? The ones who are fighting?"

"No, but we figured they got to have some older kids like him or adults, if only to teach them how not to blow their heads off. Here." Sharon handed Alex the cardboard box containing her packet of spaghetti and meatballs. "Eat up while it's hot."

The cardboard box was soggy and the packet inside just the near side of scalding. Carefully, she tweezed the pouch apart. Fiddleheads of steam unfurled in a stomach-churning stench of hot plastic and stewed tomato. Inside, the noodles shimmered in a slick, oily, copper-colored ooze, like ropy nerves and torn veins in a puddle of old blood.

"Something wrong with that spaghetti?" Sharon asked.

Maybe I am cooked and stick-in-the-fork done, or pretty close. "No," Alex said, and shoved in a squelchy mouthful of oily pasta. *But I'm not there yet, and when it's time, it'll be me that does it, not Spider or Leopard or anyone else.*

"It's great." She chewed those noodles to glue. "Just great."

An hour later, the Changed came for her.

44

The reek of sex and booze hit a good hundred yards from the front door of the old Victorian, while she was still shuffling after Slash through the snow. Yup, Saturday night, and time to get down, get dirty, get funky. Not that she'd be partying. She studied Slash's back as the girl lumbered against the wind. The girl's scent was more sour than ever but void of useful information. Alex had been mystified until Slash toed the medical supplies Alex had gathered into neat piles.

"Looks like they want you to play doctor," Sharon had observed, then gestured toward the stash of pills. "Leave me a bunch of them painkillers and sleepers, you don't mind. Just in case Ruby wakes up."

"Sure." The rest—gauze, bandages, sterile packs of instruments, ointments, a bottle of peroxide—Alex shoveled into a camo pack. "But go easy. Ruby's pretty small. You don't want to overdose her."

"Don't you worry. I'll take care of both of us. Now you go on and do what you have to. And Alex?" Sharon's eyes had battened on hers for a long, disconcerting moment. "That boy, Daniel . . . he's just lost his little brother. He's got some dark days ahead. No matter what comes down the pike, you stick by him."

She had said something noncommittal, like *okay, sure.* But what had that been about? She would help Daniel. No problems there. But if they were taking her to Beretta, they had another thing coming. That kid could rot for all she cared. Besides, if she helped *them,* that brought her one step closer to *being* them.

And I'm not. I'm not going to let them or it win.

The house was much warmer than the guest cabin, and feverish with the odor of sex. Both fireplaces were going. In a place this size, there had to be a couple woodstoves, too. In the dance of orange light and dark shadow, she saw a tangle of bodies, mostly naked, and the glint of empties. Someone had definitely puked in the far right corner. A girl, one of Leopard's crew, was sandwiched on an ottoman between two writhing boys. Acne slouched on a sofa with his pants puddled around his ankles, a girl's head bobbing between his legs.

Too much information. She'd actually braced herself as she entered, expecting her mind to do its slewing swoon again. But nothing happened, which made her wonder if her hypotheses were all wrong. Maybe this had nothing to do with hunger, sexual or otherwise. *Because if ever there was a time and place . . .* she sidestepped two drunken boys fondling one another on the stairs . . . *this is definitely it.*

Once on the second floor, Slash turned right. Which was interesting. From the odor, she knew Beretta was behind her, in the far room to the *left.* So this was not about him. They passed a display table with doilies and bric-a-brac, a blur of framed photos. Bedrooms up here, too. She caught Spider's scent almost at once, from behind a closed door. From the mélange of odors, she thought there might be two others in there with her, and one, she thought, might be . . .

Almost on cue, the knob turned, and then Spider and Leopard ghosted into view. Spider's blonde hair was tousled, and Leopard had an arm twined about the girl's waist. Both were completely naked and reeked of sex and garbage. When he spotted Alex, Leopard actually leered, his eyes dragging lazily up and down Alex's body, lingering, taking inventory. As Sharon would say, no mystery what itch that boy wanted scratched.

Oh shit. Alex's heart stilled. *God, please, I really could do without a little side trip, thanks. Concentrate on something else,* anything *else.* She screwed her eyes to the hole in Spider's cheek and stared so hard it was a wonder Spider's face didn't burst into flames.

What Spider did instead was smile, and that was somehow much worse, because her grin was slow and so satisfied Alex half-expected the girl to purr. Spider's was the kind of gleeful smirk every kid's seen a hundred times on the lips of the most popular girl in school: *So sucks to be you.*

A minute later, after Spider and Leopard had closed the door again, Slash led her to the threshold of the room at the very end of the hall. Here, the odors were very strong, too: a boy's sweat and blood and . . .

Oh God. Her heart tried climbing out of her chest, and for just a moment, the slightly metallic aftertaste of prefab spaghetti sauce took on a rankness that brought a surge of sour bile into her throat.

Because now she thought she understood just exactly why Spider had smiled.

45

Slash left a few seconds later, probably heading downstairs to knock back a few, hook up, make up for lost time. That she left Alex alone should have made her less anxious—*nothing to see here, folks, move along*—but Alex could feel the tension fizzing on her skin like an electrical charge.

Just take it easy. She wet her lips, grateful for the taste of her own salt. Anything was better than the scummy sludge coating her tongue. *It might be nothing. There are so many of them in the house, the stink's everywhere.*

This room, she saw, had belonged to a boy with eclectic tastes. A poster of LeBron James competed for space with Derek Jeter. A baseball mitt butted tennis balls. There was a red and white electric guitar in a corner. A poster of some drummer she'd never seen playing in a band she'd never heard of was taped to a closet door.

Daniel was on the bed, propped against the headboard in a tumble of blue and brown striped sheets that his blood had stained dark purple. A Coleman lantern fizzed on a nightstand. In the harsh, unforgiving white light, the shadows beneath his eyes were black. His eyes were distant and unfocused and did not meet hers even when she said his name twice and touched his face. His skin was waxen and greasy with sweat.

Daniel's wound was low on his left flank, a through-and-through, which probably accounted for why he was still alive. Working as gently as she could, she cleaned away the blood on his stomach, most of which had dried to a crust and now peeled away in large rust-flakes. She splashed peroxide over the purple lips of the entry wound. The liquid hissed and bubbled into pink foam. Daniel reacted to that. His lids twitched, and something fleet and fast chased over his face. His eyes ticked away from whatever horror they were watching, swept past her face, then wavered back.

"Hi," he said.

That settled something in her mind. Daniel was right here, right now, and he needed her help. Besides, her brain kept snagging on what Daniel had said on the snow: *You said you'd let him go.* If Daniel *could* actually hear and talk to the Changed, that alone was worth the risk.

"Hi," she said. "Can you roll onto your side? I want to clean off your back. I'm pretty sure the bullet went right through, but I want to be certain."

"Sure." Wincing, he eased over. From the way his flesh jumped, she knew the peroxide hurt, but he said nothing. The Coleman's light bleached his skin bone-white. The quarter-sized exit wound stared at her like a wet, black fish eye. After patting the wound dry, she smeared on antibiotic ointment and used surgical tape to tack down gauze. She fed him an erythromycin, then made him drink half a bottle of water in small sips. With the remaining water, she wet one of the towels and sponged his face.

He said, thickly, "It was my fault."

She paused, the cool cloth pressed to his cheek. "Because you led the ambush?"

"Yeah." His eyes stumbled to her face. "Mellie told me not to do anything stupid, but I did."

"Mellie?"

"The woman who gathered us all together. Kind of like the mom in the *Terminator* movies, you know? Only more like a group grandmom."

"She taught you how to fight?" When Daniel nodded, she asked, "Where'd you get all the guns?"

"Oh, lying around." Daniel sounded as used up as old chewing gum. "You can find almost anything you want. We even got some grenade launchers."

She remembered those Uzis and that kid from Leopard's crew with the bandolier. Definitely loaded for bear. "Where's Mellie now? Is she dead?"

"No." Daniel's head rolled on the pillows. "Gone."

"Why'd she leave?"

"She said she'd lost a couple kids before we joined up with her outside Hurley."

"Where's that?"

"Wisconsin. At the border. Bounty hunters is what she thought."

"Bounty hunters?" Scooping up kids as barter made a terrible kind of sense. Harlan had seen Spared as a meal ticket, and that was months ago. Rule certainly thought Spared, especially girls, were of immense value. "For whom?"

"Depends. There are so many stories, I never know what to believe. Some said military, like . . . you know . . . army? One girl, Sandra, thought people were trying to figure out why *we* were still okay. Like, experimenting."

Her stomach dropped. It suddenly occurred to her that maybe, for all its problems, Rule had the right idea. There had been no question that she was safer in the village than outside, and the Changed were only one of many enemies.

Wait, what am I thinking? Lena was right. The Council saw us as baby-makers. We were still barter, something to be used.

"So they got rewarded for bringing kids in?" she asked.

"Uh-huh. I was the oldest, so Mellie left me in charge. She said to take the others to this camp she knew about, where we'd be safe."

And how, she thought, would Mellie know? The idea of a grandma scooping up kids and leading them to sanctuary gave her pause. What made Mellie more trustworthy than any other oldster? Probably best to save those particular questions. Second-guessing wouldn't do Daniel a whit of good, and she needed information. "Camp? Where? What kind?"

"With other kids here, in Michigan, but way south of where you . . . we are now. Maybe . . ." Daniel's eyebrows tented with effort. "Another week? On foot?"

Other kids. Sharon had talked about groups of children fighting the Changed. So they were gathering together? And south meant *they'd* gone north, but how far? "So where are we, exactly? I mean, are we close to any towns? Because I've lost track. We've been on the move for . . ." She thought back to the notch she'd made that morning. "Eight days. Nine, now. It must be past midnight, and Sunday now. I figure we went six or maybe seven miles a night, depending."

"I don't know much about Michigan. I'm from way west, in Wisconsin, near Mellen?" When she shook her head, Daniel added, "About halfway between Clam Lake and Hurley?"

The names meant nothing to her. Other than her aunt's hometown of Sheboygan, the rest of Wisconsin was just a through state, a long expanse of highway she blasted through to get from Chicago to Michigan. "Why come here? Why not stay in Wisconsin?"

"We heard it was better, safer in the U.P."

Well, not so much. "Okay. So where are we?"

"Real close to the border. Maybe . . ." Daniel let out an almost disinterested sigh, as if the math was just too much. "Two days away? On foot?"

She hated peppering him with questions, but she had to know. "Which direction? Do you remember any towns? Is the border west?" Wisconsin was due west of Rule. "North?" She thought that might be right. Was Hurley west of the Waucamaw? God, she wished she'd paid closer attention to the maps she and Tom had found.

"We're east of the border now. Wisconsin's a straight shot due west," Daniel said. "The camp we were heading to is"—his parched lips moved as he did a mental tally—"about a week out and south of this old mine, which Mellie said was where all these Chuckies were hanging out and—"

"What?" Hadn't Chris's grandfather operated a mine? Yes, that was right; some of the older miners had been living in a wing of the hospice. Chris read to them when he was in town. "Do you know the name of the mine?"

"No. Just some old iron mine, I guess. I had a map, but I lost it somewhere. All I know is we're about five days northwest of the mine, and there are supposed to be a ton of Chuckies there, too."

"You mean, like a big tribe?"

"More like a lot of smaller groups moving in and out. Kind of like a home base, I guess. Mellie said they probably chose the mine because they knew it from before and mines are warmer the deeper you go."

She thought about that. Would Spider and Leopard circle south, too? Go hang with their friends, maybe toss back a couple brews and carve up some nice juicy steaks, throw some hamburgers on the grill? There was no way to know the answers, and in some sense, it didn't matter. Without Wolf, Alex thought her time was nearly up. Spider needed her for Daniel—no question about that—and in more ways than one. Unless the Changed figured on Alex becoming their camp nurse, Spider had no incentive to let her live indefinitely. But if this was the Rule mine Daniel was talking about, they were still relatively close to the village.

Got to figure out where I am. Her mind was already leapfrogging ahead, ticking off the steps. *This might be my best and last chance. Even a rough map will do.* Her eyes settled on that desk across the room. "If I got paper and pencil, could you draw it from memory?"

His head made a weary shake. "I'm not so good with that."

She squelched a pulse of irritation. "Could you at least try?"

"Can we not do this right now?" Daniel's lips trembled. His face was pinched, the strain and his grief carved in deep lines across his forehead and along his nose. "Can't we do this later?"

She had to snatch back the impulse to grab him by the shoulders and give him a good shake: *No, don't you get it? We really can't.* But she forced herself to slow down. "I know it's hard, but this is important, Daniel. I know you feel bad. I've lost people, too. There was this little girl and then . . ." She felt her eyes welling. "Then I failed someone I really cared about, and I tried the best I could, but it still wasn't good enough, and he's dead now because of me. So I *do* know what it's like to want to give up, I really do. But you can't. Please." She put a trembling hand on his chest. "Please, Daniel. Think. Try to remember. Where's the camp?"

The boy's eyes were pools. "Alex, I . . . I don't know, I really don't. I wish I did, but all I remember is that once we got across the border, Mellie told me to keep heading south."

"Did she say why?"

"Only that going too far east and deeper into Michigan would be bad. I didn't think to ask any more. I thought there was plenty of time, and I was so tired out and scared. Jack and me, we were on our own for so long. It was a relief to have someone tell me what to do. I only wish I'd really listened."

"What do you mean?"

"I mean . . . ," he began, then stopped. A huge tear trembled at the corner of his left eye.

"Daniel?" When he still didn't reply, she touched his cheek.

His skin was clammy and slick as cold marble. "Daniel?" she said softly. "What did you mean? Why didn't you listen to Mellie? Why didn't you do what she said?"

She watched the tear swell then splash to his cheek, and the sour scent of his loss and despair—and, worse, the scorch of his self-contempt—balled in her throat.

"Because I . . . I just c-couldn't," he choked. "Not after I saw you."

46

That knocked her back. "Me? What are you talking about?"

"I . . . we spotted your guys—the wolf-people? Like three days ago, and then we . . ." His streaming eyes meandered away a moment then drifted back. "We tracked you."

"You—" she began, then stopped. Three days ago, Brian was still alive. "Are you kidding me? You tracked us? For three *days*?" She wanted to slap his face: *You had guns! You had grenade launchers! What the hell were you waiting for, an engraved invitation?* "Why?"

"I told you." Daniel lifted a quivering hand to his lips. "I tracked you because I saw you. I couldn't let the Chuckies have someone normal. You're one of us. I . . . I couldn't let them just *have* you. So we followed you and then waited for an opportunity to take them out."

Oh my God. Daniel had talked the other kids into a rescue mission. Kids would want to save their own. The really young ones, not yet old enough to understand how bad things could get, might've been pumped. For them, a rescue would be like playing a kick-ass video game.

"What I don't get is how the wolf-people knew we were coming." Daniel said. "We stayed downwind and everything, just like Mellie taught us. That other tribe—"

"Tribe." Sure, like Wolf's pack, Leopard's crew might be called a tribe. "The kids in white?"

"Yeah. They came out of nowhere. We only got off a couple shots and then Jack . . ." He put an arm over his eyes and turned his head toward the far wall.

Her anger vanished. What the hell was she doing? She had no right. Daniel was no older than she, and all he'd tried to do was help her—and look how well that turned out. She felt sick again, and weak. This really wasn't her fault. She wasn't to blame. She couldn't control everything. Shit happened.

Yeah, right. God, first Tom, then Chris gets hurt because of me. And now Daniel's friends get themselves killed, and Jack—

Daniel reeled in a watery breath. "They surprised that wolf-guy, too."

Through the bitter fog of her guilt, it took her a second to register. "The guy. You mean, Wolf?" The sudden tightness in her chest was something she could've done without. Why she should care about a monster was still beyond her. "You saw him?"

"Yeah. The girl, the one with the face." He tapped his cheek. "She shot him."

"Shot . . ." The word dried up on her tongue. "Spider *shot* him?" When he threw her a questioning look, she added, "It's what I call her. She's got that designer gear, so . . . why did she shoot him? What for?"

She could see Daniel thinking about that. "She was . . . angry. Like she didn't want to be there at all. I'm not exactly sure how I know that, but she was."

"Be where?"

"A clearing maybe a half mile from here. They were doing this really weird ritual thing. You know those wolf skins they wear? Well, they had a real live wolf, this great big gray guy they'd probably trapped or snared. I couldn't see everything because it was getting on dark and the snow had already started. But the wolf was really strong, fighting the ropes. The girl, Spider—she had that big honking knife and so did the guy. I'm sure they were going to kill and then skin it."

This was news. She knew nothing about this side of the Changed. She thought back to that arena near Rule, the way flanked by flayed wolf carcasses. "What happened?" she asked. "To the wolf, I mean."

"I don't know. In the confusion, it might have gotten away. But the way the wolf-people were gathered around, it felt like . . ." He groped for the word. "Religious. Except for the girl, Spider? She was pissed, like it wasn't her idea."

Hmm. That was the second . . . no, *third* time Daniel seemed to either know or intuit how the Changed felt.

"So I was thinking, great, hit 'em now when they're distracted," he continued. "Only the other guys swarmed all over us, and then I saw her with one of them, a real tall guy—"

"Leopard."

"Okay." Daniel accepted the nickname. "Leopard went right up to her, and then she was yanking out his pistol. She turned fast, popped off a couple shots at the wolf-boy. He was moving before she got all the way around, and then he made it to the woods, but you could tell he got hit. She started after him, only the little guy tried to stop her, and then she popped him in the back."

The little guy would be Beretta. She thought about that. She had assumed the Changed could read one another like telepaths, in a way. But that wasn't quite right, was it? Wolf never saw Spider coming, or by the time he did, there wasn't enough time to save himself. So the Changed couldn't be, well, broadcasting all the time, if that's even what they did.

But that's why I'm here with Daniel. It was another hunch, a brain-ping, but she thought she was right. *Spider killed Wolf. Slash took me to* Daniel, *which means Spider's just as happy if Beretta gets neglected to death.* Why? Because Beretta was loyal to Wolf? That was plausible. Of the pack, Beretta and Acne seemed closer to Wolf than Slash was. Guys tended to hang with guys. Slash and Spider were the only girls. Maybe Slash was a minion, the kind of high school kid grateful to be a remora to Spider's shark.

And how had Spider gotten word to Leopard in the first place? How did she *know* Leopard? From before? Unless . . .

"Daniel," she said, "you told me there were other Cha . . . uh, Chuckies at the mine, right? Do you know how many? Are they, like, tribes who cooperate with each other, or . . ."

"I don't know." His lips wobbled. He averted his face again. "Really, I have to stop now. I don't want to talk about this anymore."

"All right." And it really was. She wasn't sure she could bear any more unexpected revelations anyway. She fished an MRE from her camo pack of medical supplies. "It's chicken with noodles. I brought along a bouillon cube, too. The doctor I worked with said chicken noodle soup was good when you'd lost blood."

He gave the packet a listless glance. "I'm not hungry."

"You should try." When he shook his head again, she persisted. "Are you thirsty?"

"A little." Tears trickled from the corners of his eyes to wet the pillowcase. "I just want to go to sleep and not wake up."

She said nothing.

"Why haven't they killed me yet, Alex?" he whispered. "Why are they keeping me alive?"

To those questions, she had no answers he would want to hear. When his shoulders began to shake, she felt an impulse to put her arms around him, but she wasn't sure he would want that, or if it was even the right thing to do. She had never seen a boy cry like that before. Well, not since she'd accidentally on purpose elbowed Scott Rittenhouse off the jungle gym in first grade. The sound of Daniel's grief was terrible, like a hacksaw through her heart, and he cried a long time.

"S-sorry." His voice was thinner and no more substantial than worn tissue paper. *All cried out,* she thought. "Would you stay with me for a while?" he said in that same, fragile voice. "I don't want to be alone with them."

She thought of Sharon and Ruby back at the guesthouse. If they were lucky, Ruby would sleep through the rest of the night.

After that, well, she didn't know what she could do for her, other than top Ruby off with antibiotics and all those painkillers and hope she healed.

"I'll stay for as long as they let me," she said. "You should try to sleep."

"I don't want to sleep. Every time I close my eyes, I see Jack. I s-see . . ."

"Shh, it's okay," she said, hating how lame that sounded. Things were definitely *not* okay. She put a hand on his arm. He was trembling, and his eyes were bright and desperate. Too late, she thought of the painkillers she'd left behind with Sharon and Ruby. Maybe it would be better and more merciful if he just went to sleep and never woke up.

What am I thinking? That's not my decision to make.

"Alex." He was shuddering as if with a sudden fever. "I'm afraid to sleep. If I sleep, what will I find when I wake up?"

"You're just tired," she said. "You're hurt."

"I want to *die*," he said, fiercely. "If I had a gun, I'd b-blow my b-brains out. I would kill myself, but I'm a c-coward and now J-Jack . . ."

This time, as he wept, she held him. He still had plenty of tears.

Eventually, he relaxed in her arms, his body draining of tension. She sensed him drifting off and decided that sleep was a mercy. In her heart, she thought she knew why the Changed had kept him. She might be wrong. Maybe if she held onto him that would help.

Because nothing's written in stone. Look at me. She'd read it in her aunt's face and behind all her doctor's look-on-the-bright-side bluster: both were amazed she'd lasted as long as she had. By all rights, with the kind of monster living in her head, she ought to be dead. Whoever said "where there's life, there's hope" was spot on, though.

There was, however, one thing she *did* have to know. Because it might be important. A clue? A way to understand what was happening to her? She wasn't sure.

"Daniel?" she whispered. She saw his lids twitch. "Daniel, are you still awake?"

He muttered thickly. Beneath his lids, his eyes rolled. "Mmmm . . ."

She hitched up until her lips brushed his ear. "Daniel, you said they told you they'd let Jack go. How did you know that, Daniel? Did they speak to you?"

He didn't answer and didn't answer, and she thought it was too late, and he might already be asleep. Then a bedspring creaked as he stirred. "No," he murmured. His eyes were still closed, but his throat moved in a hard swallow, and his tongue skimmed his lips as he worked to speak. "I don't know." Pause. "Maybe."

Not really an answer. "What about smell? Is that how? Do you smell them? Daniel?" She stroked his cheek, reluctant to bring him back to the horror that sleep would take away, if only temporarily, but she *had* to know. "Daniel, what do you smell?"

This time, there was a long, *long* pause.

"You," he said.

47

According to Mickey, Slash dragged in to fetch her at seven. By then, the room had brightened, and through the slits of venetian blinds, Alex saw that it was still snowing. She'd slept on and off for perhaps five hours, mostly off. Her mind was just too full, the thoughts jumping from one to the next like crickets. As bad as she felt, she drew some small satisfaction from how Slash looked even rougher than usual: a hangover in motion, if those dark patches under the girl's reddened eyes were any indication.

Daniel didn't stir as Alex slid from the bed. She drew a quilt around his shoulders and laid a light hand on his forehead. No fever yet, but sweat greased his skin. Would the Changed let her come back? That was more likely than not. They wanted Daniel alive for the time being. She left the bottle of erythromycin where Daniel would see it when he awoke, just in case she was wrong about what Spider might have in store.

She followed Slash into the hall. The house was dead silent, but the choking fug of roadkill was stronger than ever from so many Changed in relatively tight quarters. Spider's door was closed, thank God. In the light of early morning, the photos on the display table gave off an enticing glimmer. She ached to study them. She eyed Slash shuffling a few paces ahead and thought, *Might not get another chance.*

Moving quickly, she slipped off her pack, tugged open the top, closed the gap, and then mock-stumbled one lurching step, then two. Slash grunted as Alex slammed into her back. Alex's supplies—pill bottles, packets of gauze and instruments, a roll of surgical tape, the plastic bottle of peroxide—bounced and skittered down the hall, and the two girls went down in a heap. Slash's shotgun rifle clattered, and Alex had just a second to think how lucky she was the thing hadn't gone off. Her knee gave a small shout as she banged against hardwood, but in another second, Slash cut a vicious slap that rang her ears, and then a scraped knee was the least of her problems.

"Cut it out!" With her good arm, she shoved the other girl, then shrank back, both hands up, palms out in surrender. "It was an accident, okay? It was an accident."

Slash was breathing hard, the irritation practically fuming from her pores. She'd retrieved that shotgun, and there was no mistaking from the way Slash's shoulders tensed that she'd be just as happy reducing Alex's head to mist. Alex didn't move, and she thought now that this had been a really dumb—and maybe her last—idea. Then Slash lowered the shotgun a smidge and backed away, the big girl's upper lip peeling back in a silent snarl.

Okay, so far so good. Her knee complained a little as she clambered to her feet, and she played up the limp. The knee really *did* hurt. She gathered her supplies thoroughly and slowly, which allowed time for her gaze to sweep the walls and that display table—and those photographs.

As it turned out, she'd risked getting plugged for nothing because, in the coming days, Alex would see and study these pictures more than once.

What she didn't and wouldn't know for another five minutes, although the lack of smoke chuffing from the guesthouse chimney ought to have been a clue, was that Sharon and Ruby were dead. Judging from the rigor—they were so stiff that it took Slash and Acne and a couple of Leopard's kids quite a while to jockey the bodies out of the guesthouse—they'd been dead for hours. How Sharon had done it was easy enough to parse. A smoggy chemical reek of vomit and half-digested painkillers and sleepers hung in a cloud, and small drifts of pills the women hadn't swallowed were scattered over the hardwood. Knowing Sharon, Alex thought the old woman had probably started just as soon as Alex was gone, doling out the pills like M&Ms: *one for you, two for me; two for you, four for me.* Alex could see it.

After that little debacle, Alex would be ensconced in Daniel's room. No one tied her to a chair or anything, but they didn't let her leave for long either, and then it was like that stuff she'd learned way back in elementary school about spiders that cocooned their prey to snack on for a rainy day.

But this was all in her future. Now, by the time she made it downstairs and was threading around morning-after bodies draped over chairs and sprawled on throw rugs, she knew a few things. Big things.

One: Judging from the resemblance, Wolf's mother's name had been Emily. The last time they'd all been at the summerhouse was four years ago this past August. That's what the photo said. So Wolf would've been thirteen or so.

Two: Wolf had grandparents. This wasn't news. Until now, she'd thought they were Jess and Yeager. But Jess wasn't in the picture. Instead, Yeager stood with a plump, small woman, with hair done in a platinum sweep, named Audrey. So if Jess was Wolf's grandmother, that raised all kinds of interesting questions.

Three: One photograph had not been taken at this lake house. She didn't know where, exactly, although she spotted what looked like, what? A cave? Or maybe just a cleft in a rock face; she couldn't be sure. There had been a party, though. She spotted a grill, discarded platters and cups and wrappers; a couple of kids clutched sodas and burgers.

The kids were arranged in the kind of haphazard groupings that signaled pecking order, who was tight with whom, who was on the outs. Later, when there was time, she would count forty-seven kids. Some she recognized as the same faces staring from those white ninja outfits Leopard's crew was so fascinated with. Others, she didn't have a clue. All were mugging for the camera, and someone had helpfully penned names in a tidy hand. That was how she learned that, pre-Zap, Spider's name had been Claire Krueger. Judging from that satisfied little smirk, she'd been on top of the heap even then. But it was the names and faces she knew best that clinched her suspicions about what Rule had been doing, and even why.

Acne was Ben Stiemke. Andrew Born would die within a day, but Alex knew him as Beretta. Slash was Beth Prigge—and pretty in her own right back then: thinner, not as sullen, and, most importantly, smooth-skinned. No scar, nothing slashed. For some reason, Alex's mind jumped to Wolf and that half moon on his neck where his skin had been flayed open from ear to throat. For the first time, she wondered if maybe the two scars were parts of the same story.

But it was the fourth thing that was, she later thought, the most telling and perhaps damning, because it explained so much.

There were two other kids—two boys—whose faces leapt into a kind of crystalline clarity. They'd shucked their shirts; this was summer, from the looks of all those bare legs and shoulders and midriffs, and probably very hot. The boys' arms were draped over one another's necks in that kind of clowning-around headlock guys got off on.

Because his chest was bare, she could see that his skin was smooth. No scars at all. She couldn't tell a thing about his neck because of that headlock, but she would lay odds that he hadn't tried filleting his flesh with that knife or, maybe, a dagger of razor-sharp glass. Just a hunch.

Back then, Wolf's name had been Simon.

Standing a little ways to the right were two very beautiful girls, both doubled over in laughter. Penny, the honey-blonde, was willowy and tall. The other girl was sloe-eyed and small, and her name was Amy? Anna? Amanda? The ink was smeary and she couldn't tell.

But it was the buddy—Wolf's friend, seemingly older by several years—that captured her attention. His hair had been shorter back then, but she would know that boy anywhere, and there was something . . . Her eyes clicked back and forth between the buddy and the pretty honey-blonde, Penny. Yes, the jaw, maybe, or the cut of her cheekbones or the eyes, but something made Alex think: *Sister?*

Whatever the case, Peter Ernst had known Simon Yeager, very well. From the looks of it, they might have loved one another like brothers.

The evidence was right there in neat black ink: Stiemke, Prigge, Born, Ernst, Yeager. The proof was built out of pyramids of skulls and the bones of the Banned. The story was written in blood. There was no mistake.

These Changed were the children and the grandchildren of Rule.

48

The night they left Rule—eight days after Alex ran and Peter disappeared—was a nightmare and nearly killed them. Even if Lena hadn't been ill and queasy, she still would have been in trouble almost from the beginning, and knew it. They all were. The snow kept coming, riding a vertical razor of wind. The maps were a waste of time. In the snow, landmarks blurred, and the trail was nothing more than a hope.

Then, four hours out of Rule and too few miles east, Lena's horse plunged through deep snow and into the well of a fallen spruce. Her skittish mount had been giving her trouble the whole time, rearing and dancing, bucking a few times, and, in general, being a nuisance. Lucky for her, she was hunkered down low and forward, her hands knotted in the animal's mane and her knees so high she was practically crouching on the saddle when the horse let out a shriek. She couldn't hear the snap over the churn of the wind but felt the sudden jolt. So she knew. She'd watched the same thing happen on Crusher Karl's farm. As the horse swooned to the snow, she launched herself from the saddle. If the horse rolled and pinned her, she might not get up again. There was a moment's dizzying flight, and then she plowed a good two feet into a deep drift. Chris had to brace his feet on either side of the hole to drag her out. By then, the horse was dead and Nathan was holstering his handgun.

No one rode after that. It was pitch-black, and they might be crazy, but they weren't suicidal. The wind was too strong to even attempt a tent unless one of them had a sudden urge to go parasailing. Instead, they bunched the horses, hobbling them close together, and then used the horses' bodies to block some of the wind as they zipped the bivies together and burrowed inside. She spent what remained of that first night sandwiched between Chris and Nathan, shivering hard enough to make her teeth chatter.

When the sky began to lighten, they slogged on through the storm, leading the horses, moving east. Weller had packed snowshoes only for Chris and Nathan, so she and Chris had to share. Eventually, Chris found a good spot on the lee side of a small hill. She used the snowshoes to tamp down powder as Chris and Nathan took turns with the shovel, one digging while the other scooped snow with his hands. Lena wasn't used to the work, and she was drenched with sweat and huffing in less than thirty minutes. After that, she couldn't stay warm. The wind was a stiletto. Her body heat leaked from her pores, and she was already weak from lack of food and sleep. She went from shivering to shuddering. A monstrous exhaustion grabbed her by the throat and just wouldn't let go. All she wanted was to curl up and sleep. So she sat down—only to rest. At least, that's what she told herself. She didn't remember lying down.

The next thing she knew, someone was shaking her, hard. She thought someone was shouting, but her thoughts were like wet watermelon seeds that kept slipping between her fingers no matter how hard she tried to hang on. She wasn't cold anymore, even though snow pecked her face. That was a relief.

"She can't sleep," Nathan said, but the older man's voice was gauzy and seemed very far away.

"I know that. She's all sweaty." Chris. "Maybe we should go back. I could try to find help."

"Might as well lie down and die then. You know the Council won't let this pass. Besides, you wouldn't get two miles without getting lost."

"You mean, more lost than we are already?" Chris snapped. Even through the strange fog settling over her mind, she heard his anger. "Come on," he said, giving her a rough shake. "You got to stay awake until this is finished."

"Screw off," she said, but her voice was colorless and wan. She was more tired than she'd ever been in her life.

"Damn it," Chris said, and then he slapped her face. Twice. Not hard, but enough that she gasped.

"Go away," she said, pushing at him with arms as limp as over-done noodles. "Just let me sleep."

"No." Chris dragged her to her feet. Her knees kept unhinging, and then she was sagging back to the snow. "Come on, wake up!" Chris shouted into her ear. "Get up! Do you want to die?"

No, she just wanted to sleep. She heard the sound of a zipper—nothing more than a soft hiss—and then Chris was drawing the sleeping bag up around her legs and over her body.

"That's not going to do much," Nathan said. "She's all wet. She'll soak the bag and then we're—"

The voices faded again. That was all right. She wasn't that interested. Instead, her mind drifted off like a bit of dandelion fluff. Or maybe she just passed out.

She came to as someone manhandled her to sit. The stink of something sweet slapped her nose. Her stomach turned over.

"Drink it." She recognized Chris's voice. "Come on, it'll warm you up."

"Noooo," she moaned, and then she felt something hot and sickly sweet against her lips and then in her mouth. She flailed, but Chris jerked the cup back in time to avoid scalding them both. "Ow," she said. Her tongue felt parboiled. "What is that?"

"Hot chocolate." Chris had one arm around her, and was bracing her up with a knee. "We got enough of a windbreak from the hill and the snow that I fired up the camp stove. Come on," he said, bringing the cup back to her lips. "Drink."

The chocolate smell made her queasy, but Chris insisted. She choked down a mouthful and then another and kept it up until the cup was empty. Her stomach did a slow somersault, then decided to stay put. Little by little, either because of the sugar or the warmth, she started to wake up. She saw that the day was brighter now, although the snow was still falling in a thick, billowing curtain. Off to her right, the two remaining horses were dark blurs in a clutch of hemlock and pine.

"Wow." She burped, then grimaced at sour bile and gluey cocoa. She turned aside and spat. "That's a lot of snow."

"Yeah. Nathan says he's never seen it this bad."

"Where is he?"

Chris inclined his head to the left. "Smoothing out the snow cave and cutting in some steps so we don't fall. We're almost done. Come on," he said, stripping the sleeping bag from her legs and then hooking his arms under hers. "Let's get you inside."

The entrance was a hole maybe three feet in diameter. The tunnel, troughed out of snow, was dark and seemed very long and just wide enough for her to squirm in on her back. For a second, she froze in place. The snow was only inches from her nose and she couldn't breathe. The tunnel seemed to collapse around her, growing smaller and smaller.

"Come on." Nathan's voice drifted down. "It widens up once you get all the way through."

She pushed herself in the rest of the way. She wasn't sure what she expected, but the cave was small, maybe eight feet long and not very high, leaving only enough room for them to shamble around.

"Up here." Nathan knelt on a wide shelf about two feet from the floor. He'd covered the shelf with the tent and then positioned a sleeping bag on top of that. Most of the gear was stacked on the platform as well. It was very dim inside, but she could see that the cave arched overhead with just enough clearance for them to sit comfortably.

She clambered up the steps Nathan had cut in the snow. Now that she was out of the wind, she realized that she wasn't as cold anymore. She wasn't toasty, but she was no longer freezing. "How come there are two levels?"

"Heat rises." Nathan was working a stout branch in and out of one of two holes punched in the roof. "We'll stay warm enough up here. There'll be some melt, but as long as we keep the gear dry, we should be okay."

She turned as Chris shouldered his way through the tunnel and into the cave. Turtling onto his back, he positioned a saddlebag and one of the empty packs across the entrance, leaving a gap of half a foot. "Here." He handed her the sleeping bag he'd dragged in after him. "Spread that out. I don't think it got too wet, and you need to get out of those clothes."

"And into what?" she said.

Chris had worked his hunting knife from its scabbard, and now he aimed the tip at a small stack of clothes on the platform next to the rest of their gear. "You can wear some of my stuff. It won't be the best fit, but it's dry."

"Ah." She looked around. "Where should I change?"

"What you see is what there is," Nathan said, with just the faintest trace of amusement. "You can strip down in the bag, put your clothes on the same way."

Her cheeks heated, but Nathan was already working his stick into the adjacent hole, and Chris was plunging his knife into the snow near the entrance. Neither looked at her. After unlacing her boots, she grabbed up the clothes—camouflage pants, a fresh set of long underwear, socks, a long-sleeved black tee, a green scarf and matching sweater—and then ducked down in the bag until only her head showed. Working quickly, she stripped off her damp socks, her jeans, the sodden thermal pants, and then, after a moment's hesitation, her underpants. *Might as well go all the way.* She hitched up her butt and started working her legs into the silk drawers. "What are you doing?"

"Notching out space for the stove." Chunking out a square with the knife, Chris stamped the snow flat with his boot. "This way, it vents to the outside and any melt is down here, not up there with us."

She was swimming in Chris's camo pants, but they were nylon and fleece-lined, with a drawstring closure and elastic around the ankles. Most importantly, they were dry. Still deep in the bag, she shucked her shirt and silk top and unhooked her bra, then pulled on the dry silk shirt. "What about the horses?"

"They'll be all right," Nathan said. "Lucky for us, we haven't blanketed them much, so they got good winter coats. Long as they keep their butts to the wind and stay in the trees, they'll be fine."

"What about food?"

He hooked a thumb over his shoulder. "There's feed in the saddlebags. That runs out, we'll strip bark."

"We can stay here that long?" She slipped on the sweater, then pulled her long hair free and began to finger-comb the tangles.

"We'll stay as long as we have to," Nathan said as Chris swarmed up the snow steps. With the three of them, the fit was tight, but there was enough room to lie flat and turn. "This is one helluva blow. Storms like this get stalled around Superior, and then we could be in for four, five days. Even if the snow quits, unless the wind dies down, we'll have to stay put. That windchill will kill you just as fast. So we could be here a while."

"Won't they come after us?" she asked.

"Probably not," he said. "Even if we didn't have Weller to make sure Rule keeps looking in all the wrong places, no one is crazy enough to come after us in this weather."

"But *we're* out here."

Nathan shrugged. "Like I said."

They were stuck in that snow cave four miserable days, which was, Lena thought, about three and a half days too long. With no privacy and nothing to do but think, she was starting to go a little crazy. Her head was really no place she liked living very long, and her dreams were so bad she kept jolting awake, convinced she'd been talking in her sleep. Or screaming. Neither Chris nor Nathan ever mentioned it, but she'd caught the old man turning a quizzical eye her way more than once. For the most part, Chris just kept to himself and simmered. Which meant things were awfully quiet.

On the morning of the fifth day, Nathan squirmed through the tunnel and said, "Blow's over. Pack up. I'll get the horses ready."

"Thank God," Lena said as Nathan ducked out again. Rolling to a sit, she had to hold herself still a moment and wait for the wave of nausea to pass. Weird. Her stomach still wasn't settling; she'd managed broth but very little else. Too long to be the flu, and no one else was sick.

Could it be her period? Maybe. The problem was, she had no way of knowing. When she was thirteen, her pediatrician had put her on birth control pills for her periods, which were irregular and

so ghastly she understood why it was called the curse. She sometimes wondered if the pills were the reason Crusher Karl dared.
No inconvenient little pregnancies to try and explain away.

She'd told no one about the pills, and certainly not Jess. What
was the point? Once the world crashed, no one was going to be
churning out birth control pills anytime soon, that was for sure.
She had no way of getting more anyway. Now that she was off, she
didn't know what to expect. She'd thought her periods would start
right up again after the first month, but nothing.

*So maybe that's why I don't feel well. Maybe this is what happens
after you've been on the pill for a long time.* Which would be just so her
luck to have the world's worst case of PMS. Stifling a sigh, she slid
off the platform, grabbed up one of the backpacks, and started
stuffing in gear. She eyed Chris, who was working over a sleeping
bag, and said, "Are you going to keep this up forever?"

His back stiffened, but he didn't look round. "Keep what up
forever?"

"Oh, come on, Chris. You haven't said three paragraphs in four
days. I know you're pissed. You might feel better if you talked
about it."

"Lena." Chris slid his sleeping bag into its carry sack and jerked
the drawstring tight. "Just let it go, okay?"

"No," she said. Chris muttered something she couldn't quite
catch. "I'm sorry?"

"Nothing."

"*What?*"

"God!" He pitched the sleeping bag toward the tunnel. "You

always *push* things. Can't you just leave me alone? There is nothing to discuss. This is not about you, okay? For once?"

That stung. "But it is. You're here because of me. Because you wouldn't, you know, *tell* that I was the one who told you about the kids still around Oren."

"Ratting you out to my grandfather wouldn't have made a difference. He'd made his mind up before he even walked in the room. Of course, it didn't help that I told him to go to hell." Chris gave a bitter laugh. "My big stand. Let it go, Lena. It was my choice to keep going back."

"But I shouldn't have kept pushing you." There was a quick twinkle of pain as her teeth worried skin from her lower lip. "If you'd only stuck with Peter and the others . . ."

"I'd be dead, too. And Alex would still—" His throat moved in a hard swallow. He looked away again. "Anyway."

"Chris." She put a tentative hand on his arm. His flesh jumped, and she half-expected him to shake her off, but he didn't. "You don't know that she's dead."

"I'd like to believe that. The thing is, I don't see how she can be alive, not if Weller and the others are right. Even if they were wrong, it's been, what, twelve days now? And snowing for the last four? The only reason we've done okay is all that gear Weller scrounged. Alex had nothing but a rifle and a backpack."

"She's pretty smart."

"Alex is good, but she's one person, and her ammunition wouldn't last forever. Lena, it would take incredible luck for her to avoid the Changed. She must've run into them by now."

"Or maybe not. Weller said they were just guessing. You heard them. Not one of those guys has set foot outside the Zone."

"I'd say it's a pretty damned good guess, though." A long pause, and then he raised his eyes. The skin beneath them was darker than coal, and the whites were bloodshot with pain and, she thought, regret. "I think I always knew, Lena. About what was outside the Zone, I mean. Why we didn't need to post as many guards, why raiders never seemed to come from that direction. If I'd given it two seconds' thought, I'd have seen it. Hell." He let out a bleak laugh. "Peter pretty much laid it out for me. He made sure we steered clear. If Rule's the center of a watch, then this big region, from seven o'clock to eleven, is crawling with the Changed—and Peter saw to it that we went through only at very specific times. It doesn't get any more obvious than that, Lena."

"Look, it's easy to realize this, you know, in hindsight. But, Chris, the world died, okay? People dropped, for God's sake. Peter was doing the best he could. He was trying to take care of us."

"There were plenty of other ways. He didn't have to go this route. I just wish I understood *why*. Because I don't get that. What *made* Peter think this was a good idea?"

"You don't know that it was his idea." That sounded weak even to her ears, and she added, "Maybe he was just following orders."

"Well, they were terrible orders, and he shouldn't have gone along with them."

"That is so lame, I can't stand it," she snapped. "*You've* followed orders. You did what Peter said. You let your grandfather enforce the Ban; you didn't complain when Peter and the Council decided who got to stay and who got turned away."

His cheeks went hectic with color. "That . . . that was different."

"How? Because *those* orders weren't *terrible*, just bad?"

"Jesus, you don't think I've thought about that? *God*." He pulled his arm from beneath her hand and knotted his fists in his hair. "How could I have been so *stupid*? There were all these signs I decided to ignore. Like when that guy, Harlan, the one who had Alex's stuff and shot her friend, Tom, and all that . . . when my grandfather threw Harlan out, I knew the chances were pretty good he'd die out there. I was fine with that. He'd hurt Alex. I thought, okay, dude, sucks to be you."

"All that means is you cared about Alex. She got hurt, you were pissed."

"Lena, it's not like someone dissed her in the cafeteria. I decided it was fine for Harlan to *die*. And I had a pretty good idea how it was going to happen, too. We all know the Changed are out there. I just didn't know they were *there*-there; that Peter had this system going, and it was right in front of me, the whole time. Like, a couple times, Peter split off by himself. You know, the same way I would go to Oren? He'd take a wagon with supplies and just leave—and always around the same general areas. He'd come back, and the wagon would be empty. When I asked where all the supplies went, he wouldn't say. I mean, it was *obvious* he was giving food away, and I just let it go."

"Chris," Lena said. "You couldn't have known."

"Only because I chose not to." Chris's lips twisted as if the words had curdled on his tongue. "*That* makes me just as guilty. But Peter's gone now, and I *do* know. Someone's got to be responsible, Lena. Someone has to try and make this right. The only way to do that is tear it all down. The way Rule runs, I'm the only one left who can."

His jaw set in a new, hard line she had never seen before and would not have thought possible. This steeliness would have looked at home on Peter, who saw the world in black and white. Chris was different, though. He was, she thought, the closest thing she had to a friend. But she didn't recognize this stranger taking shape before her eyes, the way his skin had drawn so tight she could see his skull, or the fury that nipped her nose like pepper. This was not the boy with a good heart who had risked so much to find her little brother.

"Chris." Her tongue was so dry she felt as if she was talking around a mouthful of dust. "Chris, you're talking about *war*."

"Yeah," Chris said. "I guess I am."

49

After they left the snow cave, the day only got worse. The snow was too deep for the horses. Weller's roan had studs, but the sorrel didn't, and it was a small horse besides. Nathan cut up a shirt to wrap around both horses' fetlocks and cannons, but it came down to walking. With only two sets of snowshoes, one person had to ride the roan, which Chris thought ought to be her. From the look on his face, Lena knew Nathan wasn't wild about that. "We already lost one horse," he said.

"That wasn't my fault," she said.

The look Nathan wore suggested he thought otherwise, but then he nodded. "Okay. I was going to lead it to break trail anyway."

"I'll lead," Chris said.

"You know, I can be in charge of my own stupid reins," Lena said, but the roan seemed to be no happier to have her on its back than the horse Nathan had been forced to shoot. Chris finally snatched at the horse's bridle, but Lena had barely boosted onto the saddle when the roan began to buck. "Cut it out," Lena said, and gave the reins a vicious twist. "*Quit* it."

"Stop yanking the reins," Nathan said. "Give it its mouth."

"I know how to handle a stupid *horse*," Lena shot back.

"Yeah, I saw how good you did the last time," Nathan returned, and then sighed and flapped a hand. "Fine. Suit yourself. I'm not going to argue. Let's just go before we lose more daylight."

Fuming, Lena watched Nathan flounder back to his gelding with their packs. Chris said, "Don't let him get to you."

"The horse wasn't my fault," Lena said, although even she knew she hadn't handled the animal well. The roan had quieted a little, but stood blowing and quivering. She could feel the roan's hide trying to flinch away from her legs, as if she were a noisome fly it just couldn't get rid of. Maybe it sensed she was sick. Could horses know something like that? God, she hoped this passed soon and everyone could settle down.

But that did not happen. After an hour, she had to slip off the roan and duck into the woods. Her stomach emptied itself in heaves, not only of a measly half of a power bar she'd forced down before leaving the cave but of the broth from that morning and whatever else she hadn't managed to digest—which, she thought, might be everything.

After, she hung, jackknifed over the snow, her gloved hand clutching a spindly aspen. She'd waded well into the woods and behind a screen of hemlock, so she didn't think Nathan or Chris could see. A ball of sour mucus jumped into her mouth, and she spat. God, she had never had PMS like this. Cramps, yes, and some vomiting, but she'd never been so sick for so long. Could you get withdrawal or something from birth control pills? Hell, she didn't know. Unless . . .

No. She closed her eyes against the idea as much as the nausea. *No, God, come on, that's so unfair. We only did it twice. That's not fair.*

"Lena?" Chris called from beyond the trees. "Are you okay?"

"Yeah," she managed. "Just a sec."

Maybe I'll fall again, she thought as she boosted herself back onto the prancing, complaining roan. *Or maybe riding will do it. There's got to be something I can take or do; there's got to be something.*

Someone had to know what she could do. If she ever saw him again, she might even ask Kincaid. She could tell Chris, because he *was* a good person and he would want to help. Yeah, but he had enough on his plate. She'd be just one more problem for which he'd feel responsible. Better to wait until she was sure. No use jumping the gun. It wasn't like Chris could do anything about it now anyway.

"Hey." She looked down to see Chris, the roan's reins in one hand and a look of concern on his face. "Lena, you going to be okay?"

"Oh, sure," she lied. "No problem."

But what she thought was: *Oh, Peter. I think I'm in so much trouble.*

50

He knew *H-Q* and *C-Y*: *headquarters* and, probably, *Chucky*. The rest meant nothing to him. But even if Peter hadn't understood Morse code, he was getting good at reading Finn's moods, and that black look was story enough.

"B-b-bad . . ." His throat, already dry, closed down almost immediately, and he began to hack in great, shuddering heaves. Every breath felt as if someone had slipped stilettos between his ribs.

He'd been a prisoner going on twelve days. They'd only started feeding him horse-pills a day and a half ago, which he'd hoped would knock out the pneumonia. But now he thought he was getting worse. Whatever they were injecting into him probably wasn't doing him any favors either. Judging from the colors—sickly yellow, chalk-white, liverish brown—the injections might be killing him that much faster. Peter spat a thick, green gob of phlegm and chunky mucus into an emesis basin already a third full of the same goo. To his complete lack of surprise, he saw streaks of bright red blood. His fever was spiking again, too. He was burning up and shivering at the same time. What amazed him was that his bullet wound was actually healing, the bruises shading to a mottled green and yellow.

Exhausted from his coughing jag, he fell back against his sweat-soaked pillow and tried again. "B-bad n-n-news?"

"Let's just say that you'll be our only normal guest for a while." Finn looked at Grier. "Can he be moved?"

"I . . . uh . . ." Grier was a tiny, elfish man with bad myopia. Plucking up the emesis basin, Grier gave it a swirl, squinted at the mess, shrugged, and said, "Couldn't hurt."

"Good." Finn snapped his fingers at Steiner, the newest guard. Two days ago, Peter had seen his chance and gone after Lang. Peter had only gotten a few precious seconds, but that was all he needed. After the mincemeat he'd made of Lang's face, they slapped Peter back in ankle and wrist restraints. That was all right. Beating the shit out of Lang had been worth it. Peter just wished Weller had been around, too. "Take him," Finn ordered. "But get him some warm clothes first."

Steiner and two other guards returned with a bundle of clothes that were identical to their own: olive pants and a shirt, socks and underwear, a thick sweater, and even a camouflage parka and watch cap. They gave him back his old boots, which were blotchy with rust-colored stains of blood: his, Fable's, Tyler's. Peter was so weak his fingers shook as he tried working the buttons, and Steiner had to do it for him.

"Wh-where," he wheezed, "are y-you . . ."

"Can't say," Steiner muttered, but Peter saw the fine film of sweat start on the guard's upper lip. "You might still do okay," the old man said.

"What?" He twisted his head around until he found Grier standing a few feet away, his hands in the deep pockets of his doctor's coat. "Why?"

"Not up to me," Grier said. His voice was like a caricature of a cranky old farmer, the kind with steel-rimmed specs and a long-tined hayfork. "I got nothing to do with this."

Still, it never occurred to him to be afraid. He didn't think they would execute him; Finn thought he was valuable, and Peter was certain he hadn't seen the last of Finn's little experiments. So he didn't fight. Then again, he didn't have the strength. His legs were so wobbly that Steiner and the other guard pretty much carried him from the tent.

This was Peter's first time out of the infirmary. If he were well, he'd be scanning right and left, memorizing the layout just in case. After four days, the storm finally seemed to be spinning itself out, although snow was still coming down. He couldn't see much: a handful of sagging tents; a few sturdier-looking, snow-mantled huts. A black wall of trees behind a gauzy drape of blowing snow. It occurred to him that he didn't know whether he was still in Michigan. A long storm usually meant a stall, which happened around the Great Lakes all the time. He'd been pretty far gone when they found him, so they still might be relatively close to Rule, but he doubted it, and his surroundings gave him no clue. He caught the steady chug of a generator, and from the thumps, he thought there might be two more to his right, out of sight.

The guards dragged him left and down a semi-cleared path hemmed on either side by dense evergreen forest. They trudged through snow for what felt like a long time. The generator thump faded almost completely. Ahead, the path flared. A dark wood cabin, the sturdy kind made of Lincoln logs, hunched in a clearing. The cabin was a perfect but very long rectangle with two stone chimneys trickling gray smoke. The windows were shuttered. A black lattice of iron bars had been fixed to the apron of each with a thick layer of cement. Two guards manned the door. Each had an assault rifle: M4s and illegal as hell when laws had mattered. He had a feeling Finn had been making his own rules for a long time.

Steiner nodded at one of the guards, who turned, rapped on the front door, and waited. A second later, an eye-level window set in the door brightened. Peter saw the quick white flash of a face. There was the rattle of hardware as whoever was inside threw back a bolt.

The stink that ballooned out—feces, old urine, and stale flesh—was bad enough to make even Steiner's eyes water. They crowded in: Steiner on his right, the second guard on his left. They were met by two more guards, both of whom wore handguns and expandable batons in a slide sidebreak scabbard. Judging from the dings, those batons saw a lot of use.

The space inside was much larger than he'd expected. The design wasn't all that different from every other jail he'd ever visited. To the left, a plain wooden desk and two chairs for the duty-guards squatted behind floor-to-ceiling iron bars. A fire crackled in a deep hearth behind a wrought-iron screen.

To the right were cells: five to a side, ten total. The cells were simple, barred cages, each with a drain that must lead to a septic tank. No one had taken a hose to that concrete in a long time, though. Piles of shit—some very new and some so old they'd desiccated to stone—were everywhere.

The Changed were crouched there, too. He recognized the kids from the infirmary. Davey was the only Changed with any kind of clothing, and that just a dingy pair of tighty-whiteys. He wore a collar around his neck, too: black leather, with shiny D-rings right and left, and a small padlock. As they entered, Davey's head swiveled. A moment later, the other Changed turned and lifted their heads, the better to sample the air. As one, they unfolded from their squats in a silent, eerie synchrony that made the hairs rise on Peter's neck and arms.

Nine Changed. Ten cells.

And bones. Lots of little bones. Fingers. Toes. Vertebrae. Some teeth.

"N-no." Fear bolted up his throat. He was already drenched with sweat, but now a new wet oozed and trickled over his ribs. He tried to fight. Even with panic to lend him strength, he was no match for all those guards.

"Stop," one said. The muzzle of an M4 dug into the back of Peter's head. "We won't kill you, but we'll mess you up. Don't make this harder than it has to be."

No, mess me up, Peter thought, crazily. *Pull the trigger. Please, kill me now.* But his body wouldn't listen, and he froze. He just couldn't move. He understood what a very small rabbit must feel when a fox is near.

"Pl-please." He was shaking so badly he heard the hard tick of his teeth. His eyes rolled and fixed on Steiner. *"N-n-n-no."*

"I'm sorry, boy," Steiner said, not unkindly. "But really, I'd save my strength if I was you."

51

Four days after Jed's house went up in flames and two days shy of the Michigan border, Tom found bones.

He'd stayed to the woods and avoided roads. The few long-abandoned homes and farmsteads he gave a very wide berth. So he knew these people hadn't just wandered out for a stroll. Judging from the size of the skulls, some were very young, only children as well as a few babies. Many had been dead a good long while, the bones like ivory against the snow. But a surprising number still had meat, frozen hard as rock, and that wasn't right. A brutal winter meant plenty of hungry animals. Gnaw long enough, and there was dinner. Apparently, scavengers wouldn't eat a Chucky's leavings either.

What *really* bothered him: the bones shouldn't be visible. He was chasing the storm, and the snow was fresh but also trampled by prints so new he made out treads and the make of the boots.

They must be coming back to the same spots to feed. At the realization, he felt the air leave his lungs. The Chuckies were like animals returning to a den or dogs that hid bones beneath a particular tree—and they were in the woods, *with* him.

Well, Tom thought, *no help for it. Just be careful.*

That awful night on Odd Lake, the dog had saved his life, nudging and pawing him back to consciousness. It took him a while, but he'd finally rolled over and slithered on his belly, snaking over the ice, using his knife as a pick, every crack and creak sending his heart crowding against his teeth. By the time he made it back to the wind sled, his clothes were boards, and the dog's fur was chunked with ice. He changed right there, stripping out of his frozen jeans and socks and shirt and thermals, even his underwear. His parka was in the water, at the bottom of the lake with that old bounty hunter. After dragging on an extra set of thermals and doubling up with just about every scrap of clothing he owned, he'd shaken out a black contractor's bag and carefully slit the thick, tough plastic to make an opening large enough for his head. Throw in a shopping cart, and he'd look ready to hunker down around a trash barrel fire under an overpass with the rest of the homeless, which was pretty close to the truth.

He and the dog spent the night huddled together in his bivy at the bottom of a snow pit in the woods and out of the wind. He didn't want to risk a fire or the stove, but he made hot chocolate from MREs, using meltwater for the heater pack, and gave the dog warm water to drink. They even slept.

The hunter came at first light, as Tom knew he would. It's what he would've done. Rounding the jink on foot, the hunter stood there a good long time, scanning the far shore through binoculars, twisting slowly back and forth. Tom and the dog were well back, swathed in the sleeping bag and hunkered down in the trees. On the ice, Tom spotted the cigar shape of the wind sled lying where he'd left it and, beyond, the darker gap that was the break in the ice. If he was lucky, the hunter would think he'd gone through, too.

Eventually, the bounty hunter moved off. Tom waited another hour according to Jed's Timex. He heard nothing but the susurration of the wind and saw even less. Finally, he decided he would just have to chance it.

First, he hid the wind sled, dragging the craft off the ice and then through the woods for a long, long way until he came to a tumble of boulders at the base of an esker. The stones butted up to form a cave. Flipping the Spitfire onto its side, he shoved the boat through the wedge-shaped opening, remembering—too late—that this was black bear country. But nothing came out to eat him. A good omen, maybe.

If the hunter came back—and he would; that sled was worth something—one look and he'd know Tom was still alive. A gamble, but one Tom had to take. No telling if or when that sled would come in handy, but he wanted it safe, where he could find it again, just in case.

There was also no way he was leaving Jed for scavengers or, worse, the Chuckies if they wandered through. Maybe it was stupid and a waste of time when he should be running, but he covered Jed's head, shouldered the Bravo, and dragged his friend all the way back up the hill.

The cabin was a ruin: a skeleton of scorched timber and charred debris floating on a gray moat of refrozen snow and ash. Stepping carefully, he started from the fireplace and worked his way in a rough diagonal until he found the bodies. There were three: blackened limbs tucked and crimped, like babies in a womb, as the tendons cooked, fleshless lips revealing too-white teeth in eyeless skulls. Despite that, Grace was easy to identify because she was small and the only body with the charry remains of an apron and a gold diamond wedding band.

He laid the two of them together at a pretty spot overlooking the lake—and then paused, staring at Jed as Raleigh nosed the body and whined. Tom had no parka; Jed still did. Just thinking it over made him guilty and ashamed, but he *did* need the jacket and Jed was past caring. Hell, the old man would probably insist.

"I'm sorry," he said. Getting the zipper down through all that iced gore took some time. Tugging it off Jed's stiff, frozen body was worse. Tom had to roll him like a log from side to side to work the parka free. The jacket was too big and smelled of Jed and blood, but it would do. Then, using bricks and stone from the fireplaces, he fashioned a low cairn. He worried the stones might not be deep enough, but he did the best he could.

Jed once explained why a Marine sniper called his weapon a Kate. The name had nothing to do with a girl. *Kate* meant "Kill All The Enemy."

Tom spread his hand over the tomb's cold stone.

"I can do that," he said.

* * *

Their patient, standardbred mare stood in the woods next to the garage that Jed had transformed into a makeshift stable. Left alone, Dixie would starve to death. The other, Grace's Shetland, had panicked and leapt from the cliff to shatter on the rocks below. Although that pony had to be dead, he shouldered the Bravo and climbed all the way down to make sure. No way he'd leave her to suffer.

Thankfully, Jed stored the horses' feed and Raleigh's food in the stable and not the cabin's cellar. He scooped hay pellets and oats into saddlebags, dumped dog kibble into a canvas carryall. Wisconsin was a four- or five-day walk in good weather, a week or more in bad. A horse would be faster, but follow the main roads and he'd be asking for trouble. Where there was one hunter, there would be others. He was bounty, and worth killing for. So he'd have to stick to the woods, and that meant more time and added distance. No straight shots.

Despite what Jed said, he'd had no intention of seeking out a soul. Look where helping *him* had gotten Jed and Grace. He didn't want to be responsible for any more death. But now he had to factor in the animals. While his supplies would last two weeks, the animals would run out of food well before then. Hell, another storm and even he'd be in big trouble.

In the stable, he drew out Jed's list and the maps as Raleigh nosed in to be fussed over. There were three names, evenly spaced, like pearls, between here and the border, and a fourth in Michigan. By then, he might not have a choice but to stop. Sighing, he folded the list and slid it into one of the parka's inside pockets. *Damned if I do, damned if I don't.*

Moaning, the dog laid its chin in his lap. "Yeah, I know, boy. It'll be okay. Come on." He ruffled the dog's ears. "Let's go see about a girl."

Now, after four days on the road, he was still in Wisconsin, traveling beneath the bilious glow of a crescent moon.

Too slow. He ripped open an MRE of Mexican mac and cheese. With the possibility of Chuckies in the woods, a fire was out. Slopping water into the heater pouch, he slid in the MRE, then tucked both back into the cardboard container. *Almost out of feed for the horse.* He set the box up so the chemicals could work their magic. *She might eat bark, but—*

At his side, Raleigh suddenly bristled. The dog let out one very small *wuff* which it choked off almost immediately, as if realizing that making any noise at all was a big mistake.

Tom knew, in an instant. *Oh shit.* He had a moment to be thankful that he had not started a fire. A glance at Dixie showed that the mare's eyes had gone pearly with terror. She was chuffing. *Please, be still*, he pleaded, silently, stretching for Jed's Bravo. The rifle was already chambered, and he eased back on the safety, wincing a bit at the soft rasp of metal.

He listened, ears straining. Nothing. No sound. The moon's gangrenous glow turned the snow deep pewter, barely distinguishable from the darker trees. His breath clouds were tangled gray webs. He let go of another, longer breath, blowing as if through a straw, watching where it moved. Off to his left, and Raleigh was staring right. So he was downwind.

Good. If these things go by smell, I might be okay.

Something rustled. Tom's heart jumped like a hooked fish.

A whisper of snow and then a thud. Footsteps. Another thud.

Not snowshoes, he decided. So there must be a well-traveled trail he hadn't seen. He pivoted right, from the waist, slotting the rifle so his cheek rested against the stock. He let his eyes drift off-center, the better to see in the moon's ashen glow.

Two shadows ghosted through the trees not fifty yards away. Both had long hair, and he thought the smaller, slighter one might be a girl. Her right hand clutched a stubby rifle, maybe something with a pistol grip. The larger one was broad and very big across the shoulders like a linebacker in full gear. Then the boy Chucky made a misstep, staggered—and suddenly sprouted a third arm.

Oh my God. Gooseflesh pebbled his skin. *They've got a body.*

Stooping, the boy hefted the body, shrugging it back onto his shoulders, grunting a little at the weight. Now that he understood, Tom could see that the body had only the one arm, the right. The left ended in a blacker-than-black hole at the shoulder joint.

Then the head fell back, and the dead girl's long hair fanned away from her face—

Alex. Horror blasted through his mind. *Alex?*

Turning, the girl Chucky raised her rifle to her mouth—and tore off a bite.

Not a rifle.

An arm. The girl ripped at the meat. Her jaws worked, and in the gleam of that sick light, he saw the white ripple of her throat as she swallowed.

No. NO. Tom felt the earth suddenly split beneath his feet, and then he was falling and falling and he would never stop, never, and Alex . . . and Alex . . . and *Alex* and—

"NO!" he screamed. His finger convulsed. The night broke apart with a roar. A tongue of orange flame shot through the dark like a comet. Behind, he heard the horse bray in alarm. The girl's head vanished in an instant, but the explosion lingered in purple afterimages burned onto his retina: her skull bursting in a chunky halo.

Pivoting, already adjusting, he shot the Bravo's bolt and fired again. Another roar. In the bright muzzle flash, he saw the boy, caught as if in a strobe, half-turned, his mouth open in a look of stupid shock—and then the bullet drilled into his chest and he went down.

As the roar died, he heard the dog barking. Dixie was still rearing, screaming, trying to tear from her tether, her front legs jackhammering the snow.

Alex! In the next second, he was lurching as snow grabbed his feet and whippy twigs slapped his face. Air tore in and out of his lungs. The dog churned alongside, working so hard to keep up it had no breath to bark. Perhaps ten yards away, his feet registered the sudden change in the snow. He stumbled out on a path already broken and tamped down with repeated use. Ahead, he saw all three: the body, the Chucky with no head, and the boy. He spotted the half-eaten arm, too.

"Alex," he said, brokenly. *"Alex."* He fell to his knees by the dead girl with only one arm. She was facedown, her long hair dragging

over black, bloodied snow. Reaching out with one palsied hand, he
eased her over.

"Ah, God." Not a girl. Not even close. In the bad light, he couldn't
tell how old she'd been, but the woman's cheeks were weathered.
Her hair was the color of gravel and dragged from a large flap
of scalp peeled from forehead to crown, revealing skull that was
smooth as a cue ball. Her nose had been gnawed away to bone.
The eyes, too.

Oh Christ, oh God, oh shit. He was gasping. Sweat poured down
his neck; he could feel his clothes sticking to the skin of his back
and chest. And he was weeping, too: huge, ripping sobs of relief.
Stop, stop, stop! He tore off a glove, jammed a fist into his mouth,
bit down until his teeth sawed through and his mouth went coppery with blood. *Stop, you've got to stop. It's not her; it's all right to be
happy that it's not her, but you've got to—*

Then. The boy. Coughed.

More gurgled, actually. Tom heard the boil and splash of blood
and a hissing rush of air with every breath the boy drew.

That sound sobered him in a way nothing else could. Live
through enough firefights, see enough buddies go down, and any
soldier recognized a sucking chest wound when he heard one.
With every breath, the boy pulled air into his chest. Eventually,
the pressure would stop his heart unless the boy bled out first,
which he just might.

He could end this. Tom stared down at the boy. A bullet to the
brain; a quick slice across the carotids. Either would be the merciful thing, the right thing. Or, hell, he could try to save him. Well,

in theory. He knew what to do. Every soldier did. Any soldier could.

There is no right. His mind was burned white, hot as a neutron star. *There are no laws and there is no god. There is only here and now, and what I do next . . . what I do next . . .*

The boy's eyes were dark pits, and his face was gray. A black viscous pool was spreading beneath his body, leaking over the snow. The boy coughed again. Blood boiled onto his lips and ran over his chin to dribble down his neck.

I can't save you. He slid his knife from its sheath. *Not even I can justify that.*

Tom tugged open the boy's parka. The Chucky didn't resist but only stared with eyes as dark and shiny as polished obsidian. The boy's blood smelled of sweet iron. The bullet had cored midway down the right side of the boy's chest. Straddling the boy, Tom slid his knife just beneath the sternum, then up and left. The muscles parted easily, and he went as fast as he could. Still, the boy flinched and Tom hesitated.

He could do this. The pommel ticked against his palm in time with the boy's heart. He had to do this.

The boy's gaze locked on his. His lips moved.

"No, don't," Tom said, and then he rammed the knife home, pierced the heart through, and gave the blade a savage twist.

A tick.

Another tick.

Tick.

Nothing.

The boy stared. And stared.

The dog growled, and that brought him back. "No, Raleigh," Tom said. Taking back his knife, he plunged it into the snow until the blade was clean.

Then he got the hell out of there as fast as he could.

Two days later, he was in Michigan.

52

Venus was a hard diamond in the east. The air was dry as dust and going crackly with cold as the light drained from the sky. It would be dark pretty soon. But Tom had to think this one through. Once done, he couldn't undo it.

Through the Bravo's scope, he studied the farm from a screen of new birch and thick hemlock at the very edge of a wide, sloping, snow-covered field. The two-story farmhouse was solid, native stone with gable dormers, but looked to be in need of some serious work. The limp tongue of an American flag hung from a very tall flagpole mounted on a rise to the right. Thin, haggard smoke dribbled from a single, moth-eaten chimney that had lost its cap and teetered like a stack of kids' blocks ready to fall with the touch of a finger. A low woodpile butted against a fenced-in rectangle that must be a vegetable garden. The ax-half of a sturdy splitting maul leaned against a pile of uncut rounds. To the left of the garden, a dead truck showed as a glint of windshield peering from humped snow, and at the end of a sinuous path stood three garbage-can-green Porta-Johns.

A cluster of outbuildings hunched beyond a wide, unbroken expanse—a road leading to the farm, probably, but one that hadn't seen traffic in months. Of the two barns, a peaked gray prairie barn had seen better days, too; the southwest corner of the roof had caved in. In a paddock of trampled snow, a lone horse and solitary cow drooped over an old cast-iron, white-enameled bathtub while a trio of goats and six chickens drifted and scratched around a stone trough. Left of the prairie barn was a much smaller stable with sliders, and a longer, low concrete building running north-south with some kind of metal feeder silo. Adjacent to that, five enormous hogs huddled in an outdoor pen. Three more pens were empty, the snow undisturbed.

Balanced on his snowshoes, he gnawed his lower lip and thought about it. The Kings were the last people on Jed's list. So far, he'd avoided people . . . well, the Chuckies didn't count. So he *could* bypass these people, backtrack into the woods, and spend the night there.

But the animals were running on fumes. Raleigh was down to a handful of kibble. Dixie had run out of food two days ago. He'd stripped bark and dug down until he found mantles of moss he could tear from fallen trees, but Dixie only nibbled. Today, she'd stumbled and opened a large gash on her left foreleg from knee to fetlock. He'd used up two gauze rolls and an ace wrap before the bleeding stopped.

God, but he was so close! He could taste it. Finding Alex would be a good omen. A fresh start. Not atonement so much, but an embrace of his fate. Maybe, with Alex, the dreams would finally die. He *had* to get to her. Stopping for any reason felt like a mistake.

If he knocked on that door, he would rack up another debt he didn't want to pay. It wouldn't be right to take food and feed from these old people and give them nothing in return. From the looks of the place, they could use the help. So, there would go another day, maybe two. Maybe more. Lost. Poof. Just like that.

He could be selfish. God, hadn't he earned it? But the animals needed rest. He rubbed a gloved hand over cracked lips. *They* had to do what he wanted—and he, of all people, knew what that felt like. It wouldn't be right to drive them any further.

Anyway, if I can get Dixie healthy enough to ride, it ends up being the same amount of time, right? Just a couple more days.

"All right, guys," he said, gathering up Dixie's reins. "Let's go say hi."

Just as Tom knocked on the front door, Raleigh's head jerked left. A rumble rose from the dog's chest. Craning around, Tom glanced toward the ruined prairie barn with its stone silo and caught a quick orange slink moving right to left.

"Hey, come on, boy," he said to the dog. "It's just an old barn cat."

Then the door opened, releasing a ball of warmish air that smelled of fried onions and something ripe and yeasty, like bread or maybe homemade beer, and he forgot about it.

Big mistake.

53

Wade King was passionate about swine. By the afternoon of the second day, a Monday, Tom knew more about hog farms than was probably good for him.

"Last coupla years haven't been too good for the other white meat." Wade King was as large around as his Berkshires, with a belly that could have used a wheelbarrow. Dumping a load of corn and barley into a bin feeder, he waddled out of the pen as the hogs jostled and snuffled around their dinner. "First, people decide hogs are good eating. Then they decide they're too dirty. But pig manure, it's gold for a farm you do it right, only people don't want to hear . . ."

Count me in on that. Tom slid a shovel under the third and last pile of pig doo. The floor was sloped, poured concrete and designed for easy drainage in the days when water came out of pressure hoses. As the winter got worse and Wade just couldn't keep up, the manure pile had multiplied from one to three, each nearly up to Tom's knees. Wade had propane heaters for the hogs, so the shit was only partially frozen and a lot still steamed. The smell coated his tongue; he'd gone through a half tube of toothpaste already.

"Thing gets to me," Wade said, as Tom turned back for another shovelful, "is those jackboots in the EPA . . ."

Jackboots? He had no idea what Wade was talking about. That the man should rail against a nonexistent government struck him as vaguely ridiculous. God, he hoped Dixie appreciated this. At the moment, the mare was stabled with the other horse, her nose deep in a feed bucket.

Raleigh was a real problem, though. Neither Wade nor Nikki cared for dogs, which struck him as odd for working farmers. They hadn't wanted Raleigh in the house, much less running loose around the animals. In the end, Tom had nailed together a rough shelter and put it and Raleigh out in the fenced-in vegetable garden. Raleigh had barked for half the night on the first day. When he'd let the dog out to run around, the golden had taken off for the ruined barn. Wade had a fit: *That dog scares my layers out of letting go of their eggs, it'll be eating buckshot for dinner.* After that, Raleigh stayed in the dead garden. He only hoped the dog wasn't getting sick. Maybe it was just excited by all the unfamiliar smells.

He was only aware that Wade had asked a question because the pause had spun out too long. "I'm sorry. What?"

"I said if you could see your way to stay a couple more days, I could use the help. Got that roof to fix, and I'm just no good on a ladder."

"Yeah. Look, Wade, about that." Tom slotted the shovel into the side of the wheelbarrow. "I think I've put you and Nikki out enough."

"You still upset about the dog?" Wade flapped a hand larger than a ham hock. "Things are so quiet around here and then the dog starts in. Just got on my nerves." Wade brightened. "You know, we have some hamburger set by. I don't know a dog doesn't like that. We need to be friends is all. Get Nikki to mash some up with a couple eggs and—"

"No," Tom said. "You should save your meat. I really need to be moving on come tomorrow."

"What's your hurry?"

"Just like to get where I'm going."

"Where to?"

"East, I guess." Lifting the wheelbarrow, Tom pushed for the open barn door. "Then south."

Wade waddled after. "East Coast? Bad idea. They're going to glow for about ten thousand years from what I heard."

"Oh, I probably won't go that far." After the relative shelter of the barn, the wind cut his skin, and Tom blinked away tears. A gust snatched at the flagpole's halyard rope. Snaps clanged against aluminum. Both the U.S. and now an old Colonial flag rippled and snapped like sheets on a clothesline. "I'll probably stay in Michigan for a while and then maybe head down into Wisconsin again," he said, only half of which was a fib. Once he found Alex, they were heading north and away from this craziness: Minnesota, or Jed's place on that island. Canada. "We'll see."

"Family?"

Tom tipped the wheelbarrow, then began raking out the load of pig manure. "No. I need to find someone, that's all."

"Oh?" Wade was balding, but he had eyebrows thick as furry caterpillars. One crawled toward his scalp. "Where?"

"I'm not exactly sure, but . . ." He hesitated. He'd been deliberately vague about where he was headed. Why, he wasn't exactly sure. "She went to Rule the last I know."

"A girl? In Rule?"

His tone made Tom look up. "There a problem?"

"You might want to reconsider." Wade wore glasses with thick lenses and the kind of birth control goggles only the military could love. Wade *hawed* on a lens and scrubbed with a dingy red kerchief. "Way's lousy with Chuckies. Thicker than ticks on a ginger mutt."

Tom thought of the two he'd killed, and the half-munched corpse of the old woman. "How many are we talking?"

"A lot. Look, Tom, I don't want to tell you your business." Wade hooked his glasses behind his ears. "But it wouldn't hurt if you stayed put a couple more days. Smells like another storm coming anyway."

That Wade could smell anything over pig manure would be a miracle. "Maybe that's a reason to go. The Chuckies will probably hunker down, and Rule's only a few days away at most. If the weather holds, I can be there even sooner." Tom scraped out the last of the manure and tossed the shovel back into the wheelbarrow. There were still the cow and horse stalls to clean out, and if he wanted a jump on the weather, he needed to get his gear together. "I appreciate your offer, but I really do have to leave in the morning."

"Suit yourself." Jamming his hands in the pockets of his worn barn coat, Wade shrugged. "I'll just go tell Nikki to put by some hardboiled eggs, and I know we got a couple jars of—"

"You don't have to do that, Wade," Tom said, feeling instantly guilty.

"Forget it." Wade waved off his objections. "Least I can do."

By the time he got to the chickens, he was working by flashlight. The straw in the coop hadn't been changed in months, and the ammonia reek almost knocked him over. For such a slovenly farmer, Wade was very particular about separating out his manure, and chicken crap went into the woods to compost.

Which figures. Pushing the wheelbarrow through deep snow was impossible, so he'd had to go out on snowshoes first, follow the trail he and the animals had already broken, and stomp until the base layer was firm enough for the barrow not to sink. On the way out, he'd spotted Nikki slogging toward the vegetable garden with a bowl for the dog and returned her wave. Now, huffing toward the woods with the loaded barrow, he swung the yellow beam toward the garden and saw that the dog had tucked itself into the shelter, its tail fluffed over its nose.

"Right, sleep it off," he said, but he was also relieved. Better that the dog should rest up and start out with a full belly.

It was when he was scattering scratch feed for the chickens that he noticed something.

Wade had a *lot* of feed: barley, corn, good hay, scratch for the chickens. He stared down at the handful of seed and cracked corn raining between his fingers. But how was Wade getting it? Wade's only wagon had a broken axle. Even if the wagon had been in good repair, there was no way that one horse—not even a dray at that—could pull very much for very long in deep snow. Plus, there just weren't enough animals to justify all this feed. Despite his talk about maybe building up his hogs, Wade wasn't exactly energetic. The old guy couldn't care for the animals he already owned.

And why wasn't the feed stored in that stone silo? It was perfectly sound, yet Wade kept all his feed binned in the barn off the main paddock. *All* of it.

Then Tom really thought about all that manure he'd shoveled, all those poop piles scattered around. So much crap—and not one burn barrel. Instead, the Kings had Porta-Johns: not one or two but three.

So he hauled those here? That was a possibility, and it would be good thinking. Emptying chamber pots would get pretty old, and he bet there weren't many farms with outhouses before the Zap. He and Jed had built an outhouse with a removable barrel just like Tom had used in Afghanistan, and traded off on burn shitter duty. But if Wade *had* hauled the portable toilets to his farm, how had he done it?

Maybe another wagon in that old barn? After closing up the coop, he trudged out to the wheelbarrow. That was probably it. At the back of the hog barn, he slotted the wheelbarrow, then glanced in the direction of that prairie barn. He couldn't see it beyond the limits of the flashlight, but he sensed it silently brooding in the snow.

Of all the jobs Wade mentioned, he'd never once suggested they work on the barn. Why was that? Sure, there were more immediate problems. But any farmer took care of his tools and machinery.

He flicked a quick look at the house. The front windows were dark, although the kitchen window in back fired a dull yellow. Nikki would be there and Wade, too.

He slid the flashlight out of his hip pocket.

Just a peek.

54

It was a machine graveyard.

Tom fanned his light over a tractor, a manure spreader, and two Ford F-150s. Racks of farm implements and tackle lined the right wall. He even spotted a branding iron, which made him pause. Had those hogs been branded? He searched his memory. No, a farmer notched a pig's ears. Some complicated system; he didn't know what. Branding was for cattle and horses. So maybe the milkers or that bay. He just couldn't remember.

A loaded Peg-Board was mounted above an elaborate tool bench with two vises. The cave-in had dumped snow over a large electric band saw with a circular blade that Tom thought was used for slicing through meat and bone. If so, that saw hadn't seen action for a long time.

But the ax and that cleaver had.

Both rested on a freestanding workbench that reminded him of the butcher block his dad had used to hack beef ribs. The hand ax had a thin stainless-steel blade and leather grip: lightweight, easy to swing, well-balanced. The steel was clean but nicked in places, as if the ax had seen heavy use. Purple splotches stained the leather grip, and more blood had seeped into the cleaver's handle, swelling and then cracking the wood. A slop bucket rested on the concrete next to the butcher block. Stiff rags stained with dark, oily splotches were draped over the rim, and smelled of old gore.

Alongside the workbench was a large white chest freezer. Of course, it wasn't plugged in. The barn was colder than any meat locker. Rust-red tongues drooled from the freezer's lip.

Nikki had served pork stew the first night. Wade had offered to feed hamburger to the dog.

No, that's crazy. He felt his mind flinching away even as the suspicion formed. So the Kings did their own butchering. So what?

But would I know? Aiming the flashlight at the dried blood, he felt suddenly queasy. *God, shouldn't I be able to tell if it hadn't been pork or beef . . . but a person?*

Heart thumping, he levered open the freezer—and his breath left in a white rush.

Empty.

Then, across the barn and to the right, something scuffed.

Startled, he pivoted, raised his flashlight, expecting to see the bright coins of the cat's eyes, or maybe a rat or raccoon. The light broke over a trio of what might once have been long-abandoned horse stalls, with doors on sliders. Something winked from the back corner. Stepping around the freezer, he aimed the light, caught the sparkle again—and frowned. A fourth stall, completely closed off, with a heavy, shiny, stainless-steel padlock dangling from a black ring latch as thick as his thumb.

Scuffling. Then, a low whine.

A puppy. That was his first thought. The Kings had locked up a dog, probably muzzled it. He thought back to that growl Raleigh had aimed toward the barn. No wonder Raleigh wouldn't stay away; there was another dog locked up in here.

Maybe it was sick. That was possible. When he was a kid, his dad had rented *Old Yeller*. He remembered how after the wolf fight, when the dog went rabid, the boy had locked Old Yeller in the corn-crib and then shot him. Tom must've cried for a week. Knowing Wade, Tom thought he'd have gotten rid of a rabid dog, but it would be perfectly in character for the Kings to simply sequester a sick puppy and maybe neglect it to death. Save on a bullet.

Poor thing. "Hey, boy," he called, softly. The dog responded with another whimper as he crossed to the stall. He played the light over the lock, then the rest of the door and the adjacent wall, look-ing for a key. Two keys dangled on a thin wire ring from a nail just to the left of the door. He reached—and then paused. This was none of his business. He was leaving. The Kings had the right to run their farm however they wished.

The puppy whined again.

"Hey, boy." Slipping the ring off the nail, he slotted one of the keys into the lock. "Hang—"

That last word never did leave his mouth.

He saw now that the door was oak, and sturdy but not com-pletely solid. There was a large knothole about two-thirds of the way down, near the level of his right knee. It was dark, and he shouldn't have been able to see a hole. By definition, no one ever did. A hole existed because of where it wasn't.

But there *was* something here: grimy and very thin but completely recognizable.

A finger.

And then, it moved.

55

"Shit!" Tom sucked in a quick, startled gasp. The keys tinkled to the frigid concrete. Every hair on the nape of his neck stood on end. Then he knelt. "Hello? Are you hurt?"

The finger slid away and then he saw a flash of white as the kid—he was convinced it was a child—briefly pressed an eye to the knothole before wincing away from the light.

"Sorry." Tom aimed the flashlight away. Now that he was closer, he smelled stale flesh and ammonia and moldering straw mixed with feces. "Kid, kid, are you okay? What's your name?"

The child might've said something, but Tom's heart was pounding so hard he could barely hear. *My God, he sounds hurt.* He swept his light back and forth over the floor until he found the keys. *Get him out, then saddle up Dixie. Find my gear, get the guns and then Raleigh.* His hands shook. Clamping the flashlight under an arm, he used both hands to sock the key home. If he had to, he would herd the Kings into a room and lock them up until he was ready to go. *Wait until morning when it's light.* His wrist turned. The lock snicked open. *Then we get as far from he—*

A wide spotlight pinned him in place. On the door, before his eyes, his shadow sprang to life, black and perfectly defined, as if Tom were an actor backlit on a stage.

Then, there came a loud, unmistakable sound of a shotgun being racked: *ka-CHUNK-crunch*.

In the stall, behind the door, the boy whimpered.

Tom turned, slowly, a hand up to shield his eyes.

"Oh, Tom," Wade said. "I wish you hadn't done that."

56

Nikki made him strip. Unlike Wade, his wife was thin as a whippet and brittle as broom straw. Her gray eyes showed absolutely no emotion, but when Tom stopped at his underpants, she said, "No, no. All the way. Every stitch."

The woodstove kept the kitchen and this small back room very warm. Fear-sweat slicked his body and ran down the sides of his face, but he was shivering. Jed's tags rattled on their bead chain. "Why?"

"'Cuz we can't have you running," Wade said, from the kitchen. Through the open door, Tom watched as Wade withdrew the brand, inspected the iron, then slid it back into the firebox.

"That's bullshit. I'm not running in my shorts," Tom snapped.

"Oh, I don't know." Grunting, Wade planted his hands on his thighs and heaved himself up. "I saw this one National Geographic about this Eskimo who run over the ice for miles with not a stitch."

"Come on, Tom." Nikki gestured with the shotgun. "Shorts, too."

"No," Tom said.

"Fine. Right knee or left?" When he didn't respond, she said,

"Don't think I won't. So long as you're alive, they don't care what shape you're in. It's all the same to us, but . . ." Her eyes trailed over his body, first down and then up again, her gaze touching on every scar left by shrapnel, lingering on the divot in his right thigh. Her lips curled when she saw the scar on his neck. "That's a nice hickey. Girlfriend get a little carried away? Well, she probably won't mind another ding or two, considering that you're kind of tore up already." Her face blanked again. "Don't make me waste a shell, Tom."

All right, this is about domination. He hooked his thumbs under the waistband of his underpants. *Come on, this is right out of survival training. Don't let them get on top on you.*

But what could he do to stop them? He let his underpants fall to his ankles and then kicked them away. They had the gun, and he'd been an idiot.

"That's good." Nikki lifted her chin toward a straight-backed chair bolted to the floor. "Now, you sit down and put on those plastic thingamabobs. First your ankles to the chair legs and then whichever hand you want to do first. Last hand you'll have to use your teeth."

God, how many times had they done this before? His heart was trying to thrash its way out of his chest. He didn't move toward the chair. He might already be finished, but if he put on those plasticuffs, he was as good as dead. "What did you do to Raleigh? Did you kill him?"

"With any luck." Nikki shrugged. "Shame to waste a good farm dog, but can't have him barking every time he scents a Chucky."

What? Something cold settled in his chest. The ax, the blood on the freezer . . . *Oh God, the* kid . . . "You're *feeding* him."

"Sure. Get more if you can deliver a Chucky alive." Then Wade saw his face and hawked out a laugh so hard his belly jiggled. "No, we're not going to chop you up into burgers, if that's what you're worried about. Although we kinda run out a day ago, and I know that little bastard's hungry. Thing is, you're worth a lot more alive than in some Chucky's gullet. *He* starves to death, I don't know I care very much. They'll take him no matter what, and he'll keep just fine in the cold. Hunters are due real soon anyway."

"How do they know when to come?" Tom asked. He didn't really want the answer, but every second he stayed out of that chair was one more when he still had a chance.

"Run up the old flag when we got something. I guess they got spotters."

The *flag.* Tom clamped back on a moan. My God, it was so *obvious*, right there in plain sight. He'd wanted to believe he was safe—and now he was dead.

"I don't ask a lot of questions. They go about their business, I mind mine." Wade pulled open the stove's firebox. "All I care about is getting what's owed me."

"That's where the feed's coming from, isn't it?" Tom asked.

"Oh, yeah." Wade reached into the firebox with a hand sheathed in a thick red leather glove. "I turn you in, I bet I'll get a nice new wagon and maybe a good dray."

A barter system, that had to be it. Capture a Chucky or young people who hadn't turned, and you'd be rewarded. With mounting horror, Tom watched as Wade inspected the brand. The black iron—an open V that Wade said represented a broken bone, which Tom thought very apt—was turning a soft gray. The choke of scorched iron lodged in his throat . . .

It's the smell of SAWs going cyclic; of spent brass cascading over rock; of a gun barrel so hot it jams and he has to spit into the breech as he works, desperately, to clear his weapon; and there are voices, always the voices, streaming out of the merciless sun and through the speaker in his helmet: "Jesus Christ, cut the wire, cut the fucking wire and grab the kid or you're dead, you're dead, you're—"

"Tom." At the sound of his name, Tom blinked away from the horror-show of memory to find Wade there in this nightmare of the present. The broken-bone brand was not red-hot the way it was in movies but ashen. Tom felt the heat-shimmers from five feet away. "Time to sit down now," Wade said.

"You don't need to do this," he said, already knowing it was a waste of breath.

"Well, I don't brand you, I can't prove I turned you in. Don't want to get cheated."

They had the gun, and there was nowhere to run. The one thing survival school had drummed in over and over again was that unless the mission was in jeopardy, choose life.

Another thing he'd learned: eyes always gave you away. Control your eyes, and unless your opponent was a mind reader . . .

Wade was closer. Nikki had the gun.

He looked at Nikki.

He went for Wade.

57

He moved fast, aimed low, his right arm flashing out and sweeping up. He screamed as the metal brand sizzled into skin, a quick lick of fire that seared his flesh and burned hair. But Wade lost his grip. The iron clattered to the floor as Tom drove forward, twisting at the waist, pushing off from his back foot, left elbow cocked. He rammed the bony point into Wade's gut so hard he felt the impact all the way to his shoulder. Wade let out a breathy, low grunt, and then the old man was staggering, his weight pulling him off-balance. Tom stayed with him, bare feet slapping wood, his hands knotted in Wade's shirt, driving, driving. . . . Out of the corner of his eye, Tom saw Nikki pivot, the shotgun coming up, and then he vaulted around the old man.

The roar was enormous. The room jumped in a brilliant burst of light. At close range, the shot from a twelve-gauge ought to penetrate straight through and tag him, too. But Wade was huge: a three-hundred-pound human shield.

The big man jerked; there was a sound like the burst of a water balloon on cement as Wade's blood splattered against wood. He felt Wade beginning to crumple, heard Nikki shrieking over the ringing in his ears. He was already moving again, pushing off with his stronger left leg, rounding the body, staying as low as he could. He saw Nikki just ahead, less than ten feet away—eyes wide, mouth open. In her shock, her arms had loosened, and the shotgun was pointing down and away.

Go, go, go, go! He sprang, left hand clawed for a grab, right elbow cocked. *One good punch—*

His right foot came down on the thick slick of Wade's blood.

It was like slipping on a patch of glare ice. He felt his balance going, his right foot shooting out. He let out a startled grunt, twisted, tried to break his fall but failed. He crashed down hard, his left hip jamming against the solid wood floor. A rocket of pain exploded into his pelvis, and then he was gasping, rolling, trying to find his footing. On all fours now. Then his eyes jerked to the right, and there, on the floor, six inches away . . .

Above, over his shoulder, he risked a single glance. Nikki's face twisted in a mask of rage, and then she was dragging the shotgun up, pulling the trigger—

Nothing.

No shot.

Tom saw from her face that she realized her mistake at the same moment he did. In her rush, she'd forgotten to rack the shotgun. Her forearms corded as she fumbled. Her hands were wires. She worked the pump as he darted for the brand . . .

Ka-CHUNK—

. . . already thinking: *too slow, too slow, too slow!*

CRU—

His right hand snatched at the brand, still incredibly hot, and then he was sweeping around, scything the air in a vicious backhand. He felt the instant the brand connected, cutting her legs out from under. The shotgun boomed again, but the blast was wild, a spurt of fire licking at the ceiling. Nikki tumbled to the floor, and the shotgun clattered away, and she was shrieking: "I'll kill you, I'll kill you, I'll kill you, you little *fuck*—"

Hand singing with fresh pain, Tom lunged for the shotgun, grabbed it up, and then he was spinning around, racking the pump: *ka-CHUNK-crunch*—

And stopped dead.

There were two of them: a square woman in winter-weight camo and an even older man with dark eyes and wisps of steam curling from a black watch cap glued down to his skull. Both had rifles.

On the floor, Nikki crabbed back. *"No, no, we—"*

"Here," the dark-eyed man said to Tom. "Let me."

His rifle bucked, and Nikki King's face cratered.

58

No one moved. The Kings couldn't. Tom didn't dare.

"You okay?" the man said. "They hurt you?"

He was on his back, bare-assed naked in a pool of blood, a shotgun clutched in both hands, and the smell of burned gunpowder and his own crisped skin stinging his nose. "I'm all right," he said. "Who are you?"

The woman spoke for the first time. Her pale eyes darted toward the kitchen and then fixed on Tom. "Is there a boy here?"

"I think he's out in the barn, the big one. They have him locked up."

"Why?" The skin around her lips whitened.

"He's . . ." Tom swallowed. "You know."

"Oh God." She closed her eyes a moment. Her fingers rose to her lips. "*Damn* it."

"You don't know it's him," the man said.

"But we know who *took* him." She whirled on her heel. "I'm going out there."

"Mellie," the man began, "you don't—"

"He's *mine*," she shot back, and then she was gone.

The dark-eyed man stared after her for a moment and then turned back to Tom. The old man's gaze clicked to the dog tags dangling on their beaded chain, and then he cocked his head at the litter of Tom's clothes. "Why'n't you get dressed, soldier?"

"Who are you people?" Tom asked.

"Get dressed," the man said, and turned to go. "Then we'll talk."

The shot came as he fumbled the buttons of his flannel shirt. He stopped, held his breath, listened for more, but there was only the one. A short time later, he heard footsteps and the murmur of their voices.

His right palm was already blistering, but it hurt. From Afghanistan, he knew that third-degree burns didn't. He could stand the pain. Been hurt way worse. But he'd need antibiotic salve and bandages pretty soon.

He hefted the shotgun. There was no other way out of this small back room, not even a window, and there were two of them. He could shoot first and ask questions later, but they could have killed him already, twice.

On the other hand, the Kings had said he was worth more alive.

When he walked into the kitchen, the woman was sitting at the kitchen table. Her rifle was flat on the floor. The old guy had shouldered his.

"There you go, soldier," he said, setting a basin of water in front of a third chair. His manner was cowpoke-friendly. "Best you stick that hand in there. It's cold, but that's good for burns."

Tom didn't move. After what he'd been through, he wasn't going to make the same mistake of trusting *anyone* twice. He held the shotgun by his right hip, the business end pointing toward the guy's center mass. The woman would have to bend, snatch, grab, and aim. He could rack the pump again and get off a round before she knew she was dead. "Are you the bounty hunters?"

The woman let out a watery laugh. "Only in a manner of speaking. That boy out there, Teddy—I've been searching . . ." Her voice trembled, and she stopped a moment, swallowed, passed a hand over her face. When she looked back up at Tom, her pale eyes were glazed with tears. "He was in a group of children I'd been taking care of since . . . you know. Hunters took him from *me*."

That was plausible. The poor kid had to come from some-where. "How did you know to come here?" Tom asked.

"You'd be surprised how fast word gets around," the man said. "There are only so many farms out this way. When we met up"— he nodded at the woman—"I had a pretty good idea where we ought to look."

Tom thought back to Jed and Grace. They had been careful and isolated, but all it had taken was one very nosy neighbor. Again, plausible. But what were these people doing out here to begin with? Were they working together? The old guy said they'd *met up*. What did that mean? What were these two old people doing wan-dering around in the dead of winter to begin with? The woman's story, he understood. But what was the story with the wannabe cowboy?

"But to tell you the truth," the old man continued, "I wasn't sure until I saw the flag. A lot of militia groups use something similar. Played a hunch, that's all."

Militia? A small finger of unease nudged his chest. Jed had warned him about this, but Tom had been naïve enough to believe the militias were local to Wisconsin. Of all people, *he* ought to know better. Wherever there were civilians, there must be militias, some more organized, entrenched, and better prepared than others. Some might even have been expecting and hoping for the world to go ka-boom, and planned accordingly. Surviving members would naturally come together. Sick as the logic was, he understood why he and other, younger survivors might be valuable, if for nothing else than to generate replacements. But why would some want Chuckies?

"The Kings said it was a signal. It's been up two days," he said.

The man looked at the woman. "Then we got to move. Sooner we get going, the better."

"I'm not going anywhere with you," Tom said.

"It would be safer," the man said.

"I don't know who you are."

"I'm Mellie Bridger," the woman said. She held out a hand, speckled with age. When Tom didn't move, she folded her hand back into her lap. "We're going to our base camp. That's where I was headed with my group when Teddy was taken ten days ago. The other kids should already be there."

Uh-oh. A base camp implied a much bigger operation. If these people were scouts for what was left of the military, this could be very bad for him. *Might have gotten rescued from the frying pan to land in the fire.* "What camp? Where?"

"Where you headed?" the man asked, his tone still cowboy-friendly.

"I'm not sure that's any of your business."

"Listen." The aw-shucks expression the old guy wore slipped just enough that Tom caught a quick glint of something almost predatory. "In case it's kind of escaped your notice, we just saved your ass. We're trying to help you."

"Thanks. I appreciate it. I really do." He really did. "But why should you care about me?"

"You rather we side with the bounty hunters?"

This guy, Tom thought, was very good at deflecting questions and putting people on the defensive. He had just the right amount of bluster. "That's not an answer."

The old guy opened his mouth, but Mellie put a hand on the man's arm. "Back off a little. Can't you see he's scared and hurt? Cut the boy some slack."

The guy looked like he wanted to say something, then shrugged. "Whatever. He wants to end up bait, no skin off my butt. I'd advise not heading east, though."

East was precisely the direction he needed to go. "I'm headed to Rule." Tom watched them toss a look. "What?"

"Well, he's right," Mellie said, tipping her head at the man. "I don't think you want to go there."

That was what Wade had said, too. "Why not?"

"You feeling lucky?" the guy asked. "The way's real thick with Chuckies. That's why we're fighting them and Rule."

"Why fight Rule?"

"Why do you want to go there so bad?"

Tom debated a half-second, then said, "There's a girl I know. We got separated a while back, but she was headed there."

He saw something spirit over the man's weathered face, like he was adding two and two to make four. "She have a name?"

He didn't see how it would hurt. "Alex."

"What?" The old man's mouth actually dropped open in an expression of genuine shock. "Did you say *Alex*?"

"Yes." Tom saw that Mellie was studying the old man with a look of appraisal, her eyes narrowed. "Why?"

"Well, I'll be a son of a—" The old guy seemed almost confused, at a loss for words. He ran a gnarly, calloused hand over his mouth, but Tom couldn't tell if the old guy was searching his memory or trying to decide what might be the safest and best thing to say. But the eyes that found Tom were as dark and bright and canny as a buzzard's.

"I'll be damned. You're the soldier, aren't you?" the man said. "You're the kid who knows explosives, the one we went looking for months ago. You're *Tom*."

59

He knows me. Hearing his name drop from this stranger's mouth cut his legs out from under. Tom thought Mellie sucked in a quick, startled breath, but he was so shocked he couldn't be sure. Later, he would decide he'd been mistaken. Now, he felt the blood leave his face and the world tilt. This stranger, this old man, knew him, knew his *name*. And *months ago* meant . . .

"H-how—" he said, hoarsely. "How do you—"

"Because I've *met* Alex," the old guy said. "I *know* her."

Oh, thank God, she made it, she's safe. Surviving his first firefight was exactly the same: a wash of exhilaration and then relief that left him sick and shaky and sweaty as a junkie. Tom's knees wobbled, and he felt the sudden tightness in his throat and the burn of tears. *She's alive.*

"Easy, easy." The man was up and now wrapped his arm around Tom's shoulders. "Come on, son, you're all done in. Let's sit you down."

"No, we . . . I need to see her. We should *go*," Tom said, but he felt suddenly weak, the combination of shock and relief and all that had happened that day finally draining him of strength. He let the old man jockey him into a chair. "How far? How long will it take us to get there?"

"Not so fast." The man looked away, jaw working, as if trying out the right words and seeing how they fit in his mouth. He returned his attention to Tom. "It's not what you think. We got to talk about what you and us are up against here."

"Up against?" A flare of panic now. "Why? What's wrong? Is Alex all right? Is she hurt?" Something clicked in his brain. *They went back for me, but I was already gone. They'd assume I was dead, and Alex would . . .* "Is she still there? Did she leave? What's going on?"

"More than you know." The man's face seemed to close. "Alex talked them into a rescue. Believe me, it wasn't easy, but she was a pit bull about it. Everyone knew it was a huge risk, but when she told the boys in charge that you were a soldier and knew explosives . . . well, you shoulda seen their faces light up. They couldn't hustle out of Rule fast enough. But when we got there, you were already gone. Everyone figured you were dead."

So he'd been right. A terrible, black foreboding washed through him. *If Alex thought I was dead, would she stay? Oh God, what if she didn't believe it? What if she went looking for me?* "Is she . . . did she leave? Where did she go?"

"Where did *you* go?" Mellie had been so quiet and watchful that Tom had forgotten she was there. Mellie laid a hand on his shoulder. "Where were you, exactly?"

"Wisconsin." Blame the shock and his confusion, but the word tumbled from his mouth before he had time to think.

"*Where* in Wisconsin?" Mellie asked.

"Uh . . ." He ran his good hand through his hair. "A couple . . . Jed and Grace, they came through on their way west. I was pretty out of it. I honestly don't remember much. All I know is I woke up four or five days later, and we were at their cabin. Grace was a nurse and—"

"Cabin?" Mellie echoed.

"Odd Lake, yeah." Still reeling, Tom returned his attention to the man. He could feel his brain trying to put all the pieces together. "I don't understand. You're from Rule. You came to find me. So why are you fighting Rule now? What's going on? Why are you here and not in Rule? Who *are* you people?"

"My name's Weller, Tom. And I hate to say, but Alex . . ." Weller showed his teeth in a grimace.

Oh no. I'm too late, I waited too long . . . "What? But *what*?"

"I'm real sorry, Tom, but the last I knew, Alex was in the prison house."

"What? *Prison* house?" he cried, aghast. That she was alive should've buoyed him, but this was five times worse. If *prison house* had the same meaning in this village as it did in Afghanistan—if they tortured people—Alex might be as good as dead. "In Rule? *Why*?"

"Well . . ." Again, Weller's hand slowly wiped his mouth. It was the reluctant gesture of a man thinking, and very carefully, about what he should say next.

"Jesus," Tom said. He could feel the sweat beading on his upper lip. "Just *say* it."

"They're . . . let's just say they've got some real bad actors in that village," Weller said, finally. He looked straight into Tom's eyes. "We're not only talking the way the village has been run before everything went to hell. I'm talking *now*: how they treat people, the things they've done to secure the borders, in particular."

"What does that have to do with Alex? Why would they throw her in a prison?"

"Let's just say she, ah, wouldn't *cooperate*." Weller's features arranged themselves into an expression of regret.

"Meaning?"

"You seem like a smart boy, Tom," Mellie interrupted. "You've been to war. You've seen how fast things break down. So what do you think happens to young girls at the hands of old men?"

"And not all of 'em old," Weller added, softly. He and Mellie traded another long look before he repeated, "Not all."

Oh my God. He had to close his eyes. Now Weller's reluctance, how carefully he'd seemed to search for words, made perfect sense. *This is my fault. If she hadn't been alone, if I hadn't gotten myself shot, none of this would've happened.*

He heard his voice rise as if from the hollow blackness at the bottom of a well. "Tell me what to do to get her out, and I'll do it." He opened his eyes and found Weller. "I'll do whatever it takes."

There was a tiny, nearly invisible tug at one corner of Weller's mouth, a look of satisfaction there and gone in the blink of an eye. "Well, the kid who *called* the shots," he said, "his name was Peter. But you don't have to worry about him. He got himself killed in an ambush, and good riddance. But the kid who's taken over? Son of a bitch is a psychopath."

"What kid?" Tom asked. "What's his name?"

"Boy by the name of Prentiss," Weller said. "Chris Prentiss."

60

"Are you all right?" Still huffing, winded from the desperate struggle, Chris pushed up from the bloodied snow. He looked toward Nathan, who sprawled against the school's north wall. Nathan was breathing hard, a hand clamped to his left bicep. Blood oozed between his fingers. His parka was shredded from shoulder to elbow. "He bite you anywhere else?"

"No. Lucky his feet went out from under on the ice, though." Nathan's face was the color of ash. "Little bastard latched onto her like a damned leech." The old man pulled his head around his shoulder and called, "He get you bad?"

"No." Lena huddled in a heap of clothing at the corner of the building and beneath the breezeway where they'd tethered the horses. The breezeway ran on the east wall and led to a snow-covered jungle gym and the tatters of a lonely basketball hoop. The Changed had torn her parka open at the throat. Livid, bright-red scratches stood in parallel tracks on her neck where his nails had first stripped away her scarf before clawing at her sweater. That he hadn't used his teeth was a miracle. "Where did he come from? Why was he here? The school's all by itself. No houses nearby, nothing."

"I don't know." Chris stared down at the boy. The Changed wasn't quite dead but still gulping, trying to pull in air through the blood pulsing from his mouth and around the knife jammed half-way in his throat. His feet scraped snow in a slow shamble. Then the boy managed a faint, gurgling caw, and Chris couldn't stand it any longer. Kneeling, he wrapped his hands around the knife, felt it move against his palms as the boy's throat convulsed—and rammed the blade home. He felt the tip scrape bone, the slight hesitation as it parted tough tendon and muscle along the boy's spine. Chris let his weight fall.

The boy flopped as the steel found his spinal cord. A bright crimson gusher boiled from his mouth. His hands were fluttery starfish that twitched and jumped before folding, going limp, and, finally, dying. Chris waited a few more seconds to make sure, then tugged out his knife. There was blood everywhere: on the snow, the boy, his own hands.

"She's right. I don't get it," Nathan said. "There are no tracks out here. He had to be in the school."

Which meant that the boy had bypassed *them* to get to Lena, and that made no sense. When Lena screamed, Chris had been on the second floor, slipping from room to room. There had been many bodies, people-popsicles, really: all of them frozen solid and only some with portions—an arm here, a foot there—gnawed to bare bone. The halls were filmed with a fine cover of ice and snow, but he'd seen no tracks except his own. So there had been plenty of food and no need for the boy to show himself at all. From his tracks, the Changed had vaulted out of the school's library, which was the way both he and Nathan had entered. Still on the ground floor and at the back of the school, Nathan had made it out first.

But Nathan was right there. Why not go after him, or me? We were inside and much closer. Why leave? Why go outside for Lena? Hell, why go after her in the first place?

He looked back at Lena, still cringing, a hand bunched to her scratched throat. Although he'd had plenty of time, the boy hadn't bitten her anywhere. *It's like he wanted to get at her.* He eyed the tangle of green scarf and that torn parka. *Like maybe he wanted to . . .* A chill shivered over his skin. The idea that the boy might have had rape on his mind disturbed him almost more than if the Changed had only wanted to tear out Lena's throat.

"Do you think there are others?" Lena asked.

Good question. He rifled a glance at the horses, but they'd quieted. Not that horses were all that reliable an indicator: dogs were much more sensitive to the Changed. "I don't think so, but we probably should get out of here. Even if he was by himself, there are a lot of bodies in there. Might be others who decide to drop by for a meal, you know? Our horses were pretty loud and so were we."

"Move? *Again?*" Lena's skin was milky, the circles under her eyes as dark as charcoal. She was sick, eating barely enough to keep a tick alive, but she wouldn't talk about it. He was starting to have a nasty suspicion why. The question was, what could—*would*—he do about it? "Chris," she said, "we haven't gotten any rest in—"

"In days. I know." Trotting over to the roan, he unhooked his pack and then came back to kneel by Nathan. Through the rip, he could see the blood welling through a jagged rip but no pumpers. He dug out a medical kit. "But we can't stay here, Lena. Not now."

"We're in the middle of nowhere. The school's all by itself. There are no other tracks, so he's probably the only one. Chris, we have to rest *sometime*."

He bit back an impatient reply. Getting angry wouldn't help. Instead, he turned his attention to Nathan, easing the old man's injured arm from its sleeve and then setting about sponging off blood. He had no answers for Lena, and she *was* right. They were all tired. Although they'd finally decided to start looping back north and west, they'd been on the road for eleven days now. At their current rate, Oren was still a good ten days in the future if they were lucky, and two weeks if they weren't. They had to get some rest.

"Has it ever been so bad?" Lena persisted. "With the Changed coming after you? This is the fourth kid in two days."

"I don't know much about this area," he said, unrolling Kerlix around Nathan's wound. "Any time I've gone east of Rule, it's always been with a big group where we had lots of guys and guns and dogs. Nathan?"

The old man only shook his head. "All those prints and bone mounds we've found are old. We haven't run across a single homestead or group of survivors, young or old."

"Maybe they ran away," Lena said.

"Or they're all dead," Nathan said. "My point is this: there's no fresh meat, anywhere. There shouldn't *be* Changed around here at all, right? So what's the story with that little stash of bodies we found in the school?"

Oh boy. He'd never considered that possibility. "You're talking a storehouse, like a . . . a meat locker."

"I'm talking exactly that." Nathan pulled in a sudden hiss of pain, exposing yellowing teeth and gums that were the color of putty. "I don't think that's a very good sign, do you?"

"You mean, there'll be more?" Lena's voice was tremulous. "Like, they might be coming *now*?"

"There are no fresh prints," Chris said. This private school was secluded and lay at the end of a quarter-mile driveway, and theirs were the only tracks. From the lie of the land, this whole area looked like it had once been pasture. Other than a football field and bleachers humped with snow, there were no other buildings, and the nearest woods were a good half mile distant.

"I don't know enough to understand what that means," Nathan said.

He didn't either. "So what do you think? Stay or go?"

"We should stay," Lena said. "You said yourself, the prints are old. Look at this." She used the toe of her boot to scuff a white bloom of icy powder. "It snowed again just last night. This is all fresh. You can tell we're the only ones who've been through."

"I'm not wild about either choice," Nathan said, "but we've been on the move almost continuously for the last twenty hours. The horses are done in, and humping it back into any kind of woods with good cover means another two, three hours. If the animals were rested and we had some decent moon to light the way, it might be a different story." After eleven days on the road, Nathan's skin was drawn and his cheeks hollowed from lack of rest and poor food. "Even if we make it to the woods, sun's gonna go before we can make camp."

"We should stay," Lena repeated. "He was probably alone. This might just have been this kid's private stash. The others would've come out already, right? With no fresh tracks, that means there's been nobody else in at least two days. We can barricade ourselves in somewhere on the second floor. If we get rid of the body and bring the horses in, maybe no one will know we're here."

Those were all good points. Chris's eyes flicked back to the dead boy. The Changed was young, no more than thirteen, and looked healthy—well, aside from being dead. He was dressed for the weather, too. He studied the kid's face, which still had a trace of baby fat under the chin. *Eating pretty well, too. So maybe he was only defending his stash. But he had to know we're no threat to that. And the only person he went for was—*

"Chris?" Lena said.

"Give me a second." *The kid chose Lena. He could have taken Nathan or me. He could have left us alone. But he had to get at her—and he risked his life to do it.*

God, he didn't like where this line of thought was going. It might be nothing. But he thought he knew a way to test that.

"Okay." He let out a long breath. "I vote we stay. Nathan, there's a corner room on the second floor just above us, with windows east and north, and another on a diagonal south and west. We'll have a good shot at seeing anything coming." Stooping, he bent and hooked his hands under the dead boy's pits. "Lena, let's get him out of sight and then cover over the blood."

Lena looked about as thrilled as if he'd asked her to pick up dog crap, but she only nodded. "It'll be okay," she said, grabbing the kid's ankles. "It can't be any more dangerous than the woods."

That was when he lied to her for the first time.

"Yeah," he said. "Probably not."

61

"Here." Sliding to a sit beside him at his lookout, Lena handed him a steaming aluminum camp cup. "I made you some tea."

"Thanks," he said, mildly surprised. He'd left Lena and Nathan next door in what had once been a chemistry lab. The room was downwind, but they'd used duct tape along the seams and under the door, just in case. The horses were in the gym because there were no windows and the one exit was easier to block off. The horses would leave mounds of crap on the basketball court, but he couldn't think of a soul who would care. He cradled the hot metal in both hands. The steam was sweet and smelled orange. "How come you're awake?"

"Couldn't sleep. I'm too wired, and my ears are cold. I can't remember where I put my scarf either. Nathan's out, though." Her face was a dull silver glimmer in the darkness. "Anything going on?"

"Nope." Full dark had come six hours ago. A thumbnail of moon sprayed the snow a dank, dim verdigris like corroded bronze.

"So maybe there are no others."

"That would be nice." He sipped. The tea was very hot but tasted good. "How are you feeling?"

"Not so great." She paused, then added, "I need some decent sleep."

And something in your stomach. "So go back to bed."

"In a little while," she said. "I don't want to be alone in there."

"Nathan's there."

"You know what I mean. I feel better when I'm with you."

He wasn't sure how to reply, and didn't. They sat in silence a moment longer, and then she said, "Do I talk in my sleep?"

"Uh." He blew on his tea and said, carefully, "Sometimes."

Her face swiveled his way, but he might as well have tried reading the expression of a shadow. "What do I say?"

He sipped tea as a delaying tactic and scalded the roof of his mouth. "Just stuff."

"Hunh," she grunted, then hugged herself. "I thought so. Sometimes I wake myself up and I know I've been talking."

"Everyone has bad dreams, Lena."

"Not like mine."

He thought of that horrible morning when he was eight and had wandered downstairs to find no breakfast on the table and his father alternately sucking on bloodied knuckles and a bottle of Maker's Mark. There had been no Deidre, his father's girlfriend of the month, either. "I wouldn't bet on it."

"Do you dream about stuff from, you know, before?"

Oh, the nightmares had begun well before the world died.

His dreams were raw and violent and very loud: shouts and a woman's pleas—and then a weird, rhythmic noise that started out hollow and dull and went on and on, becoming wetter and meatier and, finally, sodden, as if someone had taken a bat to an overripe cantaloupe.

"None of what I dream about from before is very good," he said to Lena.

"Me neither. I guess that's why all my dreams are bad: because *it* was bad. Isn't that weird? I mean, the world goes to hell, kids have Changed into these monsters—but my life wasn't so great before."

He'd never thought about it in quite that way, but she was right. Getting to Rule had been the only good thing to happen to him in years. Peter and he got along from the start. In fact, now that he thought about it, when they'd first met, Peter's face had shifted from shock to, well, *joy*. He made Chris feel like he'd finally found his way home. Brothers could not be closer. "You know what's really freaky? In Rule, I was probably the happiest I'd ever been."

"Makes one of us," she said. "How come you never ask me anything about before? Living with the Amish?"

Because he knew there was nothing good there and he had enough dark memories of his own? "I don't know. None of my business? Besides, you and Peter were, you know, pretty tight. I figured you talked to him."

"Some but not much." She gave a little laugh. "I'm, like, totally in love with the guy, but he never asked what a pagan like me was doing with the Amish. I only wanted to forget it."

He could feel that she wanted to tell him. "So why were you there?"

"My mom was this complete druggie," she said, matter-of-factly. "Crystal meth and cocaine to go up; booze to come down. She flunked rehab, like, ten times or something stupid. I guess she thought that being Amish was her ticket to getting clean, so she married this drooly old perv named Crusher Karl."

Karl was a name she muttered in her sleep. "What kind of name is that?"

"His nickname. Almost all the Amish have them, like this guy they called Pig John because he raised hogs. Crusher Karl used to work a quarry crushing stone, and he had these huge hands. He was a complete asshole, but my mom married him anyway. My brother and I never had any say."

"That sucks."

"Tell me about it. You know the Amish don't send their kids to school after eighth grade? I kept running away, as often as I could, just to hike five miles to this bus stop so I could go. Can you believe it? Karl always dragged me back and locked me in the barn. Finally, the bishop told him to just leave me alone. But, boy, that old bastard made sure I paid. Used to hit me with this riding crop he kept for the buggy horses. Of course, my mom knew, but she only told the bishop, and he didn't want the *English* involved," she drawled in a broad German accent, and snorted. "Asshole."

This was stuff he didn't need or want to hear, but he had no idea how to stop her. "I'm sorry."

"Oh, he was the one who ended up sorry. Know what I finally

did?" she asked, then went on without waiting for his answer. "I stabbed the bastard."

He blinked. "You stabbed the bishop?"

"*No,*" she said, as if he was a moron. "Karl. One night when he came by to *visit.*" She punctuated with air quotes. "He *visited* a lot."

"Oh," he said, wishing she would just shut up. "Honestly, Lena, it's none of my business."

She went on as if he hadn't spoken. "It was the bishop and the ministers who decided to get rid of the body. The whole 'no *English* police' thing—and, you know, the Amish have this reputation for being so pure and all. I have no idea what they did with Karl or told the people at the quarry, but that was that. Karl was just gone, like he'd never existed. I think they were secretly glad I'd gotten rid of the asshole."

He said nothing.

"I never told anyone before," she said.

"Why are you telling me now?"

"I don't know. Maybe it's a last confession or something."

"What are you talking about?"

"I don't know. Just talking." Her voice was ragged, and she sighed. "I'm really tired, but my head's crowded, like everything's kind of flooding out at once. Then, other times, I just go . . . blank. Like a white sheet of paper. It's so weird. Can you die if you don't sleep?"

The only thing he knew was a person could go crazy, and she was definitely headed there. "You should get some sleep," he said, praying that she would listen. "Please."

"Okay." She put a hand on his arm. "Can I stay here? I know Nathan won't hurt me, but I'm kind of freaked out. You know, being alone with him?"

He was just as uncomfortable having her stay, but he shucked out of the spare sleeping bag they'd found. "Here. You can use this. I'll be okay without."

"Thanks," she said. He turned away to study the snow again; heard the bag rustle then still. After another moment, her voice floated on the darkness. "Chris? Can I ask you a question?"

"Lena, please, go to sleep. I mean it."

"I will, but I keep meaning to ask this and I always forget. I don't know why."

Some things—like his past and, from the sound of it, hers—were best left forgotten. But he had a pretty good feeling what she would ask. On the way back from Oren, he'd gone over it in his head, rehearsing how he would break the news. But then Alex had run, Jess had clobbered him, and the rest was history. "What is it?"

"You remember the boy? The one Greg brought back the morning Alex left? Was it—"

62

And then, in mid-sentence, Lena blanked. Just . . . fizzle, pop, gone, as if her brain had thrown a circuit breaker as a connection failed. It was the strangest, *weirdest* feeling, like her thoughts were words on a page that had been suddenly erased. Her mind bleached completely white.

Where am I? She swept her eyes around the room, spotted a tumble of chairs and desks. Books on the floor. And this boy on a stool . . . *Who is he?* Her gaze shot to the sleeping bag puddled at her waist. *Sleeping bag, on the floor . . . What am I doing here?*

Dark. She remembered that. Dreaming—yeah, that was right. And then she'd snapped awake. *Tea.* She'd made tea for . . . for this boy because she wanted company.

Who is he? Why can't I remember? A lance of fear stabbed her chest, and she began to tremble. *I must be sick.* Her forehead was wet. Why couldn't she remember?

"Hey." A white shimmer sailed from the dark, and his hand touched her shoulder. The voice said something more, but it was all so much gibberish and black sound.

What's wrong with me? The words were all locked up some-where. Nothing made sense: not where she was or why, or even the shadowy figure of the boy looming over her. *Who is he?*

Then: *Who am I?*

"Lena?" The boy gave her a little shake. "Are you okay?"

Whatever grabbed her suddenly let go. "Yeah," she said in a breathy little gasp. "I'm . . . I'm okay." She put a hand to her temple. Her head throbbed. "I'm not feeling very well."

"You haven't been eating," the boy said. "You really need to get some sleep, too."

Chris, it's Chris; what's wrong with you? Then the last half hour suddenly rushed back like pent-up water released from a dam. Embarrassment washed through in a hot flood that heated her skin. *God, why did I do that? I've never told anyone about Karl. What's the matter with me?*

"Yeah." Tears burned, and she bit her lip to stop a sob. "Sorry."

"No problem. Just go to sleep." Kneeling, he pulled the bag up around her chin. "Come on. You'll feel better in the morning."

Her throat clenched. "C-Chris?"

"Hey, hey." He gave her shoulder an awkward pat. "Don't cry."

"I'm . . ." She gulped. Felt the wet rolling down her cheeks. "I'm scared."

"Hey," he said again, and then he stopped talking and just let her hang on while she hiccupped into his shirt.

"S-sorry," she said, finally. She dragged a hand over her swollen eyes. "I-I'm sorry."

"It's okay." His hand cupped the back of her neck, and she

let her head rest on his shoulder with a grateful sigh. "We're all scared," he said.

Not like me. You're not losing yourself. A weird thought that she didn't understand but felt, somehow, was exactly right. She didn't want to let go of him either. This was a bubble in time that was no more than a gasp and as fragile as the thinnest, most perfect glass. *I'm real; right now, I'm here and I'm me.* She was afraid to move or speak, because then time would start up again and the moment would be gone, forever. Maybe her, too. For the first time in weeks, she was real; there was no other word that described how she felt, as if his arms not only held but defined her, gave her limits, kept her from falling apart, blasting to bits. She heard the steady thump of his heart, and his scent was . . . indescribable.

It's Chris. Pressing closer, she breathed him in. *This is the smell of Chris, and he is real and so is this, so am I.*

Before she could stop herself—what a lie; she didn't want to stop—she was reaching up. Her trembling fingers feathered his neck and she heard him suck in a small, startled gasp.

"Lena, I—" he said. "We—"

"Please, please, please," she whispered. Her body was shuddering, humming, warming. She brushed her lips over his skin, felt the hard throb of his pulse against her mouth, tasted the salt tang on her tongue. At her touch, he made a sound that was very far back, deep in his throat; she felt the sudden shock of it in his chest, the tremor rippling through his body like a bomb. She put a hand behind his neck, pulled his mouth to hers, and then they were kissing, and kept kissing, and his lips were warm and tasted of sweet oranges, and she focused on that, gave herself over to the feel of his mouth and his hands in her hair, the scorch of his fingers over her cheeks, her neck. She was tingling, all over, greedy for his taste, moaning into his mouth, and they were breathing in one another, and then he was saying her name and she needed that almost more than breath.

Yes, this is real and I'm Lena, I am Lena, I'm—

"Lena." He pulled away, panting a little. "No. I can't. I'm sorry. We shouldn't. This isn't me."

But it is me. "Yes, it is," she said. Her voice broke. "Please don't, please don't."

"Lena." He sounded out of breath. His hands tightened on her arms. "This isn't right."

"It *is*." She heard the plea and didn't care. "Chris, it doesn't have to mean anything more than what it is. It's not wrong."

"Lena, I just . . . I *can't*. This isn't me," he said again.

"You love her." Her voice was used up and flat as paper, and she let her hands fall away. An enormous sense of defeat washed through like black water that might just sweep her out to sea, or drown her. Same difference.

"I don't know," he said. "I think so. I care about you, I do, but—"

"Great." She gave a broken laugh. "What every girl needs to hear."

He was quiet for a moment. "That's not fair."

"Fair? Hey, news flash: life isn't fair." She heard the cruel cut in her voice, but she'd take anger over fear any day. "*Nothing's* fair."

"I know that. But I don't have to make things worse. That doesn't mean I shouldn't do what's right."

"So now I'm wrong?"

"*No.* I'm saying I can't let Alex go just yet. If I'm going to, you know, *be* with you or anyone, it has to be *you*, not who I wish you were."

She couldn't believe this. "So what? Who cares? What about what *I* need? Don't I count for something?"

"Lena, you do, but—"

"But *what?*" she spat. "I'm not good enough? I'm not *her?* Have you stopped to think, for five seconds, how *I* feel? We are going to *die* out here, and you're worried about being faithful to a *dead* girl?"

"Lena." His voice had dropped to something low and dangerous. "Don't."

"Don't what? Don't say she's *dead?*" She hurled the word, like the quick hard crack of a whip.

"Stop," he said. There was a warning thrum to his tone. "Lena. *Please.*"

"Stop. Lena. Please," she mimicked, and then in her new and cruel voice: "She's dead, Chris, and if you want to think about something, think about this: she didn't love you. She used you and then she ran *away.*"

"No," he said, sharply. "She wasn't you, and I'm not Peter."

That hurt, but she was glad. Anything was better than this bone-deep fear. "Oh, you got that right," she said. "Peter wasn't a scared little *boy.*"

"I'm not scared—"

"Oh, bullshit."

"What's going on? Why are we fighting each other? Why are

you *doing* this?" he asked. She didn't hear anger there, only a species of betrayal and wonderment, as if from a puppy that couldn't believe its owner had just kicked it. "What do you *want* from me?"

I want you to make me real. It was the first and most urgent thought. *I want nothing else to matter but right now, right here, on this goddamned floor, in this awful place.*

But what she said was, "I want to be safe." As soon as the words left her mouth, she felt her fury dissipating, like a storm finally blowing itself out. "I w-want someone to tell me everything's going to be all right. I just . . ." A sob boiled into her throat. "I w-want the world to c-come back. I kn-know it won't, but that doesn't mean . . ." She was hitching now, her shoulders shuddering. "That doesn't m-mean I d-don't want—"

This time, when she felt his arms hug her to his chest, she did nothing but weep as if there would be no tomorrow. The chances there would be weren't very good anyway. And this time, nothing happened between them, but that was all right. That was just fine.

Later:

He wanted her to sleep. "Things always look better in daylight."

Oh, she doubted that. But she stretched out again and let him run the zipper. When he was done, he lingered, then laid a tentative hand on her shoulder. "I don't think it was him, Lena."

"Him?"

"The boy from Oren?" He paused, maybe expecting her to say something. When she didn't, he prompted, "The one Greg brought back the morning Alex ran away?"

"Oh." Her memories were gauzy and a little unreal, as if her life's story were penned in an old book belonging to an extinct race from another planet. "Yes. I remember that."

She could tell that wasn't the answer he'd expected, but he continued, "The kid was eight, maybe nine. But your brother's thirteen, right?" She took so long to answer that he said, "Lena?"

"Yes, that's right," she parroted back. "He's thirteen."

"That's what I thought. So . . . I'm pretty sure it wasn't him, Lena. That means we might find him once we get back up toward Oren."

"Okay. Thanks, Chris." She paused. "I'm sorry."

"I know." He gave her shoulder a gentle squeeze. "Me, too. But it'll be okay, Lena. Everything will work itself out. Just get some sleep, okay?"

"Okay," she said, a little surprised that the tears stayed put this time. As he rose, she added, "Watch out for that tea."

"What?"

"The tea." She pointed. "The cup's by your left foot, next to the stool."

"It is?" There was a tiny *snick*, a spray of light. The cup seemed to leap into being from the darkness. "Wow. Thanks. I didn't see that."

"No problem." The bright yellow wink bouncing off the aluminum dazzled her eyes. Wincing, she rolled away and onto her side. A second later, she heard the click as Chris switched off the flashlight, followed by the shush of fabric, the slight squall of cold metal, a small sigh as he settled on his stool.

Pulling the sleeping bag up to her chin, she stared into the darkness, first at the fuzzy blue ghost images of that aluminum cup and then, as they dissipated, at the blocky silhouettes of lab tables and stools. Her gaze panned over gas spigots and chromed faucets, a glassy heap of broken beakers, a tumble of textbooks, a fan of torn pages from a lab book. The white face of a clock, its hands frozen at twenty-one minutes past nine, floated above the classroom door.

It's dark. I shouldn't be able to see this, but I do. Her eyes burned, but she had no more tears. *Something's happening to me, and I don't know what, and I want it to stop; I just want things to be okay.* Yet this she understood: things would never be *okay* for her again. Whatever memories of a brother she'd possessed were gone. She knew, beyond the shadow of a doubt, that she must *have* a brother. The feeling was right. But there was an . . . an *emptiness* inside, the way there was when you chunked out the pit of an avocado then scooped out all the soft innards, leaving only skin. Where there had been *brother*, now there was a blank, a kind of grayed-out mental afterimage with no face, no name, and not a flicker of memory.

There was, instead, nothing.

Nothing at all.

63

They came three hours before dawn.

Chris hadn't woken Nathan to take a shift. After what had happened with Lena, he couldn't have slept anyway. Instead, he waited, alternately guilty and hollow-eyed with dread.

He'd been so *stupid*. He did like Lena, just not *that* way. Did he? No. He had to protect her. Lena was sick and scared, as confused as he was. She wasn't thinking straight. No matter what she said, she was in love with Peter; he knew that. He couldn't shake Alex either, and didn't really want to, not just yet. Maybe hope was a terrible thing, but he held on to it anyway, despite what he'd said to Lena. So, better to let this whole thing just go and concentrate on what he had to do next. One step at a time.

He flicked a glance at the dim huddle beside his stool. Her breathing was even. Sleeping. No more dreams either that he could tell. He returned his gaze to the snow. God, he hoped he wasn't right, but he just couldn't get past the idea that the Changed boy had *chosen* to come out of hiding when he hadn't needed to—and he had gone for Lena.

She was unraveling before his eyes. Before they'd kissed—stupid, stupid, stupid—what was all that other stuff? It *had* sounded like a confession. Yet when they were talking about her brother, he'd sensed her sudden uncertainty. Could be dehydration, maybe. Factor in no real sleep for days and she was apt to be a touch confused.

Wait. He raked his teeth over his chapped lower lip, considering. Could she be dying? Oh, boy, he'd never thought about that. And if she was dying, they all were. He was just as exhausted, and Nathan was so much thinner—one stiff breeze and he'd blow away.

But she's sick to her stomach. He chewed off a strip of dead skin. *Mornings are worst. So maybe*—

Movement. On the snow. His gaze snagged on a dark slink. Even without the binoculars, he knew this was no wolf or coyote. He thought it was another boy, but one kid in a bulky parka looked pretty much the same as any other.

He watched as the kid made a beeline for the bodies. When Chris had come up with the idea of piling a goodly number of the dead out there on the snow, he'd simply told Nathan that he didn't want to risk any Changed trying to get into the school. That had enough truth that the old man hadn't questioned him. They thought ten bodies ought to be enough for the night, but Nathan hadn't understood why Chris decided that two piles of bodies were better than one.

Now, he held his breath as the dark, distant figure crept toward the first pile, which Chris had deliberately positioned closer to the woods. The shadowy figure lingered there for a long moment— and then kept going.

Shit. His stomach iced even as his brain argued, *Relax, you don't know what this means; it might not be anything more than he's checking them both out.* He watched as the kid knelt over the second tumble of bodies. *If more of them come and most head to the second pile, then it counts.*

Within minutes, more slinks did appear, the Changed making their way across the open field, trickling over the snow like black ants homing in on spilled sugar. In total, he thought there were about thirty. Only a few stayed with that first pile. Mostly, they clustered around the second. From what he could see through binoculars, these Changed were pretty primitive, too: baseball bats, golf clubs. He spotted one with a human femur. Another had an ax. No guns, though, and no throwing weapons. Knives would be tough to see in the bad light, but he thought they mainly used their teeth and their hands, gnawing flesh from joints, snapping and twisting off arms and legs the way you tore apart a turkey's carcass at Thanksgiving. A wing here, a drumstick there. Skulls weren't like hips or knees, where you really had to work to get past thick protective ligaments. A head was like a bowling ball balanced, precariously, atop a flimsy tower of vertebrae, held in place only by cords of thick shoulder muscle and sinew that were easily chewed through.

He turned away from two kids playing tug-of-war with a tangle of intestines and looked down at Lena, now deeply asleep. *Please,* he pleaded silently, *please, Lena, keep sleeping. Don't wake up. You shouldn't see this.*

Mercifully, she didn't, but he saw plenty. The Changed remained for what was left of that night, squabbling over the bodies, with no real cooperation that he could see. They were more like a flock of vultures. Not once did they look at the school.

The worst moment was when one Changed—he was almost positive it was a boy—reeled out something long and ropy from the pile of bodies, then looped his prize around his neck: once, twice. *Oh boy.* Chris felt his stomach plummet. He squinted through the binoculars but couldn't be sure. Might be guts. From a distance, you might almost think the kid was double-looping old-fashioned linked sausages. That would be weird; he'd never run into any Changed who actually wore body parts. But this kid might be doing nothing more complicated than carting off a mid-morning snack.

Or . . . it could be way more complicated. He wouldn't know until first light.

A half hour before dawn, the Changed oiled their way across the snow and into the darkling woods, vanishing like smoke. The night drained away. The moon had long since set, so he had to wait until a smear of thin morning light appeared. That second pile of corpses reminded him of the wreckage of a platter of chips and dip. Not a whole hell of a lot left, only leavings strewn over trammeled snow and ruined clothes. He looked hard but didn't see it. That wasn't necessarily bad. He lowered the binoculars. His arms were lead pipes and his eyes raw and gritty with fatigue. They had a long day ahead and he should rest, but he had to be certain, which meant he had to go out there, alone, right now, *before* Lena and Nathan woke.

Lena stirred only once as he slid from his stool. His heart scrambled into his throat, and he froze, the hackles along the back of his neck spiking with alarm. *No, no, no! Not now, not now!* After a moment, Lena sighed and let out a thick, incoherent mumble before falling still once more.

It was the longest walk of his life, like marching to a scaffold. Outside, the air was deeply cold but dry, and his eyeballs seemed to shrivel. Breathing hurt. The hard crunch of his boots over icy snow was so loud that he winced. There was a pressure at his back, like someone watching, but every time he glanced back, only the school stared. With every step, he half-expected hands to slip around his throat from behind or look up and find faces staring from the thick gloom of those woods. He had never felt more alone. What would he do with what he found—or didn't find? What then? He could turn back. He was probably wrong. If he found nothing, that didn't prove anything. Even the Changed got cold.

But, God, I hope I find it, he thought. *I really, really do.*

But he didn't.

Two hours later, they led the horses from the gym. The sun was out; the snow glittered, diamond-bright. Chris's eyes, already raw, began to water.

"Chris," Lena said. They hadn't said much to each other all morning, but now her eyes brushed over his with a look he couldn't decipher. "I'm sorry. I've looked everywhere, but I can't find it. Are you *sure* you don't know where my scarf is?"

Slipping on his sunglasses, he hid his eyes and lied a second time.

"Nope," he said. "Can't say I do."

64

"You should leave the dog," Mellie said as Tom hefted Raleigh onto the swayback's saddle. Catching the dog's scent, Mellie's horse, a mild tobiano paint, nickered. Mellie gave its poll a reassuring scratch. "An extra horse only slows us down."

"I don't care," Tom said, briefly. Turning aside, he began laboriously tying off the ropes securing the bulky blue tarp with its sad bundle. His right hand complained, but he forced the muscles to obey. Dixie's wound had healed enough that he felt comfortable riding her, but he worried that Raleigh's body would upset her, so he'd settled on the Kings' horse. As he worked, a solitary crow perched on the flagpole let out a mournful cry that sounded like a person hurt bad: *Oh. Oh.* Or maybe it only sounded that way to him.

"But the ground's frozen." Weller was astride a big, very muscular blood bay. "You won't be able to bury him."

"Then I'll burn him. Or I'll pile rocks. That dog saved my life. He belonged to people I care about, and I am not leaving him here to rot." Tom gave the last rope a grim tug. Even with the bandage and salve, his hand bawled. Be a while until it healed. "What about the other animals?"

Weller looked impatient. "I told you. I know a farm we can stop at on the way. Three old guys. Brothers. They'll care for them."

"You sure they'll come if there are hunters on the way?"

"As sure as we can be," Mellie said. "Tom, we can only do our best."

"But the animals didn't hurt anyone," Tom said, stubbornly. "They don't deserve to die for this."

"And they won't," Weller said. "But we have to leave now. You want to save that girl? You make the bombs and we blow that mine, and then we march in there and you get Alex out of that prison house."

He looked up at Weller. "It's never that simple. We have to get in without getting caught. I have to position the explosives just right, and they have to go off in the right order. I'm not even sure it can be done. A building with good concrete support columns would take at least a couple hundred pounds of explosives."

"Look, we've been over this too," Weller said.

"All we've been *over* is that there's a mine you want me to help you blow up. What *I* want to know is why I should. How will blowing a mine full of Chuckies help Alex? How do you even know they're in the mine to begin with?"

From the way Weller's whiskered jaw jutted, he could tell the old man was impatient. "Because I've seen 'em," Weller grated, "and we've tracked groups. Way before all this happened, kids were always hanging around there. Had their parties, explored the tunnels. It was a meeting place. I know my grandkids, especially Mandy, she . . ." Weller looked away, his mouth working, then hawked and spat. "Anyway, that's where a lot of Changed—"

"Changed?"

Weller moved one shoulder in a half-shrug. "It's the name Rule's given the little bastards. I prefer Chuckies, tell the truth. Changed makes it sound too much like a Hand of God thing."

"How many are there at any given time? Do they live there?"

Weller's face folded in a thoughtful frown. "No, it's like they rotate in and out in these packs and gangs, just like kids in a high school cafeteria. I'd say, maybe, two hundred, two fifty? Sometimes more or less, depending."

"That's a lot of kids." Yet what Weller said echoed what Jed had mentioned on more than one occasion: Chuckies orbited the familiar. What better place to hang than where there'd been great parties and good times? "And they don't get cold?"

"It's like I said, Tom. Once you're deep enough, mines stay pretty warm, and they get hotter the further down you go. Hell, there were days I wasn't wearing but skivvies, boots, a hard hat, goggles, and gloves. There's a lot of space to spread out in that mine, too: cut rock rooms for machine shops and storage areas. Places to rest, stretch out a while, even have lunch. There's this one big stope—"

"Stope?" Anything Tom knew about mines came from movies. "You mean a mine shaft?"

Weller shook his head. "You ever seen one of those ant farms they got in schools? All those hollowed-out chambers? That's a mine right there, in miniature: nothing more than a big anthill with tunnels that lead to rooms, only the rooms are called stopes and they're carved out of rock instead of sand. Some are real small, only big enough for a man. Others are huge. In this particular mine, there's one room about five hundred and fifty feet down that's nothing more than a big, hollow ball of rotten rock with only these spindly pillar supports holding up the ceiling. There are stress fractures so wide in some of the walls you could drive a truck."

"Five hundred and fifty *feet*?" That was just about the height of the Washington Monument. "How deep does this mine go?"

"Just a little over two thousand feet, not that the little bastards can get that far down. Mine's been flooded below a thousand feet for years. I wouldn't be surprised if the water's crept up even higher. In mines as old as this, you can have water on the level above or in the next chamber over and not know it, so long as the rock holds. People who go exploring in abandoned mines around these parts drown all the time."

"So what, exactly, are you thinking about blowing up? The entrance? That room?"

"Not exactly. We want to take out the room *underneath*. It's not as big, but it's just as unstable. There's only sixty feet of rock between the two of them."

Meaning anyone planting bombs would have to drop down even deeper. "Sixty feet's still a lot of rock," Tom observed.

Weller snorted. "In a mine like this, sixty feet is nothing, and like I said, the rock is rotten, like bad ice, all cracked and broken-up with stress fractures." Weller cupped air with his left hand. "So you got this great big room, and sitting right beneath it"—he slotted his right hand beneath the left—"you got this other smaller chamber. Both of them are under a tremendous amount of stress. So you make the bombs, you blow out the pillars in the room *beneath* this larger room—"

"And you knock out the legs." He now understood where this was going: blow out the supports and everything would come crashing down.

"Exactly. You do it right," Weller said, "we bury those sons of bitches."

"It's a nice theory," Tom said, "but there are a lot of variables, and you still need a high explosive, time fuses, igniters, blasting caps—not to mention a way in and out of the mine."

Mellie stirred. "We've got that covered, Tom."

"Really?" He squinted from her to Weller. "If you guys are so covered, why haven't you blown the mine already?"

"Don't think we haven't considered it." Leaning forward, Weller straight-armed his saddle's pommel, the aw-shucks cowpoke coming on strong. "But it's like this. You can give a little kid a broken-down pistol and bullets. If he's smart and given enough time, he might eventually put it together so it works. But the chances are also excellent that little tyke's gonna peek down the barrel and pull the damn trigger just to see what happens. Understand what I'm saying? We got components; we have all the fixings. But none of us is an expert. Takes a long time to learn how to build a bomb without blowing your head off. That's time we don't have."

We got components. Of course they would. There had to be lots of weapons lying around nowadays. Easy pickings if you knew what you were looking for—and Mellie had said that they were *covered.* That meant they'd been amassing matériel and planning this for some time. He was their lucky accident, a piece of fortuitous serendipity. If he hadn't fallen into their laps, what then?

"But what's the point?" he asked. "What will killing them accomplish? You said yourself, they don't all stay there at one time; they move in and out."

"Yeah, but it's efficient; more bang for the buck. Sure, we won't kill *all* the little bastards. They're like rats. There've got to be hundreds out in these woods. But that mine *is* familiar territory and a meeting place. We chop off the head of this snake, and we accomplish two things." Weller held up one gloved finger. "First off, we disorganize the little shits and kill a bunch of them in the process. A lot may scatter and that's good. Second and more important, this helps clear one path to Rule. Not entirely, of course. Rule's got a pretty strong defensive perimeter set up."

"So how does destroying the mine clear a path?"

The old man cracked a nasty grin. "Because the Chuckies *are* part of the perimeter. Think about it. When you bait game, you can be pretty sure whatever you're drawing in will stick even closer. There's no incentive for that game to wander off. Now, who in their right mind is going to want to take on both the Chuckies *and* Rule's guns? See what I'm saying? It's like Rule's built up this guerilla force, this buffer, which leaves them free to concentrate their firepower in other areas." Weller let go of a disgusted grunt, but Tom thought he heard admiration there, too. "You got to admit, Peter and Chris had one hell of a brilliant idea there."

Brilliant—and pretty sick, too. *Talk about lions at the gate.* "Even if this works, we won't just march into Rule. You said this kid, Chris, is pretty tough, right?"

"Oh yeah, he's a sick son of a bitch; real smart, real sneaky. There's almost no one there knows him well. You ask people, they'll tell you how wonderful he is. He's got them all brainwashed, but they haven't seen the stuff I have. That prison house is where he really *cuts* loose, no pun intended. You should've seen the last girl when he was done with her. I'm just glad the poor little thing didn't make it. Turned my stomach, and I saw a thing or two in 'Nam. I did Tet; us Rangers was at Da Lat and Phu Cuong and . . ."

"Yeah, yeah, and I've been at Masum Ghar and Korengal and Paktika. So what?" As much respect as he had for vets like Jed, he was getting a little tired of Weller always playing the Vietnam card. "This isn't a contest about which of us has seen worse. But you, of all people, ought to know that *killing* our way in—"

"Is the *only* way," Weller said. His skin had gone chalk-white with rage. "Or haven't you got the stomach for it, soldier?"

"You know, that *soldier* jazz is getting really old really fast," he snapped. "Don't bait me. All I'm saying is that *you* got out of Rule."

Weller stiffened. "I see where you're going, but getting out wasn't *that* easy. I had to arrange a . . . a search, then figure a bogus excuse for splitting off from the men who can't be trusted, *and* cover my tracks."

"But you're not doing this out of the goodness of your heart. This is about some beef you've got with Rule."

"What do you care *what* my reasons are? I'm offering you a way *in*."

"But only if I do what you want," Tom countered. "Regardless of whatever grudge you've got going, there has to be a way of getting to Alex that doesn't involve murdering innocent people."

"Chuckies ain't people."

Tom shook his head. "I'm not talking about them. You're condemning an entire village, Weller. Not all the people there are guilty."

"They're complicit in their silence," Mellie put in. "The survivors who have bowed to Rule's conditions, who have decided upon survival at any cost, are as much to blame as the monsters on that Council. You think about *girls and boys* passed around. You think about *Alex* and some perverted, twisted man old enough to be her grandfather taking her into his *bed*."

Her words set his teeth. "All I'm saying is that you need to think very, very hard about what you're asking. There's got to be another way."

"There isn't and we're wasting time," Weller snapped. He gave his reins an angry twist. The blood bay let out a startled snort, then pranced and stamped as Weller brought the animal around. "From where I'm sitting, it's pretty damned simple, Tom: you're either in or you're out. You're for us or against us. So, what's it gonna be?"

And if I'm out? He doubted that Mellie and Weller would simply let him refuse and go on his merry way. Refusing might even be a death sentence. Weller hadn't revealed everything, and Tom trusted neither him nor Mellie. By his own admission, Weller was a traitor. Once you'd betrayed a friend, it was like a part of your soul crossed this invisible point of no return.

Yet the math was clear. Alex was in trouble and he needed a way into Rule. These people were his best shot. Once he found Alex, they would both go somewhere far away, where no one could touch them—or hurt her—ever again.

"Tell me what to do," he said.

65

"Good news?" Peter croaked. Those two words cost him. Breathing hurt. Every swallow threatened to close his throat. Peter lifted his bruised hand to inspect the damage, finger-walking the margins of a flap of moist flesh and torn muscle beneath his left ear the size of a Post-it note. Pretty bad. A little deeper and Davey would've ripped his carotid in two, but the kid's impatience saved his life. Peter still felt the ghosts of the kid's thumbs, which had jammed, dug down, and struggled to break his windpipe before Davey had given up and lashed out with his teeth. As soon as he felt the pressure let up and Davey's teeth batten down, Peter rammed the heel of his right hand into the kid's jaw. He would've finished the kid if the guards hadn't intervened.

No doubt about it, though: Davey was getting stronger and smarter. Either that or *he* was getting weaker. Probably both.

"Oh, yes." Finn clipped his walkie-talkie back onto his hip and then reached into a deep pocket and withdrew a canteen. "I tell you, boy-o, natural selection is a wonderful thing."

"Yeah?" The canteen was mesmerizing, a candle flame to a

moth. Peter watched, transfixed, as the old man unscrewed the cap.

"Mmm-hmm." Finn drank in big, languid swallows. The knuckle of Finn's Adam's apple rolled and bobbed and hitched. A trickle escaped to dribble onto the old man's chin, and Peter's tongue wormed to the corner of his own mouth in an effort to catch the drip. All he got was dirt and dried salt. His mouth tasted like an old toilet, and his breath reeked of rotted fruit. That wasn't good. He knew the stink of starvation.

Today was Tuesday: almost two and a half weeks since the ambush and now seven days in this cage. The last time he'd tasted water was two days ago. Since then, he'd had nothing to drink that wasn't his own piss. This morning, the half cup he'd squeezed out was dark as caramel, but he choked it down anyway. Last time he could pull that stunt, though. His pee was too concentrated now. Drinking any more would make his kidneys shut down just that much faster—which might be a relief, come to think of it. Slip off into a nice, quiet, lethal coma.

Finn let out a satisfied sigh, just like a guy getting a taste of the day's first cold brew. He placed the open canteen on the grimy concrete, then reached into his pocket again. This time, he came out with a plastic bag. "Take our little experiment," Finn said, teasing open the plastic and releasing a bloom of peanuts, salt, chocolate, and sugary dried fruit. "Our exploration of pressure, for example."

He wasn't sure which ache was worse: the desert dryness in his throat, or the way his gut knifed. "Pressure?"

"Well, isn't it?" Finn tossed back a handful of trail mix and munched. "Evolution is the study of environmental pressures. Either the individual adapts, or he doesn't. Adaption is Mother Nature's idea of"—Finn smiled—"torture."

"Yeah, you're really good with that." Water, Peter decided; the need for that was much worse. He watched Finn wash down his trail mix. If he'd had any tears left, he might have wept.

Across the width of the cell block, he saw Davey, in his usual spot, squatting at eye-level and watching *him* with the same avidity. The kid was patient as a spider in a web: all glittery-eyed, just waiting for a nice, juicy fly to blunder by. The other Changed also kept an eye on him, more or less. When he fought, that really seemed to grab them. But Davey was the only one who actually *studied* him.

That morning, Davey had dragged on a pair of olive-green pants for the very first time, too. His chest was still bare and he hadn't quite figured out shoes, but those pants were a step up. The only other kid anywhere close was a pimply boy who'd draped on a girl's bra so the cups covered his ears.

"I'm not trying to torture you." Finn inclined his head in Davey's general direction. "Or him or the other Chuckies. I agree the metaphors are the same. But torture someone and all you get are lies, because everyone wants the pain to stop. What we are doing *here* is truth. We are studying how the Chuckies and normals adapt under selective pressure. Some Chuckies, like Davey here, will adapt better. Choking you was, well, a new skill. They can learn." Finn smiled. "Just like you."

This was true. Davey's method wasn't quite how Peter had

killed Wendy but close. After two rounds with the girl, he realized that she was a southpaw and always led with the left. So he'd waited, timed the blow just right, ducking and then pistoning out with his balled fist to fracture her windpipe.

He could've ended it right there. A quick snap of the neck, and it would be over. It was the way he'd dispatched a flabby kid with a bristle of broken braces the day before Wendy. But Finn hadn't liked that. Hadn't told him why, but when Peter didn't get water that day, he realized that he either had to deliver a killing blow first time around or step back and let nature take its course.

So he let Wendy suffocate, slowly, for three very long minutes. He didn't look away either, because he worried that would cost him, too. He got his water and a little food that day, but nothing since. This fight with Davey was the closest he'd come to actually losing.

"Why are you keeping me alive?" he asked Finn.

"I'm not."

"Bullshit." Peter tried to laugh, but all he managed was a dry wheeze. "The guards pulled Davey out before he could finish me. You won't kill me outright but make me fight for food and water. If I can't fight, I'll either die from thirst or because one of *them* finally kills me. So, yeah, you're keeping me alive. Why?"

"Well, I'll tell you what, Peter." Finn planted his hands on his thighs and pushed to his feet. "Next time, don't fight."

"What?" Peter stared. "What are you talking about? How can I not fight?"

"Easily. You just don't."

But that was crazy. He *had* to fight, because that was his one shot at food and water. He might die; he might not. Don't fight and he'd die for sure. A Changed would have him for lunch, literally.

"If I don't fight, it's suicide," he said. "That's not an option."

"Well, if you want this to stop, it is," Finn said.

Kill himself? The idea had never occurred to him. Anyway, letting a kid tear him to pieces wasn't suicide . . . was it? No, suicide was a bullet to the brain, a knife across his throat, a noose. Murder wasn't suicide.

"I can't just *stop*," he said.

"Yes," Finn said. "You could. It's a choice, right? Not fighting just happens to be a choice you don't like. You're very *vince aut morire* that way. Conquer or die."

"But I've always fought," Peter said—and then he got it. "That's what you want them to learn: how to fight until they win. How not to give up. You want to see which ones *can* learn."

"I knew you were a smart boy," Finn said, and turned to go. As he did, his boot collided with his canteen, which overturned, sending water sheeting over the filth. "So you see? I'm not keeping you alive, Peter. You are."

But Peter wasn't listening anymore. He was on his belly, lapping water like a dog.

PART FIVE:
KILL ALL THE ENEMY

66

Ten days ago, Tom had still been dubious about the whole plan. In part, this was because he didn't trust Weller or Mellie as far as he could throw them. But he was also uneasy because of his reliance upon Weller's memories and assurances about the mine and its layout. By his own admission, the old man hadn't set foot belowground in the more than thirty years since the mine ceased operations.

"There are things you just don't forget, though," Weller had said, unfurling a grubby roll of yellowed paper over a low workbench that reminded Tom, too much, of Wade's butcher block. Considering that Mellie and Weller's camp was situated on an abandoned farm whose hog barn had been converted into a command center, Tom thought this wasn't such a great omen.

Weller's map was crap: just a rough pen-and-ink schematic with virtually no detail and nothing to scale. Yet the old man's description had been accurate. With its rough grid of vertical shafts and horizontal tunnels, broken up by cartoonish balloons where the biggest chambers were located, the thing *did* remind Tom of a glorified ant farm.

"When it comes to hard rock mining, you basically got two options," Weller said. "You can either tunnel in from the side and then truck ore out on a decline ramp—"

Tom shook his head. "I'm already lost. What's a decline ramp?"

"Just a big underground road. But you get to a point where you're down deep enough that using only the ramp becomes real expensive and inefficient." Weller's finger jumped to a vertical line. "So you drop a shaft, like what you see in movies."

"And that's how they hauled up the iron ore?"

"Not iron," Weller said. "Gold."

"Gold?" Tom's eyebrows rose. "In Michigan? You're kidding."

"Nope," Weller said. "Ropes Gold Mine is the most famous; that's way, way east, near Marquette. We're in the second-best place in the U.P. for gold, in Gogebic County. When the original Yeager—this would've been the current reverend's dad—started the first iron mine—"

"The one they eventually turned into Devil's Cauldron, right?"

"The lake, yeah. It's pretty common in these parts to fill tapped-out pit mines with water. Anyway, looking for gold was the brothers' idea, and once they did find it, they first tunneled *into* the mountain and then dropped shafts later. A shaft is a way of cutting down on distance. This ore body runs west to east, so it's better to drop a shaft over top and work your way down. Besides, once you're that far over, you need other escape routes in case something goes wrong—and in a mine, something *always* goes wrong. Plus, you situate the shaft right, you catch the air for better ventilation."

"With cross currents." He understood that. It was the same principle as opening multiple windows in a house depending upon the prevailing winds. "So how many shafts? I see three here."

"The biggest ones, yeah, going west to east." Weller touched the vertical line left of center on the paper and closest to where he'd labeled the entrance to the mine. "Shaft One, the Yeager Shaft, is the oldest, and goes down to eight hundred and fifty feet. Further east, they drilled Shaft Two, which peters out at twelve-seventy."

Tom studied the name scribbled next to Shaft Two: *Ernst*. That rang a bell. "Wait a minute. Isn't that the last name of that kid you told me about—the one who got killed in an ambush?"

"Peter." Weller made a face like the name smelled bad. "Yeah, that's him. The Ernsts partnered with the Yeagers from the get-go. Those families have always been tight."

Tom's eyes skated to the third shaft, which was both the deepest and the furthest east. "Who's Finn? Is he on this Council of Five you were talking about?"

Tom thought he saw something spirit through Weller's eyes, but it might just have been a trick of the light. "No," Weller said. "Tell the truth, I don't know much about the Finns, other than they went in on the mine as partners and then there was some kind of falling out. There is no Finn in Rule now."

"Okay. And you're sure these are the only shafts?"

"No, but they're the only ones that matter. I know there are others, but they're real straws by comparison, probably only big enough around for a couple people to get in and out. I don't even know *where* they are, tell you the truth. Most will have caved in or filled up with water by now anyway."

"What about the kids? Which shaft are they using to get in and out?"

"Near as we can figure it, they're not using *any* of the shafts. I think the Chuckies are holed up in the oldest chambers around the Yeager Shaft." Weller traced the rough rectangles outlined in ink that lay less than a finger's width to the right of the Yeager Shaft. "Those are right off that underground road, and the easiest to get to."

"If this rock is as rotten as you say, why haven't these chambers come down already?"

"Oh, parts of this mine already have, way back in 1962, and pretty much around this same general area, only *left* of the shaft. You can't see it now because the Yeagers backfilled the thing, but the ground just collapsed. No warning, not even a rumble. The hole was a hundred feet deep and four hundred feet wide. Lost a couple trucks and one of the change-out buildings. Killed seven miners," Weller said, then added, "One of them was my dad."

Hmm. Tom had a feeling there was a lot about Weller he just didn't know. "What's keeping this one from caving in now?"

"Whether or not a mine caves in depends on how well you shore it up. You can backfill the space with sand, but it's expensive and Yeager Brothers was a cheap outfit. What they left behind instead were these real spindly rock pillars." Weller skipped a finger to another rectangle penned immediately below the larger chambers. "The pillars in this one, where we'll plant the bombs, are even worse."

Like trying to hold up the second story of a rickety old house with toothpicks. "How are we going to get underneath and into *that* room without being seen?"

"We get in and out through the Ernst Shaft. You can't tell on this drawing, but the Ernst is actually a little southeast of the mine's main entrance. It connects up with the mine at regular intervals, starting at six hundred and seventy feet. We climb down the shaft, then hike over and up, plant our bombs, and hustle back out the same way. It's about a half mile one way, so not bad. Might be a few stray Chuckies around, but we can handle them." Weller shrugged. "All we need's a little luck."

"I don't believe in luck." Luck was just a synonym for a random event that didn't kill you. Tom saw a dozen things that could go wrong. Designing the bombs to deliver maximum force where it was required would take doing. Without more sophisticated electronics, he'd have to figure out a way to time the explosions. Even if he managed to do that, the bombs might go off early, or not at all. And what if the Chuckies posted guards, or they ran into more than *a few*? Weller had said that groups moved in and out of the mine. This particular kind of plan meant *they* could send out only a very small strike squad: three people at most. Stumble on a crowd and things would get interesting in a hurry. Or what if they succeeded but ended up trapped? Or say they made it out of the mine only to die when the ground opened up under their feet? Knock out underground supports and the surface might cave in, too, as Weller said had already happened back in 1962.

"Weller, even if we manage to collapse the room just beneath the kids, they'll still be above us," he said. "What's to stop them from using Shaft One or working their way over to that big underground road to escape?"

"They can't. If you collapse the room, everything drops *down*. You knock out the guts of an apartment building, there's no way to get to the fire escape unless you climb *up*. Same thing here. The Chuckies' only choice will be to go *down*, but there's no direct connection with the Yeager Shaft or the road at all. They'll be trapped good and tight. They won't be able to go down or up, and then those Chuckies either get crushed or suffocated or even drowned . . ." A nasty grin oiled over Weller's lips. "I don't care how they go, Tom, just so long as that mine's gone, the way to Rule is clear, and those monsters are dead."

67

Ten days later, Tom planted his left pole in the snow and kicked off hard, skating on his right ski before shifting his weight to his left and driving forward. He had a rhythm down now, and Jed's old Timex told him that he was making excellent time. He'd passed their first lookout post, the bell tower of an abandoned Lutheran church, an hour ago. He was panting now, but the work felt good, his muscles limber and warm. The snow was perfect, three inches of fresh powder atop an icy, heavier two-foot base like frothy whipped topping on ice cream.

His destination was a different lookout post snuggled into the east rim of Devil's Cauldron. The lake was man-made, and all that was left of the first Yeager Brothers mine: a rough, bowl-shaped gouge chunked from the earth that the Yeagers backfilled with water when the iron ore tapped out. The tailings—monstrous piles of rubble—had been covered with a thin layer of topsoil and were now home to snow-laden scrub and thin saplings on their way to becoming hardwood forest in another century or so. For now, the scrub offered good cover and an excellent view of the second mine to the west. The last quarter mile to the rim was all uphill, and he pushed himself, bounding up the slope, poling hard. By the top of the rise, Tom's heart was banging. His breaths came harsh and fast as he armed away sweat from his forehead, but he could feel how much stronger he'd gotten. A good thing, too: he would need every ounce of muscle he could muster, because in three hours, with any luck, they would be deep underground.

As he slid to a stop, a muzzled dog slunk from a blind. A scruffy boy, all in winter-white, followed a moment later. "Hey, Tom," the kid said.

"Chad." Tom unclipped from his skis, then ruffled the dog's ears. The kid had an Uzi carbine fitted with a suppressor—another of the toys Weller and Mellie had in abundance. "Is Luke here?"

"Yeah. He and Weller showed up twenty minutes ago." Chad lifted a chin toward Tom's pack. "Those them? Can I see one?"

"Okay." Kneeling, Tom opened the pack and withdrew a steel cylinder the size of a soda can. Three metal legs, secured with duct tape, protruded several inches from one end.

"Whoa, that's pretty funky," Chad said. He ran a finger in a copper concave divot capping one end of the cylinder. "So this is like Iraq and Afghanistan, right? An IED?"

"On a smaller scale, yeah." Tom pointed to the divot. "That's your penetrator. Same principle as a bullet. Throw a bullet at a deer, it bounces off. But if you put a lot of force behind it, the slug punches through. A shaped charge channels energy. It's why bullets are so destructive. It's not the hole that kills you. It's the energy transfer to the rest of your body—or, in this case, the rock." It actually wasn't that simple, but Tom wasn't wild about giving any of the kids a crash course on explosives manufacturing. Bad enough that he was forced to take Luke, but working alone or with only Weller would take too long.

Returning the charges to his pack, he cinched the drawstring, then stood and offered his hand. "Later, dude."

"Is it okay to wish you luck?" Chad asked.

In Afghanistan, guys had all kinds of superstitions, like never eating the Charms from an MRE. M&Ms were okay, except the blue ones. But Charms were the kiss of death. Charms they dropped in the burn shitter. Wish someone luck, you got your ass kicked.

"Oh, sure," Tom said.

The others waited on a small rise behind a screen of scrub. Luke heard him coming first and tipped a wave. Weller only nodded. Mellie and the other lookout didn't turn around. Ducking beneath brush, he squatted in the hollowed-out snow at Mellie's shoulder. "Anything new?"

Mellie didn't look up from a pair of 26×70s mounted on a low tripod. "I see some movement to the north, and there might be another group looping in from the west. Cindi?"

"Too far yet." Peering through Big Eyes 40×100s, Cindi, a freckle-faced twelve-year-old, nibbled her lower lip. "But I think those guys dropping down the north approach road have prisoners."

Tom's stomach tightened. "How can you tell?"

"The flashlights." Luke was fourteen and the oldest after Tom. He'd attached himself to Tom almost right away; nearly all the kids had decided Tom was their big brother. He really didn't mind. All these kids made him feel a little better. He worried, too, what would happen to them when he and Alex left. Maybe . . . take along the kids who wanted to come? Yeah, but could they really all manage?

One step at a time, he thought. *Do this and then find Alex. The rest will sort itself out.*

Luke sipped watered-down instant coffee from a mess cup. "We've been watching for a couple weeks. When there are flashlights, that usually means prisoners. The Chuckies don't seem to need a lot of light to see where they're going."

That was interesting. It might be another reason why the Chuckies favored the mine. "Do you know how many?" Tom asked.

Cindi did a one-shouldered shrug. "Four, five in that group. Maybe more. The Chuckies have really stocked up, though. There are a lot of people already in the mine for . . . you know . . ."

"A snack," Tom said. "Innocent people they're putting by for a rainy day."

"Aw, Christ," Weller muttered.

"Tom," Mellie said.

"Ah . . ." Cindi's cheeks flushed a sudden, furious scarlet. Her eyes pinged from Tom to Mellie and back again. "Yeah. Anyway, when this group gets a little closer, I can tell better."

"Tom, we knew there would be prisoners," Mellie said. Her tone sounded more like a warning. "You're okay with this, right?"

"Which part? The killing innocent people part, or the burying Chuckies alive part?" He knew it was the wrong thing to say, but he didn't want this to be easy either. "This isn't a video game, Mellie. Real people are going to die."

"Well, isn't it good we got ourselves a group conscience?" Weller growled. "Tell me something, Tom: you get all soft and gooey on patrol?"

"I got my job done," Tom said.

"Glad to hear it." Weller unscrewed the thermos and splashed coffee into his cup. "I guess that explains why you're *here* instead of *there*."

He saw Luke and Cindi exchange startled glances, and a surge of anger brought the blood to his face. "Listen," Tom began.

"Tom?" Mellie pushed to her feet. "Let's walk. Weller, why don't you come with us?"

Weller's expression suggested he'd rather hug a cobra, but he recapped the thermos and followed. Mellie waited until they were behind a thicket of denuded scrub oak and a lonely jack pine. Then she crossed her arms over her chest. "Something on your mind, Tom?"

"You know what's bothering me," he said.

"Yes, I do. So let me be clear. This is not a rescue mission. We need to make sure those monsters do not survive."

"At the cost of innocent lives?"

"Don't tell me about innocent lives. You know Daniel and the rest of my kids never made it."

"But that doesn't mean they're dead," Tom said. "They might have gone their own way."

"Unlikely."

"Then has it occurred to you that they might be there, in the mine?"

"Of course it has, but we've seen no children. Even if we had, that changes nothing. This has to be done."

"I don't know what your problem is," Weller put in. "You're not a cherry fresh outta basic. Collateral damage is part of the game."

"It's not a game," Tom said. "This is like storming a concentration camp."

Weller snorted. "Jesus."

"No, Weller," Mellie said. "He's got a point. But, Tom, those people are dead men walking. If we succeed, some might live. Many won't, but we don't have a lot of choices. You're a soldier. Don't tell me you never fired on enemy targets when there were civilians around."

Not as a first choice, no. They were under orders, although his captain had changed his tune after an ambush killed his sergeant and wounded another. Tom hadn't fired the javelin; that wasn't his job. But he saw the house cave in and, later, the three small bundles of bloodied sheets. The father was dead, too, and so were four Taliban holed up inside. No one fired a shot from that house ever again.

Now he said, "It wasn't my call to make then, but this will be. We go through with this, it's *on* me."

"This is a war," Weller said, like that was supposed to be explanation enough. "Us against the Chuckies. Us against Rule. Taking out that mine is the first step."

Hard choices. Collateral damage. Mellie and Weller were very fond of catchphrases. "What about the people who have no say? The ones trapped in that mine who can't get out?"

Weller cursed, then tossed the dregs of his coffee onto the snow. "I'm not debating this anymore. You're not in charge of this operation."

"You're not my CO either," Tom said.

"Well, lucky me, 'cuz ain't he dead? In fact, it's a good bet your entire brigade's gone, isn't it?"

The words dropped like hammer blows. "What does that have to do with anything?"

"Because we're what's left. I was in 'Nam before your parents were in diddies. There is nothing about war I don't know. You want to see Alex again? *This* is how we do it."

"Weller." Mellie planted a palm on the old man's chest. "We need to work together here."

"Don't worry about me," Tom said, roughly. Later, when he was alone, he'd probably put a fist through something, but right now there was Alex to think about. "I'll do my job."

"All right then." Weller's mouth worked as if he'd like to spit. "No harm, no foul."

Liar. But he kept his mouth shut. He'd taken his best shot. There was absolutely nothing he could say to this old man that wouldn't be a mistake right now.

"Oh, Tom," Mellie said. She reached for him, but he sidestepped and left her grabbing air. Her sympathetic expression slipped then firmed, but didn't quite leak into her eyes. "We're all on the same side," she said.

"Sure," he said.

68

Cindi feathered the mag on her Big Eyes. "Hunh."

"What?" Luke asked.

"I think . . ." Yup, she was sure of it. The sun wasn't below the horizon yet and the light was behind her, so she could see pretty well. The image coalesced and resolved. "Remember that pack of Chuckies, the ones who wear those wolf skins? They're back."

"Yeah? How can you tell?"

"Come here." She waited until he wormed over on his belly and peered through her tripod-mounted binocs. "It's the flutter. You know, the wolf skin is loose, so it catches the wind? Dead giveaway. It's still the same girl, but the guy she's with is new."

"Okay, I see it . . . whoa," Luke said. "What's going on with her face?"

"Dunno." Either the girl had the world's worst zit or she was sprouting another eye on her cheek. And who was this new guy? What had happened to the old one? Dead, maybe. Boy, that would be okay. The more Chuckies that bit the dust, the safer they all were. Besides, those wolf-people were a little freaky, kind of *Mad Max*-y with those wolf skins.

"There are a *bunch* of new guys with those wolf-people," Luke said. "Check out the hardware."

"Yeah, I saw them." Some serious firepower there: a couple Uzis, for sure, or maybe MAC-10s—she wasn't that much into guns. One kid wore this very funky bandolier slotted with what looked like huge bullets. Those brass heads must be the size of her fist. "Scoot over. I want to check on how many normals they got."

"I think at least five," Luke said, making room. "The way they kind of walk, you know? All shuffly?"

"Uh-huh." She eased her eyepiece into focus, then said, "Oh boy."

"What?"

"I think there are two kids. Like, you know, old enough to be Chuckies."

She could hear Luke's eyes go wide. "Really?"

"Yeah." Up till now, she'd never seen any normal kids walking into that mine—and now here were two. They were still too far away for her to make out much detail, but she thought one was a girl. The other kid wasn't walking right. Hurt? Maybe.

"What's up?"

She jumped, then looked over her shoulder at Tom, who was staring down at both of them. God, he was quiet as a cat. "Nothing," she said, hoping Luke would keep his trap shut. Mellie said Tom needed to focus: *Don't make him feel worse about this than he already does.* Telling him about two normal kids suddenly being on the Chuckies' dinner menu would not be cool. "I mean . . . you know."

A frown crept over his face. "You okay, Cindi?"

"She's okay," Luke said. "We were just looking at the wolf-people. They're this tribe into wearing wolf skins. We think something happened to the lead guy, that's all."

"And there are more Chuckies than we thought," she added. "Like they hooked up with some friends and all came here together, you know?"

"Oh." Tom was quiet a second, then said, "Luke, we better get going. I want to be in position by the time the moon rises. See you soon, Cindi."

"You bet, Tom." Okay, if she was honest, she knew that the fluttery feeling she got whenever Tom was near was incredibly lame. Like, hello, she was *twelve*. But Tom was *so* hot, with those dark blue eyes and wavy hair that was this incredible shade of brown with a lot of red, like really expensive cinnamon. And muscles. Like, real guy muscles. And he was so *brave*. No way she'd make things worse for him. "Be careful, okay?" She cringed as soon as the words were out of her mouth. *Of all the things I could've said, that's, like, complete girl.*

"You, too." Tom's expression remained serious. "Things go bad, you get out of here, okay? Don't let Mellie talk you into sticking around."

"Nothing's going to go wrong," she said. "Good luck."

Something swept through his face, fleet and fast. "Yeah," he said, but the tight smile looked more like a grimace. "Luck."

Much later, Cindi saw something that changed her mind about those two new kids. The one she'd thought was a girl definitely was, and probably a junior or senior. Nice hair, too: long and red. She'd kill for hair like that. Anyway, the girl, Red, was helping this seriously good-looking blond guy. But what got Cindi's attention was when Red suddenly pulled up at just about the same moment as the wolf-girl, the one with the messed-up face and blonde hair.

That was when Cindi knew for sure: Red wasn't a prisoner. She was a Chucky.

Well, thank goodness she hadn't said anything to Tom. The knot in Cindi's gut unraveled. If Tom had found out, he might not have gone through with bombing the mine. But there was no doubt in Cindi's mind now. Only Chuckies acted like dogs catching a scent. So Tom and Luke and Weller blowing Red and her friends into eensy-weensy pieces was fine.

Oh, Red, Cindi thought, and smiled. *Sucks to be you.*

69

The mine complex was like a ghost town or something out of a news report on Iraq or Afghanistan, cluttered with decayed and bombed-out-looking buildings that were mostly broken shells of native stone and red brick. In the distance, south and east, the rusting girders of a steel headframe reared. But it was when she caught her first glimpse of the entrance to the mine that Alex was certain. She'd seen this before in all those photographs on the display table in that lake house. Why the Changed would gather together in the first place was anyone's guess, but if they kept to the familiar, then coming here made sense. This must've been a favorite hangout, not only for the kids from Rule but for those of surrounding villages and towns. Actually, the scene reminded her, crazily, of a huge high school courtyard mobbed with students just before that final morning bell.

End of the road. She trudged along, following the sashaying sway of Spider and Leopard in their wolf skins. She should've been frightened, but she was too tired. Her shoulders ached from Daniel's weight, and she was drenched in a hard sweat. She'd practically carried him, semiconscious and feverish, these last ten miles. He'd only dragged along, his boots scraping over snow, like a malfunctioning robot. The closer they got, the more the heavy smog-stink of boiled roadkill clogged the air, churning into a general fug. She could feel her throat trying to close against the oily stench. She spat, working to clear her mouth, but the fetor was stubborn and had glued itself to her tongue.

Then she caught something new. The contact was very brief, the product of the merest shift in a light breeze. Considering Daniel's sickness, the fume of sewage, and the salt grime of her own skin, it was a wonder she snagged any stray scents at all. But she did, and when she caught it, just that little whiff, she went instantly rigid, Daniel's nearly dead weight around her neck forgotten for the moment.

No, it can't be. Alex threw a wild glance to the west. The moon wasn't up yet, but the horizon was a wash of scarlet and neon orange. The day was dying and the breeze, too, and yet the scent feathered her nose, just for an instant: an aroma that was early-morning mist spread across the dark shadows of a mirrored lake, and just as evanescent.

Chris? The realization coalesced in her throat as a hard lump. An image of the last time she'd seen him—unconscious in a startling splash of blood that stained the snow—floated from memory. Chris was alive and he was *here*? No, that couldn't be right. She sucked in another breath, but the breeze must've shifted, because that fleeting odor was gone. She worried what was left, letting the smell ball and roll around her mouth. No, it wasn't quite a match, was it? There were elements of Chris there, though. Maybe it was the general fug of the Changed, but the smell reminded her of—

No. The idea was so stunning she sucked in a sharp gasp. *He's dead. It can't be—*

Spider suddenly stiffened. A moment later, a hot, noxious odor, sharp as a quill, needled Alex's nose. The stink was bitter with fury and frustration and reeked of dread. At his place by Spider's side, Leopard had also gone very still. Their heads were thrown back and their mouths hung open as they drank in that strange scent. Then Spider swiveled. Her silver eyes, glittery with hate, pinned Alex with a glare. Alex stumbled back a half-step as if struck, and she felt herself drawing in, trying to grow small like a geeky kid anxious to avoid the notice of a class bully. Spider's wound was better, probably because they'd taken their sweet time getting here. Leopard and the gang kept the larder stocked, so Spider had eaten well for over two weeks, when she wasn't screwing her brains out. (Being Daniel's roommate had been a mixed blessing, considering. But the way Leopard's gaze continually scraped over *her*, Alex was just as happy that Spider kept him busy. God help her if Leopard ever got her alone.) But the rip in Spider's cheek would never heal completely. Honestly, Spider looked a little bit like the villain in that Batman movie, the one who'd gotten half his face eaten away so you could see naked teeth and bone and muscle. Two-Face?

At that moment, Alex felt Daniel twitch and try pulling out of his slouch. His eyes, sick and bleary, fluttered. His breath was foul from vomit. "Wuhhh?"

"Daniel?" He hadn't said much all day. She gave him a little shake. "Daniel, it's Alex. Can you—"

"Uhhh," Daniel groaned, and then his knees tried to fold.

"No, no," she said, bracing him up. "Come on. Try and walk, Daniel. We're almost there, and soon you can rest." Ahead, she saw that Spider and Leopard had started on their way again, but they were worried. The smell of it fizzed like soda bubbles popping against her nose.

She could see the entrance clearly now: a maw, bristling with icicles, ready to eat her alive. Its breath was a stale fog of death and blood, of grimy flesh and sweat from the many other prisoners who must be down there, of cold stone. And the Changed, of course.

She shifted Daniel's weight across her shoulders. Behind, she heard the slow, resigned shuffle of the older prisoners as they came abreast and then broke around her and Daniel. None looked their way. Having spent the last two weeks virtually sequestered with Daniel, she hadn't had a chance to get to know them at all, and they'd kept their distance, especially now that Daniel was so sick. She wasn't sure she blamed them.

If I go in there, I'm not coming out again. This, she thought, was her last chance. Run for it, or not. She eyed the Changed milling around the entrance. An easy fifty right there, and all of them armed, although she was fairly certain they wouldn't shoot her. Spider had other plans.

Besides, even if she somehow made it past all these Changed, what future would she be running toward? Rule? Chris? No. She'd never make it to either. She knew because she had smelled him, just as Spider and Leopard had on that stray finger of wind. And Alex wasn't entirely sure how she felt about this or what it meant.

Because it wasn't Chris out there.

It was Wolf.

70

"And they always leave a symbol?" Nathan's skin was drawn so tight, his cheeks were knife blades. "Never a name or address?"

"No, it's always a hex sign," Chris said. He pressed a finger to his temple, trying to massage away a headache that just wouldn't quit. The red line of his pack's mini-thermometer just kissed freezing, but night was coming on and the temp outside the two-man was dropping fast. Turtling deeper into the sleeping bag, Chris jerked his chin at the drawing of a blue and red pentagram set against a white circle and done in rough strokes of colored pencil. "The colors are important, too, because the first time I went into a barn with the same design but different colors—a blue background, and alternating red and white for the star—there was nothing."

He looked up at the sound of a zipper. The tent grayed and then Lena squirmed through the double flap, dragging a gout of frigid air and just the tiniest hint of sour bile in her wake.

"Cold." Her breath steamed. Quickly zipping the flap shut, she burrowed into the only other sleeping bag. "It feels like it's minus a hundred out there, and it's getting windy, too."

Nathan tugged at his right jowl. "Everything come out all right?"

"Ha. Ha." The tip of her nose was windburned, but her face was nearly transparent. "Bet I haven't heard that since second grade."

Nathan spread his hands. "Just trying to lighten the mood."

Chris said nothing. They were all exhausted, but Lena was getting sicker, and her breath was heavy with the stink of vomit. A creep of dread walked his neck. *The longer we stay out here, the worse it's going to get. I can't keep putting this off.* But he still might be wrong. Nathan was just as experienced, and yet he'd said nothing, not a whisper. When a girl got sick every morning and stayed sick all day, there might be another reason that a man old enough to be her grandfather might be uncomfortable mentioning.

"I think there's another storm coming, too." She drew the bag down tight until only her face showed as a pale oval. "The sky's kind of inky north of us."

"Better hope not." Nathan's fingernails rasped over salt-and-pepper stubble. "Bad for us if we get stuck again."

"God, it's been *weeks*. How much further?" Lena asked.

"Maybe another two days if the weather holds and we stop for a whole night. The Changed are pretty thick, though, so I think it's best if we keep moving. Rest for shorter periods, stagger our hours. Be to Oren that much faster, and then we can find a place to hole up while we figure out where to look. Speaking of which . . ." Nathan proffered the penciled drawing. "You know all these hex signs?"

"Sure. I just don't know which barns have what." Still swathed in the bag, Lena cocked her head and gnawed at her lower lip. Most of the skin was chewed off. Ugly scabs beetled over her mouth.

"But it's like I told Chris. They call that one the Five Wounds. Most barns have a bunch. I don't know what they all mean, but . . . yeah."

"Oh, I know this one. Five wounds of Christ. Pentagram was an early Christian symbol, way before the Cross," said Nathan. "Is it always the same symbol?"

Chris shook his head. "It's like I said. When they want me to find them, they leave a drawing in the bookmobile's dictionary. Then it's a matter of going barn to barn until I find the right one. Takes a while."

"Well then, I guess the bookmobile's our first stop. Unless we get lucky and they got sentries posted." Nathan eyed him. "Anyone ever take a shot? You get the sense of someone keeping watch?"

He had, but that wasn't new. Ride out of Rule often enough where there were raiders or Changed or both, and his eyes never stopped pinballing. "Sure. On the other hand, I've never come in this way before or brought anyone with me—to the bookmobile, anyway. I made Greg and the others wait just outside town. Plus, I'm early. There may be nothing."

"God." Lena let out a long sigh. "What do we do then?"

"Panic." He meant it as a joke, but when she didn't smile, Chris put a hand on her shoulder. What he didn't like was that he had to think twice about that. "The big difference this time is you. If they see you, they may realize it's okay to show themselves."

"Maybe." Lena's tone was as dry and lifeless as a shriveled corn husk. "But it's not like I was all that popular."

"What about this guy, Isaac Hunter? You're absolutely sure you never heard the name?" When she shook her head, Chris looked to Nathan. "You've got to know something. Yeah, yeah, I know you trust Jess and if she says he can help, you believe that, but we're not in Rule now and Jess isn't calling the shots. So even if it's only rumors or educated guesses, anything you know or suspect might help."

He watched Nathan think about that. "I never knew the name," Nathan said, finally, "but there *was* this story floating around from when I was about your age. So . . . sixty years ago?"

"About Hunter?"

"No." Nathan ran a hand over his chin. "About these wild kids. No, no," he added when he saw Chris's expression, "it's not what you think. We're not talking kids going native or something. It's something the Amish kids do, though."

"You mean *rumspringa*," Lena said. She propped herself up on an elbow. "I know about that."

"Well, I don't," Chris said. Merton was far enough southeast that anything he knew about the Amish came from movies, which translated to *not much*. "What is it?"

"An Amish custom," Nathan said. "It means 'running around.' The Amish are different in a lot of ways, and especially when it comes to baptism. Children aren't baptized into the church at birth. It's a lifestyle they have to choose with their eyes open, and the Amish believe that only adults, who've experienced the world, can do that. So at sixteen, they let the kids run free to do anything they want. The theory might be sound, but it's a terrible idea."

"How come?"

"Because they don't know anything. None of those kids has

the faintest idea of what's beyond their settlements, in the *English* world, and when they get cut loose like that, with no one to guide them, they run wild." One corner of Nathan's mouth tugged down in a wry grimace. "I met . . . quite a few girls. That was something we boys took advantage of, because no girls *we* knew would go as far as those Amish girls. All those kids partied hard. Looking back, it's not something I'm real proud of."

"Okay, I think I get it." Chris felt his own skin heat with embarrassment. The last thing he wanted was to hear a guy his grandfather's age reminiscing about all those great hookups from the good old days. "But what's *that* got to do with *this?*"

"Maybe nothing," Nathan said. "In the end, most Amish kids run around for a couple years before choosing to follow Amish ways. They get themselves baptized and that's the end of it. But there are always kids who don't want to come back or do and *then* leave, which takes a thousand times more guts."

"Guts?"

"Yeah," Lena put in. "If they leave after they're baptized, then they're *shunned*."

"Shunned." A small *ding* of recognition. "You mean, like the Ban?"

"I mean, almost exactly that," Nathan said. "It's called *meidung*. Basically, it's the Amish version of tough love. People will still talk to them, but that's about it. They can't take communion, participate in the community, any of that. The idea is to get them to repent and change their minds. I don't remember how long a person's got before it becomes permanent."

"Permanent? As in, no going back?"

"As in excommunication. If that happens, it's like you're a shadow, or dead. These poor kids got nothing: no education, no family, no resources, nowhere to go." Nathan paused. "But it would be natural for them to stick together and try to help each other."

"Like an underground railroad." The slow dawn of an idea glimmered in his mind. Chris could feel his brain grinding through the implications, making connections. "Is that what I'm looking for?"

"Well." Nathan paused. "Jess thinks you found it. A piece, anyway."

"I don't get it," Lena said.

"A breakaway community. A settlement of kids made up of those who chose to leave. But they'd need help, maybe even someone who knew what they were going through because he or she had been excommunicated . . ." Chris's voice trailed away as another idea bubbled from whatever stew his mind had been brewing these last few weeks. He looked back at Nathan. "They'd need *help*."

"You said that," Lena said.

"*Jess*," Chris said.

"What do you mean?"

"I mean that *Jess* had to be one of them." He looked back at Nathan. "That's right, isn't it? She's Amish, or she used to be." He saw the hesitation cross Nathan's features and added, "Come on. The only way she could know about them in so much detail, enough to give you a *name*, would be if she'd lived there."

Nathan gave a slow, almost reluctant nod. "That's the theory."

"Theory?" Lena asked. "Why would this even be a secret? So what if she was Amish and then shunned or excommunicated or whatever? Who in Rule would even care?"

"Well, if their leader's the Reverend's brother," Nathan said, "they just might."

71

"Brother?" Chris echoed in surprise. "My grandfather's *brother*? I thought he was dead."

"He is," Nathan said.

"But you just said—"

"Wait, I get it. It's not dead-dead, Chris. It's dead, as in excommunicated," Lena put in. She'd pushed herself all the way to a sit. Her skin was milky-white, and the circles around her huge eyes were a dusky purple. "To the Amish, it's the same thing."

"But his last name is Hunter, not Yeager," Chris protested.

"*You're* a Yeager," Lena said.

"Only half," Chris said. "My dad wasn't from Rule at all."

"Once you've left the Amish, you've crossed into the *English* world," Nathan said. "*Yeager* is German for 'hunter.'"

Chris let that sink in for a moment. If his grandfather's brother had provided a refuge for shunned or banned Amish kids, then that meant Rule had to be some kind of crazy breakaway community, too. It would explain some of their customs, how cult-like the village was. But which split came first, Rule from Oren, or

Hunter's group from Oren? *Or even Rule.* "Do Amish have, like, I don't know, a council? Some group of guys who run things?"

"All I ever heard of was the bishop," Lena offered, and then she pulled in a gasp. "Wow. Wait a minute, that's not right. The way the Amish did it was like this committee." She held out a thumb. "There was a bishop," she said, and then counted the rest off on her fingers: "Also three ministers, and . . . a deacon."

"Five guys," Chris said. "Just like Rule."

"Not like Rule." Nathan wagged his head. "As far as I know, a bishop never makes the laws. Any big issues have to be put to a vote in the community. Rule was never run that way. What they had instead was a sixth chair, which was supposed to *represent* everybody else. Go take a look at the Council chamber sometime. You'll see. It doesn't look balanced."

Now that he thought about it, Chris remembered that, way back, *Alex* had once pointed out the same thing—a sixth chair, set by itself, behind the others: *Six chairs, but only five men, Chris. It's like there's someone missing.* And the missing man was Rule itself?

Something else Alex had mentioned also floated out of memory. His grandfather was very fond of Biblical brother stories: Cain and Abel, Jacob and Esau. But his favorite was Isaac and Ishmael, and what had he once said about the world outside Rule? *The followers of Satan have become as beasts; they bear the Mark of Cain and the Curse of Ishmael.* But if Isaac *was* his grandfather's brother, then which brother was really the beast?

"What's Jess's connection to Hunter?" Chris asked. "Why does she think he can help us, or even will? It's got to be more than just him giving sanctuary to a bunch of kids."

"I honestly don't know, Chris," Nathan said. "This is what me and Doc have been able to piece together, and it's still mostly guessing. But you find him, and then I think we got a shot at putting what's gone wrong with Rule to rights."

"And if he's dead?"

"Then I don't know," Nathan said. "We just got to hope that he's not."

"What do you think?" Chris asked a few moments later. Nathan had ducked out, ostensibly to check the horses, but Chris knew the old man was giving them space to talk things over. Not, Chris thought, that this would change much. He couldn't see any way out of the box but to continue on toward Oren.

"I think it's still pretty crazy. Oh, man . . ." Lena unzipped then reluctantly peeled back the flap of her sleeping bag with a grimace. "It's so cold my teeth hurt whenever I breathe."

He watched her make her slow, careful way out of the bag. "How are you feeling?"

"Bad." She paused. "I'm sorry I'm slowing you down."

"That's okay. Weller was right. We had to put down some serious distance east before hooking back. It would have been the same either way."

"Maybe." She stuffed the bag into its carry sack and cinched down the drawstring without looking up. "Do you ever wonder what's going on in Rule? Like if they've found Peter yet?"

"I don't think about Rule much at all, not as a place where I belong anymore. I think about what it's doing, what it's *done*. But Peter? Sure." Chris snapped his pack shut. The sound was loud in the cold, like the crack of an icicle. "Whether it was his idea to feed the Changed, or the Council's . . . it doesn't matter. He should've fought it, and he didn't."

"So, if he *is* alive . . ." She fell silent a moment, then continued, "If he's alive, and you *do* decide to fight Rule, would you fight him?"

"I guess I'd have to." Turning aside, he unzipped the tent flap. "I don't know. I just hope I don't. To tell you the truth, Lena . . . I hope he's already dead. Then it won't have to be a choice."

"But what if he isn't?"

"Then I hope I could talk to him."

"What if he won't listen? You know how Peter gets."

Yes, he did. Cold pillowed against his face. The air was so dry he felt his eyeballs pucker. He could almost make himself believe that he was past rage and sorrow for his friend even as the pang in his chest gave the lie. *God, why is this up to me? I can't kill Peter; I'd rather blow my own brains out first. I'm not even sure I can fight Rule.* "Is there a reason you care?" He didn't look around. "Maybe . . . something I should know?"

"Maybe. Yeah. I . . ." Her tone was flat and dull. "It . . . it only happened twice. Sarah doesn't know, but . . . yeah. I think . . . I think so."

That has to be it. They're not tracking us because she's Changing. The wash of relief left him so weak he clutched the tent flap. He remembered the boy winding that scarf around his neck—the one Chris had planted in the bodies because it was the only explanation that made sense. *They're able to find us because she's* pregnant, *and* Peter's *the—*

"So what are you going to do?" Lena pressed. "If Peter's alive and he won't listen and you have to fight?"

"Let's hope it doesn't come to that," Chris said.

72

"Oh shit." Luke retched again but brought up only watery phlegm. In the glow of that green moon, the boy's face was the color of moldy cheese. *"Shit."*

"Keep it down, unless you want every damn Chucky to hear us," Weller hissed. He still had both hands clamped around the dead boy's head, and a knee planted behind his shoulders. The boy was no older than Luke, and had made the mistake of wandering away from the pack to enjoy a little snack. They'd heard him slurping and gulping while he was still a good twenty yards away from their hiding place, a snow trench behind thick scrub forty feet from Shaft Two. The boy was so focused on his treat—a double fistful of brains—that he didn't see Weller until the very last second. The boy had fought and thrashed and nearly bucked the old man, but Weller ground the kid's head into the deep snow until the boy suffocated.

"Sorry." Luke was gasping. He shot another glance at the spongy goo splattered over the snow. "It's just . . . I never . . ."

"Isn't the worst you'll ever see," Weller said, using the back of his hand to smear a wormy snail slick from the underside of his chin.

"Lay off." Tom put a hand on the kid's shoulder. "We had to do it this way, Luke. Didn't want to get blood on his clothes." But he was angry. A good headlock and the boy would've been unconscious in ten seconds. A quick twist of the neck right and then left and it would've been over. That boy had suffered all so Weller could make a point. Tom had known guys like him in the Army, too.

Don't let it get to you. His heart was pounding too hard. He willed himself to ice, felt the change as the adrenaline tailed off and his pulse slowed. *He's an asshole, but he knows the mine and Rule. You need him just as badly as he needs you.*

"All right, let's get his shirt off, and that jacket, but I'd avoid the pants." Huffing, Weller levered himself from the snow. "Chucky took himself a little dump."

Weller was enjoying this way too much. "I'll do it," Tom said. He rolled the body, then quickly unzipped the boy's jacket and stripped him from the waist up, taking not only the clothes but the boy's flashlight, knife, rifle, and spare box cartridge full of ammo. He tossed the shirt and parka to Luke. "He's about your size."

"Oh. Yay." Luke handled the clothes as if they were rattle-snakes. "We sure I got to do this?"

"No, but it can't hurt." Weller kicked snow over the ruin of gluey brains. "If you two smell like Chuckies, it's all to the better. Remember, once we get inside, *I'm* bologna."

"You can do this, Luke. Leave the thermal top for me. Now, be quick." Hooking his hands around the dead boy's ankles, Tom dragged the body into the trench, then scuffed snow until the boy was invisible. The rifle, a scoped Browning BLR '81, was a good weapon but useless for their purposes. Their Uzis were silenced. After thumbing out the bullets, he broke the weapon down and threw all the hardware in different directions. By the time he returned, Luke was just zipping up the dead boy's jacket.

"This feels kind of creepy." Luke gave the cuffs a tug. "Like, you know, I'm wearing him."

"That's the idea," Weller grated.

"You can burn it after, Luke," Tom murmured. His eyes were focused on the rolling, brushy terrain between their hiding place on this rise and the shaft. In the moonlight, the snow glowed with the soft phosphorescence of a firefly and reminded him of the view from night-vision goggles. Ahead, the swell of a snow-covered mound bulged. "You sure that's the shaft?"

"Yeah," Weller said. "Stick close. Last thing we need is to take a tumble."

They shambled over the snow, awkward because of the packs and ropes and Uzis, and Tom felt the terrain change under his boots. The mound wasn't solid but ice-encrusted rubble. They crabbed over the snow, and then Weller reached for a small, jury-rigged headlamp. A tiny *snick*.

In the sudden spear of light, the shaft yawned in a black, circular sore: a wide tube of concrete about twenty feet across. The headframe and hoist were gone. Only an iron ladder bolted to the concrete remained. Weller scratched through snow for a rock, then opened his hand over the shaft. Tom counted, silently. Five seconds. Fifteen. At thirty, he said, "I didn't hear anything. You?"

Weller shook his head, then swarmed to the ladder. Everything looked solid, but up close, Tom could smell rust and see where the rungs had oxidized and crumbled. Thin fractures spidered around some of the bolts where water had seeped then frozen, breaking open the concrete.

"Only one way to test it," Weller said. He threw a quick clove hitch onto a carabiner, then clipped in. Luke grabbed Tom's waist and Tom braced himself, the rope looped across his back and firmly gripped in both hands, as the old man carefully lowered himself onto the first rung, shifted his weight. Took the second rung. The third. "Think we're good to go."

Luke ran a hand over the iron. "Feels pretty rotten to me."

"Boy, I was dropping down cliffs in Quang Ngai while Charlie rained fire," Weller said. "This is nothing."

Yeah, yeah, and you picked your teeth with a bayonet. "We don't have much choice, Luke," Tom said.

"But there's nothing to tie the rope to," Luke said. "If the ladder goes—"

"It's a long way down," Weller said. "You backing out?"

"Just do what I do," Tom cut in. He'd be damned if he'd let Weller embarrass the kid. "Except if I slip . . . don't do that."

Luke exhaled a shaky laugh. "I'm good. Uh, how far are we going again?" The kid's voice broke on the very last word.

"Far enough to knock the legs out from under those little shits," Weller said.

"What if we can't?" Luke asked.

"Then it's going to get pretty exciting," Tom said.

73

Way back, her parents took her to the Iron Mountain mine out-side Vulcan. After donning red hard hats and yellow slickers, they'd ridden a small tram into the mine through a rock straw so narrow she could put out either hand and touch stone. Caged bulbs hung from a low-slung ceiling, but pockets of thick shadow and inky tunnels pushed in. She hadn't thought she was claustrophobic—but then, in the main stope, the tour guide turned out the lights, just for show. The darkness closed down like a fist, and was so absolute it was all Alex could do to keep from screaming. Her eyes opened wider and wider and wider. If this had been a Road Runner cartoon, they'd have popped right out of the sockets on little springs: *ka-boing, ka-boing.* But there was nothing to see, because there was no light. At. All.

She wasn't a wuss, but that had been bad.

This was way, way worse.

They'd split her and Daniel off from the others, driving them further and further into the mine; down through endless turns, through a warren of drifts and tunnels festooned with spray-painted numbers and letters, and then down gated stairs. She lost track of the turns, and the greater reek of the Changed faded away.

Now, though, she was in complete and utter darkness. Well, except for Mickey, who said she'd been crouching on a nubbin of rock in this isolated side-chamber for over seven hours. No sound either, except the splash of water over rock, Daniel's rapid breaths, and the thrum of her heart. Oh, and the bats. Even if she hadn't caught their scent—dry and dusty and a little sour—she would have heard their papery rustle. Sometimes, they squeaked. No problem. Just . . . she really didn't need to run into them. *With my luck, I'll get rabies.* She wondered if rabies was passed on in meat and then decided she was being morbid.

Job one was to get out. But how? The Changed obviously knew their way around. So, it occurred to her, did the bats. Both must only go as deep as the air was good. Except this air wasn't so great. Not bad, but every so often she caught a whiff that reminded her of sulfur from a match head. But she hadn't keeled over and the bats were here, so the air must be okay. She rifled a glance behind. Nothing to see, of course. *But I wonder if . . .* She licked her finger and then held it up. *Hunh.* Maybe just a hint of air from back where the bats hung out. Could be them flapping their wings. Or just breathing.

"Good job, Alex," she said. "Creep yourself out, why don't you?" The bats rustled at the sound of her voice, and then Daniel groaned: a long, low sound.

"Daniel?" She leaned to her right, her fingers feathering the dark. Her hand traced a cheek. His skin was too hot and damp with sweat. "Daniel?"

No reply. Not even a groan. She waited a few more seconds, then took her hand back. His scent clung to her fingers, and her stomach did a little flip.

She still had another option. Reaching into her jacket, she found the lump she'd zipped between lining and shell. Twenty Percocet, nine Percodan, and one Valium, wrapped in gauze. Those were all the pills she'd managed to gather from the guesthouse floor in the short span that she'd been left alone while Leopard's crew dragged out Sharon's and Ruby's corpses. The pills were . . . insurance. A way out that could be at a time of her choosing. Of course, waking up as a gork in a pool of vomit would be so her luck. But could she do it? Kill herself if there was no other way? Maybe. Pills were lame and guns more her speed, but if she had no other choice . . .

But what about Daniel? No matter how much she turned it over in her head, she just couldn't decide. It was one thing to promise Tom. Daniel was a whole other story. She didn't know him well enough, and he was his own person. She also might be wrong. They had been virtually inseparable for two weeks and Daniel was sick, yes, but he was still Daniel. So what *if* . . .

"Stop," she murmured. "You want to think about something? Think about finding a weapon."

Okay, there were rocks, but what else? This little side tunnel had timber supports. There must be nails she could pry free. How to dig them out was a problem. She thought about that. Her fingers played over Ellie's Mickey Mouse watch and then the buckle. There was that little prongy thingamajig. Not very long, but it might work. What she really needed was something strong, made of metal . . .

Wait. Her hand went to her neck, and then she reeled out her silver whistle on its chain. She fingered the mouthpiece. It wasn't exactly sharp, but the slight curve would help, and the whistle was strong enough to—

Her thoughts choked off at the crunch of boots. The darkness in the main tunnel, dead ahead, grayed—and then grew brighter. She pulled bolt upright, eyes wide, her body quivering like a cornered bunny's. Oh God, this was trouble. Her heart catapulted into her throat. She knew because she recognized his smell. He was alone, too. No Slash, no Spider. None of his usual crew along at all, because he wouldn't want to share. If she'd had any lingering doubts about just *what* he had in mind, her vision chose that moment to go a little muzzy, like a movie doing one of those queer little dissolves between one scene and the next—as the monster in her head came alive and flexed and shifted. Because like recognizes like.

Leopard.

74

"Hold up," Weller hissed. Hooking an arm through the ladder, he dug out another rock and let it fall into the yawning darkness below.

Tom counted off the seconds. This time, the splash came when he got to six. "About two hundred feet."

"Yeah." Weller's beam cut across the concrete below. Twenty feet down, a grated metal platform and set of stairs leapt into view. The platform fed into a wide bore, and Tom saw a glint of metal track at the lip. In case there was any doubt, H L and 540 were stenciled above the bore in dull yellow spray paint, indicating that the haul level was five hundred and forty feet from the surface. "This is where we get off."

"I thought you said it didn't access the mine until further down."

"Guess I was mistaken. Been a while and the map's rough."

Terrific. "Weller, we have to make it almost two hundred feet *deeper,* then work our way west to get under that big rock room. Can we do that from here?"

"Think so. Only we got another problem."

Tom didn't like the sound of that either. As they'd gotten deeper, the shaft's condition had worsened, with concrete chunked off and bolts so loose they rattled. The shaft wasn't uniformly smooth; lengths of corroding iron, thick insulated wires, and pipes ran along the sides. The rotting hulk of the original hoist's support structure jutted here and there in broken metal fangs. Dark heaps of what looked like rat droppings but which Weller said was bat guano pilled from the struts and around the metal collars that supported the pipes at regular intervals. The air had changed, too, growing a little warmer and so moist Tom felt its fingers drag over his face.

The air also smelled, and not just of stagnant water. The stink was more like a rank, intermittent, very faint exhalation, as if the mine had a terminal case of morning breath.

Luke's light speared down from three rungs above Tom's head. "What is that? It's like . . . rotten eggs."

"Hydrogen sulfide. Swamp gas." Weller paused, and when he spoke again, Tom heard the first hint of worry. "I shoulda thought of this. All this bat shit—it's the perfect food. We're only getting a little whiff now and then, but the gas is heavier than air. The further down we go, the more concentrated it'll get. Then again, maybe not. Might just be isolated pockets here and there."

"Will it hurt us?" Tom asked.

"Gets too thick? Oh yeah. Kill ya like cyanide."

Great. "What else?"

"It, ah, explodes. Like soda under pressure? Only it also catches fire real easy. If a chamber breaks open when those charges go . . ."

We'll be flash-fried. Fireballs traveled fast, eating oxygen and crisping everything in their path. If they had to shoot, the muzzle flash might spark an explosion, too. Tom chewed at his lower lip. "Will we know it if we get into trouble with the gas?"

He could hear Weller thinking about it. "Eyes and nose should burn, and the smell will get worse, and then it'll change, get almost sweet. Other than that, I don't know."

"Do we go back?" Luke said.

Another long pause. "Look, I can't guarantee, but . . . Luke, you want out, there's no shame in that."

"No," Luke said, a little unsteadily and too quickly. "I'll be okay. Besides, if there are three of us, it'll go faster."

"Well, remember I said we have another problem? I wasn't talking about the gas. Look down at the ladder."

They all did, and in the bright ball of their combined light, Tom saw what Weller meant.

Decades of corrosion had done their damage. The ladder simply ended, broken off like the peg of a rotten tooth. Between the break and the platform, there was a gap easily twenty feet wide, and it wasn't a straight drop either. The platform was secured in a bolted bracket to the concrete and stuck out in a tongue, ending ten feet to the left of the break.

"Oh boy," Luke breathed.

"Way I see it," Weller said, pulling off his coil of two-inch rope, "one of us shimmies down, then swings over and ties off for the other two."

Tom glanced up at Luke. "When was the last time you hung around a jungle gym?"

"How does 'so long ago I don't remember' sound?" Luke said. "I just hope I don't piss myself."

"Remind me to tell you about swinging across a gap of fifty feet, thirty feet off the ground."

"They make you do that in the Army?"

"Oh yeah. Then the smart guys figured out how to make a rope bridge." He looked down to see Weller already tying off rope to several rungs above his head. "I can go first."

"Better let me." Weller gave the rope a final tug, then furled the coil to which he'd tied off another, thinner rope. "One less old fart to worry about if I don't make it."

"What's the other rope for?" Luke asked.

"Watch and learn, boy." Wrapping his hands around the rope, Weller got a good footlock, trapping the rope under his right boot and looping it over his left before easing off the ladder. The rope let out a squeal as the knot tightened with the added weight, and the iron squalled. There was the bounce and ping of rock against rock and then a distant splash as the dislodged concrete found the water. "Don't come down until I'm across."

Don't worry about that. Tom's breath hung in his chest as Weller inched down, but the old man clearly knew what he was doing. Getting up or down a rope wasn't about arm strength; the legs did most of the work. Five feet before his rope played out, Weller tucked so his feet were nearly at the level of his chest.

"What's he doing?" Luke asked.

"Grabbing the other rope." Tom watched as Weller made a one-handed snatch. Then, still hanging by his free hand, Weller used his weight as a pendulum, folding at the hips and bucking. The rope complained: *cree-cree, CREE-cree* . . . The rope's swing widened, and then Weller was sweeping over the platform: once, twice. On the third swing, he let go. His arc was perfect; the second rope unspooled behind, and he landed on bent knees with a dull *bong,* fell to his knees, then staggered to his feet.

"No sweat," he said, but he sounded winded. "Hang on." Weller unreeled the second rope, walked backward, then tied off the end to a platform support.

"Whoa." Luke made an impressed sound. "He made a bridge."

"Use your hands and feet," Weller said. His voice echoed in the shaft. "It's got enough give for a good lock. Just don't look down."

Easier said than done. Tom was sweating by the time he was midway, hugging the rope to his chest, nearly bent at the waist, feet firmly locked around the rope. He did exactly the wrong thing then, thinking about the water below and the drop—and felt cold sweat lather his face. His arms trembled, and he thought, *I'm going to slip, and then I'll fall—*

"Tom," Weller said, sharply. "Keep moving! Come on!"

That snapped him back. "Right," he breathed, swallowing back a ball of fear. He kept his eyes focused on the rope, tried not to think how much further he had to go. He heard Weller scuffing over metal, and then the old man was moving alongside, bracing him up as Tom dropped onto the platform. "Thanks," he said, gulping back air that tasted, very faintly, of scrambled eggs. "I froze."

Weller clapped a hand to Tom's shoulder. "Everyone freezes once in a while."

"Why are we going uphill?" Luke whispered as they moved in a single file through the tunnel. "Don't we need to go down?"

"Opening's actually a little lower than the level you'll be working," Weller muttered. "It's easier to move skips—these big metal buckets—down instead of up."

"But we'll still end up below the Chuckies, right?" Tom asked. The tunnel was much smaller and tighter than he'd imagined. He'd had visions of expansive, soaring ceilings; instead, a network of wires and hoses ran only three feet overhead. He felt the weight of all that rock and earth pressing down.

He noticed something else. They weren't walking on dry earth but splashing through puddles on the tracked floor. The air was very moist, almost humid, and he could feel and hear the dull patter of water as the ceiling wept onto their heads and shoulders. *We're below the water table, but there must be enough air pressure to keep the water from rising any further.* Or this might only be an isolated pocket and there was water all around them. Not a comforting thought. Break through the wrong wall and they'd be caught in a flash flood.

Moving out of the tunnel, they hooked right. Tom immediately felt the change, how the tunnel was higher and wider. Bits and pieces of machinery were scattered here and there: a square metal bin, lengths of metal protruding from rock, frayed nets strung along the stone. His light caught a flash and sparkle, and he heard Luke: "Whoa, is that gold?"

"No, that's fool's gold: pyrite. Real gold's a little dull, and you find it with a lot of quartz." Weller trailed his light over the rock and then pointed to a thick, milky-white buckle. "Right there's a bit. That kind of dirty orange stuff."

"That's it?" Luke sounded disappointed.

"People have died for less," Weller said.

Tom opened his mouth to say something, but then he heard a scratchy buzz. Not footsteps. This was like a hive of bees. Then, from somewhere very far away came an airy scream.

Luke gasped. "What is that?"

"Voices," Tom murmured. He felt the hairs rise on his neck.

"Chuckies don't talk."

"I don't think they're Chuckies." Tom turned, straining to hear above the thump of his heart and the crack and pop of damp rock under his boots.

"You mean, *normal* people?"

"Yeah." Protruding from the rock was the mouth of a yellow metal duct. It reminded Tom of a ventilation system, but this opening was very wide. Through it came a fitful, intermittent buzz: a distant ebb and flow like the susurrant whisper of the sea stirring stone. *People talking.* "What is this?"

"Ore chute. Coming from pretty far above us." Weller paused, then said, grimly, "Sounds like those little bastards got a fair number of prisoners."

"We need to do something." Luke's eyes were liquid. "Can't we *help* them?"

"We're going to." Weller jerked his head. "Come on."

★ ★ ★

They found what they were looking for twelve minutes later, which, Tom thought, was cutting it pretty close. Any further and they could kiss any chance of getting out in time good-bye. Weller had led them down a flight of gated stairs—first one level and then another—and then they'd moved fast, ducking through corridors, Luke stopping to chalk Xs to mark the turns.

The first room was smaller than he thought it would be, and the pillars weren't exactly uniform either, but mushroom-shaped, dropping from the ceiling in a taper before spreading out in a wide, rocky footprint. The layout reminded Tom a little of a very large, very low-ceilinged basement held up with two-by-fours and jackstraws. "This is it?"

"No. Worst stope's further west and not exactly on the same level. We just got to find it," Weller said.

"I thought you knew where it was," Tom said.

"It's been a while."

"You keep saying that."

"We'll *find* it."

"Well, let's do *something*." Luke was unhooking his pack. "Where do we start?"

Tom pointed. "Two charges right there next to that big pillar just off center. Put 'em behind the main entrance here, out of sight. That way, if anyone does smell something or come by—"

"They won't see." Luke nodded and moved off. "I'm on it."

"I'm going to scout ahead," Weller said.

"You should wait." Tom had dropped to a knee and opened

his bag, but now he stopped and looked up. "One of us should be with you."

Weller shook his head, then glanced over his shoulder and lowered his voice. "This is taking too long. You see that kid's eyes? How they're getting a little red? I think that's the gas. *You're* starting to look like you need to sleep off a bender."

"What?" Only when Weller mentioned it did Tom feel the slight burn and tingle. "The smell isn't worse."

"It may not have to be, or maybe it kills your sense of smell after a while," Weller muttered. "How's your breathing?"

"Fine, until you mentioned it."

"Yeah, I'm getting tight, too." Weller flicked a look at his watch. "How much time you need?"

"No more than five minutes."

"See you soon," Weller said.

He'd already prepared the blasting caps, carefully crimping each shell onto time fuses with SOG needle-nose pliers and then using the C4 punch to core a hole for the detonators. He'd timed the burn rate—forty-five seconds a foot—and under more normal circumstances, this wasn't necessarily a problem: just pull the igniter and run like hell. But they didn't exactly have a lot of open space in a mine. For more elaborate preps, there was remote detonation. But Tom's only option had been to rig a time device.

"Done." Luke dropped beside him.

"Okay, give me another couple seconds here." He glanced at his watch. Almost five minutes gone. "Here, hold this one straight out.

The rock's pretty uneven." He waited until Luke got his hand around the charge, then unspooled a few lengths of duct tape around the legs, securing them to the stone. Uncoiling the time fuse, he used tiny strips of duct tape to keep the waterproof cord from curling on itself. "Let's go."

"Where's Weller?" Luke asked at the entrance. He squatted and scratched two large Xs in white chalk.

"Scouting ahead for that room he's hot to blow." Tom glanced at his watch again. Seven minutes gone. "How many charges you got left?"

"Eight."

He had eleven, plus two blocks of C4 and time fuses, because you just never knew. "Come on. If he's marking the way, we can catch up. Better than just waiting here."

"Okay," Luke said, then coughed. His nose was red as Rudolph's, and he looked as if he'd just staggered back from a serious bar-crawl. "Chest feels funny."

"You're doing great. We'll be done soon." Tom trotted down the tunnel with Luke on his heels. His lungs burned with the effort, and he coughed, and thought, *Maybe ten, fifteen more minutes; then we got to get out no matter what.* To his right, he spotted stairs, an X chalked low on the wall, and a down arrow. The stairs sounded too loud, their footfalls ringing and echoing against the rock. At the bottom, Weller had chalked a small, left-facing arrow. *We're moving either west or south.* Tom pictured the terrain overhead. This would put them closer to the decline ramp and further from the first set of charges. They would have ten minutes max before the first charges went off. By then, they had to be well on their way toward the shaft. *Just hope we have ti—*

"Whoa, whoa," Luke hissed, and then slowed down. "You hear that?"

Tom had been so focused he hadn't noticed, but now he did hear: a grunt and then a harsh gasp, the scrabble of feet over rock. *Weller.*

He darted down the hall, running on the balls of his feet, then grabbed Luke before the boy could spurt ahead. Together, they flattened against a rock wall just left of another X—

In time to hear Weller groan.

75

Flicking the Uzi's selector, Tom pivoted, weapon at waist level, each hand on a grip. He felt Luke move to flank him.

There were four. A boy at each arm, and another draped over Weller's waist. The girl straddled Weller's chest, and Tom and Luke had arrived in time to see her rip a chunk of Weller's shoulder with her teeth. There was a harsh tearing sound, and the old man bucked, trapping an abortive scream behind his teeth. In the bad light, Weller's blood was oil, and his skin would've looked at home on a shark.

The girl heard them, the scuff of boots against rock, and she twisted, a stupefied expression spreading over her face. A ragged flap of Weller's skin hung from her mouth, and she was still chewing it back like a kid with a too-large bite of spaghetti. Gore painted the girl's mouth and face in a clown's scream. Her eyes widened, and then her snack fell with a moist plop to the rock as her jaw went slack.

"Oh *fuck*," Luke said, and then he and Tom were squeezing off quick, silenced shots: *pfft pfft pfft pfft!* Tom heard the *tick-tick-tick* of brass against rock; saw the sudden blooms on the girl's chest. She fell back without a sound. The boys were halfway up when Luke and Tom fired again. The boys jerked, then drooped in limp tangles.

"Weller!" Tom knelt by the old man. The girl had gnawed off enough meat to reveal the dull glimmer of bone.

"F-found it." Weller was shaking. His face gleamed with sweat and blood. He had a hand clamped to his shoulder, but Tom heard the *drip-drip-drip*. "Down the tunnel. I was c-coming back when these little f-fucks jumped me. N-never saw th-them."

"Why didn't you call for help?" Luke asked.

Tom knew why; read it in the tears streaking the old man's face. Weller hadn't wanted to give them away. *Not just an old hard-ass; the guy's willing to go down to make sure we do this.* Dragging out the thermal top he'd taken from the dead boy, he used his knife and ripped it into strips. "This is going to hurt," he said.

"Just d-do it," Weller said. He let out a gargling, barely audible scream as Tom crammed silk into his wound. Weller panted as Tom knotted more strips of silk into a crude bandage. "L-lucky if I don't get r-rabies."

"What do we do?" Luke said.

"You finish." Weller's skin was ash and his swollen eyes were pink, but his voice was a knife. "I marked the rooms. The good one's a little further on and down one more flight of stairs. But you got to hurry."

Tom knew he was right. There were more kids where these had come from. After he and Luke dragged the bodies to a corner, he helped Weller to a spot along the far wall, then laid an Uzi across the old man's lap. "Don't use your light. You hear something and we don't say your name, you stay quiet."

"Don't worry about me," Weller said.

"Ten minutes," Tom said, and then he and Luke hustled.

The first stope was even better than the one they'd already rigged. The cored rock room was larger, the pillar supports under much more stress. Rubble and drifts of scree were scattered along the floor. The pockmarked pillars looked moth-eaten.

"Jeez," Luke muttered. "Looks like all it'd take is a good push."

"You do this room. Use every fuse. Concentrate on the pillars in the middle. Then you wait right here. Don't move until I come back." At the entrance, he turned back. "If I don't say your name, you light up whoever comes in here and blow their heads off."

"Don't have to tell me twice," Luke said. "Good luck."

Wish people would stop saying that. He took the tunnel at a run, spotted another X and a down arrow. After clattering down the stairs, he doglegged left, trotted another length of corridor—and then saw the room yawning to his right.

This chamber was very different: not only a forest of spindly stone pillars but a huge ball, rotten from the inside with stress fractures radiating out in a sphere. The walls were a warren of fissures and nearly horizontal seams in gray rock. He studied the seams, saw how the cracks tracked and split the rock. This was like the rotting timber of a neglected basement beneath a house of solid stone. Take out the timber, core out the walls, and the room above—hell, the whole house—would fall.

He got busy, first fitting two charges, one to each of two pillars. Then he climbed along the walls, digging his boots into the crevices and crannies and using his fingertips to hoist himself into hollowed-out seams where miners had scraped rock with chisel and hammers. He set charges as far back as he could maneuver, using the points of his toes to push himself into the seams. Jagged stone grabbed and scoured his back and stomach, bit into his legs. He worked feverishly: squirming into a seam, backing out, flipping onto his back at another, and fixing a charge to rock that was just inches from his nose.

He was on his sixth seam when a new idea occurred to him. Setting off the delay devices to each and every charge would take too long.

But if I only have to set off one . . .

He wriggled out and squatted on the rock; pulled out four, five, and then six lengths of time fuse. Thought about it. Then he went to work with his knife and the duct tape, knitting the lengths together until they radiated in a huge spiderweb. Thirty feet, forty-five seconds a foot: almost twenty-five minutes. No need for a time delay. With all this extra fuse, this room might actually go last of all, but the explosion would be the most powerful and concentrated. If Weller was right, all that separated this room from the Chuckies were sixty feet of lousy rock. The floor would simply give way.

Might even punch through to the flooded levels, and if there are *pockets of hydrogen sulfide, they'll explode.* He ripped off another strip of duct tape with his teeth, then scooped up the rock he'd used to keep the fuse from curling back. *If they ignite, then—*

He heard a sudden loud scrape of rock against rock as some-one kicked aside stone. At the noise, Tom turned, a little annoyed. Hadn't he just told Luke not to *move*? To stay *put*? God, if *he'd* been just a little bit jumpier, he might've shot the kid.

But that was when Tom registered two things at once.

For one thing, he couldn't have shot Luke, because *he'd* been stupid enough to leave his Uzi propped next to his pack.

And for another, he had visitors.

The girl had probably been in a lot of trouble before she turned. Maybe she'd been into drugs or a gang. Or maybe it was abuse. The scar slashing across her face could have been from a knife.

The jittery boy's outfit reminded him of a ninja's. A bandolier of M430 grenades sagged around the kid's scrawny shoulders. Without a launcher, the grenades wouldn't arm and weren't a problem.

Scarface's shotgun, though . . .

76

Alex had only gotten good and hammered once, and all alone: the very first time she'd ventured with her friends, Glock and Jack, into her aunt's basement. There was nothing fun about her being drunk—no sense of relaxation or euphoria or even the giggles—just a sickening swoosh in her head: not spinning so much as falling backward, in place, and being sucked into very deep water. Closing her eyes only made things five thousand times worse, the black-ness behind her lids going round and round and round. She didn't get sick or weepy, but the next time she got cozy with the Glock, she took it easy with that bottle of Jack.

That feeling—of tumbling into a black whirlpool—was *this*.

God, no, why now? She gritted her teeth, fighting against the vertiginous swirl. Of course, she knew why. He was thinking about *her*, planning what he would *do*. Worse, the movie in his mind was already running, the images flickering in a blistering, bright montage: Alex, flailing, as Leopard pinned her to the rocks, clamped a hand around her throat to keep her from screaming while the other hand ripped and tore away her—

Stop. She slapped her right cheek, a stinging blow that jerked out a breath and cut tears. For an instant, the images broke apart the way a pond's perfect reflection of sky and trees fractures the instant you shatter the surface with a rock. *Come on, come on, stay with it. . . .* She slapped herself a second and then a third time, much, much harder, enough that the sharp *crack* echoed. Something seemed to snap in her head; a jagged flash of white sliced through that deadening swirl, and that awful feeling of falling evaporated as her mind cleared.

She was panting. Leopard's aroma was hot and heavy and cloying, like boiled honey laced with sewage, and he must have just eaten because his breath was foul, thick with the greasy stink of fat and wet copper. The yellow spray of his light was a dusty glow growing firmer and more coherent by the second. She scrambled back like a crab, stumbling over Daniel in her rush. She heard Daniel's breathing change, and she had a split second when she thought maybe now *would* be a good time to scream, while she still had the chance. Stupid. No one would hear or help, and she was too deep anyway. The only person who gave a damn about Leopard was Spider, who must be busy somewhere. Maybe filleting steaks for the chow line.

The spear of light swept into the drift like a searchlight and tacked her into place. Squinting against the sudden brilliance, she put up a hand to shield her eyes but couldn't see anything. The light left her for an instant and found Daniel, who barely reacted. His eyelids twitched and his head rolled; he swallowed. But that was all. No help there. No help anywhere. The light slid back and held on to her for a good five seconds. Now that she knew what to expect, she braced herself against another mental slip, but the monster was either playing possum or she really might be able to control this after all. Anyway, nothing happened. If she lived through the next ten minutes, she might even figure out why it had happened at all.

Click.

Full dark. All she saw were purple afterimages of Leopard's head and shoulders and the outlines of his Uzi. Could she get the gun? Her ears tingled. She heard a slight shush, a whisper of cloth and leather, and then the grind of metal against rock. *Putting down his gun.* His boots crunched closer. Rock squealed.

She got her feet tucked under in a crouch. The geometry of the tunnel was simple. Daniel was on her right; Leopard was ahead and a little to her left—because he was right-handed, he'd worn the Uzi in a cross-carry that could be shrugged off his right shoulder. So his weapon was on her left. One gun down. Leopard normally wore that Glock tucked in his waistband. Had she seen it earlier in the day? She couldn't remember.

She felt him move closer. His smell was huge now, a boiling black fog. His breath was ragged and sour with excitement.

Click. Light, hot and bright, shining directly into her eyes. The brightness was so intense it felt like needles, and she could feel the tears spilling down her cheeks.

Leopard was only ten feet away, no more, and he had a decision to make. If he stayed true to the brief glimpse she'd seen of what he *wanted,* then he needed both hands. Hard to take a struggling girl one-handed. So, either he'd turn off the light, or put it down to free up his hands. She bet he put it down. From what she'd seen, the Changed didn't absolutely need the light, but she thought he'd brought it so *she* would understand just what was going to happen, or maybe he wanted her to not only feel what he would do to her but see it, too. He might also leave the light on out of habit. In his previous life, Leopard was probably the kind of guy who liked to watch.

Then Leopard surprised her. Sidestepping to his right, his eyes on her the whole time, he wedged the flashlight between two timber supports at waist level. Smart. Keep the light on her and behind him. But when he sidled away, her gaze clicked to his waist and she got a good look because Leopard wasn't wearing a jacket. After all, the mine was relatively warm, and he figured on working up a swe—

All of a sudden, he was there, so fast she had no time to spring from her crouch or knee his balls or jam her thumbs into his eyes. One minute he was ten feet away and the next he was slamming her into the rock. Her head bounced against stone. Pain detonated in her skull, and the air bolted from her lungs.

Breathlessly, she bucked and flailed as he rode her: his weight on her chest, his hands scrabbling to grab her arms. She swiped with her left hand and felt her nails, jagged and cracked, rake his face. He jerked away with a grunt of pain, and in the light, she saw sudden rails of blood. His grip loosened, and then she was rearing up, cocking her right fist, aiming for his Adam's apple.

His hand shot out. Deflecting the punch, he grabbed her wrist, then jammed his knee into her bad left shoulder, grinding the bone into the rocks. She screamed. He hit her, a fast open slap and much harder than she had managed on her own. A bomb of pain exploded just beneath her left eye. Her mind blanked, and her arms loosened up. In a kind of haze, she saw him winding up to hit her again—

From somewhere beyond the tunnel came a low boom, faint but unmistakable: a shotgun.

Leopard stiffened, and she felt his weight shift. Felt the pressure against her shoulder ease as he craned over his shoulder.

Grab it! Her left hand pistoned, her fingers found hard polymer, and then she was yanking the Glock free. She jammed the muzzle into Leopard's stomach, right at his navel.

A Glock is a Glock is a Glock, and the beauty of a Glock: no active safety, nothing the owner has to remember to flip off and on. Just point and shoot. So Alex knew Glocks, very well. She'd had days to study this one. She'd watched Leopard kill Ray with it. She knew a Siderlock when she saw one, because she'd installed the very same on her dad's Glock herself. So her father's Glock had a cross-trigger safety.

But Leopard's didn't.

The only gamble was whether Leopard kept a round chambered. No time to check or even jack the slide, because that took two hands, and she only had one.

Big gamble.

Her best and only shot.

She took it.

77

The rack of the pump was a nightmare that echoed and bounced off rock: *ka-ka-CHUNK-CHUNK-crunch-cru—*

Tom let the rock fly in a hard, vicious cut, a Frisbee throw that was two parts arm, three parts wrist. The rock whirred and struck the girl square in the chest just as she swung the shotgun up—because Tom had seen that she was sloppy and overconfident, racking the shotgun before she'd even slotted the butt or brought the muzzle to bear. Total time, maybe a two-second jump—but he grabbed it.

The shotgun *baROOMED*. He was instantly deafened. Light sheeted in a bright tongue of muzzle flash, but he was still alive to see it. He would not have a second chance. Either his Uzi or her shotgun, and his Uzi was closer. He hurtled to his right, but now she was pivoting, racking the shotgun, leading, anticipating where he would land.

He just had time to think: *Too late—*

He never heard the shot because the sound was small and his hearing was still gone. But the pain he expected—the rip of buckshot through his body—never came. In another second, he banged to the rock and swept up his Uzi . . .

The girl was falling. Her shotgun slipped from her fingers. In the dark of the tunnel beyond, Tom saw another quick flash as someone shot at the jittery kid, but the boy was already peeling away in a brassy twinkle. His heart boomed, something he felt but could not hear over a loud, burring hum. A crazy thought bounced around in his skull: many more shots in close quarters and he was going to go deaf. He waited, quivering, his breath tearing in and out of his throat, as the light grew brighter, and then he saw enough to understand who was there.

"I'm over here," he said, not bothering to whisper now. He aimed his Uzi at the ceiling.

Luke rounded the corner. His skin was pale. His lips moved. *You okay?*

"Yeah. Thanks for not listening." Tom heard a faint hissing as sound started leaking through the hum.

Luke's worried face broke into a lopsided grin. "I would've stayed put, except I spotted the kids and saw they were headed right for you." His eyebrows lifted as he saw the jury-rigged network of time fuses. "Whoa. That's cool."

"Yeah." It hit him that all his work might be for nothing. When the jittery kid got back with his friends, all they had to do was cut the fuses. He thought about the two spare bricks of C4 in his pack. "Come on, we got to block off this room and then get out."

He had Luke slap a brick on one side of the entrance as he fixed the other to the highest point of the arch. Jamming a blasting cap on a time fuse into each, he used his knife to cut the det cord in half. "All right, go. Get to your charges and start the delays. If I don't show in thirty seconds, don't come back this time."

Luke's eyes raked his face, probably to see if he was serious. "I mean it," Tom said.

Luke's head jerked a quick nod. "But please come, Tom. Please."

Oh, believe me, I plan on it. As Luke pelted off, Tom darted back into the room, pulled two M60 igniters from his pack, then dug out a lighter and flicked it to life. He touched off the spiderweb. *Just hope the explosion at the door doesn't blow this stuff early.* If it did, he would never get clear in time.

Dashing to the entrance, he looked down the tunnel. Luke was already out of sight. Maybe a minute had passed since the shotgun blast. Tucking his lighter into a hip pocket, he pulled out an igniter, removed the shipping plug, then threaded in the loose end of the time fuse as far as it would go. Tightening the cap, he removed the safety pin. Wash, rinse, repeat with the second fuse.

Do it right the first time. The M60s could be rearmed in a pinch, but he really didn't want to do that. Grabbing the pull ring, he pushed, rotated, pulled. Heard the sharp *pop* as the igniter fired.

Hurry, hurry, hurry. He knelt by the other igniter, grabbed, pushed, rotated, pulled the ring.

Pop.

He ran.

78

The boom was enormous, a roar that crashed and broke and reverberated against and over the rocks. The Glock bucked as the round ripped into Leopard's gut. He flopped in a sudden, spastic, loose-limbed jerk like a marionette whose puppeteer had just been goosed. In the yellow light, his blood spray was dark orange. Blowback splattered her hands and drizzled over her face. Leopard began to crumple, already so much dead weight. Bucking him off, she rolled and hung there on hands and knees, the Glock still fisted in one hand. She knew she was panting, but she couldn't hear herself well; the sound was muffled and far away.

How long since she'd squeezed off that shot? Five seconds, ten at most. Was there someone else down here? She couldn't tell. That shotgun had sounded very far away, but if she could hear them, they might have heard the Glock and come running. She had no time; she and Daniel had to get out—

Movement. Left. She jerked, the Glock coming up . . . "Daniel." She knew she'd spoken because she felt the air leave her mouth. The stench of burned gunpowder and Leopard's blasted guts filled her nose. Blinking away blood, she scuttled to where Daniel had levered himself to a sit, his back against the rock. He stared at her with wide eyes, and she realized how she must look: blood glistening on her face and hands, slopping over her chest. "Daniel, it's Alex."

His lips moved. She thought he mouthed her name. *No time for this.* Laying the Glock aside, she grabbed his shoulders and shook until his head flopped. Put her face right into his. "Daniel, *Daniel!* Can you stand? Come on, *talk* to me!"

"Alex." She heard that. His eyes pulled together, zeroing in on her face. His eyebrows crawled to a frown. "Alex. What . . . what . . ."

Time, time, time! "Daniel, come on, get up, *stand,* stand *up!*" She took fistfuls of parka. "We've got to go! Can you walk? Can you *fight?*"

"F-fight?" he said, as if she were speaking Swahili. "I—"

Something shot out of the dark off her right shoulder. She gasped, startled, and then she saw the fluttering outlines of a bat flash in and out of the light before darting into the main tunnel. *Shot must've spooked it.* More bats hurtled through the drift. The roof of this tunnel was arched but not high, only ten feet at most. Ducking, she felt the air whisk over her hair as the animals pin-wheeled past.

She would have to get them both out. If Daniel could walk, that would be good, but she'd drag him if she had to. Kneeling, she rolled Leopard, her eyes noting the fist-sized hole the bullet had chunked in line with his spine. His blood was leaking over the rocky floor in a purple pool. Working fast, she stripped off

Leopard's leg sheath and knife, then slapped the pockets of his cargo pants. Her fingers found the familiar outlines of two spare magazines for the Glock in the pocket on his right thigh and then another full mag for the Uzi. *All right.* She slotted the mags into her own pockets, and then she was buckling the sheath around her right calf. *We don't have any choice but to go back the way we came.* She gave the straps a yank and cinched them tight, but her mind was already jumping ahead, planning their next moves. *Got to find the stairs . . . maybe I'll smell more Changed when we're closer, and that'll point us in the right direction.*

She heard Daniel moving, the grind and squeal of stone, and she froze—

Because his scent was suddenly bitter and rank, and there was no mistake. Her mind slewed and skipped, and then she saw herself, on the rocks, a splash of crimson coating her throat from where he would bite and tear. She could feel the sharp spike of phantom stone against her back, and taste how very salty and yet sweet her blood was in his mouth and—

This was the smell and the sight of her death.

Her gaze inched right. Daniel was slumped against the rock. The ghosts of her hands were stenciled in blood on his shoulders. The Glock's black eye wandered because Daniel was shaking, but it stared right at her, more or less.

She opened her mouth. Nothing came out, not even air.

"I—" His face clenched in panic and new dread, and she saw—and smelled—that he knew, finally, what was happening to him.

She'd guessed right, then, about why Spider had left them

together. Alex didn't hunt, but she knew kids who had. Bag that first deer, and you were blooded, wearing your kill as a coppery smudge on your forehead like ashes the day after Fat Tuesday.

Daniel was to be blooded with her. Or maybe it was no more complicated than a spider making an egg sac and then cocooning a great big bug. Once Daniel was hatched, Spider knew he would need a nice, fresh body upon which to feed.

"I c-can't," Daniel said. "You . . . you know. I know you d-do. Alex, you . . . you sh-should've . . ."

"No." She dragged up her voice from where it had fallen. "Daniel, you're talking to me. You *know* me. You're still here, *with* me. Maybe it'll be different for you. We don't know if—"

"N-no." His head moved from side to side. His hand was oily from Leopard's blood, and now she watched in numb horror as he brought his fingers to his nose. A second later, the pink snake of his tongue slithered out for a taste. *The Changed don't eat the Changed.* Every molecule of air left her lungs. She watched the emotions race across his face: revulsion and fear and . . . hunger. His cheeks worked and then he spat a gobbet of red foam.

The Uzi was behind her and too far away. She had the knife, but she'd never get to it in time. She didn't know how to throw it anyway.

"A-Alex." His voice thrummed with need. His teeth were orange. His eyes were too bright, and she smelled, exactly, what would happen next. "I don't think I can s-s-stop it. I don't know that I even w-want to."

"Yes, you do," she said. "Daniel, you've fought them all this time."

"But I'm so tired," he said. "I can feel it *gr-growing*. I think . . . I *have* to."

No, she thought, wildly. *This is a cancer, too; this is a monster.* "Daniel, you *know* me. You're *talking* to me. You're not one of them. You're still *you*."

"But I won't be for much longer. I can feel me . . . going away. Like trying to c-catch f-fog. Can't . . . can't *grab* myself anymore." His chest heaved and then he was panting, forcing out the words. "Y-you can't . . . you don't kn-know what it's l-like to l-lose yourself piece by p-p-piece."

But she did. She pulled in a shuddering, sobbing breath. "You have to *try*. Daniel, if you do this, it *wins*."

"I kn-know." His head sagged back against the rock and he closed his eyes, but only for a second. "Jack, oh, Jack . . . all m-my fault. I'm s-so *sorry*."

"Daniel," she began.

He pressed the muzzle under his jaw.

"Oh, *God*," he said.

79

She heard it twice: the blast five feet away and then, ten seconds later, its shadowy distant cousin—*that*, she thought, must be her mind finally blowing itself apart.

The burn of gunpowder hung in a hazy curtain. Everything else was a shock of red and black. Then the walls shuddered and the ground twitched. She was shaking that hard. Her first—her only—thought was that she was in shock. She was falling apart, her mind splitting into pieces, maybe for good. Maybe the monster was tired of the game and had decided to flex its muscles, take that great, big, drippy—final—bite. She thought that might be all right. But the world didn't fade. She didn't pass out, or die, or go crazy. Her eyes were a camera, and with every blink, the snick-snap of a shutter took the same picture: red and black, and red and Daniel's eyes, and black and Daniel's eyes, and Daniel's dead, dark eyes.

The rock shimmied again. This time, she heard the tick of stone bouncing over stone.

And the distant rumble of an explosion.

80

Chris might have seen it coming if he hadn't insisted that Nathan sleep first. He'd pulled the last watch before they moved out, and he wasn't on top of his game or thinking very straight.

Big mistake.

The trail they followed was a line of utility poles erected down a narrow stripe of clear-cut hemmed by a thick tangle of hard-wood and pine on either side. The woods knit together at intervals in a dense canopy, but the way through was largely obstacle-free. At ground level, the clear-cut was a straight, open shot and might shave off a good five miles that they would otherwise spend in a looping meander through woods. The trail was a temptation that, in other circumstances, Chris would've been smart enough to avoid. Staying under cover and blending in with the darkling shadows was always a better option. It was that canopy that gave him a false sense of security as well as the fact that they were moving at night. Both would hide them well enough, and the full moon was painting the trail into a glowing Green Brick Road that was just too good not to take.

Two more days, just two more. Chris's head thumped with weariness. The wind was a knife, the cold making him stupid. His snowshoes were lead weights. He was dead on his feet, moving out of habit more than design. *Then we'll be there and maybe we can find those kids.*

Nathan's sorrel was breaking trail about forty yards ahead, just past a wedge of ghostly verdigris shadow. A big gap. Normally, they were no more than ten yards apart. But Lena had been sick again, and Chris waited for her to finish.

"Just another couple hours, and then we'll stop to rest," Chris said as he helped her back onto the saddle. The roan did an unhappy tap dance as Lena sank into the saddle, and then Chris saw the horse's ears pin back and felt the animal tense. "Lena, pull its head up and tighten the reins . . . easy," he said as the roan tried an abortive buck and then settled, blowing hard.

"Maybe it's tired out, too," Lena said. There was a small yellow splash of vomit on her jacket. "We should stop."

From further on, Nathan called back: "There a problem?" Chris turned. Nathan was now fifty yards away, and he saw Nathan starting to turn the animal around. "She bucking on you?" the old man shouted. "Want to stop and rest awhile?"

"Yes," Lena muttered.

"We're fine," Chris called back. They needed to catch up. All this shouting made him nervous. Nathan should know better, too, but they were all tired. He waved the old man on, saw Nathan's head move in a nod, and then the sorrel was angling back around and heading toward a small rise.

He was just turning back to Lena when he saw Nathan's sorrel stumble. A quick hop. Nothing fatal.

Then something very large blurred off to Nathan's right. The shape was so out of place and so far off the ground—head height—his mind couldn't make sense of what he was seeing.

The log bulleted from the woods, so huge and fast it cleaved the air with a whistle.

"Nathan!" Chris shouted, but he was much too late. It had been too late the moment the sorrel stumbled over that trip wire.

The mace—a huge battering ram fashioned from a single, solid log—slammed midway down Nathan's right side. The log swept through, the arc of its swing driving it completely across the trail to crash into the trees opposite. Nathan's head snapped left, some heavy bone *cracked,* and then his body lifted from his saddle—but did not fall. His right boot tangled in the stirrup, so when the mace's tethers spun out and caught and the swing reversed, Nathan was already slumping as the sorrel panicked and reared.

So Nathan's head was just at the right spot. Maybe he was only stunned or already unconscious. It didn't matter.

The heavy butt of the log smashed into Nathan's left temple with a wet, hollow *thunk.* This time, Nathan's head spun fast enough that Chris heard the *snap* as the neck broke. A jet of blood spurted from Nathan's mouth, and then a spongy, black crater of gore and pulverized bone formed from the implosion of his skull. Screaming, the sorrel went down, tumbling to the snow.

All this took no more than four seconds, but Chris was already moving after one. "Nathan!" He churned through the snow, his shoes slowing him down. Behind, he could hear Lena's horrified shrieks. He stumbled, then swarmed up again. This was his fault; they should never have tried moving at night, and now it was too late, too late, too *late*.

And also, too late, he remembered: where there is one booby trap, there is, frequently, another.

His left foot plunged into the snow. An instant later, something thin bit into his shin, grew taut, and then snapped. He was pitched forward. At the last second, he rolled to take the force of the impact on his shoulder instead of his outstretched hands, but the snowshoes slowed him down. He smacked down on hands and knees, the tips of his snowshoes jammed tight in deep, hard snow.

Above, he sensed movement. Then he heard a loud, snapping, crashing whir as something barreled out of the trees. His head whipped right, but there was nothing coming for him. Not another mace. Not from the side. Not there. But there *was* something, because he heard a monstrous, splintery smash—and then he understood.

Too late.

The deadfall hurtled down from above: not a log like the mace but a flat, heavy wooden square. If this had been day instead of night and he *had* thought to look up instead of side to side, he still wouldn't have spotted it because of the thin, dark green net strung just below as camouflage. Now, in the green of the moon, the thing was near invisible.

The tiger trap rocketed for his face. He saw nailed boards, a green twinkle of glass—

The bristle of iron spikes.

81

A five-foot time fuse with a burn rate of forty-five seconds per foot meant four minutes, give or take, and he'd cut his in half. By the first minute, Tom was pelting down stairs. By the second, he was racing down the tunnel toward the stope where Luke ought to be.

The boom was very loud, and more than just a quick double-bang. The explosion tore the air, and the rock shook hard enough that a rain of dirt and grit bounced and showered from the ceiling. A few seconds later, a gush of pulverized rock and spent gases spilled into the narrow tunnel in a choking rush. Coughing against the grit, he careened down the tunnel, not bothering to be quiet, ears alert for another bigger blast—but none came.

Okay. He thought the stope itself had not gone up, and that was very good. That also answered a question about the concentration of hydrogen sulfide, too. But he had a feeling that if there was another way in, this part of the mine was going to get crowded pretty soon. The clock in his head ticked. *Eighteen minutes.*

Close to the stope, he smelled Luke's work as a tarry sting of nicotine. "How many more you got?" he called.

Luke was just lighting up another cigarette. He sucked, the tip crisping to an angry coal. "Six," he choked, and then hacked. Using duct tape, he secured the filter end of the burning cigarette to the time fuse. "God, these things are *nasty*."

"Tell me about it." He'd been the only nonsmoker in his platoon. "I had to go through six brands. Then I figured it was Luckies or bust. Keep testing brands much longer, I was going to die of lung cancer."

Luke coughed out a smoky laugh. "Think you blocked it off?"

"Sure hope so."

"Good. Thought I heard another shot, but—"

"No one here but us." Tapping out a smoke, Tom lit up, sucked, felt the acrid taste balling in his mouth, and quickly exhaled. His mouth instantly pooled, and he turned aside and spat as he taped his cigarette to a time fuse. "Not yet anyway."

"Can they get here from somewhere else?"

"I don't know," he said. "Just have to hope not."

Weller was waiting, propped in his corner. "What'd you do?" the old man rasped. "First I heard the shotgun and then that explosion. You hadn't called out, I'd have taken your head off."

Tom gave a hurried explanation, then held out his hand for Weller to grab. "We got to get going. Can you walk? What about the rope? Can you manage it?"

"Oh yeah. You don't worry about me." Grimacing, the old man hauled himself to his feet. "Coulda sworn I heard another shot."

"Me, too," Luke said.

"Might be the Chuckies. Is there another way around?" Tom asked Weller.

The old man frowned. "Shouldn't be, but maybe. Hell, they really want us, they could backtrack to the ore body and shimmy down chutes. I can't see them being that smart, though."

I don't know about that. Tom thought back to Scarface and her little buddy with the M430s. *They've figured out guns. How long until one of them gets curious about a grenade launcher?*

Weller was slower, and it took them almost nine minutes to get back to the very first stope. With the three of them puffing away, the room looked like a smoker's convention, but they were done in less than a minute-thirty and they were still alone.

"We're not going to make it back to the shaft before the first charges go," Luke said. They were in the tracked tunnel with its scatter of discarded machinery and treasure of fool's gold winking in and out of their lights, Weller at point and Luke sandwiched between them. Ahead, Tom saw the wide mouth of the ore chute opening to the left. The boy's face flashed a look over his shoulder. "We'll be trapped."

"One room shouldn't do it," Weller said, but Tom heard the note of uncertainty. "No use worrying about it now. We got to—"

From somewhere above came a series of muffled, throaty booms so close together they nearly sounded like one animal. But Tom knew: the second room had blown. He felt the change almost at once as the explosions raced through the rock to shake the air and shimmy up his feet into his shins. A stream of rotten rock cascaded down the walls with a sound like beans over tin, and in a few seconds, his mouth was filmed with dust and grit. The air was even heavier and harder to breathe. There were new sounds, too: a kind of grinding rumble, like a distant cement mixer, and then another, stranger sloshing, like a gurgle.

"Rock going!" Weller called, but he sounded excited now, almost gleeful. "I think we got 'em, I think we got those sons of bitches, I think—"

To the old man's left, a jet of water suddenly spumed from the mouth of an ore chute. Not quite like the blast from a fireman's hose, the pressure was still enough to sweep Weller off his feet, and then the old man was bent over, clawing at the rock wall, unable to stand.

"Holy shit!" Luke shouted. Ducking under the chute, he and Tom fished Weller out of the gush, hauled him to his feet, then battled their way further down the tunnel.

This, Tom thought, *was very bad*. The water, frothy and gray, kept coming, and they were headed downhill, which meant that the water would chase them the whole way. They were also soaked through to the bone now.

"What's happening?" Luke shouted over the roar. His hair was matted to his scalp, and water ran down his neck in rivulets. "Where's all the water coming from? Why is it flooding?"

Tom knew, and he saw that Weller did, too. They were below the water table; the deeper levels of the mine were already underwater, and this gusher was sheeting down from somewhere above. So they might not be buried alive or blown to bits or even keel over from swamp gas.

But they just might drown.

82

Only an idiot runs *toward* an explosion, but that was the way out and there was no choice.

Peeling out of the drift, she darted right, racing down the tunnel, following the flashlight away from the bodies and the blood and the stink of Daniel, of Daniel, of Daniel.

Why did you? Tears streamed down her face; she could hear the phantom of that shot still rebounding in her brain, an echo that just wouldn't die. *Daniel, maybe it wasn't too late; maybe you could've fought it.*

She cut that off. No point. Daniel and his odor had been so close to Leopard's and Spider's and Wolf's: almost a match as he Changed and kept Changing. She'd known that very first night. Well, it was done now. Over. Too late for Daniel, but not for her, not yet.

Run.

The bats massed in a black scream. They slapped her face, scrabbled through her hair, their nails biting into her scalp, scoring her face. She couldn't fend them off; she needed to hold the light, and there were too many of them. So she just plowed through, swimming against a panicked tide of screeching bodies. Some shot down the tunnel before her and others just as quickly streamed the other way. She thought there were more than before, and their fear was liquid and just as sour as hers. Bats gushed out of open seams and rocketed up from jagged fissures.

She ran. Her stride was awkward because of the flashlight in her left hand and the Uzi, down low at hip-level, in her right. She didn't kid herself. Only film gangstas and Arnold Schwarzenegger could do a full mag, an Uzi in each fist, and that was because actors pumped blanks. No kick, no climb. If she had to fire, she'd need both hands, and that meant losing the light.

The Glock was a fist in her back. Its muzzle was still hot and sticky with Daniel's blood, and Leopard's. She almost hadn't taken it, almost let it lie after Daniel's fingers relaxed—but then she thought of how stupid that would be. Daniel had made his choice, and now she made hers.

The ground twitched and then she heard another, longer rumble that was almost a growl: louder and closer. Another explosion. She thought it must be from ahead and above.

A sudden cloud of bats belched up from an open seam to her right, like the cork blowing out of a champagne bottle under too much pressure. Her nose was full of dead Daniel and dead Leopard, but that burned-match stench was much stronger, and she could feel the air rasp over her throat. Her mouth tasted muddy, and she heard the pop and grind of grit between her teeth.

First a shotgun blast and now two explosions.

An attack? Someone storming the mine? She slowed for just a second.

She could picture it: battling her way to the entrance only to be cut down in a hail of gunfire. She looked every inch the Changed, and she had weapons. To anyone out there, she was the enemy.

No one knows I'm here. She smelled the bats' desperation, and hers. *If I stay and the mine* does *come down, if that's the plan . . .*

She had to get out. Take her chances. Go up, find that big ramp again, see if maybe she could shoot her way out. No one coming yet either. Sure, of course not. There was a lot going on, and no need to worry about her.

To her right, she caught a glimpse of spray-painted numbers, and thought, *Just ahead, there's a turn, and then I ought to be at the first set of stairs and then—*

As she whipped past a chute, her ears snagged on something stranger still. She skidded to a halt. Backed up to the chute. Put her hand to the metal and felt the jump and skip as the metal lurched and the stone shook.

Sound is physical. Vibrations cause sound that the ear's sensitive machinery translates. Even a deaf person knows sound by feel.

And every kid knew Chutes and Ladders. Ladders you climbed; chutes shot you down. So what she was hearing now—what she felt—was happening somewhere over her head.

What churned from the chute was a roar: thunderous and remorseless and unstoppable. For once, smell was unnecessary. She recognized this.

Water. A lot of it.

The mine wasn't just collapsing.

It was flooding.

83

The deadfall hurtled down, an engine of death. Chris screamed. Then he bucked, his bent legs pistoning against his mired snow-shoes. He catapulted away, but it was as if he were a frog whose back legs had been pinned to a specimen board. He was locked tight.

The deadfall plummeted into the snow. He felt the heavy *slam* against his back, and then he was sinking, the weight of the iron-spiked boards palming and forcing him down through softer snow into hard pack, like a plunger squeezing grounds in a coffee press. Snow jammed into his mouth and up his nose and into his eyes, and then he was coughing, pushing the snow out and away with both hands so he could breathe.

And then, he stopped. The deadfall either had hung up some-where—maybe the ropes holding it in place had snagged—or the pack had been dense enough to save him. Without the snow, the only thing that would've stopped the deadfall's downward progress would be solid ground.

His pulse was thunder. He let out a breath, thought: *I'm still here.* He hurt and it was bad. He was pinned, and that might be worse. Was his back broken? He sent a command down to his feet, had a second's fright when nothing happened, but then felt his toes curl. Okay, that was good. He was alive. The spikes missed. Too far apart? Didn't matter. He was mired in deep snow under a very heavy weight, but he was still alive. Lena was here. She could help. He'd get out of this.

If I can just wiggle out . . . He tried to squirm forward, just an inch. To see.

An enormous tidal wave of pain roared up his throat and crashed from his mouth. The shriek went on and on, spinning itself out on his breath. His legs were fire. His whole body was nothing but a red blaze.

Oh my God, oh my God. Something wet and warm leaked around his thighs, and then his brain was gabbling: *Blood, I'm dead, I'll be dead in minutes, I'll bleed out, I'll—*

"Chris!" It was Lena, but he couldn't tell if she was close, because he was too deep, the snow muffling sound like cotton.

Balling his fists, he gathered his breath and shouted, "Lena, stay back!" That slight movement cost him. Fresh fléchettes of pain cut him to the bone. And, oh God, he didn't want her to stay back. He wanted help; he needed someone to *help*! But if there were two booby traps, there might be a third—and if Lena was hurt or killed, he would be beyond help. His legs were pinned and he would die for sure: either freeze to death in the snow or bleed out. "Stay back!"

"But . . . but . . . what should I do? How can I help?"

Behind him, he thought, but then he realized that she was closer. "Are you on the horse?"

"No. I . . ."

When she didn't continue, he tried to move, only a little, and regretted that, instantly, as the pain noosed down, stealing his breath. His throat locked, and then he could make no sound, not even a scream. He waited, trying to ride the pain the way a surfer followed the swell of a wave—and then the pain eased to something just the near side of agony.

"Wh-where?" The word came out in a guttural croak. "Did you tether it?"

She paused for so long he knew the answer before the words left her lips. The roan had been bucking before, and Lena wasn't that strong.

"It threw me. I guess it was all the noise." A pause and then she said in a small voice, "When I got close, it ran back the way we came."

Oh no. His gear, his gun. He had a knife, but it was sheathed at his waist, and he didn't know if he could reach it. Not that it would help much, unless he wanted to cut his throat before a Changed ripped off his head. He couldn't roll over. Even if he hadn't been tacked in place, he didn't think Lena could lift the deadfall high enough for him to squirm free.

Might be the wrong thing to do anyway. He'd seen a movie about aliens landing in cornfields or something, and he remembered that when the preacher's wife got pinned to a tree by this honking huge truck, the police hadn't dared to move it because it was the only thing keeping her alive. So that might be the same thing here.

"Listen." He was starting to shiver. *Blood loss, shock . . . the* cold . . . "We're not far from Oren. You . . . you c-can m-make it. But you're going to need g-gear . . ."

"The only gear left is with Nathan," she said.

He tried to nod. He knew that.

"I can't, Chris. He's dead and so is his horse and I can't touch him. I . . ." She was crying. "I'm not like Alex. I'm . . . I'm *scared*."

Me, too. He made the mistake of trying to move and had to wait until the tidal wave of pain passed. It seemed to take longer this time, and he was panting when it let go. Sweat trickled down his cheeks to seep into the snow. "Y-you have to keep . . ." He lost track of what he wanted to say. The words unraveled in his mouth. He laid his cheek on the snow. *Just a second. Just . . . need to rest.*

She said something else, but her words were just so much sound. Cottony gibberish, like the lyrics of an unknown song dribbling from someone else's earbuds, or his father swearing in electric, red noise that fizzed and burned into his brain. He couldn't place the song. Those shouts had been only rage.

Passing out. A blanket of sticky cobwebs drifted over his mind, the same type of gooey stuff he tore apart with bare hands to scuttle behind the furnace down cellar as his father rampaged and bulled through the house. *Got . . . got to help her . . .*

"I'm afraid," she said again. "I'll be alone."

"Hurt." He sucked in a breath. "Bad." Forcing the words, ordering them in his mind, stole his strength. He was so tired all of a sudden, and cold. *Rest soon. Help her.* "You . . . close to . . . Oren. Find . . . get help. I can't . . ."

"Chris."

"I . . . can't." *I can't help you anymore.* That's what he wanted to say, but the words wadded up behind his teeth and just wouldn't come. She said his name again, and he tried to answer, tell her what to do; there was so much.

Stick. Snow. Search for . . . He was slipping; his mind couldn't hold on. *Watch out . . . for more traps. Careful, Lena, be . . .*

Lena's voice was very far away. "Chris, please, don't leave me."

Take . . . gun . . .

"Chris—"

. . . go, Lena . . .

"Chris—"

. . . run . . .

84

Run.

Shouldering the Uzi, she darted for the steps. She could feel the metal jumping and quivering, and then she was clattering up, taking the steps two at a time. There was a long metallic scream, a huge *POP* as a bolt spurted free of the stone. The ladder hitched; she slipped, barking her right elbow against rock. The electric shock of it streamed into her hand. Another explosion and she was knocked off her feet.

Get out, get out, get out! She swarmed up the stairs on hands and knees. Leopard had left the gate wide open, and then she was through, jinking a hard left and running for the second set of stairs, one hand up to protect her face, crashing headlong into the bats as they streamed the other way. Dust thickened the air and rock showered down in a constant stream. The earth shivered and jerked. Chunks of the wall came bouncing down. Now it was a choice between the bats and the rock. One good blow to the head and she was done. Ducking, she threw up an arm to protect her head, let out a yell as stone banged off her back. *Where is it, where* is *it?* Her panicked gaze strafed the wall, and then she saw spray paint, glanced ahead, spotted the junction. A left would take her to stairs. Wait, was that right?

Another rumble, but this time she heard the distant *bang* and then the jump and tink and slide of rocks slithering down the walls. The tunnel shook, then groaned and popped as the overstressed stone began to buckle. The ground lurched, and she actually staggered as a shower of debris spilled from overhead.

Then there came a huge, long bellow that she couldn't begin to describe, followed by a slithering hiss of rock streaming against rock and then another, louder rumble: a series of hard, insistent thumps. She had time to think that *this* was a sound the movies got dead-on. What she was hearing were bombs going off.

At the junction, to her right, the tunnel crashed down. The sound was tremendous. A gray cloud pillowed in a choking smog. Her eyes stung with dust and needle-fine grit. She clapped a hand to her face; her tongue was instantly coated with dirt, and she was retching and coughing. She staggered down the left junction, fighting the swell of dust and debris. Through streaming eyes, she saw a flash of something yellow and straight.

Stairs. She stumbled up to the first landing, but she was slowing down, her lungs struggling to pull in air that would actually do her some good. The next flight of stairs was dead ahead, but the air was still thick with bats, though there were fewer now as they darted past her and back the way she'd just come.

Then, over the growl of rock behind and the screech of the bats, she heard that roar again—from above. *And* ahead.

"Oh my God." She stood there, paralyzed with shock and the sudden realization that the bats were going the other way because they knew what she was only now beginning to understand.

Water: below, above. And coming right for her.

Wheeling around, she clattered down the steps, hooked left, pushed through a fog of dust. The smell of rotten eggs had faded, and now the air was strangely sweet. She didn't think that was good. She raced after the bats, the Uzi banging against her hip. Behind, she heard water churning and splashing, and knew it was sheeting down, building to a torrent, and then she would either drown or be crushed by the rocks. She made it to the second set of steps. Another jolt as some other level or wall gave way, and she was spilling down in a tumble of stone and larger rocks.

To her mounting horror, she saw that there were more and bigger boulders in the tunnel than before. She threw herself at a tumble piled high, almost to the ceiling, and scurried up, digging in with hooked fingers, scrambling over the rock. The opening seemed wafer-thin. Shucking the Uzi, she dropped to her belly and then socked through the weapon, the flashlight, and, finally, the Glock. Then she eeled, feeling the rock scour and bite her skin through the parka. She made the mistake of imagining herself caught here as the water rose and filled the tunnel all the way to the ceiling—and she panicked. Pulling in a huge breath, she screamed and kicked out with both hands and pushed and punched and batted, and then she was tumbling, bouncing, flipping down the other side. She landed on her back with a smack hard enough to drive knuckles of rock into her spine.

Get up, get up, get up! Staggering, clawing her way to her feet, she bent over her thighs and dragged in a breath, choked, then dragged in another as she swept up the weapons and her flashlight. *Go, go!* All this rock would buy her some time, but there was a lot of water coming, and eventually that dam just wouldn't hold.

The floor was strewn with loose stone. She slowed down, afraid to turn an ankle—or break it. If that happened, the next bullet out of that Glock would have her name on it. Ahead, she saw a bat flash in and out of the light, heading to the left. Less than a second later, so did two more, and then so did she, wheeling into the drift she'd left only minutes before. Her light flicked over Leopard's body, then Daniel's, and then they were in her past as she scrambled further back into the drift.

Air. I felt air before; I know I did.

The smell of bat guano was much stronger here, and the tunnel seemed to slope up. She fanned the light right and left. The rock was streaky with bat shit. As she pushed on, the ceiling seemed lower, and soon she was crouching, duckwalking, dragging the Uzi with one hand because the tunnel was no more than four feet high. Then she felt the shift in the air, smelled the difference, sensed space opening up—and she slid into a large chamber. Her light strafed the walls. The room was large, maybe the size of a decent living room with a cathedral ceiling. The walls were solid. No other openings. No tunnels.

Oh hell. She aimed the flashlight toward the ceiling. *Bats fly, you idiot.*

The way out must be there: far above and out of sight. She could never hope to climb this.

Then her light snagged on a craggy horizontal bracketed by two verticals.

A ladder.

You watch. She darted over. *It'll be a tease; it'll be broken.* But the ladder wasn't—not completely—although it was wood and very old. Corroded chunks and splinters speckled the rock to mingle with a thick mat of bat droppings.

Her odds were crap. She was hundreds of feet from the surface. There was no guarantee the ladder reached that far. If this tunnel slanted, she might be able to scuttle up the rocks, but she hated rock climbing. She always, always slipped.

So her choices were two. Stay here and die. Or try and maybe she'd make it. Or not. Maybe she'd only die trying. Well, maybe. There was still the Glock. Hell, if she was really worried, she could flip that Uzi to full auto and dump that mag in two seconds flat.

But not just yet.

Hooking her hands onto the boggy wood, she began to climb, racing against time.

Fighting for her life.

85

Well, they weren't dead yet: not buried or gassed or drowned. Tom had miscalculated by a minute or so, and they were across the rope bridge—Weller using that one good arm—and monkeying up the ladder when the big stope collapsed. They were too far away to hear it go, but they felt it. The ladder bounced and jounced under his feet, and Tom gasped as the metal bawled. He heard the air split as something big—maybe a part of the shaft itself—bulleted out of the dark to his left. A second later, there was a huge *boosh* as something plunged into the churning water below.

"It's starting to shake!" Luke screamed. He was five rungs above, but now he'd frozen in place. "It's shaking, it's shaking, it's shaking!"

He felt it, too: a constant, monstrous ripple shuddering through every bone. His body, obeying instinct and reflex, tried to lock up, but he clamped down hard. This was combat—this was exactly the same—and he would not survive if he listened to fear.

"Come on!" Weller roared. He was in the lead, and his voice boomed down like the voice of God. "Come on, Luke, you can do it, boy!"

Please, God, just get us out. He shot one glance above to make sure that Luke's feet were still moving, and then he fixed his eyes on the ladder, his arms and legs moving, always moving, hands wrapping around iron, boot pushing off against the last step. . . . *Keep moving keep moving keep moving* . . . the roar was huge and constant, and *they* were east of the main cave-in. God only knew what was going on down there.

Water crashed and spewed against stone, but he couldn't tell if that was below or from the side or sheeting down from above. Something bounced and rebounded against concrete, and he thought about all that loose stone above them. Weller had said that the last time there'd been a cave-in, the ground itself sank a hundred feet. *This* was larger, bigger, more powerful, and it was a very, very long way to the bottom.

So this might not be over, even if we make it. He was practically running up the ladder now, up and up and up. His lungs were tearing and working hard and his muscles shrieked with fatigue, but he kept going as the ladder quivered and bounced and the water below bellowed.

"Hey!" Luke was shouting. "I see sky, I see *sky!*"

He spared a look, craning his head back as far as he could, and then gasped. Beyond Luke, he saw Weller's head, haloed with stars. He was shocked by how close they seemed. It was like coming the wrong way out of an eye, like that movie from way back—only they'd come out through the guy's tear duct, hadn't they?

Gogogogogo . . . he felt air now, very cold, washing down over his head and shoulders, and he heard Luke shout again. He glanced up, saw that Weller was gone. Then the boy folded, and Tom saw only his feet as Luke scrambled out of the shaft. *Keep going, keep going* . . . he was forty feet away, thirty feet, ten . . .

He felt a hand clamp onto his left wrist, and then Weller had his right. Luke and the old man gave a mighty heave, and Tom flopped out of the shaft and sprawled belly-first onto the snow. For a few seconds, all he could do was gasp, and then Luke pounded his back hard enough to jar loose his breath.

"We d-d-did it," Luke said. The boy was grinning and shivering at the same time. "W-w-we did it, we d-d-did it!"

"Uh," was all Tom could manage. He could feel the earth shimmying under his stomach, and from far down in the shaft came the echo and rumble and roar of disintegrating stone and churning water.

"Hey," Luke said. He was looking to his right. "I s-s-see bats, d-dude."

The moon was setting but enormous on the horizon, like the green eye of a giant. The bats were black, fluttery, spastic silhouettes bulleting in all directions.

"Must be another opening," Weller said. Sucking in air, he spat then staggered to his feet. "We got to go. Cold'll get us soon, and I don't like the way the ground is shim—" A pause. "Oh, fuck me."

Uh-oh. All Tom's fatigue—and relief—was swept away in an instant. Weller was hunched over, propping himself up on his thighs, looking southwest and down the rise. Tom did the same, and he wasn't sure now if the shuddering in his legs was only from the ground.

They weren't far away. Maybe—he squinted in the poor light—four hundred yards.

"How many do you think there are?" Luke asked.

"Can't tell." Weller glanced at Tom. "We shoot it out, or we run."

"We should f-fight," Luke said, then added, "I'm not s-scared, just c-cold. We can d-do this."

"No," Tom said. He swung up his Uzi and peered through the scope. Seven, he thought. They were spread out across the shivering snow, but they weren't coming on fast. From the way they lurched, they were having trouble on the shifting snowpack, and he thought only two were on skis. Of those, only one kid was a threat. His gaze narrowed to a laser point and fixed on the tallest Chucky. A boy, he thought. From the kick and glide, the kid knew what he was doing.

Then, three of the others from further back raised their weapons.

"Down!" Tom shouted. They all flattened just as the night sparked and crackled. Tom didn't think the bullets even came close.

He heard the *snick* as Luke thumbed the selector of his Uzi. "We could kill them," Luke said. No shake in his voice now. "We should fight. After all those poor people back there . . . they deserve to die, Tom."

"Wait. Let's think about this. We're on a rise. Gravity is working against them and their bullets." Tom pointed. "There's only that one guy who knows what he's doing. He's closest and he hasn't taken a shot. We stick around, he will."

"So we take them out now," Luke said. "Please. This is for, like, *everybody* who died, you know?"

"But we don't *have* to fight, Luke. We still have a choice."

"Well, I vote we stay," Luke said.

More sparks and crackles as the Chuckies fired. They all ducked back, but Tom knew there was no danger. These kids were firing wild.

Almost like they're trying to scare us off.

Which was strange, come to think of it.

"Come on, they want to fight. They're *shooting* at us," Luke said.

"No, they're trying to drive us off," Tom said.

"Why would they do that?" Luke asked.

"Doesn't matter. The point is, they're not firing *at* us yet, but in about three minutes, they—" He felt a sudden heave as if the earth were pulling in a big breath, and then the ground seemed to fall away. A yell of surprise shot out of his mouth, and then he was sprawling, smacking the ground on all fours. He waited to keep falling, but nothing more happened, although the snow still trembled on.

"What was *that*?" Luke yelped. He was trying to swim to his knees. "What *happened*?"

"Surface subsidence starting," Weller said. "Mine's caving in, and it's getting worse. Before, there wasn't warning, but this time . . ."

There is. "We *have* to go."

"Don't hear me arguing." Weller was already turning. "We can probably beat them and the cave-in on skis, but we got to be—" Another shock. Weller lurched and would have fallen if Tom's hand hadn't shot out to snag him. "Christ," the old man grated. "Between this and those damn Chuckies, we'll be lucky to—"

Suddenly, from somewhere off to their right came a thin, high, shrill note.

The sound was so unexpected Tom whirled on his heel, still in his crouch, the Uzi in his hands. He heard the others readying their weapons.

"Did you hear that?" Luke whispered. "Does a cave-in make a sound like that? Or was it like . . . a *bat*?"

"No," Weller said. "It sounded like—"

The sound came again, and this time, Tom knew exactly what it was.

A whistle.

86

When the distant crackle first reached her, she didn't get it. She had been climbing, steadily, in the grumbling dark for ten minutes. Every now and again, a bat spirited past, but she spared them no more attention. All they told her was this was the right way to go. Sweat streamed from her face, and her clothes were clinging. Her lungs were going like a bellows, and her thighs burned. Three rungs had given way, and now when they hit bottom, she heard a splash. The tunnel was filling and so was this chamber. The gush of water was building to a steady rumble, and this slope was shaking, too. She heard the grind and bounce and slide of rock pinging and catapulting for the water.

Then that crackle came again, a sound like crispy cellophane, and this time she got it.

Gunfire.

Her head jerked up, eyes scanning the darkness. Was it less dim? She couldn't tell, and her sense of smell was no help here. The occasional bat still fluttered past, but they seemed to have all gotten out. She was alone, making her way up a shuddering, squalling ladder.

If there are guns, there's a fight.

There might be people up there, maybe killing Changed. Or the Changed might have found whoever set off the bombs. Considering what she'd seen, she wouldn't be surprised if the Changed were killing each other.

She froze, tried to think what to do. She could squeeze out a round from the Glock or even a couple from the Uzi . . . but that didn't tell anyone up there anything except that she had a gun. The Changed had guns. If there were people up there, all they had to do was spray bullets into this tunnel, or wait until she popped out.

Not an option.

"Hello?" She started scrambling up the ladder again. "Hello, I'm down here! Help, *hel*—"

Snap. And . . . *SNAP!*

This time, both rungs gave at once. She screamed, felt her body lurch down, and then her feet were dangling, trying to climb against air. Her biceps shrieked, but then one flailing boot banged into the rock face, and she pressed it hard, balancing on her toes like a rock climber, which she was most definitely not. She hung there, her right leg shuddering, her arms quaking with the strain. Her left shoulder, still scabbed, fired with pain. Below, the water thrashed. The walls shivered and she heard the rock splintering and cracking. The rickety ladder vibrated in her hands. Lifting her left leg as high as she could, she felt the butt of a rung against her boot, and then she was leaning into the ladder.

Oh my God. Gulping, she rested her sweaty forehead against the moldering, swollen wood. *Hurry up and kill yourself, why don't you?*

"Help!" she screamed. "Help, *please*!" A waste of energy and breath. Hopeless. She was too far down, and her voice was no match against the water's ceaseless churn. No one would hear.

Wait.

She still had it, didn't she? Reaching with one trembling hand, she felt at her neck, then gasped out a sobbing breath.

Her dad: *You blow on that, honey, and I'll be there in a heartbeat.*

She fitted the whistle to her lips.

Oh, Daddy, please be right.

She inhaled—and let her breath go.

87

Oh my God. The sound knifed right through his ribs. *It can't be.*

"Where is that coming from?" Luke said.

"Where we saw the bats," Tom said. The ground twitched again and he staggered, and then he was bolting over the unsteady snow. His frantic eyes scoured the horizon. *The bats were silhouetted against the moon; they were right there!* He caught another flit, changed direction, stumbled as the earth shifted again, and then he was plowing through deep drifts, his Uzi held high.

"Tom!" Weller shouted. "Tom, wait! You don't know where—"

He paid no attention. He kept on, swimming through the shivering snow, and then he saw a bat bullet skyward just a few feet to his right. Dropping the Uzi, he fell to his knees, clicked on his light. The ground lurched again, and he swayed and then began sweeping the snow with his arms in wide arcs, looking for the opening. *Come on, come on, come on, I just . . .*

Another jolt, and he heard something new: the bang of rock against rock. Then he saw it. The opening was a dark slash in the skin of the snow, only two, maybe three feet wide, and as long.

He fell onto his belly. The earth was bucking, but he pushed at the snow, clearing it away so he could see. He heard Weller and Luke still shouting at him, closer now, but he didn't look around. From below came the rumble of a distant thunder and the grind of rock. Another bat whirred past.

This had to be part of the mine, too: a forgotten shaft, a side tunnel. Maybe, long ago, an old escape route.

The enemy was down there. But so were people.

The odds were a billion to one, but there was only one person on earth he knew with a whistle.

"Ellie?" Tom cupped his hands and bellowed. *"Ellie?"*

First, there had been a fine snow spilling like white sand. Not a lot, but enough that some sifted into her hair.

Then, incredibly, a scent of musk and sweet smoke and spice that tugged her heart.

And, finally, a voice. Distant. So small.

But she made out the one word.

Ellie.

"Oh God." For a second, she just hung there. Her heart stuttered and then banged to life.

It's him. It's him*! He's alive. He's the only one who knows. That's his scent. It's him. It has to be. It's—*

"Tom!" she shrieked. *"Tom!* It's *Alex,* it's—"

Alex? He went absolutely still with shock. *She's here?*

Her voice came again, and although he could barely hear her, knew she was very far away and out of reach, her words—his name—exploded against and in him with the force of an atom bomb. Beneath, the earth was shuddering, and so was he, all over, and then he was screaming down to her: "Alex, Alex! It's me, it's Tom! Where are you, Alex? *Where—*"

"What's happening?" Luke dropped beside him, and then Tom felt the boy's hands on his arms, trying to tug him back. "God, Tom, be careful! You're going to fall in!"

He paid no attention. "Alex!" he bawled. "How far down are you? Can you see me? Can you see my light?"

"Who's Alex?" Luke said.

"*Quiet.*" There was a very long pause, and he felt like he would burst, but he shoved a knuckle into his mouth and waited. He heard Weller thrash his way over but didn't look around. *He said she was in Rule, but she's here, she's—*

"Far." Her voice was like those silver bubbles that had boiled from his lungs to break into empty air and they were the last of his life, and he was drowning. "Can't . . . see . . . you."

But I hear you, I hear you, oh God, I hear you. "Hang on! I've got rope! I'm coming for you! Can you climb? Can you—" He broke off as Weller grabbed his right arm and twisted him around.

"You can't," Weller grated. "Tom, she's got to be a couple hundred feet down. We got twenty feet of rope and that's it! She's too far, and we don't have *time!*"

"No, give me the goddamned rope!" Tom shouted. "You and Luke go, but I'm staying!"

"To do what? You think you can help her?"

"We came together; we leave together!" Luke cried. "I'm not going without you, Tom! I'm staying!"

"You hear that? You're gonna kill this boy." Weller was right in his face. "You want to be responsible for that? You want his blood?"

"Don't put that on me!" Tom shouted. "No one's telling you to stay! Both of you just *go*!"

"Then you might as well put a bullet in your brain for all the good you'll do that girl! This whole rise is gonna go! Even if it doesn't, those Chuckies aren't going to stop, and they'll *be* here!"

"Then I'll *kill* them!" Tom roared. His face was wet, but he didn't care. One more second and he would murder this old man. He twisted away with a curse. "You said she was in Rule, you said she was in *Rule*!"

"I don't *know* about that!" Weller shouted. There was a high crack that was not a bullet but the sound of wood shattering, and then Luke was screaming something about trees breaking and Weller was shouting: "You hear that, you hear that? You're gonna kill this boy and yourself for *nothing*!"

No, no, not for nothing. *For her.* She was calling him again, but her voice was so faint. He wasn't sure now if what he heard was real or an echo. Or maybe he was trapped in some endless flashback from which he would never shake free, because there was now also dust and hot sun and gray rock and Jim's voice: *Cut the wire, cut the wire and get out, just grab the kid, grab the kid and go, go, go!*

"But, God, *please*, which *one*?" he shrieked. He was on his knees, in snow, on a dirt road, under a weird moon, beneath the blazing sun, and there were voices in his head and the pop and bang of weapons fire and the wail of men and women somewhere close and the voices of his friends—all dead now, all gone—and sweat that stung and tears that ate his eyes. "How do I *choose?*"

Because there was, in that road and on that day, not just one child with a bomb strapped around her tiny waist.

There was the boy, too.

"God, how do I *choose?*" he screamed again. He pressed the heels of his hands to his temples and squeezed. *Get out of my head, get out of my head, grab the kid, grab the kid, cut the wire, get out my head, get out get out get out!* "How can you *ask* that?"

"Tom!" Luke cried—but from another life, a different time. "Tom, please, come on!"

Oh God, Alex. Help me stay. He leapt for that crack in the earth, a distant hope, and thrust his head and then his arms into the dark. He felt quaking rubble and snow that melted beneath the heat of his hands. The roar was tremendous, as if there was something alive down there, bellowing, opening wide, ready to swallow them both. "Alex, please, try, *try!* Climb, Alex, climb!"

"Tom, don't!" He felt hands grappling for a handhold around his waist. "Leave it," Weller bawled. "Leave it, Tom! We got to go!"

Got to go, cut the wire, cut the wire, grab the kid, go, go! Kicking, cursing, he reached down the mouth of that tunnel as far as he could, straining so hard that his muscles shook and his joints screamed—and no matter what he did, it was still not enough. She was a voice in a vast emptiness so profound he might fall forever. But he had to try; he couldn't stop. He had to reach her because they would touch, and then he would save her; he would pull her from this hell and into the light; they would save each other. *"Alex!"*

"Trying." Her voice, so tiny. "Too far . . . no time." Then: "Run, Tom, run. Get out . . . get away before—"

"No!" Tom bellowed. "Don't give up, Alex, don't you dare give up! I'm here, Alex, I'm right *here!*"

"No time. Tom, please, *go* . . ."

"They're over the rise!" Behind, above, Luke was screaming: "They're here, they're here, they're over the rise!" A *crack* and then two more, the bullets whizzing by in shrieks. "Tell me what to do!" Luke shouted, his voice notching higher with panic. "Somebody tell me what to do—do I shoot, do we fight, do we—"

Fight, Alex, fight; say my name again, say my name again, don't leave me here, I'll never get out. "Alex!" His fists closed, but there was nothing to grab but the trembling dark. He tried squirming even further, but Weller was battened around his waist and he couldn't move, only teeter on the brink: nightmare above, his fate below. "Alex, *Ale*—"

With no warning at all, the ground suddenly heaved and swelled and then came down with a slam that socked him in the gut, straight through to his spine. From the tunnel came a great gasp as the earth shifted, and then he heard a hiss, a sizzle, a ballooning whisper as the rocks under his hands moved and wallowed and gave way. They bounced ahead, hurtling down the chute. Suddenly off-balance, with nothing under his hands but air, he lurched forward and might have tumbled in after . . . and maybe that was, really, what he wanted.

But Weller's grip was too strong. The old man hauled him

back from the edge and wouldn't let go, and Luke was screaming: "Tom, *please*, we got to get out; I can't leave without you. Please!"

And I can't leave her. But no one would help him. He couldn't save her. He would never reach her in time, and she knew that. *Save myself? For what?* But if he stayed with her to the end, this boy would die and Weller, too—and all that would be on him.

"Help me!" All his grief and rage burst from his chest in a loud, long, anguished wail: "God, *please*, help me! Not again, don't ask me to *do* this again!"

His answer came. In the next moment, the air shattered with *cracks* and the snaky hiss and suck of bullets. Cursing, Weller wrestled him to his feet, and then he was stumbling through snow and away from her, and Luke was still shrieking, and *he* was screaming her name over the hollow, stuttering *tatatatatatats* of the Uzis as the distance between them spun out.

It was happening again. His choice was made. The wire was cut, and he was as damned and lost now as he had been on that day, when one child would die because he could not save them both.

Then, somehow, over and above all that, he thought he heard the high pipe of the whistle again. It couldn't be, of course. It must be the sound of his mind going, a shriek that grew fainter and fainter until that one note disintegrated under an insane moon— and so, finally, did his heart.

But the ground kept on, heaving and shuddering, the snow shifting and cracking beneath their skis as they fled. Eventually, he knew even that would end: when the tired earth, like him, gave up.

He just did it sooner.

88

God, she hoped he listened. She thought he must have. She couldn't hear him anymore, not over the clatter of rocks, the jackhammer rumble, and the suck and hiss of the black water fizzing below. There was that huge slam that had nearly knocked her right off the ladder, and then he'd stopped calling. His scent had torn apart and faded. So she thought he was gone. But there'd been gunfire, too. Had he been shot? Was he dead?

No, God, please, don't let that happen. Keep him safe; make him go.

She didn't want him to go. It was the last thing on earth she wished, because now she was truly alone, with only the monster for company: lurking in her head, waiting for her to make a mistake.

Oh no you don't. She willed herself on: one more step and then another and another. *Not yet.*

It was on her, again. Maybe living always had been. She wasn't Daniel. Hell, she wasn't sure she was Alex anymore. All that mattered was Tom was alive and up there, somewhere, and *that* was worth hanging on to. They couldn't touch, but he had reached her, whether he knew it or not—because hope was enough. Hope was all she had.

She would run to him.

So, run, Tom, run, her mind chanted. *Run, Tom, pull me up, pull me up, run, run, run.* She kept the mantra up as she climbed the ladder that, somehow, hadn't decided to die just yet either. She was going on a wing and a prayer, by feel and faith, that the next rung would be there and the one after that and on and on to a world she probably wouldn't see again but would try for anyway because he was in it. Tom was alive and that was something to believe in that was as real in all this darkness as the wood under her hands and the stammer of the earth and the wild thrum of her heart.

She grabbed at the jumping, quivering ladder; felt the bite of wood in her flesh. Her hands were bloody; a rock, sharp as broken glass, had sliced her forehead on the way down, and now she was arming blood from her eyes every few seconds. Her left shoulder had gone from fire to a deadening cold numbness, and her clumsy fingers tingled with pins and needles. There was a weird hissing now that she knew was the sound of scree raining over the rocks. That sulfur smell was worse, too, and her head was beginning to go a little swimmy.

Don't lose it, don't give up. If her eyes closed, they would never open again. She willed her legs to keep moving. *Keep going, go, go, run, Tom, run, ru—*

Another *slam*, and she swayed. Her left boot slipped, and then she shrieked and threw herself forward, hooked on with both arms as the ladder lurched and bounced. From somewhere above, there was a sharp *bang* and then a crack. Something huge whirred past, and her mind just had time to squeak one word: *big*.

There was an enormous *ker-SPLASH*. Water jumped, grabbed at her ankles, then slithered away with a hiss.

Felt that. Really close. Gonna get me. Well, what if the water did? Maybe she could float. If it kept rising, maybe it would push right to the surface—because she *was* tired. The burst of elation that had fueled her was ebbing. Her head was swirly, and her lips had no feeling. The gas? Could be. Maybe that was why the water fizzed. Was it methane? No, no, that was . . .

"Coal mines." She said it just so she could hear herself and know her brain was still working. Her mouth mangled the words. "Coal mines have methane. Other mines have . . ." Hell, she didn't know. *Should've paid more attention in earth science.* Weary to the bone, she hugged the ladder. A splinter of wood nipped her cheek, tore into her already bloodied forehead. "Come on, Alex," she mumbled. "Stay awake. Don't pass out."

Run, Alex. Tom, in her mind. Not the monster, not her voice, but Tom. Maybe Chris, too. *Run. Run to me. Run to us.*

"Yeah, yeah, I'm on it," she panted. Reaching for the next rung with her right, hanging on with her creaky left, she looked up. "I'm right—"

Stars.

For a brief moment, she was so stunned she could only gape. She blinked, but the view didn't change.

There are stars. Oh my God. Got to be close, got to be. She surged up, stumbling as the earth bounced. Her head was hollow; her left arm was not at its best and even her right was clumsy. She put her back into it, heaving up in a roundhouse grab like a chimpanzee—

And missed.

Her right hand shot into absolutely nothing. Suddenly off-balance, her right boot slipped out from under, and then she was slamming into the right-hand rail. The blow caught her face. A bomb of pain detonated and her vision went white; her skin ripped, and she let out a gasping sob. Frantic, fighting to keep her balance, she tried pushing off from the rock, which she thought must be right in front of her—

But there was nothing. Just black, empty air. No rock and no wood either. Her whole body weight had shifted to a point beyond the ladder's right rail, and she was twisting, her weaker left arm providing the fulcrum about which her body pivoted. The entire right half of her body was hanging over open air, and the wood was slippery and very old, and she was still turning, her body slotting in between the rock that reared away from her back and the ladder right in her face. She felt the overstressed wood buckle. There was another crack and then a long, high squeal she heard even over that ceaseless rumble and churn of water and stone.

Oh God, please, I'm so close, please, help.

She had less than a hundred feet to go, but they might as well have been miles. Above, the stars were dimming, winking out in a sudden swarm of cold shadows darker than night. The earth began to collapse and fold, the surface shearing; the rock was coming down, and then so were the shadows, and she felt the ladder shudder and begin to break apart; it was breaking, it was breaking, it was—

The ladder disintegrated to splinters, and then there was suddenly nothing in her hands at all but air. Beneath her, the tunnel's throat opened. The water was all sound; it was everything that was left. Her mouth was open, and she knew she was shrieking, but she couldn't hear anything, and for a crazy second, it was as if the water's roar had become her voice.

Screaming, Alex hurtled straight down, and her last thought, right before she hit, was: *Feet first.*

She smashed into the water.

PART SIX:
THE DEVIL'S DOOR

Sometimes, he moaned. That was her only clue he was still alive.

She sat with him all that night. Maybe she should've gone for help, but she was too afraid to move. She called his name a few times. At least, she thought she did. For a few terrible seconds, she couldn't remember his name—or hers—and that scared her more.

And then, much later, he stopped making any sound at all.

She waited. And waited. The darkness went grainy and gray as that gangrenous moon slid west and the night began to fade. In the spray of weird light, the wood shone a dullish white. She saw that it wasn't part of a door because of that arch drawn in black paint and the half-symbol of three spiked points just above, like a setting sun cut by a distant horizon. There was a name for this, too. What was it? She couldn't quite remember. But why not?

She waited, sleepless, raw-eyed. Cold. She hunched up her shoulders, hugging herself to stay warm. Her fear was salt and metal in her mouth. And she was hungry. The snake of her stomach twisted and writhed. So hungry. The need had been building for a while. She had decided not to think about it. Now, as dawn showed in a white streak, she couldn't ignore it.

Morning soon. Full day. She couldn't stay here.

But . . . he had a scent. *He is*—she drew him in and her mouth watered—*food.*

Don't.

Yes.

Don't.

Stop.

She crept, slowly, carefully, on all fours. The wind burned her cheeks. The air was suddenly choked with the smell of iron and meat. He was far down in the snow, and she used her hands to dig at the edges of the trench. The hollow was surprisingly warm, and his smell was so rich her stomach cramped.

Stop. You're still you. Don't.

His face was turned away, his watch cap rucked up a little cock-eyed, like a makeshift shroud. That made it easier. At his waist, where the wood cut across, she made out an irregular, dark patch. She formed her hands into a scoop and lifted out a scarlet chunk of ice and sucked his blood, still warm, into her mouth.

Don't.

Warm. Yes.

"Stop," she said, and then she flung the gory handful away. Her gorge rushed up her throat, and she heaved and vomited, but she hadn't eaten in two full days, and there was nothing left.

Almost nothing left of her either.

"N-no," she said. She tottered to her feet and stumbled back, away from the blood and temptation, away from his meat, that scent, his smell. "No. Stop. Run. He said to ru—"

From somewhere down the trail, toward . . . toward . . . where had they been going? She didn't know. But the sounds, she recognized.

Dogs. From the racket, more than one, and big. She heard the new note of excitement in their cries, too, as they scented her the way hounds chased down a whiff of good prey.

She had to get out of here. Where there were dogs, there might be people, and she couldn't be caught; she couldn't be seen, she had to—

From behind came a low, menacing growl. Lena's throat closed down on a sudden scream. The small hairs along her neck and arms stiffened in alarm, and she had to force herself to move slowly, so *carefully*. Her eyes inched to the right.

The dog was not far away at all. In her panic, she couldn't gauge the distance, and that really didn't matter. With its black mask and those ears, the animal was like a small German shepherd, but the rest of its fur was a reddish-brown, like a chestnut mare's. Its lips had peeled back from its very white teeth in a snarl.

Her throat convulsed. Her mouth was open, and she thought she was trying to say something, but the only sound that came was a strangled moan. It seemed as if two giant fists had clamped around her chest and *squeezed*. She eased back a half step, then stopped when the dog's deep rumble grew louder.

It's going to kill me. "Puh-puh-puhleeez," she wheezed. She saw the dog's ears twitch, and that growl hitched and dropped a note.

To her eyes, the dog actually looked confused. "Please, juh-just let m-me g—"

"*Meeenaaah.*" Not a singsong, although the distant voice was young. "*Meeenaaah, where are you, girl?*"

Meeenaaah, or Mina, or whatever the dog's name was, faltered then. She watched as the dog threw a glance over its shoulder, and then *she* was moving back a quick step and then another. Whirling around, the dog tensed, and for a second, she thought it was going to come for her after all, but then the dog was pivoting on its hind legs and sprinting away, barking as it followed the girl's voice.

Go. Turning on her heel, she darted off the trail and into the woods. Branches whipped at her skin and tore her face, snagging her hair. *Go, go, he said to go, run . . .*

The woods still were the color of lead, but the snow was not as deep in the trees and her footing was better. Behind, she heard the moment the dogs' voices changed—heard that call again—and knew they'd found *him.* They might not follow her now. She might be safe.

Run. Then: *Lena, I'm Lena. He's Chris and he said to run, Lena, run.*

The cold air was crushed glass in her throat, but she blundered on, churning and crashing through the woods. She had no idea where she was going, or what she should do now, but she was alone. No one would see.

I'm a coward. If I had any guts, I would've shot myself or told him the truth and asked him to do it. He would have.

But she was as afraid of dying as she had become of sleeping. Because what would she be when she woke up?

You're still you. She spotted a bright smear, a break in the trees, and felt a tug in her chest, like the set of a hook. She changed direction. Why? Maybe a road. Was that what she thought? Of course she did. Who was thinking in her head but her? Her feet pounded and pushed against snow. There would be a road and she would be able to run even further. *You're still you and you can stop this.*

Liar. She dodged through a tangle of whippy alders, let them slap her face. *You can't because you won't. You're scared of dying because then there's nothing—no more anything and no God either.*

She vaulted toward the break, that glimmer of yellow-white which was the sun trying to struggle above the horizon, coming fast and very soon. Maybe *that* would kill her, like in a movie or book. Poof! Nothing left but ash and a scorched shadow, just like Hiroshima and that nameless Japanese person: painted black on a stretch of ruined concrete in a skeletal cityscape of twisted iron, pulverized stone, and naked steel. God, how could she remember *that* and have trouble with her own name?

I'm Lena, I am Lena, you can't take that. She bulleted through the snow, tearing her way through brambles and scruff. *I won't let you, I won't—*

She pulled up with a sudden, hard gasp and came to a dead stop.

In the nacreous and feeble light of the coming day, she saw only four clearly, but she sensed many more to the right and left. They faced her as the first fingers of pale light leaked into slate sky, so that they were, each and every one, crowned with glimmering halos, like dark angels fallen from grace.

Even the boy with her green scarf twined around his neck.

Her heart thrashed in her chest, and she was trembling both from fear and her mad flight. It came to her then—what that arch and symbol painted on the deadfall represented. They formed a Devil's door. A trick. The arch was an illusion, the star symbol cut in half not by a wood sash but deliberately painted to give the appearance of something whole cut in two. There was no door, and the Devil would only bang his head if he tried to enter.

Unless the Devil was clever and very, very patient and found another way.

"No. P-please," she choked as the Changed began to move, their shadows eeling over the snow, reaching for her in black fingers. "I'm me, I'm Lena. I'm *n-not—*"

They closed in.

The chirping ceased. Most had buzzed by too quickly for him to decipher through his fog of exhaustion and starvation, but Peter got some of it.

Rule. Finn and his people would march on Rule, and there was nothing he could do for them, or himself.

He sprawled in his cell, back to the iron bars. His clothes were in tatters, no more than dirty rags held together with bits of string. His body wasn't much better: a patchwork of half-healed wounds, open sores, new bites; a bag of bones in a sack of torn skin.

But he was the only one left. These last few days, Finn seemed content with simple attrition. No Changed to the right. No Changed to the left. Empty cells with just the stink as a reminder, a smell seeped into stone like blood. Only time erased that.

No Davey either, although Peter hadn't killed him. Davey had grown quick and very sure. A fast learner. Finn took Davey away . . . day before yesterday? He thought that was right. Days meant virtually nothing now. There was only living through the next fight for that half cup of water, a mouthful of bread.

Saving Davey for the end, like the cherry from a sundae.

Could he fight? He cradled his left arm, his right palm clamped to the place where the girl had bitten and ripped clean through to the bone. He didn't remember much—it had all gone so fast—but she was one of the feral Changed: all teeth and mad eyes and weird energy. Quick on her feet, too. Probably because she'd just eaten. She nearly had him.

But he could also learn. His eyes rolled to the body. The lake of blood pooling out of the crater he'd torn from her neck was so high the overflow wormed to cold concrete. All that time with the Changed paid off after all; he'd taken his cue from them and ripped her throat out. And, God, that blood was so tantalizing. It was liquid. It was wet.

Thirsty. So thirsty.

The next time they opened that cell door and Davey came through? It would be the very last. Oh, he would try, but unless he was extremely lucky, Davey would kill him, and slowly, too. Davey seemed to favor strangulation. Finn let the Changed boy practice on other Changed. Five, ten, fifteen minutes sometimes before Davey got tired and finally squeezed hard and long enough to end it. The very first time, Davey had kept poking the dead kid's eyes. Like he couldn't understand why the kid he'd just murdered wouldn't get up and play.

God, just make it quick. He felt the sob trying to work its way up his throat but swallowed it back. *Maybe this is punishment, but I only did what I thought was right, what I had to do.*

"R-Rule." His mouth was thick and sticky with gore. "Wh-what . . . are you g-going to d-do?"

"In Rule?" Finn clipped the radio onto his belt. "Oh, a little shock, a little awe. You know, the all-American stuff we're so good at."

"Why?" Peter swallowed, grimaced against the taste of dead girl. He worked up enough saliva to spit, but he had no strength and the foamy gobbet drooled onto his chin. "What have th-they done?"

"Peter." Finn did him the favor of not smiling. "Of all people, you really have to ask? But don't worry. I wouldn't dream of leaving you behind. You're coming with us, boy-o. I want your people to take a good, hard look. First, though, let's get that nasty bite taken care of. Clean you up, get you fed, put some meat on those bones. Make you right as rain. New day, new dawn, new Earth." Looping his hand through the carry handle of a knapsack, Finn dug around in a cargo trouser pocket and withdrew a set of jingling keys. He socked one into the lock. "I have a lot of respect for you. You've been through quite a trial, a journey to the dark center of the soul."

Okay, yes, this guy was nuts. Peter tensed as the cell door opened on a scream of metal hinges. Mincing around the blood, the old man squatted on his haunches until they were eye to eye and just a few feet apart.

"They say every man has his breaking point. But I haven't found yours, Peter—not yet," Finn said. "You're like the Ever-Ready Bunny that way. You just won't quit. That's admirable, boy-o. But maybe there's a difference between what you do to yourself versus what is done *to* you. Maybe my hypothesis has been all wrong."

"What . . ." Peter had to work up enough moisture to keep going. "What the hell are you t-talking about?"

"Well, I was thinking," Finn said. His hand dipped into his knapsack and came up with a clear plastic bottle filled with water. The bottle must've been put in the snow to keep cold, because beads of condensation shuddered and then obeyed gravity, rolling down the plastic to drip over Finn's fingers. "There is pressure from without—torture and environment and so on—and then there is the pressure that comes from within."

Peter barely heard. His gaze was riveted on those drops, Finn's fingers, that small core of ice bobbing in all that cool water. The need for water was so great it took all his willpower not to grab Finn's hand and lick the moisture from the old man's flesh.

"I think I made a serious miscalculation in my initial hypothesis," Finn said as his fingers worked the cap. "The will to survive exerts its own pressure. Right now, I've given you walls to push against, obstacles to overcome, someone to hate. What I neglected to consider was what might happen if those walls suddenly vanished." Finn proffered the open bottle. "If there was no one left to hate except the self."

He's giving me water. There are no guards and Davey's not here and he's not going to kill me. That was all he could think. The hot surge of gratitude, absurd and irrational, made him want to weep. He let Finn fit the bottle to his lips and hold the back of his neck as he drank, greedily, the icy water spilling around his mouth and down his neck and exploding into his empty stomach with such force that he moaned with the pain.

"Easy, boy-o, not too fast," Finn murmured, almost lovingly. He didn't take the bottle away, but kept talking as Peter gulped. "So I thought to myself: Finn, stop with the threats and the pressure. Making the boy fight for his life might not tell you what you want to know."

"What . . . what's that?" Peter gasped. Every drop of water was gone. He leaned back with a sigh. His belly sloshed. He would probably be sick; might even bring it all back up. But he didn't care. His head was spinning, and now his hunger was a roar again: something struggling to be born in the taut tent of his skin that just might tear him in two.

"Every man breaks, eventually." Finn capped the bottle. "Even Jesus cracked at the end. But that wasn't because of what was being done *to* him. His pressure was doubt and came from within, but he always had a choice. We just call it destiny when it's too late to change our minds. But I realized that I had to make *your* choice yours and not mine. In the heat of battle, all a man wants is to live."

He had no idea what Finn was going on about. His head was muzzy and, too late, he wondered if maybe the water had been spiked with something. *Killing me with kindness*, he thought, and nearly giggled. The water made him a little giddy. But the hunger was sharper now, a knife slashing at his guts, and he stifled a groan when his stomach cramped.

Beyond the cell, there was a clank of a lock and then a gush of cold air as the prison house door swung open. "Ah," Finn said, checking his watch. He pushed up on his thighs. "Right on time."

Three guards guided Davey in on control poles fitted to that wide leather collar. The Changed boy was fully dressed in the same uniform everyone else in Finn's compound wore.

Peter's heart lurched against the cage of his ribs. So it *had* been just a trick. Probably, Finn gave him water so he'd be strong enough for one last bout.

Keep fighting. Using the wall for support, he struggled to his feet as the guards maneuvered Davey down the center aisle. Davey's glittery eyes fixed on Peter, and his nostrils flared and relaxed and flared again, like those of a hound eager to have at the fox. Peter slid along the wall and then felt along the bars until he could wedge himself into a corner. If he used the bars for leverage, he could kick. Better than Davey catching him in the center of the cell. *Kick at his face, if you can.* He wrapped his hands around cold iron. *No matter what, don't just give up.*

"That's good," Finn said as the guards reached the cell. "Hold it there." Finn had his knapsack again, and when he opened it, Peter saw Davey's head suddenly jerk toward the old man. The Changed boy actually tensed, going up on tiptoe the way little kids did at Halloween so they could dig into that bowl for their favorite candy.

"Sorry, Davey boy, not for you," Finn said. Chuckling, he reached a hand to Davey's head and ruffled his hair. The Changed boy didn't react at all.

My God. Peter's heart stuttered. *He's turned it into a pet.*

"Here we go," Finn said, and withdrew a white paper packet. Waxed paper? Peter wasn't sure. He watched as Finn squatted, set the packet down, and teased open the paper. Coils of steam unfurled, releasing the juicy aroma of fresh-grilled meat and perfectly seared fat.

A moan pushed between his lips before he could call it back. Saliva gathered under his tongue, and the beast of his hunger tried clawing right into his throat.

"Yes, smells good, doesn't it? I do love a good steak. I hope you like medium-rare. Oh, and it's fresh. Just butchered this morning." Finn used the point of his knife to flip the muscle so Peter could see the crisscross grill marks—

And the faded red ink of a tattooed heart.

At first, he just didn't understand. His eyes fixed on that tattoo, and then his brain was working the problem like a complicated geometry proof. There was meat and . . . a tattoo; steak and a—

"N-no!" he gasped. He cringed back against the bars. He did not know which was worse: the steady, strong claw of his hunger that simply refused to stop—because the scent of that meat was so strong and he was really and truly dying—or the sudden, cold blast of horror. "I . . . I won't. You can't make me p-put that in my m-mouth. You can't make me *eat*."

"Wouldn't dream of it. Haven't you been listening, Peter? This is your choice now. No threats. No pain. No Chucky ready to tear your eyes out. I wash my hands of this fight. There is only you, Peter, and"—he aimed the knife—"that piece of meat. This fight is between you and *you*. There is food, and it is the *only* food. So eat, and live."

"I w-won't." And now he was weeping. His legs wouldn't hold him up anymore, and he let himself sink to the grimy, bloodstained floor. "I . . . I *can't*."

"You can," Finn said. "You could. The question is, will you? Because of the pressure, Peter, you see? In a battle, even of the soul, a man will do anything to live. The only saints exist in fairy tales and legends. So maybe you won't break today or tomorrow . . . but soon, Peter, very soon."

No. Peter turned his face to the bars. The smell of succulent roast meat was overpowering. *No, I won't. I'll die first, I'll—*

"Watch and learn, Davey," Finn said. "Watch and learn."

Dawn was two hours away, the night sky a black bowl salted with stars. Beyond the bouncing ball of her headlamp, the snow between camp and the church spun out in a brassy, bright ribbon. Luke moved easily enough, but the only one of the three who seemed to be having any fun at all was the dog, a yellow Labrador that trotted ahead, its tail whisking a mad, happy semaphore. Every twenty feet, it dashed back to give Cindi an encouraging yip.

"Yeah," Cindi huffed. She was no expert on skis, but she could tough out a couple miles. Kind of. She felt like she'd been on these stupid skis for a solid day instead of only forty minutes. "I'm coming."

At the base of the church steps, she sucked wind until her heart stopped trying to pound its way right out of her ears. When she was done gasping and spitting, Luke said, "Maybe we should just leave him alone. You know, give him space, like Mellie and Weller said."

"Screw them." She used her poles to unclip. "He's been up there two whole days. It's not good for someone to be alone so long."

Luke jammed the ends of his skis into the snow to stand them up. "How do you know what's best?"

"My mom was a shrink." She stood her skis up alongside his. "She said you had to help people want to stay. Like, yeah, someone you cared about just died, but here are all these other people waiting for you to come back. So." She shrugged the pack a bit higher on her shoulders. "We're Tom's other people now."

Luke screwed his face to a knot, like he'd just gotten a whiff of something stinky. "Maybe I should stay here with the dog. You know, make sure no Chuckies show up."

"There's not a Chucky around for five miles," Cindi said. No one knew that for sure, of course, which was why they'd taken the dog to begin with. A lot of Chuckies had survived the cave-in and flood, and there really was no telling where they might be. Weller and Mellie thought many might be heading north toward Rule. If so, the Chuckies would have company, and pretty soon. She gave Luke a withering look. "Come on. Stop being such a wuss."

Luke made the dog lie down to wait, and then they slogged up the church steps. Inside, the church was gloomy as a tomb and cold. They skirted the nave, taking a side aisle to stairs and a dusty library on the third floor. There was a trapdoor beneath the organ pipe chamber, and then they huffed up a spiral iron staircase that led directly to the bell tower. In the bell tower, there were seven landings reached by a series of iron ladders bolted to the limestone. A defunct wooden carillon console dominated the southern half of the seventh landing. To Cindi, the batons and foot pedals, with their ropes extending to the church's twenty-three carillon bells, looked like a gigantic weaver's loom. Or, maybe, a spider's web.

At the top of the last iron ladder, Cindi reached up and popped open a sturdy wooden trapdoor. The trap yawned; a wave of cold air splashed over her head and shoulders.

"Hey, Tom," she said, clambering up the last few rungs. The belfry was open on all four sides, and she tossed a glance north, her headlamp cutting a gash through the blackness. The way north gave a very good view of the mine. Well . . . what was left. But she was sure that was the vantage point Tom would choose, and he had, all right: hunched on a high stool, a bulky sleeping bag wrapped around his shoulders, that big scoped rifle with a girl's name propped against the stone. He didn't look around, but she knew from the way his head tilted that he was awake. "It's Cindi. I brought you something to eat."

No reply. She hadn't really expected one. The rest of the belfry was very dark from the bells that dangled from a latticework of vertical struts behind louvered openings. They gave some shelter, but the air up here was much colder, and she was starting to cool down. She shivered as a tongue of wind licked sweat from her neck. She heard Luke scramble up behind her and then shut the trap, and said, "Luke's here, too."

No answer. Luke shot her an "I told you so" look that she ignored. Crossing the belfry, she set her pack on the floor, unzipped, pulled out a thermos and then a cup. "I thought maybe you'd like some soup?" When he didn't reply, she unscrewed the thermos, releasing a cloud of chicken-scented steam. "It's chicken noodle. Well, not *real* chicken noodle. I used bouillon cubes and some ramen and—"

"Thanks, Cindi." Tom's voice was so low she almost rode right over it. He didn't look down at all. "I'm really not hungry."

She heard Luke shuffle but didn't turn around. She *did* wish he'd say something. *Hello* would be a start.

"Yeah, I know," she said. Was that the right thing to say? Probably not. God, she wished her mom was around. "But my mom used to make chicken soup when I was sick. So I figured you might want some. You know, eventually." Ooh, that was lame. Being sad wasn't a sickness. It was human. She carefully set the thermos next to his stool and then withdrew three wrapped parcels. "I made sandwiches, too. They're not, you know, great or anything. Just peanut butter, and I found a couple little squishy packets of honey. I would've brought coffee, but . . ." But what? *But gee, you're not sleeping and you really should? But Tom, when are you going to come down and be Tom again?*

She heard him pull in a long breath, and when she glanced up, she was so startled she nearly gasped. He had already been thin.

Now, he was gaunt; his cheekbones were razors, his skin caving into the valleys of his cheeks. His lips were crusty with blood from where he'd chewed away skin.

"Maybe you want just a taste?" She didn't know what else to say.

"No." He gathered in another breath and looked away. "You should go back. It's cold."

"You should come with us," she said. God, was Luke *ever* going to say something?

He shook his head. "I'm not quite ready yet."

"When will you be?" She didn't think there was any kind of little-kid whine in there, but who knew? This was so freaky. She wasn't her mom.

A pause. "I don't know." She heard a touch of wonderment, as if he was really thinking about that. "I guess when I get tired of looking at it. The problem is . . . I'm not ready to look away," Tom said.

She knew what he meant. In daylight, the mine was a gouge in the earth: black against the snow and very deep and ragged, like a boil that had burst to let out all the pus. The smell was a little better because the wind was blowing in the right direction, and a skim of new ice had formed over the water. Mellie said there would be two lakes now, shining up into space like lopsided eyes. The sight was the kind of awful that used to make people slow down when they passed by an accident: ugly and absolutely hypnotic at the same time.

What Cindi wondered about were the bodies. There had to be a lot of them, but she hadn't spotted a single floater. A long time ago, she'd seen a movie about a sunken submarine. The gross part was the bodies, bobbing like corks, hair as wavy as seaweed. Probably a lot of dead normal people down in the mine, too, out of sight. She didn't want to go looking for them, but it was just as impossible not to think about them.

"I just try not to think about it," she said. "My mom . . . she said that everything bad goes away eventually. You just have to want to stop thinking about it, Tom."

Tom seemed to consider the idea. "Maybe that's my problem then. If I stop looking at *it*, that means I'll stop looking at *her*. I guess I haven't been able to look away for a very long time now. Maybe I never will."

"It's only been a couple days," Luke said.

"No, Luke," Tom said. "It's been months and months and months."

"What are you talking about?" Cindi asked, mystified.

He was quiet so long she didn't think he would answer, but then he said, "Afghanistan. There was this school. For girls, actually, but people were too afraid to send their kids because the Taliban, the warlords, the local leaders . . . they're against that kind of thing. They don't want their girls educated at all. They'll burn schools, gas them, kill the teachers. They'll do whatever it takes. So we marched in there and guaranteed the village that we would guard their kids and keep that school open, no matter what. Only that's not how it worked out."

"Oh." Cindi flicked a quick look at Luke, who only shook his head, and then turned back to Tom. "What happened?"

"They bombed it."

"You mean, like, from a plane? Or an RPG?"

When Tom shook his head, Luke asked, "So was it a suicide bomber or something?"

"Yes." Pause. "And no."

"I don't—" Luke's voice cracked, and he had to clear his throat. "I don't understand. How could it be both?"

"Because," Tom said, and then he craned his head around to look at them. "They wired the bombs to the children. Two of them: a little boy and a little girl."

"Oh." This time the word came out as a horrified moan, and Cindi felt her heart drop into her stomach. "Oh *no*. How *old* were they?" And, God, did that *matter*?

"I don't know. No older than six or seven. Whoever rigged these bombs was very good. There wasn't enough time to disarm them both, only I didn't figure that out until almost too late. I had, maybe, thirty seconds left? So I had to choose. I had to decide which child was g-going to live and wh-which one I would l-let . . ." A silence, and then Tom's voice came again, angrier this time: "They were forcing me to *choose* which child was worth saving, don't you *see*?"

"Oh Jesus," Luke said, and Cindi wanted to grab his arm and shout, *Don't ask him which one he chose! Don't do it!*

"I see that every day," Tom whispered. "I dream it. I *hear* it, I *smell* it . . . the heat coming off the rocks, and the dust, and my friend shouting for me to cut the wire, cut the wire, cut the *damn wire* . . ." Cindi heard him pull in a long and shaky breath. "At the last second, when I'd made my choice and it was too late, I still looked back because I thought it would be wrong to look away, that someone should remember . . . and I s-saw . . . I s-saw her f-face . . ."

The girl, then. She was the one who . . . Cindi could barely breathe. What did you say to something like that? She tried to imagine what that was like, to watch a little girl just blow *apart*. Her mother had never let her watch movies or play computer games like that. What made people think that killing, even when it was pretend, was something you should do for fun?

"The memory is like blood. You can wash and wash and wash, but the shadow of where it was is always there." There was a long pause. "You should go," Tom said. His voice was dead and toneless now. "Really. I'll be all right."

"Well, I'm not," Luke blurted. His face was very white, and his eyes were pooling. "I don't think I will be again for a long time. It's my fault. I made you leave. If it hadn't been for me, you would've stayed. Maybe you would've gotten to her."

"Probably not," Tom said, and Cindi thought that if a voice could be a *thing,* then Tom's was a stone. "She was too far down. We'd both be dead."

You want to be. She knew that now, beyond the shadow of a doubt. *You wish you'd died instead.*

"It's no shame to choose life, Luke," Tom said.

"Then you should follow your own advice," Luke said, and now tears splashed his cheeks. "Because I want you to stay alive and I'm scared you won't. I'm scared you'll kill yourself, and I know that it'll be because of me."

"No," Tom said. "It would be on me. But you don't have to worry, Luke. I would never do that to you."

Maybe not now and not here, Cindi thought. Maybe when Tom finally looked away, he'd wander off to die alone. Just go lie down somewhere and let go.

As if hearing her thoughts, Luke said, "But if you don't come back, I'll never know. I'll always wonder. I told you I couldn't leave without you then, and I won't go without you now or when we march."

"March?" Tom asked.

"Mellie says we need to take on Rule soon," Cindi said, and thought, *These are kids. Tom is good—I know he is—and he'll want to help them.* "She says we have to rescue those other kids."

"There's nothing in Rule for me," Tom said.

"Not even that guy, Chris Prentiss?" Luke said, and Cindi grimaced. This might be the wrong thing to say, but Weller and Mellie had told them all about Chris, and he sounded pretty bad. "Weller said Chris must've sent out Alex so the Chuckies could have her. Don't you want to make him pay for that?" Luke said. "*I* would."

"Oh yes," Tom said. "I do. But that's what scares me. For the first time in my life, I really *want* to kill. I want to see Chris Prentiss die, up close. I want to be the last thing he sees on this earth. I think I would enjoy killing him."

"Well, why not?" Luke said. "He deserves it."

"We don't know that. I don't know him. But I'm . . . I can feel myself . . . *changing.*" He balled a fist over his heart. "Right here. I don't want this, and yet I do. I'm afraid that if I go to Rule, it'll change all the way."

·"It?" Cindi asked. There was nothing good in Tom's voice now.

"This monster in me," Tom whispered. "I *feel* it. I think that if I go with you, I won't be able to stop it. Maybe I won't want to even try."

Cindi was suddenly very afraid, but she had to know. "What's it *feel* like?"

His eyes were terrible: weary and haunted and far back in his skull. The hollows were as purple and pewter gray as thick clouds gathering for a storm. Looking into Tom's ravaged eyes was like trying to stare directly into the sun for too long: something so bright and horrible it could burn you blind.

"Black," Tom said. "It feels black."

ACKNOWLEDGMENTS

If I have learned anything working with Team ASHES is that these guys, they just don't quit and the book you hold now is the better for that. So, once again and with feeling, I give my sincerest thanks:

To my editor, Greg Ferguson, who always insists that I reach a little further, dig a little deeper, and uncover just exactly what it is I want to convey: your support and belief mean the world to me. And next year? Eagles, Dude . . . unless it's the Packers. Oh, all right; for you, just this once, the cheesehead goes into storage.

To Ryan Sullivan, the world's most enthusiastic and thorough copy editor: man, seriously, I love your passion.

To Mary Albi, Katie Halata, Robert Guzman, and Alison Weiss: for smoothing the way, waving pom-poms, answering panicky e-mails no matter what the hour, tweeting your fingers off, and—most important—giving my work its best possible shot.

To Deb Shapiro: Lil Sis, thank you for seeing to it that I remembered to eat.

To Elizabeth Law, for reaching out, pulling me up, making sure I understood.

To my indefatigable agent and advocate, Jennifer Laughran: whenever we get to yakking, I discover so many more things to like about you.

To Dean Wesley Smith—again and always—for being there.

And, as before, to David: all this, without you? Seriously? Not a chance. But I wouldn't say no to Tasmania.

THE ASHES TRILOGY—
HOW BOOK ONE STARTED

Need a quick refresher? A synopsis of who's who and what's going on? Well, you won't get much in *Shadows*. For storytelling purposes—plot, pacing, and all that—I decided against a detailed recap. *Shadows* pretty much picks up where *Ashes* left off, and is a bigger and broader book, with a *lot* going on—new characters to meet, new mysteries to unravel.

But I also realize it's been a while for some of you, so if you *do* need a memory-jog, read on. (If you haven't read *Ashes*, shame on you. Drop what you're doing this *instant* and go read. I mean it.) In any event, BEWARE: major spoilers ahead. Really, if you've not read *Ashes*, don't go any further. Not only will you ruin the perfectly good time you might have had—because no synopsis can do justice to a novel—but you will miss a lot of vital information that I can't include here. Just saying.

The Zap: On what starts out as a perfectly nice Saturday in October, a wave of e-bombs sends electromagnetic pulses sweeping through the sky. No one knows who did this, or why. In some ways, that's not important. All that matters are the effects.

In an instant, the vast majority of the world's adult population dies; power and communications grids are destroyed, and sophisticated electronics crippled. (So that spiffy new iPad? It's a brick.) Along the East and West Coasts, the detonation of low-altitude nukes above nuclear waste storage facilities, as well as other facilities going critical because backup generators do not kick in, spews fallout into the atmosphere, turning the moon green and the sunrises bloody. Everyone who might be able to fix anything is also history. In a flash, civilization collapses into a hellish, preindustrial black hole.

Those still alive—the very young and the very old—must find a way to battle new enemies, not only fellow survivors organized into raiding parties and rigidly ordered societies (like Rule, a very small, very insular village) but the Changed: teenagers you really don't want to meet in a dark alley. Dogs are like canaries in a mine when it comes to the Changed, acutely sensitive and able to alert people to the Changed's presence. There is also some suggestion that dogs can sense those who are likely to Change or who are actively Changing.

A very few people have changed in a different way, developing super-senses, which some are not afraid to use to their advantage. Older individuals with advanced Alzheimer's or other senile dementias are suddenly Awakened, returning to their previous levels of function. Still others are Spared, teenagers and young adults who should be dead but aren't. No one knows why the

Spared have survived, and without sophisticated computers, laboratories, or scientists, there's really no way to find out. Kids are suddenly valuable commodities, but the few Spared are also viewed with suspicion, because no one is quite sure if the Change is over.

THE MAJOR CHARACTERS

Alex Adair: living with her aunt in Illinois after her mom, an ER doc, and dad, a cop, died in a helicopter crash three years ago. Suckier still, Alex carries a monster in her head: an inoperable brain tumor that's stolen her sense of smell and many of her memories, especially those of her parents. After two years of failed chemo-therapy, radiation, and experimental regimens, Alex has decided to call the shots for a change. As the novel opens, Alex has run off on what might well be a one-way backpacking trek through the Waucamaw Wilderness in Michigan's Upper Peninsula. She intends to honor her parents' last wishes and scatter their ashes from Mirror Point on Lake Superior. As it happens, she's also got her dad's service Glock, just in case she opts out of a return. After the Zap, Alex gets her sense of smell back in spades, a super-sense that also allows her to intuit emotions and, on one occasion, catch a glimmer of what goes on inside the mind of a wolf. Which is pretty funky. Much more to the point, like the dogs, she is able to detect the bloated roadkill stink of the Changed. Oh, and all of a sudden, every dog is her new best friend.

Ellie Cranford: sullen, uncooperative, a trifle whiny, a kid Alex has to keep herself from slapping silly. What can you say? The kid's eight. Her dad's KIA in Iraq, her mother split years back, and Ellie's now being cared for by her grandfather, Jack, who might have the patience of a saint, but cut the kid a break. She hates camping, and it's not like she hasn't got good reason to be a little pissy anyway. Initially rescued by Alex and then Tom, Ellie is kidnapped by some very nasty adults who see her as a meal ticket.

Mina: Ellie's dog, a Belgian Malinois and formerly her dad's MWD (military working dog). Mina also has the patience of a saint but packs a mean bite. The nasty adults take her, too.

Tom Eden: a young soldier and explosive ordnance specialist on leave from Afghanistan; a competent guy who complements Alex in a lot of ways. After Alex fends off a pack of wild dogs, Tom saves both Ellie and Alex by shooting his buddy, Jim, who's gone through a major lifestyle change. Steady and calm, someone to whom Alex is instantly attracted, Tom also has a few secrets of his own. The biggest is just why he's in the Waucamaw to begin with. After they leave the (relative) safety of the Waucamaw—we're talking wild dogs, booby traps, and kids who've suddenly decided that people make excellent Happy Meals—Tom is shot while trying to prevent the nasty adults from stealing Ellie.

Chris Prentiss: the grandson of Reverend Yeager and Rule's de facto second-in-command, though he grew up outside the community. Dark and reserved, a bit of a brooder, Chris has an uncanny ability to find Spared, especially up north around Oren and its nearby Amish community. He falls for Alex in a big way after she comes to Rule. Despite her initial determination to escape, Alex eventually reciprocates his affection.

Peter Ernst: Rule's overall commander, although he takes his marching orders from the Council of Five, representatives from Rule's founding families who run the village. At twenty-four, Peter is the oldest Spared, and he's fiercely protective of Chris. Peter has a thing going with Sarah, one of Alex's housemates.

Sarah, Tori, and Lena: Alex's housemates; all refugees to whom Rule offered sanctuary. Of the three, Sarah's a tad bossy. Good-natured Tori alternately crushes on Greg (another Spared who is part of Chris's squad) and Chris, and still makes a mean apple crisp. Taciturn, irreverent, and originally from that Amish community near Oren, Lena's a girl with 'tude. Having manipulated Peter, Lena once tried to escape—only to be caught in the Zone, a no-man's-land buffer zone through which those who are Banned (i.e., kicked out of Rule for various offenses) must travel in order to leave Rule's sphere of influence.

Reverend Yeager: a descendant of one of Rule's five founding families. Filthy rich from having run a very profitable mining company, Yeager heads the Council of Five. (The other Council members are Ernst, Stiemke, Prigge, and Born.) Before the Zap,

Yeager was quietly dementing away in the Alzheimer's wing of Rule's hospice. After the Zap, however, Yeager was Awakened. Like Alex, he possesses a super-sense and can determine emotions and truthfulness through touch.

Jess: a tough cookie with a penchant for spouting Bible verses. Jess seems to have her own agenda when it comes to who should be making the decisions for Rule. She's hot for Chris to stand up to his grandfather. For a variety of reasons—all of them very good—Chris is reluctant. Jess also makes no secret of encouraging Chris and Alex to become, well, a little closer.

Matt Kincaid (Doc): scruffy, pragmatic, sharper than a tack, and Rule's only doctor. He is also an Awakened, though he has no super-sense. He is the only one who knows about Alex's brain tumor as well as her super-sense of smell. Kincaid has suggested that the monster might be dead, dormant, or busy organizing into something entirely different.

THE ASHES TRILOGY— HOW *ASHES* FINISHED

After Tom is shot, he and Alex make it to a deserted convenience station where Alex battles three brain-zapped teenagers and very nearly ends up as an appetizer. Already weak from his gunshot wound, which is badly infected, Tom is even more seriously hurt when a brain-zapped kid bites off a chunk of his neck. Although Alex treats him as best she can, they both know that he'll die if she doesn't go on alone to Rule and return with help. Before she leaves, they have a nice moment, and Tom, who's come close to admitting the truth about why he came north to begin with, promises to tell her everything once they're reunited.

Alex makes it to Rule, acquiring an orphaned puppy on the way and having a close encounter with a wolf pack. But she is nearly lynched by a mob of terrified adults who see kids her age as potential threats. Chris and his dog, Jet, rescue her. She convinces Chris and Peter to leave the relative safety of Rule and go back for Tom. When they arrive, however, Tom has vanished.

It is now the beginning of November. While on her way to meet the Council of Five, Alex picks up a scent she's smelled before: one of the men, Harlan, who kidnapped Ellie (and stole a fanny pack with the ashes of Alex's parents, a letter from her mother, and a Bible). Harlan confesses and says that he last saw Ellie and Mina weeks before, south of Rule. Harlan is then Banned. Alex gets her parents' ashes back, but the Bible and her mother's letter are gone. Sensibly pointing out that they don't have the manpower to mount a search and that Ellie could be anywhere by this time (or dead), Chris and Peter refuse to go after the little girl.

With nowhere else to go, the winter digging in, Ellie gone, and no idea if Tom is still alive, Alex really has no choice but to stay. This turns out to be moot, since Rule has no intention of allowing the Spared to leave; indeed, the inhabitants of the village—a fundamentalist group that could be an offshoot of the

Amish community near Oren—are encouraged to see rescuing the Spared as akin to seeking the holy grail. Furthermore, this is a very traditional society organized along gender-specific tasks, which further constrains Alex's movements about the town.

Still, not everything is rotten. She's apprenticed to Kincaid as an assistant and doctor-in-training. Banking on the day when she'll be able to escape, she squirrels away odds and ends. Yet the months slip by and life develops a mind-numbing routine that begins to wear Alex down into a kind of acceptance. What Alex doesn't count on is a growing friendship with and affection for Chris. She rejects many of Chris's overtures, but grows fond of him nonetheless.

The holidays pass and then it's January. Even though previous foraging expeditions have been successful, Rule's beginning to run low on supplies. Forced to venture out further for food, Chris and Peter leave for Wisconsin. The morning they're due to head out, Alex is unexpectedly shaken when she glimpses Chris and Lena in some sort of impassioned argument. (Alex's mood doesn't improve when Lena throws her arms around Chris.) Alex isn't prepared for how hurt and jealous she feels. Frustrated because he's made a promise to help Lena, Chris can't explain what they were arguing about. But he can kiss Alex, and boy, is it a doozy. Alex admits that she's been afraid to let herself like him because that means choosing to stay in Rule for the long term and giving up on Tom and Ellie. Chris leaves on his foraging expedition, and Alex seems content to wait for his return.

But after several weeks, one splinter of Chris's party—including

Greg, who's now happily returning Tori's major crush—suddenly arrives back in Rule with a gravely ill boy they say Chris found near Oren. This is strange, since it means that Chris broke off from the main party to go north instead of sticking with Peter and his men, who went west. In the course of taking care of the boy, Alex finds something of hers: a whistle her father gave her long ago and which she later gave to Ellie. Unfortunately, the boy dies without regaining consciousness.

Putting together the bits and pieces she's heard and learned over the months, Alex figures out that while Chris and the others might be gathering supplies, they're also taking Spared wherever they can find them, and quite possibly—very probably—by force. In other words, they're stealing kids.

Appalled by this and also galvanized by the discovery of her whistle, Alex makes the impulsive decision to hijack Kincaid's horse and leave Rule by way of the Zone, which is close to Jess's house. She is stopped, however, by none other than Jess, who Alex now realizes is an Awakened with a super-sense of her own (hearing). As it turns out, Jess has been waiting for Alex to make this decision, and now helps her escape. Jess's rationale is, however, a little suspect. She doesn't care so much about Alex; what Jess wants is for Chris to wake up to what Rule's doing—although Jess is vague about what that *really* is—and mount a challenge to his grandfather. Chris has to want this badly enough, and Alex is the tool Jess will use to force Chris's hand.

As Jess and her allies escort Alex to the Zone, Chris suddenly gallops out of the woods. He's returned early, and in the nick of time. Frantic to stop Alex from passing into the Zone, screaming that she doesn't know what she's doing, Chris is forcibly stopped by Jess's men and then clubbed unconscious by Jess. Although Alex tries to help Chris, Jess forces her out at gunpoint.

Once away from Rule and many miles into the Zone, Alex discovers a shocking tableau: a sort of processional way marked by the flayed corpses of wolves dangling from trees, piles of clothing and jewelry, bones, and a pyramid of human heads in various stages of decomposition. One frozen head she recognizes: Harlan, the man who stole Ellie and was Banned months ago from Rule.

And *she* is discovered by a pack of five Changed—all in winter gear (although two wear wolf skins and cowls), all armed, all looking very well fed.

It is then that Alex realizes the truth.

Rule isn't fighting the Changed.

Rule is feeding them.

AN EXCERPT FROM
MONSTERS

ALEX HAD FALLEN LIKE THIS ONLY ONCE IN HER LIFE. THAT happened when she was nine and took a wild leap from Blackrocks Cliff off Presque Isle into the deep sapphire-blue of Lake Superior. She remembered that the air was laced with the scent of wild lilacs and early honeysuckle. Although hot sun splashed her shoulders, her bare arms and legs were sandpapery with gooseflesh because the wind skimming Superior was, even in June, still very cold—and she was also, frankly, freaked out. Standing at the cliff's edge, her monkey-thin toes gripping rough basalt, she looked down past her new emerald green bathing suit, felt her stomach drop, and thought, *Seriously?* That cove looked pretty puny. Her dad, who'd gone first with a whoop and a leap, was only a dot.

"Come on, you can do this, honey!" She could see the white flash of his grin—a tanned, muscular, bluff, and confident man, who carried her on his shoulders and boomed out songs. "Jump to me, sweetheart! Just remember, feet first and you'll be fine!"

"Oh-oh-oh . . ." She meant to say *okay*, but her teeth chattered. Heights scared her something stupid. Stephanie's birthday party last month? The indoor climbing wall? *Mistaaake.* Not only was she the *only one* to freeze and then slip; she came *this close* to wetting her pants. And now her dad was daring her to jump from way up here? For *fun*?

Can't do this, I can't . . . Every muscle locked in a sudden, whole-body freeze, except for her head, which swelled and ballooned. *I'm going to faint*. Her brain seemed surprised. *This is what it's like to—*

There was a whirring sensation, like the blast of a jet engine gushing through her skull, blowing her sky-high. All of a sudden, she wasn't in her body at all but floating *waaay* up there, looking down at this teeny-tiny girl in a deep green bathing suit, an emerald smudge with hair as red as blood. Far below, so small he was nothing more than a mote in a very blue and watery eye, was her dad.

"Alex?" Her dad's voice was the size of a gnat. "Come on, sweet-heart, jump to me."

"If she doesn't want to . . ." Her mom, the worrier, on a faraway crescent of gravel, hand to her eyes as the wind whipped her hair. "She doesn't have to prove—"

But yes, I do. Her mom's words—her doubt that Alex had the guts—cut the string of the strange kite to which her brain was yoked. That weird distance collapsed, and Alex plunged back into her skin, faster than a comet, to flood the space behind her eyes.

Then she was out over open water, with no memory of launch-ing herself from the cliff—probably a good thing, because she'd have spazzed, *I'll slip, I'll slip, I'll bust a leg or break my face*, and only scared herself more. Long red hair streaming like a failed parachute, she sliced through air in a high whistle of wind.

Slapping the water, still icy at that time of year, was a shock. She punched through with her hip, a hard smack that jolted a mouthful of air past the corkscrew of her lips. Silvery, shimmering bubbles boiled from her mouth and all around her. Water gushed up her nose, the pain of the brain freeze scaring her even more than losing what was probably no more than a sip of air. She could hear herself, too: a choked little underwater raspberry, a *bwwwuhh*, not quite a scream but close enough. The water wasn't blue at all but murky and a really weird, brassy green. She couldn't see more than a few feet—and was she still sinking? *I'm going to drown!* She could feel a panic-rat skittering in her skull, nipping her eyeballs as she whirled, her hair fanning like seaweed. *I'm going to drown!* Wild with fear, she looked for her dad but didn't, *couldn't* see legs or feet or hands or *anything*. She wasn't sure where the surface was. Craning, she saw how the water yellowed with diffuse sun. *Go, that's up, go, go, swim!* Thrashing, she bulleted up and then crashed through, her breath jetting in a thin shriek: *"Ahh!"*

"Attagirl!" Her father was instantly there, laughing, his wet hair dark and slick as seal skin. "That's my Alex! Wasn't that *fun?*"

"Uh," she grunted. Still booming a delighted laugh, her dad wrapped her up and boosted her—shrieking deliriously now—way up high, nearly out of the water, before bringing her back down to earth and to him, because he was *that* strong.

Then, together, they stroked for the gravel beach, her father pulling a slow sidestroke, staying with her the whole way as she churned for shore, and home.

That was where the memory ended. She couldn't recall if she and her dad climbed the cliff again. Knowing her dad—how much she adored and wanted to please, be *his* girl and dare anything—they probably had. Knowing her dad, he'd treated her to a waffle cone of chocolate custard topped with Mounds and Almond Joy chunks because, sometimes, you just feel like a nut. Her dad probably stole from her cone so she could dip into his, right backatcha. She bet her dad told her mom, *Relax, honey, she's wash and wear*, as Alex crunched almonds and chewy, juicy coconut and licked sweet chocolate runnels, molten in the afternoon heat, from her wrist and forearm and the knob of her elbow. Her father was that kind of man.

More than likely, she'd been underwater less than ten seconds. She got herself out of it, too, and all because her dad dared her to try. After that leap, she really believed she might dare anything, because no matter what, if she jumped, her father would be waiting to swim by her side, stroke for stroke, into forever.

Of course, she was nine and her dad was immortal.

And nothing lasts forever.

Years later, after her parents were dead, her doctors said she'd had an out-of-body experience. Commonplace, no voodoo. For example, certain epileptics had similar experiences all the time. Hoping to walk the stars and know the gods, mystics and shamans drank potions. It was all funky brain chemistry, the doctors said, the mind's switches already primed, requiring only that you tickle the brain in the right spot, goose it just so. Easy-peasy. Figure out how to bottle it, and we'd all be rich.

In fact, her last doctor thought what happened at Blackrocks— that shove from the shell of her mind—might've been the monster, just beginning to wake. That her sleep going to hell and the smell of phantom smoke weren't her first symptoms after all. That her little baby monster was hatching, chip-chip-chipping a peephole to peer with one yellow baby-monster eye—*why, hello there*—way back then.

And she had been falling, falling, falling ever since . . .

Into now.